The Silent Call

James L Diffin

Cover illustration by Duncan Long
www.DuncanLong.com

ISBN: 0-6155-7237-5
ISBN-13: 9780615572376

Dedication

For Marguerite. My lady, my love, my life.

Epigraph

He had been born in pain and fury. His father was fire. His mother was water, who cooled him and gave him rest. He tried to sleep, but each time the battering strokes woke him. Fire and water, again and again. He grew stronger as the blows formed and shaped him.

Spawned of the fiery pit, his god was war. As he swung through the air, the sound of his passage was his battle cry. He would bite deep, through flesh, through bone and sinew, deep to where the blood ran hot. The hand that held him fused him into an invincible force. As long as there was The Gift, he would live forever. His name was Excalibur.

—The Book of Arthur

Prologue

He rose slowly out of the cold, black, oily depths, sliding easily up through the layers of water that turned gray as he approached the surface of the lake. In the darkness just before dawn, a heavy mist covered the still water. Overhead, the stars were beginning to fade. He was alone.

He turned his head slowly in every direction. The world was young and he and his kind ruled all the oceans of the earth. None could dispute his passage, but he was always alert, always on guard. It was his way.

He started to move now, easing through the mist. He was big, even for his kind, but nature had formed him well. He moved so smoothly that he barely disturbed the surface of the water as he passed silently on down the lake.

The lake was cold and deep, but he felt at ease. He had been born here and had returned many times. In the weeks since he'd left the open ocean, he had not eaten and he was eager now to depart. When he reached the north end of the lake, he would dive and pass through a series of underground caverns that opened to the sea. Without stopping, he'd swim halfway around the world before his pace slowed and he began to feed well in the warm southern waters.

With a squeak of an oarlock and a muffled laugh, it all became a lie. The world was not young. It was the twentieth century and that irritating squeak announced the presence of the true master. He knew that he had not yet been seen, but still he stopped moving. He turned his head toward the noise. He did not hurry. In the depths of the ocean where he lived, he held his own against the diving sperm whale and the giant squid and, although he could easily destroy the unseen boat and its passengers, his eyes reflected the wisdom of 135 million years of survival.

In the beginning, his kind had fought the Tylosaurus and Kronosaurus, huge dragons who terrorized the seas. They'd all watched the Pteranodon, a flying freak with a thirty-foot wingspan and, from the safety of the water, kept a wary eye on evolution's prize, the Tyrant Lizard, Tyrannosaurus Rex. Then they were gone. Of all the giants, his species alone had learned to adapt and had endured.

One key to his longevity was that he had always been secretive and his infrequent contacts with Man served to make him more so. He had retreated to the vastness of the ocean depths, rising only in search of food. This, too, was his way and here, in this lake where it all began, caution dictated that Man was to be left strictly alone.

As long as his existence was only a suspicion, he was safe. Once his presence here was proven, it would be the end. The curiosity seeker, the trophy hunter or, worse yet, the man of science could never again leave him in peace. But, sometimes, in spite of his caution, there was a certain sound that pulled him to the surface of the lake.

He saw them now—two figures in a small boat. One of them rose and turned to face him. He felt a sense of contact with something other than his own, a spider thread of recognition. There was no fear. It was lighter now, but still he remained, held on a gossamer leash by the man standing in the boat.

Finally, the thread stretched and broke. It was long past time to go. His great head lowered and he silently disappeared, leaving only a few ripples to disturb what was left of the morning mist. He was gone as quietly as he had come. The waters of the lake were still.

Then, after a time, it started again, that ordinary, reassuring sound of a squeaky oarlock keeping two early morning fishermen company.

From a rocky point on the far shore, a white-robed figure turned and vanished into the coming dawn.

Chapter I

Stacey Ryder was pushing it. The rain had been coming down heavily since early evening. When she called the airport, they told her there was a break in the weather and John's plane would be landing in less than an hour. Now the rain was nothing more than an annoying drizzle. Wouldn't you know it. She smiled to herself as she turned on the car radio. She had a thing about being late, even when it wasn't her fault.

Stacey drove easily, sitting well back with her hands at quarter to three on the steering wheel, just like John. She enjoyed watching her husband when he drove. Sometimes she'd sit facing him, her head back against the rest with her eyes almost closed. John drove with the kind of concentration that said there were a lot of crazies out there.

That was why he'd bought her this Volvo and why the Michelins were new. She'd been impatient with him; she'd insisted that new tires were a waste of money, that there was plenty of tread left and that the tires were good for another year at the very least. But John, with that little quirk of a smile she was usually so fond of, waited until she'd finished.

"Not on your life," he'd said.

She glanced at the rearview mirror. There were headlights behind her, the beams broken by the trees as the road wound down through the wooded hills to the valley. Strange, but the flickering lights made her feel uneasy. She wondered who it could be at this time of night. There were six houses on the lake and only half of them were occupied year round.

Stacey checked the rearview mirror again. The headlights were closer, so she sped up a little and switched off the radio. This was no time to be distracted. It was probably the Landers boy from across the lake. The road was narrow and, with all the curves, there was really no safe place to pass. Stacey had never told John, but even though she loved their home on the lake, she didn't feel really secure about driving in the hills. Especially at night and especially that one place. Hills were no place for a Florida girl.

The reflection of the headlights in the rearview mirror was really beginning to annoy her. The driver was much too close and he had the high beams on. Stacey shook her head with frustration and drove faster. She didn't want that stupid kid sitting on her bumper all the way down out of the hills. She was already late and she wanted to surprise John. The headlights dropped back to a proper distance. So there. Stacey relaxed her grip a fraction on the steering wheel and flexed cramped fingers.

John was going to get more of a surprise than Stacey meeting him at the airport in the middle of the night. She'd been sure for a week now, but it wasn't something you announced over the telephone. She hadn't even told her sister Wanda and they shared everything. Well, almost everything. Stacey was glowing with life and could hardly wait to tell John. She hoped it would be a girl this time. Matthew, their four-year-old, already wanted to be a professional chess player like his Dad.

Stacey touched her face. She knew her cheeks were flushed just thinking about John. He knew those signs, and they'd never make it all the way home. Well, he had been away for almost two weeks.

Those damn headlights were starting to move up again, growing larger with a rush. The rearview mirror was filled with light. He couldn't be more than a foot or two from her bumper. Stacey realized she was holding her breath.

There was only one more curve and she would be done with this foolishness. Just let her get down to the bottom safely and, late or not, that young man behind her was going to get an earful. He could count on it.

This was the place that bothered Stacey the most. There was a long, slow curve to the right, hugging the side of the hill. To the left was the valley. The trees on that side of the road had been logged, leaving a clear view. You could see the lights of the town below. The road was steep and there was no guardrail. It hadn't seemed so bad until they'd cut down the trees and you realized just how dangerous it was.

Stacey wasn't aware of how fast she was going until the Volvo began to drift toward the center of the road. She knew enough not to touch the brake. Straddling the center line, those new Michelins were holding the car steady. She was going to make it.

Stacey was so intent on what she was doing she had forgotten all about the car behind her until it nudged her right rear bumper. The impact was so gentle that, at first, she thought she had imagined it. But then she realized she no longer had control.

She tried to remember all those things John had taught her, but she couldn't think. When the car went over the side, she had a firm grip on the steering wheel and both feet braced against the floorboard.

"Dear God, no."

The Volvo sailed off into space, dipped to strike the hillside, bounced, then cartwheeled twice before coming to rest with a shattering crash. The car, right side up, was wedged in among the tree stumps on the side of the hill. Miraculously, Stacey survived, half conscious, held securely by the seat belt. Strange. The motor wasn't running, but the headlights were still burning.

She had just decided to see if she could move, when the door of the Volvo opened. Powerful hands unbuckled the seat belt and lifted her from the car. The man was only a black silhouette against the light. He held her so easily, she thought she was in her father's arms again, but that thought lasted only a moment. Her nostrils were stung with a sharp, cruel odor. Something was very wrong. Stacey touched one of his hands and shuddered.

"You had to know," said a voice from the darkness.

Somewhere below the car, she was dropped backward onto a large tree stump. She couldn't move.

There was silence. She hoped the man had gone for help, but it didn't make any sense. Why put her on a tree stump with her head and legs hanging over the edge? Didn't he realize how much that hurt her?

There was a grunt of exertion and the sound of rending metal. Stacey turned her head. She didn't really believe what she saw. It must be the angle at which she was lying, or maybe she still wasn't clear in her mind, but she could swear that the shape of the Volvo was changing, growing larger. As the car tipped and rolled over on Stacey, she struggled to speak. It was all so silly and, besides, she was going to be late. Who would meet John at the airport? The horn began to blow.

Chapter II

John Ryder felt a flutter of anticipation. At the grand master level, chess was war. Players had been crushed as surely as if they'd been poleaxed. It was will against will, legion against legion. The need to dominate aroused violent passions.

The luck of the draw had favored ex-world champion, Martin von Friedenthal, with the white pieces and first move. The referee started the time clock and the game got under way.

Immediately, with the first move of von Friedenthal's queen's pawn opening, Ryder had the feeling of being watched, of personal contact. It had nothing to do with the usual chess audience that followed every move with intense concentration and it had nothing to do with the buzz of excitement when he made one of his unorthodox moves. Someone was watching. Any professional who performs in front of an audience soon learns to ignore or filter out anything that disturbs his concentration. No, this was more—much more.

Ryder flinched as he felt a kind of invasion, a mental intrusion. He had the feeling that a presence was going through his mind making a cold evaluation of what it found there. Jesus, Mary, and Joseph! What the hell's going on here?

At first, the presence was nothing more than a curious, dispassionate intellect with a clear line of reason. Then it changed. Ryder clutched the edge of the table for support, as a wave of savage, brutal thought crashed against his mind with the force of a physical blow. An inhuman strength was smothering him, pulling him down.

Mercifully, as suddenly as it had come, the presence was gone. Maybe it was only his imagination or, possibly, the strain of the last few weeks but, whatever it was, von Friedenthal had felt it, too. He looked up from the chessboard, something he almost never did, and glanced at the audience. He then studied Ryder for a long moment and, apparently satisfied, returned his attention to the game.

Thank God, it's not just me, thought Ryder, wiping a film of perspiration from his forehead. He played bishop to king two and stood up. He generally played quickly and it was not unusual for him to leave his seat during his opponent's move.

The match was being played in a small auditorium in Ipswich, England, with the players seated at a table in the center of the stage. The referee sat behind them. To one side, an easel held a large chessboard with flat magnetic chess pieces. Each time Ryder or von Friedenthal made a move, the referee duplicated it on the board, so that the audience could follow the game.

Ryder crossed to stage right, where a table held an assortment of beverages. He was a dark-haired, athletic-looking man of twenty-eight. Deeply tanned and casually dressed in a turtleneck, slacks, and tweed jacket, he looked vaguely out of place. He poured himself a glass of mineral water. It wouldn't disturb von Friedenthal; he probably didn't even know Ryder had left the table. Ryder contemplated the magnetic chess pieces, apparently thinking about his next move. He turned slowly and looked out over the audience.

All right, you bastard, where the hell are you? But there was nothing unusual. He'd seen them in half the cities of the world. The fascination with the "game of kings" was shared by young and old alike. Hell, it was the same for him. When he'd first started to play, he'd been interested enough to trace the origin of chess all the way back to India in the seventh century. Brought by travelers and merchants, the game slowly moved west, pausing in cities along the way. Antioch, Messina, Samarkand; the old names fell easy on the tongue.

Gradually, the rules changed, and developed. During the Middle Ages, chess took Europe by storm; first Spain, then Italy, and finally, France and England. It was in France that the queen became the most powerful piece on the board. Leave it to the French, thought Ryder, as he watched von Friedenthal play king's knight to bishop three and push the button on his time clock. With a last glance around the auditorium, Ryder returned to his chair and the game continued.

The intellectual prowling began again. This time it didn't take Ryder long to discover the source of his discomfort. First row, last seat on the right side aisle. Ryder's attention was drawn to the expensively tailored man because he didn't move. He had no mannerisms. He didn't cough or fidget. He didn't cross his legs, shift his weight, or act as if he didn't know what to do with his hands. He just sat there, motionless, and watched.

Ryder found the whole business disconcerting. He mentally shook himself as he stared at the chessboard. If he didn't watch it, the tough old man across from him was going to walk away with the game. Von Frieden-thal had castled, his bishop controlled the white diagonal, and his knight was a power at king five.

Forty moves in two-and-a-half hours, then play would be adjourned until the next day. At this level of competition, the player with the white pieces and first move had a definite advantage. Besides, Ryder's open style of play brought out the best in von Friedenthal's careful, meticulous develop-ment. This, combined with Ryder's preoccupation during the opening, had placed him in an almost impossible situation.

Ryder smiled at his opponent's baited trap dripping with poisoned honey. Although it was seven moves away, Ryder could see in seconds what the average player wouldn't see in an hour. Von Friedenthal was a master's master who played the board regardless of who sat opposite him and now, only the fire of originality had any chance of defeating the German's refined logic of time, space, and force. Ryder took a deep breath. What the hell. Let 'er rip.

He began to play, conjuring up something from nothing. He didn't stir from his chair or look up from the board. The feeling that he wasn't his own man made him bring his powers of concentration to a point where nothing existed outside of the sixty-four squares and the pieces on them. He played for the sheer enjoyment of the mystery hidden in the secret squares, the sense of magic.

Time and time again he came up with the one move that held off di-saster. The move was there, he just had to find it. He retreated, blocked, and sidestepped, buying time. Every move was an adventure into an unknown universe and, by all the laws of chess, shouldn't have worked, but did.

Ryder snapped out of it as von Friedenthal signaled the end of the day's play by handing the tournament director a sealed envelope containing his forty-first move.

Ryder leaned back in his chair and rubbed his hands over his eyes. Ever since he could remember, unpredictably, it would happen like this. Some-times, when he was physically challenged or sometimes, even at the chess board, he'd suddenly have the sensation of freewheeling overdrive, of being more than himself. It never lasted but, while it did, it was always one bitch of a ride. He'd never told anyone.

He was a pawn down and his uncastled king had been hard-pressed until von Friedenthal overextended himself and Ryder was able to force an exchange of queens and two minor pieces. Now, his positional advantage was such that, if he didn't make some stupid mistake, his chances for tomorrow's play were excellent.

He would have supper alone in his room and spend the evening studying and analyzing how best to proceed the next day. He knew von Friedenthal would do the same. Played like this, chess was hard work. Ryder couldn't imagine anything else.

Earlier today, when play resumed, the Leopard's chair was empty. That's right, Ryder thought, the Leopard. It had come to mind immediately. Several years ago, he had been playing a tournament in Kenya. One night, in the hotel lobby, he'd swapped lies with an aging Great White Hunter who told tales of how it used to be. One stuck. It was about leopards.

It seems that the big cats would pick out a limb over a game trail. Hidden by the foliage, they would lie completely still for hours, never moving, until the unwary passed below. Many had been shot by hunters because the cats had the habit of allowing their tails to hang down from the limb on which they lay. For the gazelle and the wild pig, who equated movement with danger, it was nothing more than a vine. For the alert hunter, it was another matter.

After several moves on the chessboard, and without glancing up, Ryder knew the Leopard was there again. This time the feeling of mental invasion was less, perhaps because Ryder was prepared and would permit no interference. And this time, too, the presence remained surgically clean and without threat.

The game went well. Von Friedenthal twisted and turned, trying to negate the absolute power of Ryder's doubled rooks on the open queen's file. He hadn't allowed von Friedenthal to complicate the position and gave him no opportunity for counterplay. Ryder gradually increased the pressure, turn by turn.

On the sixty-third move, it was over. Even the audience knew it. Von Friedenthal looked up from the chessboard, tapped the table twice with his knuckles, and offered his hand.

"Congratulations," he said with a wry smile. He leaned across the table, knowing the applause would cover his words. "There's no way you should have won. John Ryder, you're a Yankee devil! After your first fifteen moves, you were finished—and you know it."

As Ryder accepted von Friedenthal's hand, he turned and saw that the Leopard's chair was once again empty. Ryder hadn't seen him arrive, and he hadn't seen him leave.

"Maybe you let me off the hook, Martin."

Looking at the chessboard, von Friedenthal shook his head. "Now I've seen it all!" He sighed. "You've broken something in me. It's time for me to retire and it's all your fault. Ha!"

Ryder stood up and came around the table. He leaned over and put an arm around the seated man's shoulders. There was the sympathetic murmur of voices in the theater. English audiences were always so well mannered. Even the tournament officials kept a respectful distance. A civilized American, for a change—how nice!

"Listen to me." Ryder spoke softly. "You don't know what you're saying. You can't possibly imagine what that would mean." He paused. "I can see it now—a picture-postcard day in old Heidelberg—the Castle, the Holy Ghost Church, the red-tiled roofs. And there, in his garden, Herr Professor Doctor Martin von Friedenthal, retired chess player, wearing a sun helmet while tending his roses."

Von Friedenthal raised his hands in protest. "I hate roses."

Ryder leaned closer. "You know the helmet I mean, don't you? The one with the little point on top. You fraud! The only way we'll ever get rid of you is to shoot you. You'll still be playing when they have to prop you up in your chair." Ryder tapped von Friedenthal's chest with a finger. "You'll probably drool."

Von Friedenthal threw back his head and roared with laughter. "Enough—I take it all back. Your picture postcards are terrible." Von Friedenthal clasped Ryder's arm. "All joking aside—you played a magnificent game. I wouldn't have missed it for anything."

Ryder's emotions weren't too far from the surface. "Yes, it was special. Too bad there had to be only one winner."

"Ha! Don't be silly. Capablanca didn't lose a single game in ten years. He must have been bored to tears." Von Friedenthal's voice grew serious. "We must talk. Join me for a drink when we finish here?"

"How about the hotel bar at six?"

Von Friedenthal nodded. He signed his score sheet and thanked the tournament director. Before leaving, he paused and, in a conspiratorial whisper, said, "*He* was here again today."

Ryder felt a flood of relief. "So it's you. What kind of man is that and what the hell have you been up to—cheating on your wife again?"

Von Friedenthal loved it. Five-foot-six on a good day and well over two hundred pounds, he had three passions—chess, his family, and food. Against all advice, he'd married late in life, to a woman less than half his age, and now had two beautiful little girls. Their home was filled with joy, especially when Papa was home. Von Friedenthal was a lucky man and he knew it.

His three-piece suit, of indeterminate age, struggled to keep up with the times, and his vest, well-flecked with pipe ashes, no longer fully covered the area for which it was intended. Von Friedenthal looked the part—a chess grand master and former world champion. It had been years since he'd been champion, but he was still tournament tough, playing as often as his schedule permitted.

Professor Doctor Martin von Friedenthal—author, lecturer, and teacher. His Political Science lectures at Heidelberg University were always well attended. He was in demand as a speaker and his books on chess were required reading for anyone with a more than passing interest in the game. He had a mind that defied his seventy-seven years and was a formidable opponent. Tournament chess was a young man's game, but not the way von Friedenthal played it.

Von Friedenthal patted his stomach. He was very fond of this young American who broke all of the rules of chess and so often got away with it. "My friend, who says he was watching me?" Von Friedenthal moved away to join some fans waiting to speak with him.

The spectators crowded around Ryder. His triumph was theirs and the questions came rapidly, one after the other.

"On your sixth move, how come…" "I told George, here, that you…" "The most unusual defense I ever…" "Best game since…" "For a cup of tea and then…" He nodded and smiled. It was part of the price. To the victor belong the spoils. From experience, he knew they weren't really interested in answers, just questions.

Finally, it came. Ryder knew it would. He thought he was prepared.

"I heard about your wife…"

Without answering, Ryder turned away, his eyes suddenly blinded with tears. Angry with himself, he shook his head fighting for control.

He decided to walk back to his hotel. A few blocks from the auditorium, he came to a small park. He paused, his shadow long in the late afternoon sun. The trees were beginning to flesh out with the first pale green of spring. He'd always enjoyed England at this time of year and, lured by the fresh smell of growing things, decided to cut through the park. As he strolled along, eyes fixed on the middle distance, Ryder thought about the last two days.

What the hell was happening to his world? First, Stacey's death, now this. Here he was, walking through a park in Ipswich, England, watching tree limbs, for Christ's sake. The sense of accomplishment, the satisfaction of winning the tournament, was missing. Ryder had the uneasy feeling that something had been left undone. He didn't like it.

You have seen but could not recognize me, for you do not have the power. If you are chosen, you embrace only death.

Chapter III

Shortly before six, Ryder crossed the lobby of the White Horse Inn. Once, long ago, the three sides of the room had been the outside walls of buildings that bordered a courtyard. Later, the open street side was enclosed and the whole thing roofed over with glass, leaving the three walls as they were. An open wooden staircase still clung to one wall. With the natural light overhead and the original cobblestones underfoot, it was a unique room. Ryder liked the hotel and had stayed there before.

In a small bar just off the lobby, von Friedenthal greeted him with raised glass. Using the stem of his pipe, von Friedenthal indicated a drink on the bar. "I took the liberty—"

"Thanks, Martin," Ryder said. "Cheers!"

Both men raised their glasses with the comfortable familiarity of friendship shared and a fine single-malt Scotch. Von Friedenthal, who was always on a most-favored-customer basis with the local bartender, signaled for two more of the same.

"My boy, it's good to see you," he said with genuine warmth. "We didn't think you'd play, considering your wife and—"

"They say life goes on," Ryder cut in. The pain of Stacey's death was a sharp knife in his gut. He toyed with his glass, regretting the coldness of his remark.

"I know, I know," von Friedenthal said quietly, "but now we must talk. I'm leaving first thing in the morning. One of my students will do the driving, that is, if he gets back from chasing the ladies." He smiled. "Liesel and the girls send their love."

"My love back."

Von Friedenthal lowered his voice. "What can I say, John? We were shocked, that's all. It was a personal loss for us, too. I wish you had allowed us to come to the States. We cared for her as one of our own, you know. How could such a thing happen? She was always such a careful person. Tell me about it."

Ryder knew what von Friedenthal was doing. He wasn't being cruel or curious. He was trying to help, to share Ryder's grief. Over the years, von Friedenthal had become the father Ryder had never known. Ryder shrugged, but his voice was bitter as the words came spilling out.

"It just happened, that's all. They called it an accident and said that she was killed because she wasn't wearing her seatbelt. That just wasn't Stacey." Ryder stared into his glass, but found no answers. "My flight was delayed because of bad weather. She wanted to surprise me. She was hurrying, late at night—a slippery road. I'd been away for ten days."

Von Friedenthal knew that Ryder blamed himself. The worst kind of guilt. If only I had...what?

"And your son?"

"He was lucky. Stacey wouldn't leave him alone in the house. She left him with some friends. Now he's in Florida with Wanda and her husband. The two sisters were always very close."

"How's the lad taking it?"

"He knows something's wrong, but how do you explain to a four-year-old? He misses his mother and asks for her, but Wanda keeps him busy. She has three kids of her own, so he's never alone. They all seem to get along together and Wanda insists it's best, for now, that I'm not around. She says it would only upset him." Ryder looked at von Friedenthal with pain-filled eyes. "Every time I see Matthew, I see Stacey. He has the same blond hair, the same mannerisms. I was almost glad when Wanda offered to take him. I suppose that doesn't make me much of a man."

Von Friedenthal put a comforting hand on Ryder's shoulder.

"Thanks, Martin. I only agreed to play this tournament because I knew you'd be here." Ryder's face was a mask. "I had to identify the body. She'd been thrown clear before the car rolled over on her. Stacey and Matt and chess...was that asking too much?" He took a deep breath and let it out slowly. "I've put the house up for sale. I plan to stay on in London for a few days before going back. Then—we'll see."

"You have to be patient, my boy. Sometimes we must leave in order to come back. Time is the only healer and, if it's of any small consolation, I, too, am here only because of you."

Ryder held his glass as if it were a life preserver.

Von Friedenthal gave Ryder's shoulder a shake and then slapped the bar with his hand. "Ha! What are we thinking of? Come and stay with us in Heidelberg. Better yet, leave with me in the morning. Liesel will be delighted. She hasn't seen you two since—sorry—I only meant..."

"Don't worry about it, Martin. It's easy to do. I know, I do it all the time. I appreciate the offer, but it's too soon." Ryder shook his head. "I can only take so much kindness." Liesel von Friedenthal loved to mother Martin. Ryder knew she would do the same with him. She always had.

"You're sure?"

Very much alone, Ryder could only nod.

Von Friedenthal was refilling his pipe, glancing at Ryder all the time. He seemed to have trouble lighting his brier. Finally, on the fourth match, he said, "What are we going to do with you, John Ryder?"

"What?"

"I'm very concerned. I know all this is too soon to talk about, but as I may not see you for some time, I'll say it anyway."

"I can't imagine there's anyone who could stop you."

"You are—undeniably—a chess grand master. Only your flights of fancy keep you from qualifying for the world championship. I never know what you're going to do next—for that matter, neither does anyone else. It really wouldn't surprise me if you opened with a rook pawn."

"I never thought of it."

"Try that on someone who'd believe it. No, there's always been something different about your game. You remind me of Morphy."

"Paul Morphy?"

"Absolutely brilliant. A shooting star."

"Thanks a lot. If I recall, he fizzled out in a hurry."

"I told you, years ago, the very first time we played one another, that you were different. If I wasn't such a cynic, I'd say that you don't care whether you win or lose, that chess for you is not a contest, but some kind of moral issue."

Ryder studied his glass. "I thought we were drinking Scotch, not truth serum."

Von Friedenthal snorted. "I'm not so naive as to think you don't try to win," von Friedenthal said, almost to himself. "There's more to it than that.

One day you play with pure genius and the next—well, any competent amateur could beat you."

"Win some, lose some."

"Don't try that with me, young man. I know you too well. Over the years I've played the very best and I've sat across the board from you on more than one occasion. I don't think you realize what a rare talent you possess."

"And I'll lose my marbles just like Morphy."

Von Friedenthal tapped Ryder's chest with the stem of his pipe, refusing to be sidetracked. "I know what I'm talking about and I tell you now, this past two days' contest will become a classic. I wouldn't have believed it possible, and," he added, "I do have some small knowledge in this regard."

Ryder looked off across the bar. "You're getting carried away with this whole thing. I never played like that before and I probably never will again."

Von Friedenthal was adamant. "When this game is published, there will be a great deal of discussion among the experts, trying to explain just what it was that you did. Your son will read about it one day."

"From a two-bit tournament in Ipswich?"

"Yes, even from here. If you think that all those wonderful games of Lasker and Alekhine were played in the major capitals of the world, to the cheers of the multitudes, you're being deliberately obtuse."

"You're talking about the ghosts of Christmas past."

"Which all leads to today. Chess has no boundaries. Lopez and Lombardy were Catholic priests and, at the end, Alekhine wrote anti-semitic articles for the Nazis. And there were those who should have been champion, but never were. I don't want that to happen to you. You're approaching the full strength of your craft. You could be one of the truly great ones."

"Better yet," said Ryder, trying to get von Friedenthal off his case, "why don't we talk about a champion of champions. Some German guy by the name of von Friedenthal."

Von Friedenthal nodded his acknowledgement, but said, "Don't play schoolyard dodge ball with me, young man." Martin paused with a thoughtful smile. "By the way, talking about school, did I ever tell you that I attended university not far from here?"

Ryder was happy with the diversion. "Born and raised in Heidelberg and you came to England to be educated?"

"That's the way it was done back then. Yes, in those days it was considered quite the fashion for young men of good family to be educated abroad. Young English gentlemen attended Heidelberg University or the Sorbonne. In my case, as a German, it was Cambridge. I had no choice in the matter. It was decided for me." Von Friedenthal again speared Ryder with his pipe stem and fixed him with a knowing eye. "But, as usual, I digress and with no small help from you. What I was going to say was—"

As von Friedenthal spoke, Ryder felt it again. That damned mental presence. He turned his back to the bar and watched as the Leopard crossed the barroom.

Ryder was relieved. Anything to save him from another lecture. There was no stopping von Friedenthal once he got going.

"Good evening, Doctor von Friedenthal—Mr. Ryder. Please excuse the interruption. My name is Andrew Hall. I wish to congratulate you on a fine game and to thank you both for these past two days. It was a pleasure to observe your match."

Andrew Hall stood as quietly as he'd sat, earlier, in the auditorium. He appeared to be in his mid-fifties and a couple of inches over six feet. Short, iron-gray hair framed an unlined face.

Ryder had seen that face before, or rather that look. Some high-ranking military officers had it, as did the occasional financial tycoon, presiding in splendid isolation at the head of the boardroom conference table. Ryder knew it wasn't a look so much as an attitude, an attitude of unquestioned authority, of command.

"As soon as I heard there would be a final match, I made it a point to be here. When you two gentlemen meet, the results can be most stimulating."

Von Friedenthal gestured with his pipe. "You've an interest in the game then, Mr. Hall?"

"Doctor von Friedenthal, I wasn't present when you first won the world championship, but I've had the pleasure of seeing you defend that title several times. I've spent many hours playing over your games and trying to solve the problems in your books. To my mind, you have set the standard against which all others must be measured. I appreciate excellence, especially yours."

Von Friedenthal was pleased. "You're too kind. I'm not too old to be flattered, so I thank you—but this day belongs to John. I've been telling him how his game today has opened a whole new realm of possibilities." Von

Friedenthal removed a tobacco pouch from his pocket and sat fingering the well-worn leather. "Why, I am actually impatient to get home and set up a board so that I can begin replaying the moves. Maybe I can discover just exactly what he did to me. I haven't been this excited in years." Von Friedenthal smiled fondly at Ryder. "He makes me wish I were forty years younger."

"I understand completely, Doctor von Friedenthal. Mr. Ryder has achieved more in these last two days than he realizes. That's the reason I'm here." For the first time, Andrew Hall looked directly at Ryder. "May I ask what your immediate plans are?"

It had been a tough couple of days. "Perhaps another drink and dinner with Martin. Why? Care to join us?"

Hall smiled faintly. "Frankly, that doesn't sound like an invitation. In any case, it was I who was going to invite you to join me. Early tomorrow morning, I intend to be on a lake in Scotland. I want you to be there with me."

Ryder raised a disbelieving eyebrow.

"Doctor von Friedenthal," continued Hall without pausing, "please excuse me. I mean no disrespect, but my business now is with Mr. Ryder. I sincerely wish it were otherwise."

Hall turned back to Ryder. "You're known for your unconventional approach to things. This trip will be of interest to you and, more importantly, it will give us an opportunity to talk. It's a matter of some urgency." Hall spoke with absolute confidence.

Ryder studied the man. "Mr. Hall, I seldom pack for fishing when I'm playing chess."

For the first time there was a flicker of emotion on Hall's face.

"It's been arranged. We'll dine on the way and clothing will be provided. When the trip is over, you will be returned here, to your hotel."

"Just like that," said Ryder.

Hall again turned to von Friedenthal. "Doctor von Friedenthal, please forgive my bad manners."

"Don't give it a thought," von Friedenthal said. "However, I'm a bit puzzled. I've spent some time in this area and I know that the public transportation system in England is outstanding. Within reason, one can always get from here to there. But how do you propose to accomplish all this at this time of night? It's surely much too far to drive."

"There's a small airfield just a few miles north of here. By jet, from takeoff to landing, it's less than an hour's flight. Time, in that respect, is not the problem."

Almost with an air of confrontation, Hall faced Ryder. "Well, Mr. Ryder, what do you say?"

Again, Ryder felt that tentacle of thought. He looked sharply at Hall. There was no mistaking the sardonic gleam in Hall's eyes.

Ryder knew he had unfinished business with the Leopard, but not like this and not now. He was empty inside, without purpose, adrift in swollen seas. For want of something better to do, he shrugged his acceptance. Hall could think what he wanted.

"Excellent. The hotel has been instructed to hold your room. Your driver will be here in thirty minutes. Be ready."

Hall turned to von Friedenthal and held out his hand. In flawless German, he said, "It has been an honor to meet you, Doctor von Friedenthal. But for now, *Auf Wiedersehen*. I wish you a safe journey home. You're driving, I believe, to the ferry at Felixstowe? Please give my best regards to your wife and daughters." With a slight bow and a nod to Ryder, he was gone.

Von Friedenthal, busy refilling his pipe, muttered under his breath. "Unconventional approach to things? Felixstowe? Ha! I'd like to know as much about him as he knows about us." Von Friedenthal reached for a box of matches on the bar. "Strange, but I could swear I've met him before. I don't think I would forget such a man." Von Friedenthal waved his pipe in the air like a baton. "When he looks at me, I feel as if someone is walking on my grave."

"He's a bit much, all right. And listen, you old crock—what was all that business about you can't wait to get home so you can set up the board to replay the game? You've probably played two variations over in your head while we were having drinks."

"Actually—three. You have to be careful with outsiders. They wouldn't understand."

Ryder looked doubtful. "I'm not so sure—"

Suddenly, von Friedenthal straightened. "My God, now I remember! Strange, but I haven't thought of it in years, As I told you, I went to school here. It was the usual university prank. We had a secret society and part of the initiation involved a Druid ceremony."

"Give it a break."

"I'm quite serious. Although that was many years ago, there are still some today who follow the old ways." Von Friedenthal puffed furiously on his pipe.

"I know the British are into all kinds of weird clubs, but Druid ceremonies? Get real."

"Not only here, but in Germany, too. It's not often spoken of, but there is much more to it than one thinks. Unfortunately, many of them have forgotten the Oak Tree."

"Martin, what the hell are we talking about?"

"Sorry, the word Druid means knowing, or finding, the Oak Tree. There are those who...well, never mind, it's not important and, as usual, I digress." Von Friedenthal drained his glass. "As I was saying, there was a ceremony with a Druid priest, you know, a priest in a long brown robe with a cowl. Apparently, somebody got hold of the real thing."

You're still doing it."

"I never did see his face," mused von Friendenthal, "but he gave me nightmares for years. I felt the bugger could read my mind. I've had that same feeling ever since we started yesterday's game." Von Friendenthal shook his head. "Ha! My imagination is getting the best of me." He raised his voice, "Innkeeper!" then leaned closer to Ryder. "Thank God, I don't have to do the driving."

"I never knew a little Scotch to stop you."

Fortified with a fresh drink, von Friedenthal said, "More to the point, my friend, just exactly what does our Mr. Hall want with you, and in such a rush? I really don't think it has anything to do with fishing, if you know what I mean."

"He probably wants me to teach his kids how to play chess or some other fool thing." Ryder swirled the last of his Scotch around, drank it, and set the empty glass carefully on the bar. "I wonder what you catch in Scotland at this time of year..."

"He never said." Von Friedenthal's voice was serious. "John, my boy, watch yourself."

Chapter IV

Ryder leaned on the oars and said, with a mirthless laugh, "I know the Scots are tight with a buck but, good God, just a little grease on these oarlocks—what a racket!"

"Keep your voice down," said Andrew Hall. "Let me know when you see anything out of the ordinary."

"I thought we were going fishing."

"The fishing tackle has little to do with our presence here. No one questions the actions of a pair of fishermen. Just keep rowing and do try to be quiet."

Hall had insisted that they couldn't use a motor so Ryder had volunteered to row. After some fifty minutes, he wished he'd kept his mouth shut. It was a big lake. His muscles weren't tuned for this kind of exercise.

The mist was beginning to thin when Hall leaned forward, touched Ryder's knee, and whispered, "Stop rowing. Quiet now. Look there—about two points to starboard."

Ryder turned and looked over his left shoulder. There was a long moment of disbelief. "Look at the size of him! You're not trying to tell me he's real?"

"Then why are you whispering?"

"Come on! That's the Loch Ness Monster, for Christ's sake. Those things died out millions of years ago. And, by the way, has it occurred to you that, if we can see him, he can see us."

Hall smiled sadly. "He's very old now and hasn't yet seen us, but he knows we're here. There's no danger, especially not for you. I've watched him for many years. I suppose you could say we are old acquaintances. However, I don't think I shall see him again. That's why time was so very short. He's been waiting for you. He's the first test."

As Hall spoke, Ryder thought he also heard another voice in the mist. He looked around for a moment and then turned back to face what could not be there, but was. The two men watched in the early morning mist as the beast's head turned from side to side, like a creature from some childhood nightmare. It saw them now.

Drawn by an unknown force, Ryder stood up. He should be afraid, but he wasn't. He had the strangest feeling that he was about to be judged. They looked at each other, man and beast, across the span of a hundred yards and a hundred million years. The two men in the boat were silent, each with his own thoughts, until the beast was gone.

"I've lost an oar."

"I know." Hall's voice was surprisingly soft. "It's over there. If you'll pass me the other one—"

Ryder sat down and handed Hall the remaining oar. He watched as his companion held the shaft against the transom with his left hand and set the boat in motion with a sculling stroke. In his shapeless yellow slicker and rubber boots, Andrew Hall bore little resemblance to the well-dressed gentleman Ryder had first met. He could just as easily see the man standing on the bridge of one of Her Majesty's capital ships, as sitting here in this rowboat in the middle of a lake in Scotland.

"There, that's got it," Hall said, retrieving the dripping oar. "Shall we change places? I'll row back; it can be difficult if you're not used to it. I think we could both do with a good breakfast and some hot tea. I can well imagine what you're thinking."

As they exchanged seats, Ryder couldn't resist. "Another example of the fine British art of understatement?"

Hall only nodded and started pulling for the dock with an effortless back-and-arm motion—the oars' even bite and feathered return stroke— while his eyes never left Ryder's face.

Something was different now. The last freshly baked roll was gone. Ryder sighed and reached for the teapot. He was seated across from Hall in the pleasant breakfast room of a small inn overlooking the lake. The tourist season had yet to begin and they had the place to themselves.

"You've hauled me around the countryside in your private jet, introduced me to a creature that doesn't exist—before breakfast, I might add— and then you have the balls to say you can imagine what I'm thinking. If these last couple of days are any indication, you already know. Mister Hall, what do you want?"

Hall offered his hand. "First, let's dispense with the formalities, shall we? Call me Andrew. To answer your question, it's really quite simple, I need your help."

Ryder hesitated for a moment, then took Hall's hand. "I play chess." Looking out of the window toward the lake, he added, "And that, you'll find, is a talent somewhat limited in scope."

"Perhaps. You must excuse the mental gymnastics and the abrupt introduction out there, but time was critical. I hope that I haven't erred on the side of the dramatic, but I had to know."

"What?"

"Why is it that you don't wear a watch?"

"Say again."

"Why is it that you don't wear a watch?"

"What's that got to do with anything?"

"Would you answer the question."

"I don't wear a watch because I don't need one. I've always known what time it was."

"I'm told that you only write down your moves at a chess match because it is required. It is said that you can replay, from memory, the moves of any game that you have ever played."

"Who the hell have you been talking—"

Hall interrupted. "A year ago in St. Louis against Bonner—what was your eighteenth move?"

"You can't be serious."

"Your eighteenth move?"

Ryder thought back. He didn't have to work at it, it was just there. He remembered the icy, gray slush that covered the streets that winter's day—and the game. "Bishop takes knight."

Hall nodded. "Winfield—New York—four years ago—his forty-third move?"

"Pawn to rook six. What's your point?"

Hall didn't answer, but sat looking out over the lake.

Ryder sipped his tea and waited. He wasn't patient by nature; it was an art he was trying to develop. His defeats at the chessboard had taught him not to go jousting at windmills until he knew something more about windmills. He was sure of only one thing—he no longer believed this had anything to do with chess.

At last, pointing to the lake, Hall asked, "What did you feel out there?"

Ryder didn't answer.

"It's important. I wouldn't ask if it wasn't."

"That this is his world, not mine."

"Anything else?"

To buy time, Ryder took another sip of tea, then looked straight at Hall. "I had the feeling that he was waiting for me."

"As I said."

"That doesn't mean one damn thing."

Hall sat as still as only he could. Ryder suddenly felt those mental fingers again. He closed his mind and looked steadily back at Hall. "No, you don't, my friend," he said. "Not ever again."

Hall spoke as if nothing had happened. "I'm a very rich man, John, one of the world's richest." Hall paused, waiting for Ryder's reaction. He was refilling his teacup. Hall continued.

"Wealth has been in my family for over a thousand years. Our holdings are worldwide—there is scarcely a place on earth where we don't have an interest of some sort. You've never heard of me, or my family. We take great pains to keep it that way."

Hall raised a cautioning finger. "I'm telling you this for a purpose. Should the question ever arise in your mind, let me make this point perfectly clear. I've neither the time nor the inclination for practical jokes or petty diversions. I found you again only by accident. That's the reason we are sitting here, together, at this table."

"You still haven't said what it is that you want. I play chess. It's true that I can do a couple of minor parlor tricks, but not the kind of thing you've been up to."

Hall gave a short bark of laughter. "And you accuse the British of understatement. But—to business. You planned on spending some time in London before returning to the States. Instead, I want you to join me at my home. There's someone you must meet. You'll learn what this is all about and come to understand why I need your help in a matter of vital importance." Hall cleared his throat. "If it's of any interest to you, I can't read your mind against your will."

24

"You're all questions and no answers."

"This is neither the time nor the place to speak of such things. Please bear with me." Hall waited before speaking again. "You must agree!"

With unseeing eyes, Ryder looked out over the lake. Stacey will never believe...damn it all to hell! There I go again. There was no one to tell, there was nothing to share. There was only the memory of a merciless morgue light on a stranger's white, dead face.

Ryder was using every distraction he could think of. He had to keep moving or the darkness would pull him down, too. He turned back to Hall.

"I've nothing you want. If you don't believe me, then that's your problem." A quirk of a smile appeared. "Also, you're an overbearing ass."

The two men stared at each other across the breakfast table, eyes locked.

"All right, then." Ryder leaned forward, his smile gone. "You know damn well I can't just walk away. But, I warn you—no more lakes."

Andrew Hall saluted Ryder with his teacup. "I promise—nothing like that."

Chapter V

It was early evening when Ryder opened the French doors of his room and stepped out onto a small balcony. There was a hush in the air, the last lingering light of day had a soft, golden clarity.

The manor house was built against a hill and looked out over a large park. Directly below the balcony was a white gravel driveway which led to a group of smaller buildings at one side of the main house. Across the drive were formal gardens with a grove of exceptionally large and stately trees at the center. In the park itself, sheep grazed among widely spaced oaks. A stream meandered into a large pond where ducks and geese conversed in soft night sounds.

Ryder had assumed, when accepting Hall's invitation, that he would be staying in London. Instead, he was somewhere to the west, somewhere deep in the Cotswolds. He was learning not to assume when dealing with Andrew Hall.

Earlier today, a driver had picked him up at his hotel. He was a surprised when the Rolls, an island of silence, had skirted London and headed west on the M4 motorway. The driver hadn't volunteered any information; in fact, he'd hardly spoken at all, apparently in shock over the idea of Ryder sitting up front. They left the motorway and headed toward Swindon on 419. After Cirencester, Ryder had stopped worrying about where they were going and decided to wait and see.

Finally the car slowed. To the left, a square tower of an old Norman church stood strong above the trees. To the right was a gatehouse of honey-colored stone and a pair of ornate iron gates. A white gravel road disappeared among the trees.

The gates swung open as they turned into the drive. After they'd passed through, Ryder glanced back. He watched as the gates begin to close and felt the ghost of a shiver. Come on, he thought, it's nothing more than electronics.

The road wound through thickly wooded, rolling hills. Finally, through the trees, he'd seen the mansion and the balcony, where he now stood. The house itself was large and built of the same honey-colored stone as the gate-house.

Which brought him full circle to what he was trying most not to think about. Ryder put his hands on the stone balcony railing and closed his eyes. He saw another house on a lake—empty rooms—closets filled with Stacey's clothes—her scent—the echo of her voice. Maybe, if he never went home, none of it was really true.

Ryder's internal clock told him that it was time to join his host. He took one last look around, reluctant to leave. As he watched, the day turned to a velvet dusk and then, a moment later, it was dark.

When Ryder entered the library, Andrew Hall turned away from the young woman he'd been speaking with. "Ah, there you are, Mr. Ryder. Sorry I couldn't be here when you arrived, but you were in good hands. Bentwood tells me you've settled in."

Ryder nodded. "I thought we'd be meeting in London."

"It's much more private here, don't you agree."

Ryder nodded again, but his eyes were drawn to the woman who was in her early twenties, with the flawless pale complexion that so many English women seemed to have. She was striking in a simple, but elegant black dress. Waves of sable hair were arranged on her head like a crown.

"I'd like you to meet my daughter, Katherine," Hall said.

She smiled and offered her hand. "I'm pleased to finally meet you, Mr. Ryder," she said, her voice as soft and beautiful as she was.

They shook hands. "The pleasure's all mine," said Ryder.

Katherine had the same air of stillness as her father and wore no lip-stick or jewelry. With her head tilted to one side, she looked at him with a slightly quizzical expression. "So this is the famous John Ryder I've been hearing so much about." She seemed faintly amused and a little disappointed. She was probably quite accustomed to her effect on men. "Congratulations on your tournament, and welcome to Hall House."

"Thanks."

"May we offer you a drink?"

"Scotch, please, no ice."

"How very continental of you, Mr. Ryder," she said, raising an eyebrow.

Hall led Ryder to a pair of couches on either side of a fireplace, where a cheerful blaze provided pleasant warmth against the evening's chill. "Please make yourself comfortable."

Without the distraction of Katherine, Ryder was able to study his surroundings for the first time. They were in a spacious, high-ceilinged room. The polished wooden floor was divided into areas by Oriental rugs. In a bay window, at the front of the room, a concert grand piano stood in splendid isolation.

There was a leather-topped desk, as well as several wing chairs and low tables with vases of fresh flowers. There was also a game table with a chess set, and a sideboard, where Katherine was preparing their drinks. Shaded lamps cast warm pools of light against the darkness.

The four walls of the room were lined with shelves of beautifully bound books. Where there weren't books, there were oil paintings. On the way in, Ryder couldn't help noticing another painting in the great hall outside.

Katherine handed drinks around and then joined her father on the couch across from Ryder. He looked toward the grand piano in the window at the front of the room. "Do you play?" he asked Katherine.

"Quite badly, I'm afraid. The Bechstein deserves better." She smiled. "Are you aware that the newspaper says your game with Doctor von Friedenthal will probably be the 'Immortal Game' of this century? You must be most pleased."

"I haven't seen the papers," replied Ryder. "It sounds as if someone let his imagination get the better of him or perhaps he had trouble filling his column."

"Oh, not the Times, Mr. Ryder. But, I must say, that's very modest of you." For some reason, John Ryder annoyed her and it was making her task easier. She wondered if it might have something to do with that disturbing little smile at the corner of his mouth, or with that splendid tan. From somewhere at the back of her mind came the words "fatal Irish charm."

Katherine looked at him over the rim of her glass. "Do you have any Irish ancestors, Mr. Ryder?"

Ryder appealed to Hall. "Is she going to ask what Carter's thirty-second move was?"

"No, I'm not, Mr. Ryder," continued Katherine. "But, after all, you've made quite a name for yourself."

"I have?"

"Come now. I've read that you are considered the great American hope, that you have more native ability than any man alive. You are expected to beat the Russians at their own game, to bring the chess title back to the West."

"Do *they* know this?"

Katherine, eyes sparkling, changed the subject. "My father tells me that you and Doctor von Friedenthal are old friends."

"We met over a chessboard in New York City about ten years ago. Martin was giving an exhibition in simultaneous play. He won easily. It's a habit he's continued over the years, but at least he got me to take the game seriously." Ryder frowned. "Could we talk about something else?"

Hall observed the exchange in silence, head turning from one to the other, eyes sharp with interest.

The evening passed quickly. Ryder had another drink and the conversation became general. When Katherine discovered that Ryder wasn't interested in talking about himself, she stopped prodding him. Ryder found that he was actually beginning to enjoy himself.

Later, in the dining room, he was in for a surprise. England isn't famous for its cuisine, but this was different. The dinner, and the fine wines that accompanied it, was excellent. Ryder had just the hint of a buzz on. It was pleasant to talk to a beautiful woman—Katherine's voice, the hint of perfume, the rustle of her clothes when she moved—but he would have gladly traded all the world's beautiful women to see Stacey seated across the table from him.

It was apparent that the Halls had a deep affection for one another. Every once in a while, Ryder would look up to discover Katherine studying him. In the candlelight, her eyes seemed to deepen in intensity. He began to wonder if she was only a figment of his imagination. It wasn't his imagination, though, when he saw her nod to her father in answer to an unspoken question.

Ryder was annoyed with himself at the faint pang of disappointment when he heard that Katherine was leaving for London immediately after dinner. There was mention of an early morning business appointment. She had, at her father's request, stayed on only to meet him.

In the great hall, Katherine, cool and poised, offered her hand. "Please excuse me for not joining you in the library; I still have much to do. Mr. Ryder, I enjoyed meeting you. I didn't think I would. Bright young men can be such bores; they always want to tell you about it. It has been an agreeable surprise. You're obviously level-headed." She reflected for a moment. "An attribute you're going to need. Goodbye—and good luck!" Katherine took her hand back, dismissing him.

"Father, may I speak with you for a moment?"

"Of course, my dear. John, please go on into the library and help yourself to a brandy. I'll be with you directly."

In the library, Ryder turned to shut the door. The Halls were standing quietly, watching him. Why had she felt it necessary to wish him luck? Carefully, he closed the library door.

Chapter VI

"Sorry to keep you waiting," said Hall, as he entered the library. "A matter required immediate attention—Katherine will see to it." Hall selected a cigar from the humidor on the desk. "You don't smoke, but this is the one vice I allow myself." He rolled the cigar between thumb and forefinger, then held it briefly to his nose. "Cuban—which only proves that a little Communism isn't necessarily a bad thing."

Ryder stretched his legs and, brandy snifter in hand, stared into the fire. "It wouldn't be too hard to get used to this."

"Thank you. We have other houses, but they are merely places to stay. This is our home. I lost my wife many years ago and, since then, Katherine and I have had to carry on by ourselves. We seldom have guests here."

"I'd think you'd need a large staff for an estate of this size."

"Not at all. A half dozen or so. James drove you up from London and Bentwood showed you to your room. His wife prepared our meal and their daughter Heather helped at table tonight. The others are mostly involved with outside duties. They've been here all their lives."

"I was under the impression that sort of thing had gone out of style."

There was a hint of steel in Hall's voice. "They are here by choice."

"When I first started playing on the international circuit, I made the mistake of staying with people who were considered wealthy. I don't do that anymore. All the fetching and carrying bothered the hell out of me."

"As I told you, back at the lake, we've had centuries to learn the true value of wealth. I still manage to put my trousers on all by myself and as far as Katherine is concerned—well, you've met my daughter." Hall blew a smoke ring. "She dislikes pretension of any sort."

"While you two were talking, I couldn't help noticing the Gutenberg."

"It's one of the first." Hall looked around the room. "There are so many old things here at Hall House and around the estate, we take them for granted."

"Like hanging a Rembrandt in the hall outside?"

"That, too. And did you notice the trees out in the garden?"

Ryder knew this wasn't small talk. Hall was apparently trying to make a point of some sort. He nodded.

"They're cedars of Lebanon, brought back from the Crusades by one of my ancestors and planted where they now stand. As English history goes, this house is relatively new and built on the foundation of an earlier one that was destroyed in the thirteenth century. That was the last time anyone entered these grounds without an invitation. We still have the occasional poacher, but that is easily dealt with."

Suddenly, the peaceful atmosphere—the firelight, the aroma of a fine cigar, the mellow color of the brandy in Ryder's glass—was gone. There was more to this place than rare old books, priceless paintings, and unusual trees. Ryder could almost taste it.

He'd had the same feeling this afternoon watching those iron gates swing shut. Something lurked beneath the surface—something dangerous. Although it hadn't happened again, the feeling of evil he'd experienced back at the chess match was never far from his mind. Von Friedenthal had warned him to be careful.

"Who are you?" asked Ryder.

Hall shifted in his chair to look directly at Ryder. "Not what you are."

"Come off it, will you." Ryder was growing impatient. "Let's just cut to the chase."

Hall's voice was serious. "I know more about you than you can imagine."

"Why bother? It's no big deal."

"What time is it?"

Ryder sighed and raised his glass to look at the brandy turned to amber in the firelight.

"No—no more tricks. I really would like to know."

"It's just after eleven."

"Good, then. I appreciate your forbearance. I'm not insensitive to your situation."

Ryder looked bored.

"I have waited for thirty years," snapped Hall. "Perhaps you can bear with me for five minutes."

Ryder was warming the brandy glass with his hands. "It's your move."

Hall placed a careful inch of cigar ash in the ashtray. "I know about Fletcher's gorge."

Ryder paused in surprise. "You can't. There was no one there."

"In your high school junior year, the new mathematics teacher formed a chess club. The game fascinated you. You also had offers of athletic scholarships from a number of colleges; however, your mother died and you joined the navy, instead. Afterwards, bored with university life, and with Martin von Friedenthal's encouragement, you committed yourself more and more to your present profession. You inherited a modest sum of money, which permits you to be independent. You like fast cars."

Ryder was still spooked. How in the hell could he know about Fletcher's Gorge?

"Among your colleagues, it's generally agreed that you could be world champion—if you put your mind to it. Except for your son, you are alone. You keep physically active. The last time you played squash, you thoroughly thrashed the resident professional. He's thinking of retiring at the tender age of twenty-five."

"And I know guys who run six miles every day," said Ryder. "I hope this isn't what you had to tell me. I know how it comes out."

"Do you? In the few short years since you left your home, the stories of your earlier feats, at the chessboard and on the playing field, have become so distorted that they are no longer valid. In the minutes to come, try to remember how easy it is to step over the fine line between fact and fiction."

Hall stood up and threw his cigar into the fire. "Finish your brandy. We're going for a walk."

In the hall, to Ryder's surprise, Hall turned left, toward the rear of the house and away from the front door. They passed through several rooms, finally entering a small sitting room. There were no windows.

"Close the door behind you. When I said this house was built on the site of the previous one, there was a more compelling reason than family pride or tradition." Hall crossed the room to a fireplace much like the one in the library. He placed both hands on the mantel.

There was the muted rumbling of powerful motors, more sensed than heard. Slowly, the back wall began to swing out and away from the room. The whole wall was one enormous door. The lights of the sitting room barely penetrated the darkness beyond. Ryder was watching Hall and the doorway, both at the same time.

"This will not function unless the other door is closed," said Hall. "There are several interlocking devices, one of the advantages of modern technology."

Hall threw some switches on the portion of the wall that could be seen through the open doorway, then motioned for Ryder to follow. A series of wall fixtures illuminated a wide passageway that sloped gradually downward. Ryder couldn't see where it lead.

"Come along. The door will close and lock automatically," said Hall, as they stepped through the doorway. "It's constructed much like a vault door and weighs several tons."

Ryder kept a sharp eye on Hall as he followed him through the door. He realized they were now inside the hill behind the house, that this corridor was actually a tunnel. However, unlike any tunnel he had ever seen, this one was paneled and carpeted. Finally, the tunnel leveled off and there were lights ahead.

They entered a huge chamber, a natural underground cavern so large, the ceiling was lost in the darkness. The air was pleasantly warm, dry, and faintly scented.

The cavern was hung with tapestries and brightly colored pennants and banners. Suits of armor, shields, and lances were arranged along the walls. Evenly spaced racks of swords, maces, battle-axes, and morning stars marched across the floor. At the back of the cavern, lighted candles were on what appeared to be an altar.

The thought dawned on Ryder. It's a museum. Then, his eyes widened. "Holy shit," he said, his voice loud in the silence. First the lake, now this.

Standing alone in the center of the cavern, was a round table. Suddenly, he knew. Somehow—he had always known. Ryder turned to bombard Hall with questions, but the man had vanished.

Like a moth to the flame, Ryder approached the table. It was massive, its true size lost in the vast chamber. He looked at the names carved deeply into the thick, dark wood. Some were different from what they were called now, but he recognized them all. *Percivale. Tristram. Launcelot.*

Ryder again looked around, but he was still alone. It didn't matter. The only thing that mattered was how he knew these things.

On the far side of the table, nearest the altar, was a final name. Arthur. Ryder ran his fingers over the letters worn smooth by the centuries, his thoughts racing.

Reluctantly, he turned his back to the table and looked up at the altar. Steps chiseled out of the native rock led to the platform on which the altar stood. Behind it, on the roughhewn wall, hung a tapestry, different from all the others. It was of a woodland scene, a large tree in the foreground.

Ryder slowly mounted the steps. A scarlet and gold cloth covered the top of the altar, on which lay a sword. The hilt wasn't encrusted with jewels, there was nothing written on the blade, but from the far reaches of buried time, Excalibur seemed to whisper to him—*believe.*

As Ryder straightened up again, the tapestry caught his eye. He went around behind the altar for a closer look. It seemed incredibly old, though parts of it might have been newer than others. He realized that the leaves of the tree were not leaves at all, but names.

Those nearest the trunk were blurred and faded, but farther out along the branches the colors were brighter and clearer. On the tip of a branch almost touching the ground with the weight of years, was a date, above which, newly stitched into the fabric of the tapestry, was the name "John Ryder."

Suddenly, Ryder realized he was no longer alone. On the other side of the altar stood a cowled figure in a long brown robe. It held Excalibur, blade cradled in the crook of its left arm.

Von Friedenthal's talk of Druid ceremonies and visions of human sacrifice flashed through Ryder's mind. Adrenaline surged through his body. Without moving, he was ready, eyes riveted on the sword and the first flicker of the blade that would set him in motion across the cavern and the nearest rack of weapons.

"How do you like the needlework?" said the voice of Andrew Hall. "Katherine did it after dinner, while we were in the library."

"She's supposed to be on her way to London." Ryder's voice was sharp with fear, his body bowstring tight.

"She was the second test and it was a small, but necessary subterfuge. It's a task that has been performed from the very beginning. Fifteen hundred years of history are woven into that tapestry." The brown-robed figure nodded.

"By the way, Doctor von Friedenthal was partially correct; it was my father that he met long ago. The rest is wrong. Druid priests are now teachers, not executioners." The warmth of Hall's voice suggested that he was amused. "You cannot take this sword from me by force. Someday, but not today."

The brown-robed figure with Andrew Hall's voice said, "If I may?" Slowly, so as not to trigger Ryder, he turned the blade in his hands and extended the sword, hilt first.

"Take it, John Ryder. It belongs to you now. Welcome home."

Chapter VII

He was moving better now. It was almost over before it had really gotten started. He'd never in his life been hit so hard. He peered warily through the inadequate slit in his coffin of steel, trying to locate the source of his torment.

"Where the hell are you?" Ryder was talking to himself as he lunged about, almost falling.

The object of his search was a suit of fifteenth-century plate armor. The armor looked surprisingly shiny and new. The suit of armor stood some twenty feet away, leaning on the hilt of a huge two-handed broadsword just like his own. The sword also looked new. The suit of armor appeared to be watching him. It was hard to tell.

It wasn't at all what he'd imagined. Where were the festive crowds, the gaily colored tents, the trumpets, the stamping horses, and the fair princess seated at the usurper's side?

It had sounded easy. Christ, he had trouble even picking up his sword, much less using it to any noticeable effect. And ever present at the back of his mind was the duck pond. If he fell into the water wearing all this metal, he was sure as hell going to drown.

He studied his opponent. The figure standing in the sunlit meadow had nothing to do with some dusty suit of armor in a forgotten corner of a museum. For one thing, it moved and for another, it hit. Yea verily, brother, did it hit!

In a fit of galloping insanity or still under the influence of the visit to the cavern last night, he had simplemindedly agreed to this combat. Perhaps he was hoping to relive the days when he and Bobby Clark, using fruit-basket lids for shields, had bounded around the backyard, enthusiastically whacking each other's wooden swords until someone got his knuckles mashed and, with dire threats of "I'm telling my Mom," went home crying.

Ryder was lying to himself. He was still running and knew he would someday have to stop, but not yet. He wasn't ready to face the rest of his life without Stacey.

He had allowed himself to be stuffed and buckled into this ridiculous suit of armor by two of Hall's men. For God and country and the princess, of course, he had tottered out, onto the green.

Then it began. He had seen the first blow coming and had partially blocked it, but from then on he hadn't seen much of anything. He had been struck repeatedly with forehand and backhand blows to his arms, chest, and shoulders. He had even been hit from the side. He wondered where he'd gotten the idea that this was going to be fun. This was full combat and it wasn't fun.

Finally! The sensation of freewheeling overdrive cut in. At first, because the sword was real, Ryder had been tentative about actually trying to hit someone with it. But not anymore.

With thunder in his heart, his sword feather light, he reared back and struck a mighty blow at his enemy, only to find himself staggering down the field with the force of his near miss and the weight of his sword. Ryder's sole purpose in life was instantly reduced to remaining in an upright position. What he got for his trouble was a vigorous thwack, square on the top of his helmet.

His ears ringing, and bathed in sweat, he was amazed that he was still standing. Somewhere along the line he had come to the conclusion that the knights of old hadn't been cut down but were, instead, battered into submission, blow by blow.

So much for the flower of knighthood, chivalry, and all that good stuff. The fair princess would have to do the best she could without him. It just wasn't worth it. He had to end it quickly.

From one end of England to the other, countless brave and true knights, sleeping peacefully beneath the sod, turned collectively in their graves as John Ryder, sword raised high, and looking more like a spastic robot than one of knighthood's finest, lurched to the final attack.

Dropping its sword, the suit of armor staggered back a step or two, raised its metal hands in feeble protest, and toppled backward with a loud crash. Immediately, the two attendants were at its side. They quickly stripped the armor from the body of Andrew Hall.

Then it was Ryder's turn. The men removed his helmet, exposing him once more to the glories of a Cotswold morning. One man wiped Ryder's streaming face with a towel, while the other helped remove his armor. Pieces lay strewn on the grass like some great dissected beetle—thorax here, legs there, and finally, the head.

Ryder looked sourly at Hall, who was rolling back and forth on the grass, making a strange keening noise. When Hall attempted to sit up, he again saw Ryder's two-handed sword buried, blade deep, in the trunk of a venerable oak. One look and Hall started rolling again, still making that noise. He was laughing.

"Crap," said Ryder, and the keening sound went up in pitch. Ryder shook his head as he looked at the sword. He made no move to touch it. As far as he was concerned, it could stay where it was.

Hall's men had almost reached the house. They hadn't said a word the whole time, as if suits of armor wandering around the grounds were an everyday occurrence. Jesus! What was it with this place? Ryder sat down, his back against an oak, and began examining his welts and bruises. At least nothing seemed to be broken.

It was too much. The mind reading, the beast, and last night's visit to the cavern were just too damn much. Also, last night, he'd gone along with Hall's request to wait even longer to tell his story, but this was it. He had paid full measure for his curiosity and was going to be stiff and sore. He didn't relish the prospect. He refused to be hazed any further.

"It's time to call it quits. If you'll have your driver drop me off at the nearest station, I'll catch the next train back to London."

Hall rose and came to sit by Ryder. He was no longer laughing. "I apologize." Hall wiped his streaming eyes with the back of his hand. "I wasn't making sport of you. If only you knew how long I have waited for this moment."

"To hit me up alongside the head?"

"Why do you insist in being so—so American," snapped Hall.

"Where I come from, you can be any damned thing you want."

Hall struggled to regain his composure. "I'd just about given up all hope." He indicated the armor. "I shouldn't have let it go this far, but bear with me. What you have seen here, and what I am about to tell you, is for you alone. It can never be repeated—do you understand—never!"

"If you're so concerned about what I might say, why tell me at all?"

"Because," said Hall, who looked as if he had a toothache, "I must. Your word."

"All right, then—my word. Besides, who's going to believe me?" Ryder was tenderly fingering one of his rapidly blooming welts. "I keep hoping I'm going to wake up and none of this is real." Ryder grinned. He looked very young.

"Except for the part where I beat Martin von Friendenthal."

Chapter VIII

"About fifteen hundred years ago," said Hall, leaning back against an oak tree, "quite near here, a minor chieftain had a son who we now know as Arthur. From the very beginning, the boy was special. He did things differently. It seemed as if Arthur had only to think about doing something difficult and he was somehow able to do it. While he was still a young child, he came to the attention of a Druid priest."

Ryder was massaging a cramp in his leg. "Why am I not surprised."

Hall gave Ryder a sharp nod. "Yes—Merlin. Merlin's second sight recognized in Arthur the raw material that could someday unite the warring chieftains into one strong kingdom. With the full approval of Arthur's father, Merlin became the boy's guardian and teacher."

Picking up a discarded towel, Ryder began wiping his still perspiring face and neck. He wouldn't look at Hall.

Hall paused as if not sure how to continue. "In the beginning, Merlin didn't completely understand the boy's ability or how it worked. But, by trial and error, he was gradually able to develop Arthur's skills to an amazing degree. Through physical and mental exercises, Merlin was able to communicate with Arthur at a level unknown before that time. He was able to perfect the interaction of Arthur's mind and body to the point where Arthur, now a man, actually achieved a permanently altered state of consciousness."

Tossing the towel on the grass, Ryder leaned over and picked up one of the helmets and began examining the shining steel. His own expression matched that of the lifeless metal. Someone was walking on his grave.

Hall glanced around the park, and then at Ryder. "Modern science would express it something like this—Arthur was able, through a paranormal physical phenomenon, to release a controlled psychokinetic power. The key word is controlled. It is common knowledge that, at moments of great fear or anger, some human beings have been able to perform amazing feats of physical strength. By what right does a ninety-pound woman single-handedly lift a car to free her child from beneath its wheels? It defies the laws of physics."

Ryder looked up from the helmet, glanced around the park, and then, with a guarded expression, at Hall.

"With Arthur, though, this was not a onetime or even a seldom occurrence. Plainly stated—he could, at will, draw power from the reservoir of his mind. As I said before, today there are more precise terms to describe how Arthur was different from other men, but back then Merlin simply called it The Gift."

What the hell was he doing here? Ryder stared back at Hall. He thought he'd learned his lesson about jousting at windmills. When would he ever learn?

"At the same time," continued Hall, "and encouraged by Merlin, the legend of the sword Excalibur began to spread—the sword against which none could stand. It is amazing that men prefer to attach magical powers to objects rather than to people. It wasn't the sword that was so remarkable, it was the man. In reality, he would have been just as effective with a good-sized stick, but in those dark days any unexplained condition came under the heading of magic and, as such, was readily accepted. You couldn't just go around announcing to your enemies that your leader had something called The Gift and they might as well pack it in."

Hall paused for a moment while Ryder went back to examining the helmet.

"Arthur's enemies sued for peace. How do you fight against an army that knows that its leader cannot fall? How do you fight against an army backed by an ageless magician who, they whispered, was responsible for arranging those huge monoliths at Stonehenge? Together, Arthur and Merlin proved to be unbeatable."

Ryder kept turning the helmet in his hands examining its face from every angle.

"You realize, of course, what I have told you so far basically agrees with the romanticized version of the Arthurian legend, with the exception of Arthur's unusual powers. Reality was considerably less romantic. Forget all the nonsense about Guinevere. Arthur's bride was chosen with attention to the more practical side of marriage. A king must have sons, especially in Arthur's case. It was not merely a question of succession, but of The Gift. Would Arthur's sons inherit it? Was he the founder of a new race of men? In due course,

Arthur married a sturdy girl, wide of hip, who kept his bed warm at night and bore him six strong, healthy sons."

Ryder was looking inside the helmet, as if the rest of the story was hidden in the folds of leather padding.

"As Arthur's sons grew, they exhibited none of their father's special abilities. They were all quite normal. As the king's sons, they were all skilled in the use of sword and lance, but they were not Arthur. So much for the dreams of kings. When each of the sons came of age, a place was made for him at the Round Table. They all gave service to the king, and championed his causes. Arthur and Merlin continued to watch them, hoping that one would show some sign that he, too, possessed The Gift. It was not to be."

Ryder was growing restive. Hall was beginning to annoy the hell out of him. He tossed the helmet onto the grass. It rolled over several times, then came to rest upright, where it regarded them with a baleful glare.

"The sons took wives of their own. Then it happened. In his eighth year, one of Arthur's grandsons began to display many of the same traits that had originally attracted Merlin's attention to Arthur. The boy was unusually strong and very quick. He, too, seemed to do things differently, not all the time, but often enough to catch the eye of someone watching for the signs. Arthur quietly observed the boy and then, when he was certain, went looking for Merlin."

"If you're going to do this generation by generation, we'll be here until Christmas."

Hall's voice was biting. "I'm surprised you let me get this far. I know it's difficult, but allow me the courtesy of finishing."

Ryder was slow to answer. "It's your story."

"Thank you," said Hall sarcastically. "As I was saying, together, Arthur and Merlin sought out the boy. In the privacy of Arthur's chambers, they had him repeat the simple exercises of the king's youth. It was Arthur reborn. The newly rejuvenated Merlin knew at once what had to be done. Above all else, The Gift had to be protected. The why and the wherefore didn't concern him; that it had appeared again was enough."

The more Hall talked, the more Ryder felt like he was being herded into a fast, narrowing chute.

"By this time, Merlin was very old, but he managed to live another two years and during that time he formed the foundation for what was to follow.

First, came the boy. Merlin knew that his own time was short and spent every possible moment training the youngster. Then there was the rest of it."

Ryder was rubbing his shoulders against an oak. The drying sweat made his back itch.

"To Merlin, although it didn't make any sense, it was now clear that The Gift would reappear when it would. Provision must be made to keep track of Arthur's descendants. Because the written word was against Druid belief, Merlin created a tapestry on which to record Arthur's family tree."

"I suppose that's the one in the cavern?"

"Of course, and it followed that Merlin's heirs would become the custodians of The Gift and teachers. They would monitor, test, and, whenever The Gift appeared again, be prepared to teach. As the boy was trained, so was Merlin's son Kayne, a Druid priest, and Merlin's successor. Kayne was given the secret of the mental training exercises. He quickly established a special relationship with Arthur's grandson. It has been that way ever since. The members of my family have been stewards, if you will, waiting to serve The Gift."

Ryder's mouth almost dropped open. "You've got to be kidding."

"Not hardly," said Hall impatiently. "I told you back at the lake, that I've no time or inclination for practical jokes or petty diversions."

"You wouldn't be the type."

Hall fixed Ryder with a stern eye. "The destruction of Arthur's kingdom came from within. Arthur and Merlin's obsession with the boy, to the exclusion of all else, provided the fertile soil in which the seeds of envy would grow and eventually spell the end to the kingdom. Arthur had never picked a successor. His sons could accept that, but not the possibility that one of them might be passed over in favor of the boy. They fell to quarreling amongst themselves, their vows of knighthood and chivalry forgotten. Their squabbling soon caused discord and dissension among the other members of the Round Table."

Ryder couldn't help himself. He made a derisive noise. A modern-day Merlin, for God's sake. Wait until I tell Stacey about...Ryder closed his eyes in pain. He was very much alone.

"At the worst possible moment, Merlin died. Within the week, with Merlin's magic no longer there to protect him, Arthur was murdered in his sleep. The next morning, when they came to ask Kayne's advice, he and his family were gone. Soon after, it was discovered that Arthur's grandson had also disappeared. An intensive search was undertaken, but they were never found."

"Because none of this is real."

Hall shook his head impatiently. "During the years of Arthur's reign, it wasn't unusual for Merlin to disappear for extended periods of time. Many thought that he was communing with the gods, but the truth was quite simple. He traveled. He was intensely interested in places and especially people. It was said that he ventured all the way to China. However, it was certain that he knew every part of this island. Earlier, his knowledge of the terrain had proved invaluable to Arthur in his military campaigns."

Ryder made a throwaway motion with his hand. "What else."

"On one of his first expeditions, Merlin discovered the cavern we visited last night. He stored the information away for possible future use. It was to this very place that Kayne, his family, and the young boy came. Merlin had taken everything into account, even the death of Arthur, and had planned accordingly. Merlin knew that, if it were ever necessary, the cavern would be ideal. Arthur's grandson would be in no position to defend a castle against the realm's enemies, much less against his own father and uncles."

Ryder looked across the pond and the gardens at Hall House, with the growing fear that this was all too true.

"The entrance to the cavern was well hidden, but Kayne built a house against it to make certain. No one dared question a Druid priest or even report his location. They were left in peace. Remember when I said that this house was built on the site of the previous one? There have been a number of houses since that first one, all guarding Merlin's cave."

Ryder had played too many losing chess games not to know that the next move would be his finish.

At last, Hall leaned back against an oak. "So that's the story of Arthur. Within ten years of his death, his quarreling sons lost the kingdom to forces stronger than themselves. With the aid of members of the priesthood, Kayne had the altar, the Round Table, the sword, the tapestry, and the personal belongings of Arthur and Merlin brought here for safekeeping."

Hall had finally stopped talking and was staring at Ryder. Ryder saw the look. He hunched his shoulders. "No! Whatever it is, don't say it!"

"In the past fifteen hundred years, including Arthur and his grandson, there have been twenty-eight holders of The Gift. You are the twenty-ninth!"

Over across the pond, up past the gardens and the white gravel driveway, Hall House, and the secret it guarded, looked unchanged. Out in the park, sheep cropped grass and ducks nested by the water's edge. The sun was warm, the air sweet with spring, but for Ryder, it could never again be the same.

"I really screwed up hanging around, didn't I?" He made an impatient gesture with his hand. "By what wild stretch of the imagination do you mix me up in all of this? Not only do you have the wrong man, you've got the wrong country."

"I am well aware of what country you're from." Hall didn't sound pleased.

Ryder stood up. "Great, I'm glad that's taken care of. It's time for me to hit the showers."

Hall was relentless. "Consider the tapestry for a moment. As I told you, it was originally intended to record the names of Arthur's descendants. As time went on, there was not enough room for all of them. Other methods were developed. Now only those who actually possess The Gift have their names embroidered into the fabric, as Katherine did yours last night."

"Just because Katherine sewed my name onto a piece of cloth doesn't make it so. You're both off the planet."

"All the daughters of Merlin have been gifted with second sight. She knows you have The Gift. Your meeting with her last night was a test."

"Test of what?" Ryder eased to a sitting position again, muscles already stiffening. "You get hold of something and you just won't quit, will you? You're right up there at the head of the class, along with Martin."

"Thank you. I take that as a compliment. It has been an immense task keeping track of Arthur's descendants. In the beginning, it was simple, but with the passage of time Merlin's original plan had to be modified. To complicate matters, many of Arthur's lineage migrated to other lands—France, Germany, Italy. Then came the Crusades, the opening of trade with the Orient, and the discovery of the New World."

"More like impossible."

"On and on it went, their children and their children's children scattering, as the world's frontiers were pushed back. We went with them. Wherever they were, we were there also. Of course, along the way some have been lost, but you might be surprised to know just how few of those there have been."

"You and Martin have to be related."

"Finding you again, for instance. As I told Doctor von Friedenthal, I've played over many of his published games. Your name began appearing with increasing regularity, sometimes with an absolutely brilliant performance and then the next time—well, you know the answer. This wide swing between genius and the commonplace and the combination of physical and mental abilities was so like that of Arthur's heirs, it caught my attention."

"Man, you're looking for dust under the bed."

"The final clue came when I discovered that, after your father's death, when you were an infant, your mother moved clear across the United States, assumed her maiden name, and began a new life. So simple, but we, the great keeper of records, missed it. The youngster who had been misplaced in our files and the chess grand master were one and the same person. In the past, training was always begun during childhood. We've lost precious time."

"I play chess."

"How many chess players hold records in the long jump?"

"It happens."

"Only with you. As I've said, where the children of Arthur went, we went also. We were absorbed into other cultures, we adopted their ways. We became traders, merchants, and business people. Over the years, a cobbler's shop grew into a shoe factory, a fishing boat became a fleet, a livery stable an automotive manufacturing plant, and so on. Your father was an engineer working for a construction company that I own. But everything that my family stands for and everything that we possess is for one purpose only—to serve The Gift. There is nothing else."

"What's so important about the stupid Gift? You make it sound like the Holy Grail."

"There's that, too."

Ryder held up his hand like a traffic cop. "Don't even start with that one. Mr. Hall, I have no doubt that you're rich, and with wealth comes a sort of power. I'll concede that you people have somehow kept track of Arthur's descendants and I'm a shirttail relative of his."

Hall looked offended. "Not a shirttail relative."

"I've read about mental telepathy and I know that from time to time things are fished out of the ocean that are supposed to be extinct. I'll grant you all that. But when you start using ten-dollar words neatly wrapped and labeled 'The Gift,' and when you start looking at me like I've a part missing, you become the classic example of the true English eccentric."

"But—"

"No! It's my turn. I'll accept your mental abilities, the creature, the cavern, the sword, the table, the tapestry, the whole damn bit. But you talk about what happened fifteen hundred years ago as if it were yesterday. As far as I know, it was just a bunch of guys who painted themselves blue and sat around in trees."

"Hardly that."

Ryder pointed a finger at Hall. "What I cannot accept is any personal connection with this fantasy you call The Gift. That some dude comes out of the woodwork and says that I'm the twenty-ninth holder of The Gift ought to be laughable, but why aren't I laughing. There's no sense to any of this. What you're saying is that I am going to bend iron bars with my teeth, or lift a ton, and all by using my mind. It's definitely time for me to get the hell out of here."

"Arthur was more than that," said Hall. "So were the others, and so are you. Chivalry was more than being gallant to the ladies, protecting the weak, and showing generosity to the vanquished. It was a code of justice. Then, as now, humanity didn't care for absolutes. Regardless of what they say, people are more comfortable living with compromise."

"Sure. Why not? It's something we all understand."

Hall's expression was not that of a man who understood compromise. "The Round Table and the men who sat at it were absolutes. Aggression resulted in immediate retribution, no matter what the price. Those men were judge, jury, and, when necessary, executioner. That sort of behavior can be a powerful deterrent. Naturally, one man or one small group of men could not change the world, but they had to try. Each of those who came after Arthur tried."

"To do what?"

"To carry on the code of the Round Table."

"That's no answer."

"It's the only one there is."

"Not for me!"

"Stop being a child!"

A vein throbbed ominously on Hall's forehead. "You don't fool me for an instant. You've known the truth about yourself since last night. It's something you have suspected for a long time. I could tell the moment you saw the table. You are the sum of fifteen hundred years of heredity. There's no going back. Whether you like it or not, the sword had been passed to you."

"But I don't want it."

Hall took a slow breath. "If it's of any interest, you're the first American to hold The Gift. I suspect things around here will never again be the same."

Ryder felt an infinite sadness. He had always been a loner, until he'd met Stacey. She'd made him feel he belonged. "I do not possess anything called The Gift."

"You're not being honest with me and, worse, you're not being honest with yourself. Do you want to go through the rest of your life not ever knowing the truth?"

Like some great, shining silver fish, Ryder made one last convulsive attempt to slip the gaff. Justice and retribution were not his world.

"I have a life, a career."

"I offer you the world."

"You sound like Satan. Hall, I don't believe you or trust you."

"How shall I put this? You are a motor that has been improperly assembled. The power is there, but you cannot make use of it. However, in spite of that, your abilities are so remarkable you occasionally do manage. You're never certain when it will happen and it doesn't last long. True, the others were found and training begun while they were still children. You're making a late start. However, it's a challenge that must be met."

Hall stood up, extended his hand and helped Ryder to his feet. "You're a mortal man. A knife can cut you, a bullet can pierce your flesh, but this century has seen only two other men like you."

"And they are?"

"They were Brian Harwell and Major Gordon Ramsgate."

"Were?"

"They're both dead, I'm afraid."

Ryder stared at Hall. "And you're not going to tell me."

Hall's voice was firm. "When it's the right time."

James L Diffin

"There are other questions."

"Ask."

"Back at the chess tournament?"

"What about it?"

"There was something else, wasn't there?"

"There was some mental interference. I can't explain it, at least not yet."

Ryder knew Hall was lying. The question was why?

"You'd better try."

"Oh, I shall. You can depend on it."

"And let's not forget the small matter of my son."

"English schools are the finest in the world."

"Yeah, I've heard."

"Which means?"

"That this is totally insane."

"So is life."

"You understand this is a day by day thing."

"Then let's be about our business." Hall started walking back toward Hall House. "You have much to learn. I only hope there is time."

"You keep saying that."

Chapter IX

Ryder followed Hall into a large room on the second floor of Hall House. The room was a fencing *salle*. The bare, wide-boarded floor gleamed with years of waxed care. Fencing and dueling weapons hung from pegs along three walls. The fourth wall was mirrored from floor to ceiling. A wide strip of rubber matting ran the center length of the room. Four men stood waiting at the far end.

As Ryder approached, he had the feeling he'd been weighed, measured, and classified—the length of his stride, the reach of his arm, the span of his shoulder, the way he moved.

"Good morning, gentlemen," said Hall. "I would like to present John Ryder." None of the four offered to shake hands. "John, these are your trainers."

"You can't be serious."

"If I may offer a bit of advice," said Hall, "I would be extremely selective in my choice of words around these gentlemen. From now on, your life will be in their hands. You're not here to study for the ballet. They've spent their lives, as did their fathers before them, preparing for this moment. I wouldn't disappoint them, if I were you. These are dirty, nasty men."

No one seemed offended. If anything, they looked pleased. Ryder had again underestimated the power of Andrew Hall. The way he'd held himself since entering the room, the way he turned his head—Andrew had assumed the mantle of unquestioned authority. He was not the same person who had been sitting in the grass only a few minutes ago. He was, without question, the alpha male.

"You're pretty damn sure of yourself."

"If you mean, am I sure in the power of The Gift, then yes."

"There's no end to this, is there?"

"There will be if you'll permit me to finish," said Hall with a touch of impatience.

"As soon as I knew that I had finally found you, I also realized there was a problem that had never been faced before. You are no longer a child.

All the others were discovered as children. When they were brought here for training, there was never any difficulty. Children's minds are open; they want to believe. It is only as adults that we learn to place limitations on our imaginations."

"I wonder why?" said Ryder looking around at all the weapons hanging on the walls.

Hall's voice took on a disapproving tone. "Despite your comment about all of this being the hobby of a wealthy eccentric, there is one saving grace. You immediately recognized the table and the sword for what they were."

Ryder made a winding motion with his hand for Hall to finish.

"Originally, the code of the Round Table was a system of justice, emphasizing retribution against the enemies of Arthur and his kingdom. For subsequent holders of The Gift, the code was modified and has become the basis of a particular way of life. It became apparent there could never again be a fellowship of the Round Table; that could only happen once. Since that time, those who possess The Gift must stand alone."

"I hate to appear dense," said Ryder, "but you're not going to tell me that each in his own time and each in his own way stood against the forces of evil?"

"Overstated in an overblown American way, of course," said Hall calmly, "but you're nearer the mark than you realize. You will use your skills to help those who cannot help or defend themselves."

Ryder held out his hand, palm down, and made a noise of an imaginary spaceship. There was a stirring among the trainers.

"I've warned you once," said Hall, "I won't again. Now—to finish."

Hall waved a hand which seemed to include all their mirrored images. "When it became clear that the new holders of The Gift had no one to depend upon but themselves, something had to be done. Since my Druid forebears were themselves teachers, there was a possible solution. We began to train certain of Arthur's descendants in various forms of the martial arts. We kept it in the family, so to speak. Those who were trained would, in turn, become trainers. It was also an effective way of maintaining secrecy. No one knows what we do or even that we exist."

As his gaze wandered over the four, Ryder couldn't imagine their being overlooked.

"The trainers," said Hall, "became the very best at what they did. Fathers passed their skills down to their sons. When the call came, they were required to come here and impart their knowledge to the newest holder of The Gift."

Someone was in for one hell of a shock, thought Ryder. But then again, why had he felt so strange in the cavern last night. It all made about as much sense as that creature appearing out of the Scottish mist.

"It's time," said Hall. "In the future, you will come to know these four very well indeed."

Hall gestured to the first man. "This gentleman is Harry Tanaka. Harry is from Japan, where he owns a chain of very successful restaurants. He charges ridiculously high prices and his customers feel honored to pay them."

"I know about high prices," said Ryder. "I've been to Japan."

Hall's smile reached his eyes. "Harry is the descendant of a sailor who jumped ship on Matthew Perry's second visit to Japan in 1854. Harry's family has been trying to live it down ever since. However, we seized the opportunity to include the wisdom of the East, with its unique philosophy, in our own training regimen. For seven generations, Harry Tanaka's ancestors have studied and perfected the Oriental martial arts. Harry is the consummate master. By the way, do not play cards with him—he cheats."

Harry Tanaka was built like a boulder. He wore a loose-fitting judo gi with a white belt. Ryder guessed the white belt had little to do with false modesty. Tanaka didn't smile or acknowledge Ryder. He stood, arms folded across his massive chest, and waited.

Hall continued. "Next in line is Nathaniel Hawthorne Green. Nathaniel is a countryman of yours. Nathaniel perfected his skills in the jungles of Vietnam. He makes his home in New York City, where he is the captain of a police narcotics squad. Nathaniel is a survivalist. He's able to live indefinitely in places where no ordinary human could. Nathaniel is also a world-class boxer and the strongest man I know."

Green was a tall black man with a trim beard. He didn't have the bulk of Harry Tanaka, but neither would he be lost in a crowd. Broad of shoulder and narrow in the hips, he looked like a well-conditioned heavyweight.

"Hey, Nate," said Ryder.

Ryder's countryman had been looking at the floor. His beard twitched as he raised his eyes to stare at Ryder. He spoke slowly, as if counseling his words. "The name is Nathaniel."

Ryder's emotions had been switched on and off too many times lately. "Are any of you guys for real?"

Nathaniel Hawthorne Green, survivalist, had cornflower-blue eyes.

Green ignored Ryder and spoke directly to Hall. "You mean this is what we have to work with? This is it?"

"Patience, gentlemen," said Hall, turning to Ryder. "Mr. Green does have a softer side. Nathaniel has refused promotion on several occasions. He feels it would remove him from those he's trying most to help."

Green only snorted. He was looking at the floor again.

Hall was unperturbed. "The third member of our quartet is Mahmut Asim. Mahmut is from Turkey. His European forefather never returned home from the Crusades. Mahmut knows all there is to know about the use of ancient weapons. The damage he can do with a hunting bow is quite amazing. Mahmut is a goldsmith and quite an artist with the metal."

At first glance, Mahmut Asim was lost, standing beside Harry and Nathanial. He was about Ryder's size and had the blank stare of the religious fanatic or the terrorist.

No, that wasn't it, either. Ryder studied Asim more closely. With the sharp planes of his face, the beaked nose, and shoulder-length mane, he bore a striking resemblance to a bird of prey. It didn't take too much imagination to see that Mahmut Asim would prefer to be somewhere else. He wasn't looking across the *salle*, but to some distant horizon.

"Last, but by no means least, let me introduce Colonel Brooks Cameron. He's British. We've known each other for more years than I care to admit. Brooks was with the 22nd Regiment of the Special Air Services for many years. He was in charge of training. Not many know about the beginnings of the Regiment. They were skulking around the North African desert as far back as the Second World War. Vicious lot, really."

Hall clapped Brooks on the shoulder. "Their main function now is dealing with terrorists. You're probably too young to remember most of them, but the SAS was responsible for cleaning up a lot of messes. This chap's expertise in the use of modern weapons and explosives is absolute."

Colonel Brooks Cameron nodded in agreement. He wasn't in the least embarrassed by the accolade.

Hall smiled fondly at Cameron. "He also knows another trick or two. Brooks has perfected the night stealth of the Ninja. You have to keep a close watch on him or he'll go to ground right before your eyes. The good Colonel lives here at Hall House and looks after things."

Short, stocky, sandy-haired, and dressed in heavy tweeds, the Colonel's only response to the introduction was a raised eyebrow and a world-weary sigh.

"There you have it," said Hall. "These men are here to perform their function as your trainers. Many of their forefathers were never lucky enough to meet a holder of The Gift. These fellows are truly fortunate."

As far as Ryder could tell, the trainers looked anything but fortunate. They looked pissed.

"I'm being premature," said Hall, "when I say 'holder' of The Gift. You have it right enough, but until now, using it has been a hit-or-miss affair. These men will develop your physical skills to the highest possible degree before The Gift takes over. Hall turned to face Ryder full-on. "As for me, I will instruct you in the use of the weapons you see hanging on the walls. In addition, and even more importantly, I shall also deal with the mental aspects of your training."

Ryder looked at Harry Tanaka, Nathaniel Hawthorne Green, Mahmut Asim, Colonel Brooks Cameron, and finally at Andrew Hall. Five to one. Ryder was curious now. What the hell. He'd planned on staying in London. Instead, he'd hang out here for a couple of days. Why not?

Hall turned his attention to the trainers. He spoke slowly and distinctly, giving weight to each word.

"Gentlemen, you know your duty and you will carry it out to the best of your ability. John must receive full measure. Bend him, try to break him, but you must train him."

Ryder held up a hand in protest. "Whoa there, Charlie."

Hall waved a cautioning finger. "As for you, John, I'll make it perfectly clear. The trainers do not like you. Even though they are also Arthur's children, if you will, when they are finished here, you'll have something they never will. Be careful—do not forget that these men are killers."

Late that afternoon, in the library, Ryder was pacing back and forth in front of the fireplace. Hall and Katherine sat watching him. "Killers? Killing? You must be out of your mind." Flames fought the deepening shadows of a fast-fading day.

"It sometimes comes down to that," said Hall. "It's a terrible responsibility."

"Right! I'll just whack 'em to death with a chess piece."

"You could."

"Oh, God!" Ryder threw up his hands in frustration and went to sit on a couch across from the Halls. He stared at the two, father and daughter. "So where are these killers? You somehow whistle them up, and then they just disappear. I'm still not sure they're real."

"There's no great mystery," said Hall. "They've gone down to London with Brooks. He belongs to a club where they gamble. The stakes are high."

"And I'm to play a game where I don't know all the rules."

"You only need to know that it is imperative for you to have The Gift. It may be enough."

"You've ducked this question before, but does this have anything to do with what happened at the chess match?"

"All I will say is that we here at Hall House are in grave danger."

"Then why should I stay?"

"Because you have no more choice than we do."

"Have you ever considered," said Katherine, speaking for the first time, "that your wife's death was not an accident?"

Ryder was shocked. "But that's what it says on her death certificate." He saw Hall give Katherine a warning glance.

"What happens to any of us," said Hall, "is because of you."

"I've had enough of this. I'm going home. I need to get back to my son." Ryder started to stand up, but stopped when he saw Katherine slowly shaking her head.

"Don't you realize that you're the danger? Matthew is safer where he is."

"How do you know his name?"

"I know."

"And the way to protect my son is to stay away from him?"

"If he had been threatened, it would already be too late," answered Katherine. "You are the danger and you are our only hope."

Ryder would have given anything not to say it. "Stacey is dead because of me?"

Katherine's voice mirrored his pain, but she didn't hesitate. "Yes."

He looked deep into her eyes, testing, probing, examining what she'd said. If he'd, somehow, been responsible for Stacey's death, there was nothing on earth that could now drive him from this place.

Ryder began emptying his mind, waiting for the first true gut response. He stared into the dancing flames. Long seconds passed as he struggled to quiet his racing thoughts...Stacey's death...Matthew...unknown danger... The Gift...four violent men...Merlin...Arthur. It was like pulling the plug on a drain and watching the water swirl around and around.

He watched until his mind was empty of thought. All that remained was an infinite sadness. Still, he waited. Finally, from a place deep inside came his answer.

"What do I have to do?"

Hall's voice was heavy with relief.

"Only the power of The Gift can save us. Training begins tomorrow."

Chapter X

The lights were on in the fencing *salle*. It was barely dawn outside, but Harry Tanaka was already well into the 128 postures of *t'ai chi ch'uan*. This was Tanaka's only constant. Each morning began with *t'ai chi*, the ancient Oriental martial art form whose beginnings were lost in a clouded past. It was no longer a form of combat and Tanaka used the stylized moves as an exercise and to cleanse the mind.

Ryder watched for a moment, then closed the door and took his place beside Tanaka. They were facing the room's mirrored wall. Although many of the movements were repetitive, Ryder knew exactly where Tanaka was in the routine and began doing the same postures as Harry, each position flowing smoothly from one to the next. Ryder could see Tanaka's eyes fixed on him, seeking a flaw. They did not speak.

In the beginning, it had been a game. Tanaka apparently followed some kind of Oriental philosophy that required that the teacher arrive at the dojo, or in this case the fencing *salle*, before the student.

Just once, Ryder wanted to be waiting when Tanaka appeared, yawning and knuckling his eyes. Ryder started setting his alarm earlier and earlier, but without success. Tanaka was always there first, lost in the grace of *t'ai chi*.

One morning, Ryder had looked over the third-floor balcony railing to see the *salle's* darkened doorway. He'd turned and raced downstairs, jumping the steps three and four at a time, only to find that he was too late. The lights were on and Tanaka, his back to the door, was already in the posture of "grasp the sparrow's tail." His eyes, reflected in the mirror, were the color of ball bearings.

It was a no-win situation. Ryder soon discovered that if he arrived at the *salle* at three in the morning, the day's training would begin at three and would be longer, harder, and more violent. The game quickly lost its spice.

Now, Ryder's alarm was set for six. Even that was too early, but Tanaka insisted. He had no faith in a Western diet and his teaching was done on an empty stomach. That was fine with Ryder. Most days, tea and toast was all he could handle.

The postures continued in mesmerizing silence. There was no footfall, no rasp of clothing, no sound of heavy breathing, only an endless kaleidoscope of slow, stately movements, never hurried, always the same. The routine came to an end, as the two men returned to the starting position.

Without warning, Tanaka whirled toward Ryder and let out a terrible scream. The first time Ryder had heard the "shout of doom," he'd jumped a foot.

"Good morning," said Ryder. Someday, he was going to die, but after working with Harry Tanaka, it wasn't going to be from shock or paralyzing fear. Ryder selected a wooden sword from a rack on the wall and took his place on the strip of rubber matting that ran the length of the room.

"Congratulations," said Tanaka, "you hardly flinched. But, remember, even the blink of an eye or a moment's hesitation is all the advantage a master would need." Tanaka spoke distinctly; he had no trouble with the letter L. "Why are you preparing for *kenjutsu?*"

"That's what you had in mind, isn't it?"

"Very good—perhaps the rest of the day will go as well."

Tanaka took another wooden sword and came to face Ryder. They were dressed alike. Ryder wore a white gi and belt and was barefoot. It was not the traditional *hakama* dress of *kenjutsu*. Tanaka had decided that tradition must give way, since more than one discipline was practiced each day. Time could not be wasted changing clothes.

"And why did you select the *bokuto?*"

"The bamboo *shinai* requires two hands. Why use two hands when you can use one," answered Ryder. *Merde!* The same thing over and over—lecture, question, answer. The only thing that changed was the order in which they came.

Tanaka talked from the beginning to the end of a session, telling Ryder exactly what he himself was going to do and then exactly what Ryder was going to do. All the trainers, except Mahmut Asim, ran off at the mouth. Ryder missed Martin von Friedenthal. Martin liked to talk, but at least what he said made sense.

"Whenever you are ready," said Tanaka, which was odd. Normally, he would attack without warning.

Ryder began to shift his weight back from his toes. When Tanaka had first demonstrated the position, Ryder told him he looked like Charlie Chaplin. He was promptly knocked unconscious. When Ryder had regained his senses, Tanaka calmly continued the demonstration.

"I told you to tread firmly; I did not tell you to go to sleep." There was no compromise in Harry Tanaka, nor was there the least bit of compassion. He demanded total obedience as *sensei*.

It began slowly. Ryder held the sword lightly between thumb and fingers. *Tap-tap.*

"Why do we use the sword?" intoned Tanaka. "The sword is the soul of the samurai and all things come from this." *Tap-tap-tap.* "The art of swordsmanship is only a technique. True greatness comes when one follows *heiho*, the path of enlightenment. To know—"

"—one thing is to know a thousand things," finished Ryder. "I think I've heard this before."

Tap-tap-tap. Ryder attacked and retreated and the tempo quickened.

"There are five attitudes," said Tanaka. "High, middle, low, left guard, and right guard." *Tap-tap.* "There are no others." *Tap-tap-tap.* "If you cut across, return your blade across." *Tap-tap.* "If you cut down, return your blade in proper order."

They were moving faster, pressing each other up and down the rubber matting. The wooden swords made a deeper sound and became a blur of motion. *Tunk-tunk-tunk.* "You have become skilled in blocking, *gaijin*."

"You'd better believe it," said Ryder through clenched teeth.

Tunk-tunk-tunk-tunk. "Why do you not strike? Blocking is only the opportunity to strike."

"Very funny."

Tanaka paused. "But the swords are wood, there is no cutting edge—not even a point."

"Sure, Harry, and your favorite *Bushido* guy, Miyamoto what's-his-name, killed his victims with a wooden sword just like this one."

"The way of the warrior is the complete acceptance of death. You must seek it out."

"I've told you before—not this child."

Tanaka gripped his sword. "You must—it is the basis of everything we do."

"Go plant a turnip."

Tanaka attacked. *Whack-whack-whack-whack.* He was in a fury as he beat Ryder's point down. Ryder tried, but he couldn't disengage his weapon. Tanaka's sword was on Ryder's—riding, forcing his blade to the side. *Whack-whack-whack-whack.* Tanaka was crowding Ryder, using his shoulder to push Ryder back. Tanaka gave a final shove and sent Ryder sprawling across the wooden floor. Ryder's sword flew up against a far wall.

Tanaka stood over Ryder, his sword over his head and his left fist in Ryder' face. Tanaka's face was a mask of fury.

Ryder's smile clicked into place. "Remember—no posing, the positions must flow from one to the other without thought."

Tanaka now held the sword with both hands. The blade quivered.

"Go ahead. You can kill me, but I still won't accept your warrior philosophy. I'll die, but I'm not going to seek it out."

"You would rather die a coward?"

"By whose reckoning, Harry, yours or mine? While we're at it, aren't you the one who told me that losing control betrays a loss of confidence?"

Tanaka went up on his toes and raised the sword higher.

"Stuff it, you chop suey peddler."

Tanaka screamed in rage, turned, and went back down the mat, swinging his sword in great slashing strokes. *"Hai!" Swish. "Hai!" Swish. "Hai!" Swish.*

The floor felt cool against Ryder's cheek. He was breathing heavily. He studied the wide wooden boards. If you thought about it, floors were fascinating. When you were this close, it was really neat to see how smooth the floorboards were and how firmly they were held together by those clever little wooden dowels. Pure genius. Someday, when he had the time, he would have to go into the subject in greater depth.

Ryder turned over on his side and propped himself up on one elbow. It was just as he feared. Harry Tanaka was still there, and this wasn't a bad dream. From Ryder's place on the floor, the *salle* appeared even larger than it was. So did Harry Tanaka. He was huge and very hard. His face had about as much expression as a tomb.

Tanaka put his sword back on the rack and stood watching Ryder. "Someday that mouth of yours is going to get you killed."

John rose to his feet, retrieved his sword, and placed it alongside Tanaka's. Why argue? They were worlds apart. They always would be.

"What next?"

"No floor exercises today. Today we go straight to *karate*."

Thank you, God. Floor exercises. For months now, Ryder had repeated the movements over and over and over again. There was no end to them. He even did them in his sleep, their names a jumble of Japanese words whirling in his brain.

"Begin!"

Ryder slid easily into a back stance only to have his instep kicked by Tanaka's hard, bare foot. It broke Ryder's rhythm.

"How many times do I have to tell you? Sometimes you lead with the left foot, sometimes with the right. Never the same. A habit pattern would be fatal. Now—again!"

Using more care, Ryder adopted the horseback-riding stance, and they began to fight. Full-force blows with the hand and foot, blows that could kill or cripple, stopped a fraction of an inch before contact. Blows to the middle of the body, while not full-force, did connect and Tanaka was not always as careful as he could be.

Ryder was in the best shape of his life, but against Harry Tanaka he was winded in a matter of minutes. He had no wooden sword with which to defend himself. Tanaka's face, as usual, was impassive and, as usual, he talked.

"You pant like a water buffalo. The mind controls the body. You, of all people, should know that." He faked low, then hit Ryder in the chest with a side-blade kick.

Ryder doubled over, then recovered. Jesus, that hurt.

A couple of months ago, Ryder had taken Harry at his word about always being ready. Harry had had his back to Ryder, as if inviting attack. It looked good, so he grabbed Harry around the middle and, pinning both arms, squeezed.

The result had been instantaneous. Ryder was flung violently away, so hard he'd suffered three cracked ribs. He'd been heavily bound for weeks, but the training continued. The tape had come off just last Thursday.

Ryder moved into *kokutsu-daichi*, a leaning-back stance. He took one short quick step, whirled in the air with a foot back-slash. Tanaka countered, then began circling Ryder.

"You used the same kick twice in a row."

"It keeps the wolf away."

"Never adopt a style. The Way is no way. Do not favor kicks over hand blows. Do not favor hand blows over throws. Remember—what we do here has nothing to do with sport."

Ryder was still hurting. "I never would have guessed."

"Also, do not favor the *Shaolin* hard way over the soft way. Speed and precision must never give way to power and strength. And never try the same thing twice. If it didn't work the first time, it is reasonable to believe it will not work again. But I've said all this before." With that, Tanaka turned left, came right, and took Ryder down with an ankle sweep.

"Whether you use a stick, a stone, or your body—whether the school is Japanese, Chinese, Korean, or Okinawan—it does not matter. All pots of water come from the same well."

Ryder rolled and came to his feet. He had nothing left, but still came back with a straight-arm strike, using the first two knuckles of his hand. Tanaka took Ryder's arm in an *aikido* wrist-hold, turned lightly, his back to Ryder and—one, two—struck a paralyzing elbow to Ryder's breastbone, followed immediately by a fist to the face.

Ryder went down like a shot. Again, Tanaka stood over him.

"If you defeat one, you can defeat a hundred. I always win because I have absolute belief in my powers. I am a rock and you are nothing."

Tanaka didn't bow or do any of those nice ritualistic things. Without another word, he turned on his heel and left the *salle*. Ryder lay on the wooden floor. He was no stranger to pain, but Harry had gotten him twice in the same place, his newly mended ribs. It was no accident. Ryder rubbed his chest. In all of Harry's talking about his Eastern philosophy, Ryder hadn't heard the one about the rock before. What a way to start the day! Rocks before breakfast and still three trainers to go.

Chapter XI

Ryder crouched behind the bush. He could see Mahmut Asim standing in the meadow. Asim held his favorite weapon, a composite bow. Turkish bow makers were long considered the finest in the world and Asim's weapon was a handcrafted masterpiece of wood, bone, and sinew.

Over the months, Ryder had seen him perform some amazing feats with old weapons, but nothing could compare to the magic of Mahmut Asim's bow. When he used a bow, it became a living thing. And that was the trouble. This exercise of Asim's looked deceptively easy, but wasn't.

At the edge of the meadow, on a heavily wooded slope, Asim had set up a kind of shooting range, some sixty yards wide and thirty yards deep. Ryder had to get from one side of the range to the other while Asim tried to hit him with clay pellets shot from a bow.

At first, it had seemed simple. The problem was in getting there. Ryder could cross the course by any route he chose. There were trees and bushes to hide behind and, if his success on the squash court was any indication, he already knew how to move. The problem was Mahmut Asim's bow.

Asim had restrung one of his weapons with a double bowstring. The two bowstrings were kept apart by spacers at either end of the bow. In the center, the strings were attached by a leather pocket which held whatever missile the shooter elected to use. Asim was equally adept using stones, steel balls or, in this case, pellets made of modeling clay.

The first time Ryder saw the bow set up in that manner, he couldn't believe the thing had a serious use. Without a word, Asim had reached into a leather bag hanging from his belt and, without looking, withdrew a steel ball the size of a marble.

He'd turned, drew back the bowstring, and fired. Out on the duck pond, a paddling drake was neatly beheaded. There was a flurry of feathers, then silence, as the stain of the bird's blood spread across the water.

Later, when Andrew Hall found the headless corpse, he was not at all pleased and had politely, but firmly, ordered Asim to leave the livestock of Hall House the hell alone.

That was only the beginning. Ryder had watched Asim stand out in the meadow with a half-dozen arrows stuck in the ground in front of him.

When Asim's head came up, his nostrils would flare as he tested the wind. He'd nock, draw, and fire the arrows one after the other. All six would be in the air at the same time, arcing high above the trees, only to drop down into a target hundreds of yards downrange.

Today was going to be different; Ryder could feel it. He started to reach for a branch with which to pull himself up, then yanked his hand back just in time to avoid being struck by a pellet.

Ryder was off toward the first bush. In the space of eight feet, he heard the buzz of a clay pellet. Missed. Ryder was up and away toward a small stand of saplings. He arrived in a rush, still untouched. Peering between the slender trunks, he watched Mahmut Asim.

A moment later, he burst out from behind the saplings toward the far side of the range. He reversed, then turned down the slope, angling toward the front of the range. He slammed into a tree with both hands, bounced off, changing the angle, and ended up on his stomach in a diving slide behind a clump of bushes at the front of the range.

He was closer to Asim now and also closer to the other side. Ryder congratulated himself. He was farther than he had ever gotten before, without getting hit.

Ryder's thoughts were interrupted by Asim's piercing whistle and a pellet rattling through the branches overhead. Asim was impatient.

Ryder broke from cover on the run, angling up the slope away from Asim. He stutter-stepped, crouched left and then right, but kept moving. Clay pellets were striking all around him. He had a cold feeling at the back of his neck. What if Asim got hold of one of those steel balls instead of a clay pellet?

He was almost there. There was a large clump of bushes at the back of the range. If he could just get behind them, he would be safe. He reached the first bush, but didn't stop. He head-faked as if he were taking cover, then cut left, this time angling back down toward Asim, but always going toward the far side of the range.

He was really moving now, zigzagging down and across the course at a full run. He was holding nothing back. The air was filled with the sound of angry hornets.

As he passed a lone sapling, Ryder reached out with his right hand. He swung himself completely around the tree and catapulted away. Two bounding leaps and he hurled himself through the air in a headlong dive toward the safety of the boundary marker. He was untouched.

He leaped to his feet and stood, hands on hips, facing Mahmut Asim.

Asim stared back over the strings of a fully drawn bow. Ryder knew his man well enough. There was a steel ball aimed right between his eyes.

Ryder started down the slope, keeping eye contact with Asim. The drawn bow followed his every step. Ryder walked out onto the meadow and stopped.

"This close enough for you?"

Without a word, Asim released the tension on the bowstring, threw the weapon up into the woods, and strode away.

Ryder retrieved the bow and headed back to the pavilion. The pavilion was a large, striped, lawn-party tent that had been erected beside the pond to temporarily house the various weapons, pieces of equipment, and supplies that were used in Ryder's training. It saved a lot of running back and forth.

Ryder unstrung the bow, returned it to its place, and walked down the aisle between the long tables of weapons—mute testimony to man's ingenuity through centuries of violence. There were weapons that, until a few short months ago, he had never dreamed existed—like the three-bladed Congo throwing knife. Asim could throw that knife sidearm for an amazing distance. Some of the oaks in the meadow bore the scars.

Ryder saw the grotesquely carved *kris* from Bali, with its straight-bladed knife. He'd always thought that *kris* knives had a distinctive wavy blade, but had since learned that most were straight-bladed.

Tables and tables of weapons. Over there was the Japanese *kozuka*, another throwing knife, with its innocuous inscription that had nothing to do with the actual purpose of the knife. Side by side, in a row, were the *kukri*, the Gurka's fighting knife; the *kindjal*, the Khyber knife, national sword of the Afridis; and the kidney dagger of northern Europe. There was the *bidag*, the dirk of the Scottish Highlanders; and several versions of the Arab *jambiya*, the most widely used knife in the world.

There was even an honest-to-God bowie knife. According to Colonel Cameron, the heavy blade made it unbalanced, like most Americans. Ryder had to smile, knowing the part in American history the blade had played.

Then there were the pellet bows that Ryder knew so intimately. *Bolos* from South America, even one type used by the Eskimos; throwing sticks from Australia and India—they were all there. Weapons with which to cut, slash, and stab, and all manner of things that flew through the air.

Along the way, Ryder learned that it was not gunpowder, as he had supposed, but flights of arrows thick enough to darken the sky that had spelled the end of plate armor.

In answer to his question, Andrew Hall had stressed that it was necessary to study and understand the past in minute detail in order to deal with the present. What this tent contained was only a part of one of the world's great collections of weapons, normally found in the cavern behind Hall House.

Weapons belonging to Colonel Cameron were kept at the back of the tent. As expected, there were rifles, shotguns, and handguns of every make and model. There were also automatic weapons, so favored by Iron Curtain and Middle Eastern countries, where marksmanship had degenerated into spraying everything in sight.

In his years with the Special Air Services, Cameron had used them all. There wasn't a weapon on the tables that he couldn't field-strip on the darkest night.

Ryder hadn't been surprised to learn that Cameron, in spite of his personal choice of armament, liked the magnum caliber handguns. It fit. Cameron could use such a weapon with the skill of a surgeon. When Ryder tried it, the thing kicked like hell and made a bitch of a racket. He noticed the others tended to remove themselves from the immediate vicinity, as if questioning his accuracy.

Ryder picked up one of the handguns. He weighed and balanced it in his hands. It was beginning to feel different now. He could feel the faint residue of oil on the metal surface and could sense what lay within. The weapon was loaded. He removed the cartridges, one by one, and felt their weight.

Cameron spent long hours examining the ammunition he used. He left nothing to chance and checked each cartridge, using the utmost care to see that the rounds were uniform and that each casing contained exactly the same amount of powder. He knew the information would kill Brooks, but Ryder could tell the difference between each load.

He shook the cartridges like dice, then held them to his nose. They smelled of oil, gunpowder, and...death. Before Ryder left the tent, he reloaded the weapon and returned it to its place, wiping it first with a cloth. Brooks had trained him well.

"Water, food, fire, shelter—those are the big four. It's the same in the city or in a South American jungle. You've got to be able to go it alone, to be self-sufficient, if you're going to survive."

Ryder yawned. He was sitting on the bank of the duck pond with Nathaniel Green. They'd just returned from a tracking exercise in the woods. Green was disgusted. Ryder could see his whiskers bristling with indignation.

Green scowled. "I never met anyone before who was supposed to have The Gift, but I didn't think he would turn out to be such a total waste of time."

"You're not admitting to having doubts, are you?"

"Only when the others aren't around. If I never give anything away, then the advantage is mine."

"Always looking for the edge?"

"It's called survival."

"The kind that Andrew has in mind?"

"Both."

"But I know differently."

"You don't count."

Ryder contemplated the water and the paddling ducks. He was feeling good about his success with Mahmut Asim.

"Maybe—just maybe—one of these days you'll have to change your tune."

"You mean when you get The Gift?"

"Something like that."

"It's never going to happen. The worst of it is, I have to waste my time here."

"Don't hang around on my account."

"That's pretty much what I'd expect from someone like you."

"What's that supposed to mean?"

James L Diffin

"You have no respect for tradition. I do. We will continue with all this until Andrew says we're finished or you quit." Green smiled. "Or you die. Any of the three is acceptable. My loyalty is to the brotherhood of trainers, something you will never understand."

"You forget—I've seen your brotherhood."

In the beginning, the four trainers were wary of one another, circling like a pack of wolves. Each of them scrupulously avoided infringing on another's territory, but they still had to know who was the alpha male. Most evenings found them in the library playing various games of chance. Two of their favorites were backgammon and cribbage. They always played for money and the stakes were high.

"And I've seen you," said Green. "Why Andrew keeps on with this, I'll never know. He thinks that when you get The Gift, you'll be able to hear a gnat fart."

"I can't imagine Andrew putting it quite like that."

"What difference does it make? You don't believe in any of this, much less even begin to bridge the gap between the amateur and the professional. You are totally out of your depth."

"I'm giving it my best shot."

"It's not good enough." Green made an impatient gesture. "Let's just get on with it, so I can get rid of you for the rest of the day."

"I'm enchanted with you, too."

Lying on his back, Green looked up at the sky in frustration. "You've gone through the drill a thousand times. By now you ought to know these things—how to find drinkable water on the seacoast, or in the desert, or the high country, and how to tell if a water hole is poisonous; how to build shelter and make fire using whatever is available."

Green rolled over on his stomach. "You know how to get out of the water if you fall through the ice, what to do about snow blindness, how to avoid hypothermia and dehydration—and let's not forget quicksand."

Head on his arms, Green shifted his weight several times to get comfortable. "You know that the burdock, found on three continents, will sustain life, as will the shepherd's-purse, and you know which wild fruits and berries are edible. You can catch fish with your hands and take freshly killed game from a predator, build snares and deadfalls..."

Green lifted his head. "Are you listening to any of this?"

72

"It would be hard not to."

"I work with you because it's my duty. I just don't happen to like you. None of us do."

"Thanks."

"I don't owe you a thing. The only reason you're hanging around is because you've got a case of the hots for Andrew's daughter."

Ryder shook his head. "No, that's your problem."

"The hell you say."

"When Katherine comes down here to the duck pond to read, where does she sit?"

"Somewhere around here—how the hell should I know?" Green's voice grew louder. "What are you getting at?"

"It's not somewhere around here. Katherine always sits in the exact same place, the spot where you are now lying. Ladies and gentlemen, I give you Nathaniel Hawthorne Green, defender of the brotherhood, dry-humping the grass."

"You sonofabitch!"

Ryder never had a chance. Green leapt to his feet, grabbed Ryder by the neck and crotch, and then lifted and hurled him well out into the duck pond. The last thing Ryder heard, before the water closed over his head, was the hurrying tempo of duck wings and the expletive—"Shee-it!"

Chapter XII

"I see you've changed into something dry. Still, a rather odd choice of swimming apparel, don't you know."

"It wasn't my idea."

"I realize that; I was watching."

In Ryder's opinion, Colonel Brooks Cameron was, in his own quiet way, the worst of the lot. True, he didn't inflict the physical pain that the others did. He rarely touched Ryder, acting almost as if doing so might expose him to some incurable disease. Ryder was amused, having heard of the muck-and-mire training of the Strategic Air Services.

These days, the Colonel was very much the proper English squire. He favored heavy tweeds that were as rough as his sarcastic tongue. A "no, no, dear boy, that's not the way we do things, at all" would be followed by a heavy sigh and a "but I'm obliged to try—duty and all that, don't you know." Cameron very often ended his sentences with questions that weren't really questions.

Not that the good Colonel didn't give Ryder full measure. He spent his allotted time each day expounding endlessly on the theory and practical application of various types of modern firearms and explosives.

He would lecture by the hour, explaining the history and development of a particular weapon or explosive, and then go on to demonstrate, step by step, how it worked in practice. Only then, would he permit Ryder to attempt to duplicate his genius. Ryder's ears often rang from the sound of objects great and small going *bang*.

"I don't think we'll work with explosives today," said Cameron. "The way things are going, you'd probably blow yourself up. Andrew would never forgive me, more's the pity." His expression betrayed his insincerity. "Let's have a go on the pistol range, shall we. I can keep better track of you there."

On a wooden bench at the head of the pistol range were a holstered pistol and several boxes of ammunition. The pistol Cameron favored over all others was a .45-caliber Colt Commander. When Ryder first questioned his choice of armament, in light of his views on all things American, Cameron was at his caustic best. "Can't say much about the quality of fighting man on the other side of the pond, but the weaponry is superb."

Cameron had held the Colt lovingly in his hands. "You can bring this up out of the ooze, with green things growing on it, and it will still function perfectly. And, I might add, with factory loads. Most gratifying." Cameron shook his head sadly. "America is the only country in the world with a legitimate history of handguns. Pity what they've done with it, don't you know."

"Loaded?" asked Ryder, indicating the Colt.

"Of course."

Ryder slid the Colt out of the holster and ejected the clip. He thumbed out the seven loads, then replaced them. Before replacing the clip, he pulled the slide back to check if there was a cartridge in the chamber. He loaded it, released the slide, and put the safety on. There was now a live round under the hammer. In the cocked and locked position, Ryder reholstered the Colt.

"Very good—a positive step in the right direction, I must say. I'm delighted that you no longer take anything for granted. To assume that you have a fully loaded weapon, simply because someone else says so, is the height of folly. Never trust anyone, not even yourself. Check, double check, and check again."

Ryder slipped the holstered weapon inside his waistband with the muzzle slightly forward. He knew Cameron was carrying a Colt in exactly the same position. When Ryder had first seen the weapon, he'd used the term automatic and had been quickly corrected.

"A self-loading pistol, if you please. When we have to refer to it, let's use the proper term, shall we."

Ryder faced the target and consciously relaxed his shoulders. He drew the Colt, slipped the safety and, supporting his right hand with his left, crouched and fired seven times.

"Four in the black at twenty-five yards," said Cameron. "I suppose it will have to do. Pity that none was a ten." With that, Cameron stepped to the line. In one continuous motion, he flicked his jacket aside, drew, and fired. There was the sound of a double report and two bullet holes appeared in the target—dead center.

"Why only two?" Ryder asked.

"You should be able to accomplish what you have to with two shots. That still leaves five rounds for other matters. When we know what we are

doing, we don't have to go off hosing down the countryside, now, do we."
Automatic weapons offended Cameron.

Ryder replaced the target, finished reloading, and reholstered the Colt.
He drew and fired until the clip was empty.

"Two in the black—pitiful, really pitiful. I have told you before, you
have to know your target. It works better when the target is a man."

"You really expect me to shoot someone?"

With a snort of disgust, Cameron stepped to the firing line. "Watch
the left hand." Cameron drew and fired five times. The shots were so close
together, it sounded like one long report. Now there were seven holes in the
black, Ryder's two and five from Cameron.

It was just as unbelievable as his stunt with the Colt. Cameron has
used his left hand to draw and fire a five-shot .38-caliber Smith & Wesson
Bodyguard Airweight that he carried under his right arm, suspended upside
down in a Martin-Burns holster.

It was a startling range for a handgun with a two-inch barrel. Cameron
was never without it, either at dinner or later in the library. Ryder had asked
Cameron what else he had hidden and had been put off with, "A good in-
structor always saves something for himself, don't you know."

Since Cameron seemed impressed with the damage a .22-caliber slug
could do rattling around inside someone, ricocheting off bone and tearing
holes in vital tissue, Ryder suspected a hideout weapon. The question was
where the Colonel carried it.

"Let's move on, shall we."

Ryder put in a good hour and the Colt had grown warm by the time
Cameron called a halt. "Let's pack it in; it's not getting any better. Remember
to pick up your brass." Although Cameron didn't hand load anymore, the
habit remained. "Just once, I'd like to see you put all seven in the black. I
could die happy."

Ryder picked up the shell casings, waiting for the question he knew
Cameron would ask.

"Are we on then, for tonight?"

Although it had nothing to do with weapons or explosives, Cameron
had an exercise that especially pleased him. After nightfall, Ryder could go
anywhere on the estate and conceal himself. Cameron had to find him within
one hour. It was a deadly serious game of hide-and-seek.

Ryder spent hours thinking of places where he could hide—up a tree, on a roof, under a pile of leaves or even in the duck pond, but it was no use. He would be tucked safely away where he could never be found, certain that he was unobserved. Then, without warning, would come that unmistakable oily snick of a weapon being cocked or the sting from the point of a knife at the back of his neck, followed by an infuriating chuckle.

"Okay," answered Ryder, "but I have a suggestion."

"Really? How splendid!"

"You practice *ninjutso*—the art of invisibility—right?"

"My word, this does sound serious."

"Yes or no?"

"You sound so determined about all this—suppose the answer is yes?"

"You know that Harry says the ninja are nothing but spies, thieves, and assassins."

Cameron beamed.

"How about switching roles?"

"You mean are going to search for me?"

"Yes."

"On this estate?"

"Yes."

"In one hour?"

"Yes."

"I say—I am impressed."

"How about it?"

"I think all this training has gone to your head."

"Think what you like."

"You know, old boy, every once in a very great while, you show an infinitesimal touch of class."

"Well?"

"I'll tell you what—to be on the safe side, let's make it for the whole night. Even you should be able to find me in that amount of time. I promise to stay in one place and not to enter any of the buildings." Cameron smiled. "More sporting and all that."

"Agreed."

"After dinner then?"

"Suit yourself. I'll be seeing you."

"Ah—that is the question."

Around nine that evening, it began to rain. Ryder was already in a state. He had been at it for an hour, but there wasn't a trace of Colonel Brooks Cameron.

Ryder was determined. He quartered the grounds, back and forth, up and down. There wasn't a square foot of wood, field, or pond that Ryder missed. All night long, in the icy late autumn rain, he searched. He looked in every imaginable hiding place, but found no sign of the Colonel.

At first dawn, Tanaka came looking for Ryder. "You're late."

"Get the hell out of my face, Harry."

One last time, Ryder covered the estate. He missed nothing. Finally, he had to admit defeat. He was dirty, soaking wet, and chilled to the bone. When he entered the dining room for coffee, he was in a filthy mood.

Seated at his usual place, Colonel Brooks Cameron was reading the morning paper. He was freshly shaven and smelled of bay rum. Ryder froze in the doorway.

Cameron turned a page. "Sorry, old man, but I waited as long as I could, don't you know."

Chapter XIII

It was early evening. Ryder was standing on the rubber *piste* of the fencing *salle*, wearing the traditional white uniform of the competitive sport fencer—padded jacket with knee-length breeches, long white stockings and rubber-soled shoes. He held a foil in his gloved right hand and cradled a fencing mask under his left arm. He was waiting for Andrew Hall.

The style of knee pants and stockings were a holdover from the court of Louis XIV, the Sun King, but instead of silks, these stockings were made of cotton and the pants were a heavy grade of canvas. Hall insisted on proper dress at all times in his *salle d'armes*.

Hall, also in white fencing clothes, entered the room. "Sorry about the delay—I've just finished talking with the Rome office; there seems to be a problem."

After a glance at the weapon in Ryder's hand, Hall selected a similar foil from the wall rack. At this stage in his training, Ryder had his choice of foil, épée, or saber.

Hall took his mask from its usual place and turned toward Ryder, but his thoughts were obviously still on the Continent.

"Bloody hell—it's just as easy to do things correctly, but some people never learn. Now I'm going to have to go over and straighten out their mess." With an uncharacteristic gesture, Hall ran his gloved hand through his hair.

He stepped onto the rubber matting in front of Ryder and stopped abruptly. "Something's different here." He studied Ryder closely, all thoughts of Rome apparently forgotten. "It's almost as if…" He gave a couple of practice swings with his fencing foil. "Well now—this should be interesting." Hall put on his mask. "Shall we begin?"

They faced each other in the classic fencer's position, weight evenly balanced. Ryder had discovered a natural affinity for edged weapons and he looked forward to this moment when they first crossed swords.

Small blade movements, engage only to disengage, engage again, the tip of his blade probing, testing. It was like a chess match. You created an opening in order to attack, even if the attack was only a diversion.

The blade movements became larger as Ryder advanced, forcing Hall back down the rubber matting, their flashing blades weaving patterns in the light. It ended quickly, with the blunted tip of Hall's sword against Ryder's chest.

Ryder swept his blade up to knock Hall's foil away and, in the same motion, threw his weapon hard at the wall. Steel winked across the room and ended—point first—buried in the wooden rack. He tore off his mask and threw it after the foil. The mask bounced off the wall and fell to the floor. Ryder stood with his hands on his hips and glared at the fallen mask.

"God damn it all to hell, anyway!"

Hall took off his mask, crossed the room and, using his own weapon as a pointer, indicated the still quivering blade. "Did you mean to do that?"

"Hell, I don't know. I just threw the damn thing, that's all." Ryder paced the rubber matting and watched Hall's futile attempts to pull the blade from the rack.

"Just once," Ryder said, "I'd like to see you and Harry go at it."

"He would, of course, lose."

"With his Bushido code? No way!"

"I'm afraid my advantage is too great."

"Harry claims he's ready to die for his beliefs."

Hall only smiled.

"King Arthur stuff again, right? Listen, I'm tired of hearing all this garbage about a pile of bones. Jesus!"

Hall was unperturbed. "A thousand years before Miyamoto Musashi, there was Arthur. Against him, even a martial arts form grounded in the Oriental Zen philosophy would be of comparatively small consequence."

"I wonder what Harry would say about that."

"He knows."

"But all this hoopla applies only to Arthur and the other holders of The Gift, not to Merlin, right?"

"Merlin was there from the beginning. Or better said, he was the beginning and had no small part in what followed."

"But he still wasn't Arthur."

"No, but he was enough." There was a flicker of a smile.

"And I'm no Arthur."

"You will be. I can feel the power growing. Today, I was more aware of you and had to use more of myself. That is why I defeated you so easily."

Ryder felt like screaming. "Will you—just for one second—knock it off!"

"I cannot. There is little enough time left. Forces have been set in motion and there is no way to stop them. You must be ready."

"That does it. I've got the five of you kicking ass and you tell me that there is no time." Ryder took off his fencing glove and threw it after his mask. He stopped pacing. "I wonder if I can still play chess—or have I lost that, too?"

"It's too late. It always was. We have no other choice but to continue." Hall made a gesture with his foil. "Are you ready?"

"I've had it!"

"Perhaps you're right." Hall was studying the steel exclamation point imbedded in the wall. "Change and we'll finish up."

Ryder was totally frustrated. He also didn't trust Hall. There were too many missing pieces and the feeling of impending violence was growing. Knowledge was his only weapon. He had to find out why Stacey was dead and who killed her.

There was no day or night in the cavern, only eternal silence. It was dark, except for one spotlight focused on a ordinary sword suspended, point down, over the Round Table. A metal cable attached to the pommel of the sword disappeared into the darkness overhead.

Ryder and Hall were seated at the table. Hall, dressed in his Druid robe, was watching Ryder, while Ryder was staring at the sword. Using the power of his mind, he was willing the sword to move, but nothing happened. Nothing was going to happen. Nothing had happened. Well, there was that one time.

In the first week of his training, Ryder had been seated, as he was now, staring at the sword. Slowly he rose to his feet. Brow wrinkled in concentration, Ryder stepped onto his chair and then onto the table. His eyes never left the sword. As he came erect, he was level with the heavy blade. He drew nearer, mesmerized by the hanging steel. The air was electric. There was movement and the blade slowly began to turn.

From the darkness came the sound of measured applause. "Most impressive. Now could you try it without the heavy breathing?"

"Have I failed my audition for the Old Vic?"

"Rather badly, I'm afraid. All in all, a ghastly performance."

"But you saw it—the blade moved."

"Of course, but at the moment, I'm more interested in the power of your mind than of your lungs."

"Sweet Jesus—you really mean it! I'm supposed to make that thing move just by staring at it."

"Do come down from there and be serious."

Nothing had changed since that first week. Every evening, Ryder sat and stared at the sword. Tonight was worse than usual and he was having a difficult time trying to concentrate. The sword wasn't going to move tonight any more than it had before. Ryder's thoughts began to wander.

According to Hall, this business with the sword was the original test that Merlin had devised for the young Arthur. How many times had someone else sat here, staring at that stupid sword until his brain began to fry?

The mental exercises were a washout. For all of his abilities, Ryder was helpless. Hall couldn't unlock the power of Ryder's mind. Ryder knew he would have to give it his very best, but his supposed powers proved to be useless. It didn't make any difference if the exercises were modern or those that Arthur had done. In the end, it all came back to the sword hanging there like an accusing finger. Nothing worked.

They discussed the documented feats of Palladino, Schneider, Geller, and Manning. Hall told Ryder about Nina Kulagina and her telekinetic ability, the ability to move or deform inanimate objects through mental processes alone. It was some small consolation to Ryder that none of them were able to use their powers all the time. Some considered them charlatans because they could not always demonstrate their abilities under laboratory conditions.

Hall could not penetrate Ryder's mind as he had at the chess match in Ipswich. Ryder hadn't felt that sense of evil again, but he hadn't forgotten it either. He did what he could to help, but a curtain had been drawn and not even Hall's remarkable powers could break through. For reasons known only to himself, Hall seemed satisfied.

Ryder shoved his chair back from the table. "Enough! This isn't my day."

"What about Mahmut?"

"Big deal—in all these months, I've managed to make it across his damn course just once without being hit. Those aren't great odds." Ryder rose and walked over to the stone steps leading up to the altar.

"Andrew, why is it that you've never told me anything about the other holders of The Gift?"

"It isn't necessary—when you gain your full power, you will know for yourself."

"What's that supposed to mean?"

"You will become the sum of all the others."

"You mean there are going to be twenty-eight voices buzzing around in my head? I've had enough of that stuff already."

"That's not it at all. Since there is no way to explain, you'll just have to be patient. It'll come in good time."

"I thought you told me there was no time."

Hall stared at Ryder. "It will be a near thing."

"This is going nowhere."

Ryder climbed the steps to the altar where Excalibur lay. He'd avoided it since that first night in the cavern. Instead, he looked at the tapestry on the cavern wall behind the altar. It was just as bad. Ryder felt himself sinking under the weight of history.

He turned and stepped to the edge of the platform. "Andrew?"

"Yes?"

"All this"—Ryder made a sweeping motion with his hand to include everything in the cavern—"all this is to support the holder of The Gift?"

"Correct."

"And all the money?"

"That, too."

"What if I said I needed a million dollars?"

"Of course," said Hall without a pause, "cash or check?"

"Ten million? A hundred million?"

"Whatever you wish."

"My God, you're serious, aren't you?"

"Deadly."

"Aren't you afraid I'd spend it all?"

"Not you or a hundred like you."

"I can't win, can I?"

They stared at each other. For the first time, it was Hall who looked away. "Sometimes you can be very difficult."

"It's the only thing I have left."

"Can you not understand? You're not losing anything. You are not going to be less, but more. You're not going to metamorphose into another being. You will continue to be yourself—John Ryder—with your own mind and your own thoughts. There will be no one else in that thick skull of yours but you."

"Then what has been the purpose of all this?"

"What we are doing here is preparing you to use your mental powers. It is a matter of total concentration. Then, it is more."

Hall took off his robe and put it on a chair. It was a signal that the session was over. Hall never wore the robe outside the cavern.

"Let me illustrate," he said, as they crossed the cavern toward the tunnel that would lead them back to the house. "When you enter a chess tournament, the first thing you do is find out who the other players are. You know from past experience what their openings are, what type of game they play, and you can predict with reasonable accuracy what variations they will use."

"There's one hell of a difference."

"No. It is the same in this world. There are any number of ways that a man may try to kill you and you have to be made aware of all of them. Even the way a martial arts expert stands will tell you what you need to know—what school he represents and what moves he is likely to make."

"Except Harry."

"Correct. You have learned which weapons an apparently unarmed man can carry and how he will produce them. That is why you study the ancient ways. There is little that is new. Only the method changes and, in the end, a knife or an arrow can be just as effective as a hand grenade or an automatic weapon."

They had reached the end of the tunnel. Hall touched a switch and the door swung slowly toward them. Ryder stepped into the sitting room and waited while Hall placed his hands on the mantle of the fireplace attached to the room side of the door.

The door began to close again, but they would have to wait until it was completely shut before the door to the rest of the house could be opened. The cavern would not give up its secrets lightly.

They crossed the great hall and, at the library door, Hall paused and turned to Ryder. "How about a game of chess?"

"Thanks, but not tonight."

Ryder started upstairs. His left knee was beginning to stiffen. He must have banged it this morning in one of those headlong dives in Mahmut's shooting gallery. Another day, another bruise—business as usual.

Sitting naked on the side of his bed, Ryder looked at the telephone on his nightstand, but made no move to pick it up. He was too tired to call Florida and reluctant to go to sleep. His dreams were a torment. They would begin with shadowy figures out of the past, calling his name.

Those figures would fade, only to be replaced by the faces of the four trainers and Andrew Hall, all talking at the same time. Do this, do that—dummy, dummy, dummy. In his dreams even Mahmut talked. Ryder would wake in the morning more exhausted than when he had fallen into bed. He studied the telephone.

Ryder called Florida every week to ask about Matthew. It didn't seem to make any difference what time of day or night he called. His son was either sleeping, or out somewhere playing, or at a friend's house.

When Ryder had first called his sister-in-law last spring to say he might be delayed for a few days, Wanda told him to take his time, everything was fine. She had sounded relieved. Since then, he never got to speak to his son at all. It was a sharp price. Would Matthew understand?

As he sat there, Ryder wondered what the hell was happening to him. Spring had passed into summer and now into fall. The routine of days melted one into another. Each morning started with Harry and his merciless hands. Next came Mahmut. After lunch, he had his sessions with Nathaniel and Colonel Cameron. The day ended, after dinner, with Andrew and what was left of Ryder. Seven days a week—forever.

Ryder had his moments, but they were few and far between and only served to make things worse. He was angry all the time. Some mornings he was sure he could not get out of bed. For the first time in his adult life, Ryder had run into something he couldn't handle.

And then there was Katherine. Ryder spent most evenings in his room, but a closed door was no barrier to Katherine's disquieting presence. She would be absent from the estate for days at a time, but suddenly there she was at breakfast or at dinner.

Cool and lovely, she was friendly up to a point. She always used the term "Mister" in addressing the trainers or Ryder, and called Cameron "Colonel." Often, at dinner, Ryder caught himself staring.

Katherine read a great deal and spent hours either in the library or on a blanket down by the duck pond. Sitting sideways, with her legs curled up beneath her and the sun shining on her raven hair, she was beginning to steal into Ryder's unwilling heart.

He was acutely aware of Stacey's death. The numbness that had protected him in the beginning had worn away. He was tormented not only by a sharp sense of loss, but by his feelings of guilt and disloyalty whenever he thought of Katherine.

Ryder turned off the light and slipped beneath the covers. But, as sleep claimed him, he wasn't thinking of Stacey or of Katherine.

In the cavern behind Hall House, a brown-robed figure watched with approval as the sword hanging over the Round Table began to move, swinging ever so slightly from side to side.

Chapter XIV

The pattern of shadows formed by the sun shining through the French doors crept, inch by inch, down the flowered wallpaper of the bedroom, across the bedcovers, to finally touch the face of the sleeper. John Ryder stirred.

For months now, despite his nightmares, he slept as if drugged. He hadn't heard the alarm. It would throw the whole day's schedule off. Then he remembered. It was Sunday and the first day in a long time that there would be no training. Harry, Mahmut, and Nathaniel were off to London; Brooks had gone north for some shooting; and Hall had pressing business somewhere in Italy. Ryder started to stretch and caught himself. God, he was sore.

He sat on the side of the bed, rolling his head around, trying to loosen his neck and shoulder muscles. It took a good ten minutes of careful stretching each morning before he dared to stand. Only then would he head for the shower to try and restore his lost youth.

Dressed in slacks, turtleneck, and loafers, Ryder reached into an ornately carved armoire for a jacket. He selected an old Harris tweed he'd picked up on one of his earlier trips to London. As well traveled as Ryder himself, it was always the first thing he packed. A splash of aftershave and he was ready to face the day.

Breakfast at Hall House was an informal buffet. The food was kept warm in covered silver dishes. For all his discomfort, Ryder had a ravenous appetite and did Mrs. Bentwood's cooking proud, twice over. He guessed he wasn't terminal, after all.

The house was quiet. There was no one in the library. Ryder idly picked up a stone chess figure from the set on Hall's desk. Since the trainers used the game table most evenings, the chess set had been moved to the desk.

Ryder fingered the smooth stone of the queen, wondering what stories she could tell. The queen, worth more than any other two major pieces on the board, no longer spoke to him. Ever since he had first learned to play, chess pieces had always had a certain feel, as if they were sentient beings, but not today.

The marble figure with her enigmatic expression had, after all, a heart of stone. Ryder shook his head with regret. The man, who could have been world champion, carefully put the chess piece down and headed outdoors.

Walking down the drive, past the gardens and the cedars of Lebanon, to the meadow, he began to relax. It was a lovely morning, exceptionally mild for mid-November. School was out.

On the far side of the pond, close to the bank, he saw Katherine. There was an unopened book on the blanket beside her. She was watching the ducks and geese. She looked as if she were waiting for someone.

"May I join you?"

Katherine looked up, glanced around the meadow, then regarded him with a level gaze. "If you wish." She smiled slightly. "There seems to be room enough, Mr. Ryder."

"I've been meaning to talk to you about that."

"Talk to me about what?" She knew very well what he meant.

Ryder eased himself down. Lord, he was stiff and his knee was really bothering him. "We've known each other for months. We've lived in the same house. We've even played chess together."

"You make that sound like the final word. Besides, you let me win."

He shrugged. "I don't suppose I could persuade you to call me John."

Katherine thought about it. Of course his name was John. How many times had she said it to herself? She knew of his reputation as a chess player and she could see for herself that he was not all that unattractive but, as it happened, so were a dozen other men she could think of. Then again, she could also see that smiling turn at the corner of his mouth. And it was such a nice mouth, too.

She was spending more and more time at Hall House, as if her presence could lend support. Outwardly, her attitude hadn't changed. She still addressed him as Mister Ryder and she kept contact to a minimum, but she was there. She even found herself inventing little excuses to pass by a window in hopes of catching a glimpse of him. At dinner, and later, in the library, she watched him whenever she thought he wasn't watching her.

Katherine looked at the man lounging on the grass at the foot of her blanket.

"Well?"

"Well, what?" She had to smile as Ryder shook his head in mock despair.

"It's a perfectly acceptable name and," he paused, speaking more softly, "I'd like to hear you say it."

She looked back at him. "All right, then...John."

"There, that wasn't so bad now, was it?"

"You are quite impossible, you know."

It was the first time they had been alone. The morning had gotten warmer—most unseasonable for this time of year, really! Katherine looked away. She was acting like a schoolgirl, transparent as glass.

"How is your training? Father seems pleased, although he is concerned about your attitude."

Ryder pulled up a handful of grass and was tossing it, blade by blade, onto the surface of the pond. The waterfowl were interested. "I'm just tearing them up. Andrew must be some kind of optimist."

Ryder brushed the grass from his hands and turned to Katherine. "While we're on the subject—I've got a question. You've grown up with this Arthur thing, right?"

"Of course. I have known about the cavern ever since I was ten years old."

"And that lake in Scotland?"

"It is the first test and, without him, there would be nothing. One of his kind has always been there to pass judgment."

"You mean, he actually says yes or no?"

"In his own way and only if he stays. There is a bond and not every novice is accepted. It was my turn to call him."

Ryder let his gaze wander around the meadow. He no longer questioned Katherine's mysterious, fey manner. "How?"

"As we all have done, I sang to him."

"I thought I was losing my marbles."

"Never that. I was witness to the two of you. It was splendid."

"But you don't buy this business about The Gift, do you? Even after all these months of training, I still get knocked down ten times a day."

Katherine wouldn't look at him. "My father thinks so," she said quietly, "and he is never wrong."

"I'm asking you. You're the one with second sight."

"You have The Gift." Katherine leaned toward Ryder and touched his forehead with her finger. "It is all there—waiting."

Ryder caught Katherine's hand. She didn't respond, but neither did she pull away. "That's not enough."

"It has to be. I am sorry that I can't tell you more. The last holder died before I was born." Katherine placed her other hand over Ryder's. "You must believe. I know how difficult this is for you, but there is a purpose—trust us."

"The last time I trusted someone, he sold me a bridge."

Katherine pushed Ryder's hands away, laughing. "You fool—can't you be serious for five minutes?"

"Come on"—Ryder stood up, offered his hand, and pulled Katherine to her feet—"let's walk." After all this time, he still found it difficult to believe that she was real. Maybe, in this place, nothing was.

Katherine was wearing a green sweater with a plaid skirt and matching jacket in muted blues and greens. Her black hair was caught in a twist, making her eyes look larger than ever.

"You must miss your son."

Ryder was startled by the change of direction. "Yes, very much."

"Matthew is almost five now, isn't he?"

"I call him every week, but Wanda, my sister-in-law, doesn't let him talk to me."

"Why ever not?"

"She thinks it would upset him. She says he's fine and not to worry."

"Couldn't you insist?"

"It's kind of hard over the telephone. Wanda is just as stubborn as Stacey used to be."

"I'm sorry, I didn't know."

"She says that if I insist, it could scar Matthew for life, and confuse him about the only family he has left."

"That doesn't sound quite right."

"Tell me about it. I only hope I know what I'm doing."

"What was she like?"

"Who?"

"Your wife, of course."

How do you talk to one woman about another. "We had six years together. She hated injustice in any form and had a tennis backhand that wouldn't quit."

"That's...quite a combination."

There was a long silence. "It was." Ryder looked at Katherine. "Why are you doing this?"

"I'm sorry, I didn't mean to pry. I can see that you miss her very much."

"No, Katherine." It was the first time Ryder had used her name. "You know that's not what I mean."

They had reached the wooded slope at the far end of the meadow. Katherine stopped by a large oak. "No, I suppose it's not. Perhaps I'm jealous."

"Of a dead woman?"

"She had six years. I'd settle for that, I really would."

"What are you saying?"

"John..."

The way she said his name made the hairs on the back of his neck stand up. Leaning back against the tree, Katherine was watching him. Ryder moved nearer. He'd never seen anything like it. The color of her eyes seemed to change from a light sea green to deepest unfathomable blue. He put his hands against the tree, on either side of Katherine, leaned forward, and kissed her.

They stood that way for a long moment, with only their lips touching. Ryder kissed her with all the loneliness, pain, and hunger that was in him. There was no response. Katherine stood still, hands at her sides. He could have been kissing a beautiful alabaster statue.

Just as he began to think he'd made a terrible mistake, Katherine stirred. Her lips softened, opened slightly, and she breathed of him. Again there was a long moment of stillness. Finally, Katherine shuddered and slowly raised her arms to encircle his neck. She moved away from the tree and pressed against him. She was kissing him with a fully open mouth, turning Ryder to fire.

His arms were around her waist. He slid one hand under Katherine's sweater to cup her breast. Only the silkiness of her slip separated Ryder's hand from the fullness of firm, bare flesh. His finger traced the outline of a nipple. Katherine whispered against his mouth. "Please!"

Ryder pulled her closer, so close that he could feel the subtle pulsing of her loins. He turned her slightly, took his hand from her breast and slipped it down her stomach to the juncture of her thighs. Katherine's tongue touched his lips as he caressed the fine, high ridge through the fabric of her skirt.

Ryder bent and picked Katherine up, cradling her in his arms. He started up the slope into the woods with her head against his chest. The veins in his arms were heavy and he carried her easily. When he felt something warm and wet against his neck, he drew back to look at her. Without making a sound, she was crying.

He set her down. Tears were streaming down her cheeks. With her eyes closed, Katherine began to turn her head from side to side.

"How could you?"

"I didn't mean to shock you."

Katherine struck Ryder's chest with clenched hands. "It's not that. How could you be so cruel?"

Katherine took a handkerchief from her pocket, wiped her eyes, and started back down the slope and across the meadow, with Ryder at her side. From time to time, she would glance at him.

At the pond, Katherine stopped. She looked across the water at the house and the hill behind it.

"I didn't mean what I said back there."

Ryder started to speak.

"No! Please let me finish. From the time of my birth, only my father and I have ever entered the cavern. The others who live here know only that there is something of great value to be protected." She shook her head sadly. Her chin was quivering and she wouldn't look at him.

Finally, she forced herself to face him. She was crying again, angry with herself. She held her arms stiffly at her sides, but looked directly at him. "John, please understand. No matter what either of us may want, you must know that there can never be anything between us."

"Because of this Gift thing?"

"Yes"

He smiled. "Hey, no problem. I've been telling Andrew all along that he's wrong about me. I don't have the stupid Gift and I never will." He held out his hands to her.

"No!" Katherine caught her breath as she said the word. "The Gift is closer than you realize. It is served. There is a terrible price to pay. I can never be with you. Never!"

After one last searching look at him, Katherine walked around the pond and up the white gravel driveway to the house. She held her head high.

Ryder stood and watched her walk out of his life. He noticed that the day had suddenly grown cold.

Chapter XV

The eight-fifteen from Bridgeport was late. Major General Robert E. Hartley looked at the clock on the wall, drummed his fingers on his thigh impatiently, and, as generals do, said exactly what was on his mind. "Damn it all, Martin, where the devil is that train anyway? This is a hell of a way to run a railroad. You've got to get organized around here."

Martin von Friedenthal looked up from his control panel. "Now, now, General, there is no need to get upset. If you read your train board, you will see there was a heavy snow at Adler Pass last night. We are running ten minutes late."

"Well, get on with it. I haven't got all day." The General was anxious to get his hands on that train.

They were in the basement of von Friedenthal's home in Hasenleiser, a suburb of Heidelberg, Germany. The room contained a club-sized, point-to-point, HO-gauge model railroad. The General, who'd dabbled in the hobby for years, had never seen better. Von Friedenthal's attention to detail was incredible, right down to the pigeons on the engine house roof.

General Bob, as he liked to be called (it made a good impression on the troops), was bucking for his third star. A large, aggressive West Point graduate, the General had only two ways of doing things—hard and harder. He was impatient with human frailty and went through aides at an astonishing rate. He also enjoyed popping up at the most inopportune times, when a junior officer was Xeroxing the office football pool, or having a little harmless slap-and-tickle with the new secretary, and demanding, in that steely voice of his, "I thought I told you—"

The General glared first at von Friedenthal, calmly sitting in the middle of his transistorized, computerized, miniaturized world, smoking his favorite meerschaum, and then back to the layout. The peddler freight was just now coming into sight, easing down the long, twisting grade from Adler Pass, creaking across the tall spindly wooden trestle toward the town of Mayville, where the third man was seated.

The presence of the third person came as a surprise. He sat with an unusual stillness; not even his eyes seemed to move. Then there was his smile.

That smile and the fella's tan bothered the hell out of the General. Usually people acted nervous around him and talked too fast. General Bob liked the feeling it gave him. He enjoyed his power, when one stroke of his pen on an efficiency report could destroy a man's career. To hell with the bomb—the pen was the ultimate weapon.

"You'd better be on your toes there," said General Bob. "What was your name again?—oh, yeah, Ryder. Well listen, fella, that freight is running late as it is and I don't want to lose more time on top of it—so watch it! Why have a schedule in the first place if you're not going to keep it, right, Martin?"

"Whatever you say, General." Von Friedenthal was smiling around his pipe.

After a brief glance at the General, the fella called Ryder turned to the train pulling into the Mayville station. That glance startled the General. He had the impression of twin 50's trained on him. That didn't bother him, he'd faced fire before, but what got him was the flash of something else. It was like cracking the door on a slag furnace. The General shook his head. Maybe he should browbeat a couple of colonels into a game of golf. He always won.

The General watched John Ryder's hands on the controls at the Mayville station. Freight cars were cut from the train and others added. It was done with deceptive ease and fluidity. General Bob knew there was no way to get around the slow reaction time of the momentum throttles that controlled the layout, but damn it all, here came the freight winding its way along the canyon walls, high above the river, toward the Peace River Station and the General. The man had stolen his thunder. The freight was precisely on time and all the man did was sit there and simper.

In all the General's years in the Army, he'd met only one man who was his match—a tobacco-chewing Sergeant from Tennessee who just happened to be his driver. The Sergeant had all the answers. He was inevitably in the right place at the right time. The General hadn't caught him out yet, but he would. In the end, the General would win. He always did.

The General addressed the smile. "You a chess player, too?" The implication was clear—you had to be crazy to play that sissy game. The General looked around the room at the layout. Well, a little crazy.

"Yes."

"Heard from Martin that you play squash."

"I enjoy a game now and then."

"You any good?" The General wasn't about to waste time with some fud who couldn't even keep score.

"I manage."

The General snorted. "That means you're good. How about a game?"

"Why?"

The General looked sharply at Ryder. "Why does anyone play? You look fit enough. Besides, I can't get any real competition around here."

"Hard to imagine why not."

General Bob was not noted for his sense of humor. "I play a pretty rough game. Think you can handle it?"

"Perhaps."

"Well, good. I'm pretty big and I'll crowd you. If you get a shot off me, you have to earn it. How about it?"

"We'll see."

"Done! Make it tomorrow at twelve hundred hours. I have the court reserved every day at that time, whether I use it or not. You know where Campbell Barracks is. Come along to the Headquarters Building at eleven-thirty sharp. If you need a racquet, I have extras. You'll have to use the street entrance. Can't have you civilians wandering around the place. Tell the MP at the desk I'm expecting you."

General Bob glanced at his wristwatch, slapped his hands on the arms of his chair, and stood up. "It's almost thirteen hundred, Martin. Got to get back to the grindstone. Had a game today, but you know me. Couldn't wait to see that new narrow gauge extension. Looks fine. I'll give you a call in a couple of days, and you,"—he glared at Ryder—"I'll see tomorrow. Don't be late."

Going up the stairs, the General was smiling. He was going to have his pound of flesh for those ten minutes.

Von Friedenthal's wife, Liesel, was waiting at the top of the marble staircase. "Why, General—how nice to see you smiling. Leaving so soon?"

"Duty calls, m'dear," said General Bob, taking her hand. How the devil did the old goat do it, he thought for the hundredth time. Liesel was an attractive, young-looking blonde.

"How are those charming daughters of yours?" inquired the General, thinking they hadn't affected her figure any. "What are their names again... Karen? Silka?"

"Correct as always, General. They are fine and thank you for asking."

"In school, of course?"

"Of course."

All white teeth and aftershave, General Bob smiled down at Liesel. He wondered what it would be like to get her in the sack. If he had something like this waiting at home, he sure as hell wouldn't be spending his time on hobbies.

As he bent and breathed on her hand, the General felt as gallant and continental as all hell. Only the heel clicking was missing.

"Take care, m'dear," he said, opening the door slightly.

"Oh, I shall, General," said Liesel sweetly. The General was not one of her favorite people.

General Bob was peering hopefully through the crack in the door. As the house door opened, so did the right rear door of his staff car, which was parked facing away from the von Friedenthal house.

Without a word, the General marched to the car and seated himself. The Sergeant from Tennessee quietly closed the car door and went to the front bumper to remove the cover from the General's standard. Folding the cover, the Sergeant came around the sedan to the driver's side. As he opened his door, he turned an expressionless face to look directly at Liesel.

Standing in the doorway of her home, watching the car drive away, Liesel's eyes widened slightly. Unless she was very mistaken, the Sergeant had just given her a slow, conspiratorial wink.

After lunch, Karen and Silka were excused to do homework.

"It's a good thing you don't come to visit often," said von Friedenthal, patting his stomach. "I couldn't afford to eat like this every day. At my age, I have to be careful."

"When did all this start?" asked Ryder. "You never turned down a meal in your life."

Von Friedenthal chuckled. "Listen, if you don't take me for a walk, I'm going to nod off right here." He was looking out the dining room window at Ryder's rental car parked in front of the house. "We'll take the Mercedes."

"What happened to the Porsche?"

"With the children growing up, we needed more space."

"You probably needed more room to squeeze your stomach behind the wheel."

Liesel couldn't help laughing. "Will you two stop it! John, get him out of here so I can clean up. You're the only one who can lure him away from his trains for any length of time. And John?"

"Yes?"

"Thank you for the girls' presents. That was very sweet and most unnecessary. You spoil them."

"No big deal. I bought some for Matthew at the same time."

"I thought maybe we'd walk up the Philosophenweg, behind the old place." Von Friedenthal stood up and kissed his wife. "We may be gone for a while."

It was a tight fit in the garage and Ryder had to wait while von Friedenthal eased the Mercedes out. The Mercedes was one of the big ones, in shining, spotless black. As soon as von Friedenthal was clear of the garage doors, he motioned for Ryder to join him.

"I see you've bought yourself quite a toy," said Ryder, as he slid into the plush interior. "You have to stop being so hard on yourself."

"The last one, I'm afraid." Von Friedenthal caressed the leather-covered steering wheel.

"Planning on joining an order?"

Von Friedenthal headed for the Autobahn. Humming to himself, he put the Mercedes through its paces with a practiced hand, pipe clenched between his teeth at a rakish angle. The Mercedes was surprisingly nimble for a car of its size. After several miles, von Friedenthal took the main Heidelberg exit. They came into town along the Neckar River. At the first bridge, they crossed to the north side of the river and found a parking place.

The two started up the long, winding path of the Philosophenweg, stopping every so often for von Friedenthal to catch his breath. At one of those pauses, while looking across the valley and the Neckar River to the castle ruins on the far hill, he spoke.

"Let's stop wasting time, shall we? You know it always gives me great pleasure when you visit. I was delighted when you rang up and asked if you could come by. Now, I am gravely concerned. I know trouble when I see it and there is an anger about you. I would have to be blind not to notice your limp, though you take pains to hide it. What have you been doing to yourself?"

"Don't you mean, what is being done to me?"

"*Mensch!* Something is going on, but never that. You are too strong-willed a person."

"I don't seem to have a mind of my own anymore."

"You were abducted?"

"No."

"Held against your wishes?"

"No."

"Well?"

"I was wrong to come here."

Von Friedenthal shook his finger under Ryder's nose. "I deserve better than that from you, John Ryder."

"Sorry."

"Don't complain, never explain, and leave the apologies to those who need them."

Von Friedenthal was studying Ryder with concerned eyes. "There is an illness of the soul about you, the worst kind. What you need is not my forgiveness, but my help."

"What makes you think that?"

"I'm wrong?"

"All right, I need your help."

"You have it."

"No questions asked?"

"None."

Remembering his promise to Andrew Hall, Ryder added, "Because I can't tell you anything."

Von Friedenthal took Ryder's arm. "Come, my boy. Let's go on—I think better when my feet are moving. Perhaps that is why I am no longer champion." He shrugged. "You disappear, as if you fell off the world. I made inquires and you haven't played in any tournaments. I finally called your

102

sister-in-law to learn that you were still somewhere in England. I did leave word with her, by the way, to have you call me."

"She never said."

"And you have nothing to tell?"

"You wouldn't believe me."

"I won't ask. Even though you have aroused my curiosity, I won't ask."

Ryder shook his head. "I can only say that I'm involved in something and I don't know what to do."

"Then, this isn't something to do with Stacey's death?"

"No, not directly."

"Or not being with your son?"

Ryder looked so stricken that von Friedenthal relented. "I didn't mean that. If you haven't seen your son, then there must be a very good reason."

"Thank you."

"And there is no way out?"

"Not really."

"Does this have anything to do with that fellow, Andrew Hall?"

"What makes you say that?"

"Please! Don't insult the few gray cells that I have left. You disappear after a fishing trip to Scotland with a mysterious, somewhat sinister gentleman, only to show up, months later, looking like the wrath of God."

"I'd better leave."

As Ryder started to turn away, von Friedenthal stopped him. "Again, I say, I deserve better from you." He gave Ryder's arm a shake. "I want to help. And, if it is of any importance, I am honored that you came to me."

"I just don't know. I can't play chess anymore, and I never thought I would question that. I had to get back to the real world and talk to someone who would understand. But, I made a promise before I knew what I was getting into."

"Ah, ha!" Fumbling around in his pockets for his tobacco pouch, von Friedenthal said, "Now—where to begin?"

"But, I haven't told you anything."

"Oh, but you did. You never answered my question about our Mr. Hall."

"That means nothing."

"I beg to differ." Von Friedenthal stopped walking and turned to face Ryder. "You smart-mouth to cover up, but you have known for a long time that you are different. Now, you must be honest, if not with me, then with yourself."

"Perhaps I've forgotten how."

"Never you, my friend. You might be feeling a little sorry for yourself, but not that. There is some kind of decision to be reached and you are making heavy going out of something that is basically very simple. You either do or don't do whatever it is that you can't tell me about."

"It's not that easy."

"Your mind, John, your mind. Use it, for God's sake! During the Second World War, I was imprisoned for matters of conscience. How many games of chess do you think I played in my mind to keep my sanity? Ha! In the same camp, there was a concert pianist who played scales by the hour on a tabletop. What about that fellow who invented a whole new approach to mathematics while in prison? The mind is a two-edged sword. Before I get down from my soapbox, let me say this—I have never known you not to finish what you have started."

"But—"

"Your vocabulary has declined considerably since we last met." Von Friedenthal clapped Ryder on the shoulder. "We shall commence the cure— ha! Pawn to queen four."

"A game of chess?"

"Well?"

"Martin, did the circus leave town without you?"

"There you go again," said von Friedenthal, pointing at Ryder's mouth. "We return to the basics. You can no longer think logically, so we begin at the beginning."

"Pawn to queen four is the answer? Now, why didn't I think of that."

"Don't you see? It's what the game represents. If you didn't have a mind, you might as well be a prize bull, eating grass, and chasing the lady cows. No, the game is the answer. If you move badly, you must pay; if you move correctly, you are rewarded. Where is your logic? Besides, I owe you for that last game we played."

"I was lucky."

"Luck had nothing to do with it. So, my boy—no pieces, no board, only the mind. And need I remind you that chess is a game of intellect and not of emotion?"

"Horse feathers!"

"No, thank you. Pawn to queen four."

"All right, damn it, all right. Knight to king's bishop three."

"See how simple it is?" Walking along with his hands behind his back and puffing great clouds of smoke, Martin von Friedenthal beamed. "Pawn to queen's bishop four."

Chapter XVI

"Ah, there you are," said Colonel Brooks Cameron. "Heard you were back. Rather a brief stay, but you usually do make short work of things, now don't you."

Ryder entered the dining room to find the others already assembled there—Hall, Katherine, and the four trainers. He knew it was going to be one of those nights. He would either be ignored by the trainers as they talked amongst themselves, which he didn't mind in the least, or he would be the center of attention, as every detail of the day's training was picked over.

"No, no, sit over here—at the head of the table," said Cameron, as Ryder headed toward his usual seat. "This is a special occasion and Andrew has graciously agreed to give up his place, just this once. Here, allow me to hold your chair. Tonight, dear fellow, you are our guest." Cameron included the other trainers. "Normally, the guest of honor sits at the host's right, but as spokesperson I've taken the liberty of changing things so that we can all see you, the better to share you, if you know what I mean. There...comfortable? Yes, indeed, this promises to be quite an evening."

Ryder wondered what the hell was going on. One glance at the seating arrangements told him he had been right—it was going to be one of those nights. Brooks sat at his right, along with Asim and Andrew, while Harry and Nathaniel were at his left. The only good part was that he could look at Katherine, seated at the opposite end of the table.

"Mrs. Bentwood has outdone herself tonight," continued Cameron. "We'll begin with a superb Scottish salmon. I think you'll enjoy the rest of the fare, as well. I didn't have much time, but I think the results will warrant the effort."

Heather, the Bentwood's daughter, began serving the pink, smoked fish. Paper-thin slices of salmon on buttered dark bread were accompanied by wedges of lemon and a large wooden pepper mill. The tangy aroma of the fish and freshly ground pepper made Ryder's mouth water.

"Bring the first wine now," ordered Cameron. "You know the one I mean, don't you?"

Heather, a shy girl, bobbed her head, but didn't answer. She never looked directly at anyone, except Katherine. Ryder had never seen Heather outside the dining room. He wondered what else she did. Did she go to school? Was she married? Did she have children? He hadn't the faintest idea. Like so many things at Hall House, she, too, was a mystery.

"Pensive tonight?" asked Cameron. "Aren't you going to tell us about your trip?"

Ryder looked at the man. "You wouldn't be interested, Brooks. I played a game of chess with an old friend. No one was killed, maimed, or injured."

"How is Doctor von Friedenthal?" interjected Hall.

"He's fine."

"Von Friedenthal?" mused Cameron. "Sounds like a Kraut."

"He happens to be German," replied Ryder, "among other things."

"Who won?" asked Green.

"We agreed to a draw. It was a fine game."

Cameron couldn't resist. "You must understand, Nathaniel. John, here, isn't interested in a win. He thinks it's not a question of winning, but of how you play the game, that matters. Almost British, wouldn't you say? It evidently takes a man like this German friend of his to bring out the best in him, something we haven't been able to do. But, of course, in our business, a draw would hardly prove satisfactory, now would it."

"Sorry, I wasn't thinking," laughed Green. He smiled at Ryder.

"Careful," said Ryder, "you'll give yourself away."

Green's eyes gleamed in the candlelight. "It doesn't make any difference—this farce is about over."

"Think what you like."

Asim and Tanaka were following the exchange. They seldom had much to say at the dinner table, but seemed to enjoy listening to the others. Hall was watching with guarded attention, while Katherine was clearly annoyed with whatever the evening promised.

"Don't apologize, Nathaniel," said Ryder. "Martin's a better man than all of you put together."

"Man, I didn't apologize, you—" Green's voice was rising.

"Gentlemen," said Hall, "need I remind you there is a lady present."

Cameron addressed Katherine and Hall. "No offense intended, I assure you. Relax, Nathaniel—all in good time. Drink up, enjoy the moment and be patient. I promise you, it will be worth it."

Ryder wasn't about to let anything spoil Mrs. Bentwood's dinner. Everything was delicious. And, regardless of his opinion of the Colonel, the man's taste in wines was superb.

As Ryder stretched his sore knee under the table, he listened with only half an ear. He'd heard it all before. Conversation with Katherine or Andrew was impossible. The trainers were hard at it and Ryder was going to relive his last training sessions, whether he wanted to or not.

The table had been cleared when Cameron again turned his attention to Ryder.

"Understand that Asim got you six out of six the time before last. One would think you'd have gotten the hang of it by now. Why don't you quit and we can forget the whole thing. Go back to playing chess; you shouldn't hurt yourself too badly. I do have some other things I'd prefer doing—like working with the real holder of The Gift."

"Don't say that," said Green. "There's one other thing he does well."

Cameron looked puzzled. "Whatever might that be?"

"He's an excellent swimmer."

The trainers were chuckling. Ryder's unscheduled dip had not gone unnoticed.

Ryder couldn't help smiling. Humor was infectious, even at his own expense. If he had any serious regrets, they concerned his failures during his exercises with Hall.

He took another sip of wine and thought about the hours he'd spent staring at the metal spokes of the little opened umbrella in its glass case, willing it to turn. It was another version of the sword that hung over the Round Table.

Ryder had tried everything. He pushed from the back of his mind and pulled from the front. He had channeled his thoughts to include only those metal spokes. He'd imagined the umbrella was a lawn sprinkler and his thoughts, the hose.

As he turned on the faucet of his mind, the water would rush under pressure through his thoughts and the sprinkler would start to turn. It didn't work. It wasn't a sprinkler and his mind couldn't make the stupid thing move. More often than not, he found himself staring off into space.

Was it only yesterday that he had decided to give the whole thing up? He owed von Friedenthal a debt. That wise old man had struck true.

Ryder looked down the table to where Katherine sat. Why was the unobtainable the most desired? Damn and double damn. Ryder raised his glass to her in a silent toast. He smiled at her and then looked at the trainers. He was committed. The small smile at the corner of his mouth was at its maddening best.

Cameron rose quickly, glass in hand. "Gentlemen—pardon me, lady and gentlemen, one toast deserves another." The Colonel was in vitriolic good form.

"Fellow trainers," said Cameron, looking at Asim, Green, and Tanaka, "throughout history, men have been asked to follow their kings, their emperors, their khans—warriors all, who ruled by leading their men into battle. They were always in the thick of things and their men followed to the known ends of the earth and, if necessary, beyond. Those must have been great times. Think of it, a king who never asked anyone to do what he couldn't do himself. But times change."

Cameron paused for a dramatic moment, full of mock regret. "Gradually, the kings had others do their fighting for them, while they stayed safe behind their castle walls, practicing the fine arts of war—like writing sonnets and dancing. Instead of leading their men, they waited at home for a fast rider to tell them their crown was still secure. No more dying with the men. True courage had gone out of style."

The Colonel waited. The other trainers were smiling. What was the old fox up to? Cameron looked at the man seated at the head of the table. He took something out of his left pocket and held it concealed in his hand.

"First, a word to the lady of the house," continued Cameron, who had turned to Katherine.

"I'm sorry to say that you are behaving like a silly little goose. The child I bounced on my knee, and the little girl who couldn't wait for my next visit, is now a woman and not a very wise one, at that. I've been watching you. He's not the man for you; he's really not much of a man at all. I expected more from you."

The suddenness of the attack shocked Katherine. Gone was her cool detachment. She was angry and it showed. She spoke slowly, giving each word full weight. "Colonel Cameron, your lack of propriety is astonishing. You involve yourself in matters that are not of your concern. I never realized what a prig you really are. It is only by my father's leave that you are here at all. Even so, there is no longer anything you could possibly think of, that I would toast to."

Katherine looked Cameron straight in the eye. Using one finger, she pushed over her half-filled wineglass. The crystal shattered and they all watched in silence as the red wine stain spread on the white tablecloth.

Nothing fazed Cameron. He turned next to Hall.

"We've been at it for months now. When he left, I thought that was the end of it. Now he's back. What do I have to do to convince you? I've always admired and respected you. Through the years, we've shared many things. But this time, you're wrong. I know what this means to you—we all do—but give it up. It's a hopeless situation. He's not your man. He never was."

Hall took his time before answering. "Brooks, I'd be most careful, if I were you. This is your evening, as you requested. I understand your frustration. However, your behavior is inexcusable. I didn't think that I'd have to remind you, of all people. Do you remember my warning when you first met John? It still stands. You don't know the force with which you're dealing. I'd hate to lose you."

Cameron wouldn't be put off. With a little bow, he replied, "Thankee, m'lord. I'd tug my forelock, if I had one, but you see we don't share your privileged information. In any case, I am always careful. You will shortly come to appreciate that fact."

The trainers were no longer smiling. Cameron raised his glass to them. "My final toast is to you—fellow sufferers on the wheel of John Ryder's incompetence," he intoned. "I raise my glass to each of you. To Harry Tanaka, the last of the samurai—warriors second to none. To Mahmut Asim, with the blood of sultans, and to Nathaniel Hawthorne Green, whose forefathers were kings. We may be part of Arthur's family, but we also stand alone."

"Hear me, Brooks, and the rest of you, too," interrupted Hall. "Long before the kings, there was Arthur. Before the sultans and before the samurai, there was Arthur. For the last time, stop this before it goes too—"

James L Diffin

Cameron held up his left hand. Slowly, he opened his fingers to reveal a small gray box, the size of a cigarette lighter. He held it up for all to see. "Notice, if you will, the little red button here," said Cameron.

He turned, at last, to face Ryder, and spat out the words.

"If we are not good enough to sit at that table of yours back there in the cavern, then I see no reason for you to sit at ours." Cameron pressed the red button. There was a sharp explosion and the room filled with smoke.

Chapter XVII

The smoke cleared quickly. Cameron had wired Ryder's chair with explosive charges strong enough to destroy the chair without killing its occupant. Caught by surprise, Ryder struggled to keep his balance and get his feet under him. In spite of his stiff knee, he almost made it. Instead, he fell heavily, striking his head a smashing blow against the edge of the dining table. Amid the debris of the chair, Ryder sprawled on the floor, stunned and only half conscious.

There was a moment of shocked silence, a sharp intake of breath. Then came the laughter. It rolled over Ryder, swirling and eddying around the room. Now that the danger was identified and didn't involve them, the trainers thought it funny.

Ryder struggled to sit up. Now he knew why Katherine and Hall had been seated at the far end of the table. For the first time in his life, Ryder felt like killing someone. It was a frightening thought. Above all, he had a paralyzing pain in his head whenever he tried to open his eyes. Suddenly he realized his eyes were open. He was blind.

Above the sounds of laughter, Ryder heard the Colonel's voice.

"Now, what do you think of your precious holder of The Gift?"

Katherine and Hall were at Ryder's side. He heard Katherine catch her breath in disbelief.

"John, I didn't know," said Hall. "Here, let me help you."

Ryder pulled himself up by the edge of the table, shaking off Hall's helping hands. He still couldn't see. He had to get out of there. He smiled.

"Brooks, that was quite a trick. One of these days, you'll have to show me how it works. If you'll excuse me, I think I'll go up to my room for a while."

Again, John shook off Hall's hands. "No, Andrew, I'm all right. I'd like to be by myself, if you don't mind. I do not want your help." John couldn't see the trainers, but he could sense their grinning faces.

"Sure you don't need me to show you the way?" said Green with a laugh.

It got Ryder from the room. He quietly closed the door on Hall's voice giving Colonel Cameron unshirted hell.

In the great hall, Ryder collapsed against the wall. He'd found his way out of the dining room only by memory. He felt cold and was shivering with shock and anger. He hadn't felt like this since he was nine years old and Carl and the other boys had tried to stuff a dead rat in his mouth.

Driven by pain and fear, Ryder headed toward the rear of the house toward the cavern and sanctuary. By running his hands along the walls, he found his way to the inner room, locked the door and went to rest his forehead against the marble coolness of the fireplace. The pain in his head was worse. His brain was being torn apart by some savage beast. His mouth was filled with the sour taste of fear.

The cavern door swung open and Ryder went careening blindly down the passageway. In the cavern, he ran full into a rack of weapons, setting off a terrible din as steel clattered and rebounded from the stone floor.

Ryder crawled the rest of the way until his hand touched a chair leg. Dizzy and sick to his stomach, he pulled himself up to finally sit at the Round Table. He gripped the thick wood to steady himself and tried desperately to see again.

What an idiot he had been! The power of the mind—bullshit! With one blow, the years of small, hard-won victories over himself were gone. He was afraid. The only difference was that now, he could admit it.

As a boy, there had been the running. Like every kid in every schoolyard, he'd learned that if you took one step back, you were finished.

He was afraid, so he ran, and because he ran, they chased him. Every day, after school, they would be waiting. Like hounds in full cry, they hunted him all the way home.

He was never caught, because he ran in absolute terror. With a last desperate burst of speed, his thin chest heaving, he would tear open his front door, safe...until tomorrow.

He'd been a voracious reader and, secure in his room, he spent hours reading and plotting revenge. Ryder was a late bloomer, but bloom he did. Armed with the tales of a hundred heroes, he finally stopped running.

It had been bloody at first, but he discovered the secret. He picked just one boy on whom to vent his newfound rage, no matter what the cost.

In the end they got him, of course, but not before he did his damage. Before long, it wasn't a fun game anymore. He paid, but so did they. Eventually, it deteriorated to name calling, which he found acceptable. It didn't get you all skinned up or tear your clothes. He could live with that.

But, he wasn't a child anymore. The only difference now was that he had learned not to run. Big deal!

The trainers held him in contempt and he was the butt of every joke they could devise. The chess grand master, the man who could be champion, was simply a source of amusement for four violent men.

So there he sat, sick with pain, while fear and anger fought. Until now, whenever things were beyond his control, he'd had a place to go in his mind, but tonight there was no place to hide.

At first he had been cold, now he was burning up. He shivered and shook, a man gripped with fever, drenched with sweat. All the old devils and some new ones he'd found along the way massed to begin the chase down the corridors of his mind. He supposed he was a bit mad.

Ryder was massaging his temples, trying to ease the pain, when he heard it. He turned his head to listen. It wasn't a sound, but an awareness.

He reached out. On the table before him, where he knew it would be, was a goblet. Fingers that had held a thousand chess pieces traced the raised ornamentation around the outside of the cup. It was a wide-brimmed vessel with a metallic feel. The pain in his head tightened another turn.

With trembling fingers, he picked up the goblet. It was surprisingly heavy and Ryder had to use both hands. As he held it, the goblet seemed to throb with the pulse of a beating heart.

Drawn by an instinct stronger than fear of the unknown, he raised the cup to his lips. He didn't question where it had come from or what it was doing there. He knew that if he hesitated, he was lost. He drank and then drank again until the vessel was empty.

The pain in his head was now absolute. In spite of his agony, Ryder carefully set the cup on the table. From a fragile toehold at the back of his mind, he lashed out.

"Enough!" The word was both a plea and a command.

The goblet had been filled with heaven and hell—and life. There were brilliant flashes of light in the gray cotton that covered his eyes. All the fibers

115

of his brain seemed to expand, and then contract to clasp mental fingers in a grip that only death could break.

The pain was still intense, but it no longer mattered. Gradually, he was beginning to see again. His vision was still cloudy, but he knew that it was time for him to leave the cavern.

Alone in the night outside, Ryder raised his face to the sky. The pain began to recede. Slowly, like a developing photo, faint at first, the light of a million stars became clearer. My God, he thought, I never knew there were so many. The stars grew brighter, each one shimmering and sparkling. They hung there, vivid and radiant in a velvet black sky. He realized that he was seeing with a new sense of depth and distance. The stars were now three-dimensional.

He looked out over the park. The night no longer consisted of shades of gray, but was alive with color. He could see into the darkest shadow. He flexed his leg and his knee no longer hurt. He felt good; he felt great. For the first time in years, he felt like running for pure joy.

Down the drive, around the gardens and the cedars of Lebanon, and out into the meadow he ran. Summer's first new pair of sneakers. He could fly. He could jump over the moon. He was approaching the narrow end of the duck pond. Without thought or hesitation, he was airborne. Up and across, no longer earthbound. Then he was running again.

He stopped. Just what the hell did he think he was doing? He walked back to the pond and stood looking across to the other side. He must be drunk or hallucinating. He couldn't have just done what he thought he did. From where he stood the far bank was a good twenty feet away. He hadn't even been trying. Ryder sat down.

A half hour ago, he couldn't stand up, now he was jumping out of his skin. What the hell had he gotten hold of? He realized he was smiling. Sometimes, on the squash court, he would laugh out loud for the sheer joy of being alive. He felt that way now, only more so. He wanted to kick up... hold it! Let's not start that again—one step at a time. Think! Lord knows he hadn't accepted Andrew Hall's mumbo jumbo about some super gene popping up every so many years—but something different. Ryder ran his hands over his body. It was the same. The change was within. He had a moment's panic before remembering von Friedenthal's advice—you are a thinking animal.

Okay, let's not play the middle game before we're through with the opening. First there was his eyesight. Now there was the way he moved. He had run and jumped as never before and he wasn't even breathing hard.

Ryder felt for his pulse—nothing. He shifted his fingers on his wrist—still nothing. *Ka-thump*. Thank God. Then nothing. He waited. *Ka-thump*. He estimated his pulse at thirty a minute, less than half his normal sixty-five.

Then there was the way he felt. He had been sore and aching for months, but you'd never know it now. Everything moved so nicely, all oiled and ticking over with smoothly meshing gears. Sitting on the grass beside the pond, he had a feeling of well-being and a sense of great resting power. He could see with frightening clarity.

Ryder didn't believe in ghosts, magic, or miracles. All right, damn it, he thought, let's find out. He rose and walked toward the pavilion on the other side of the pond. He entered and went to the table where Mahmut Asim kept his bows. There it was. According to Asim, no living man could string and draw this particular weapon. It was an enormous, rough-hewn piece of lumber that only vaguely resembled a conventional bow. Whenever Ryder thought he was doing well, Asim would hand him the bow.

Ryder selected a long, heavy hunting arrow with a shaft as big around as his finger. He stood in the doorway of the tent and shoved the arrow, point first, into the ground in front of him. He held the bow in both hands, feeling the heavy grain of the wood, and thought about it for a moment. Then he was ready.

With a twist, the bow was strung, the arrow nocked, and the head pulled full back to the grip of the creaking bow. Ryder used the Mongolian release, with the arrow on the right side of the bow. He had forgotten the thumb ring that Asim wore whenever he used a heavy bow. It didn't seem to matter. Old and stiff, the bow protested against being awakened from its long sleep.

The arrow was fully drawn so that the string of the bow touched Ryder's chin. He felt the great pull, but his arms were rock steady. Raising the bow until the arrow pointed up into the sky, he released the string. The shaft went screaming away into the night, arcing high into the air, silhouetted against the stars. Yes—by God—yes! He watched its flight down the meadow.

"Try that on for size, Asim!" He continued watching until the arrow was lost to sight.

The chess player, who could be champion, stood looking up at the night sky. *So this is what it's all about.* He thought about the other holders of The Gift and felt their presence. *My apologies, Gentlemen—I sold you short. I didn't know.* He thought about the Round Table and the Code and what it represented. *Mankind hadn't come all that far in fifteen hundred years.*

But first, he had some unfinished business. He had to find out more about himself and then he would deal with those four men up at the house. As he set off across the meadow toward the woods, he laughed out loud. It was going to be one hell of a night!

Suddenly, without warning, Ryder felt a searing flash of evil that almost brought him to his knees.

Once again I touch your mind. Think not that I had forgotten. Now that you have the power, I, too, can feel your presence. It begins. You shall come to know me and there will be death.

Chapter XVIII

"Got you anyway, you bloody cheat! That's a double run for sixteen points—and I'm out," said Colonel Cameron. "I have to watch you every second; you're the only man I know who pegs twelve with an eight hand."

Harry Tanaka grinned. Like Mahmut Asim, Tanaka was an avid gambler. Cameron had taught him to play cribbage and most evenings found the two of them hard at it. Tanaka took wild chances and Cameron, for all his experience, was frequently hard pressed to keep up. Tonight was not one of his better outings—this was only his second winning game.

Seated on a couch in front of the fire, Green and Asim were deep in conversation. Hall sat alone at his desk. It had been several hours since the incident in the dining room and he was feeling uneasy.

Bentwood had informed him that Mr. Ryder was not in his room. Hall decided to wait a little longer before going in search of him. He'd tried sending mental probes out into the night, but there was no response. Tonight had been a disaster. He hoped it hadn't undone all the months of work.

Katherine was seated in a large wing chair with an open book on her lap, but she wasn't reading.

Green stood up and took another log from the brass woodbox beside the fireplace. Sparks flew as he tossed it on the flames. He turned to Andrew.

"Well, coach, where's your prize pupil?" Green yawned and stretched slowly until his muscles creaked. "This country living may be fine for you, but it's not for me. We've done all that you've asked and more. I know about The Gift—we all do. I heard about it from my old man."

Green waved a hand to include the other trainers. "I've trained since I was eight. Sure, your protégé has a few good moves—now and then—but he hasn't got it. He's not operating at a level necessary to function effectively against professionals. If he's got The Gift, then your Round Table is in for big trouble. I can't imagine why you are so obsessed with him. I spend my life preparing for this and what do I get? A smart-ass with a stupid grin."

Hall studied Green's face. "Why won't you see?" Hall shook his head sadly. "Especially you, Nathaniel, someone who's been trained to use his senses. Yet you will not or can not—amazing!"

"Forget all that jazz. How much longer do I stay away from my work? At least there, I can do something." Green turned to Katherine. "You're in this, too. Can't you do anything with your father?"

Katherine shrugged. "Perhaps, Mr. Green, you should try looking past your own personal animosity."

Green made a gesture of disgust. "I should have known better. All right, then. Mahmut, what about you?"

"I can do no more. I would see my mountains."

"Well, Brooks," asked Green looking at Colonel Cameron, "with your years in the field, what do you have to say?"

Cameron was losing at cribbage again. He threw his cards down on the table.

"You Yanks usually manage to muck things up, but for once you're bang on."

Cameron turned in his chair to confront his host. "Andrew, I have to agree. I said it at dinner and I say it again. You are too close to this one. I've been biding my time, off and on, waiting for the next bearer of The Gift to turn up. I never thought it would be like this. You obviously expect the transformation of a grown man. I've trained raw recruits who showed more promise."

Cameron looked across the library at Hall. "I don't know what you see in him or even how you came up with him in the first place. You never consulted me. Perhaps you were desperate enough to create him out of whole cloth. Knowing you, Andrew, I find the whole situation surprisingly untidy."

Hall sat perfectly still, his hands flat on the green inlaid leather of the desk top. He spoke calmly. "We might as well make it unanimous. Harry, do you have anything to add?"

It took Tanaka a moment to answer, to pull himself away from the cribbage game. "I miss my wife and my family. I miss Japan. I have a fourteen-year-old son who's more proficient. Your man makes the same mistakes over and over. The only good thing I can say about him is that he has no fear."

Tanaka's eyes were opaque as he remembered. "I know, I have tested his soul." He began shuffling the cards again.

"There you have it," said Green. "Do you think all four of us are wrong?"

"You are," said Katherine from the wing chair. "You expect from John what you could not do yourselves—to master all your combined knowledge and skill in a matter of months. Not one of you really sees the man."

Cameron was the first off the mark.

"Forgive me, my dear Miss Hall, but we haven't had time to stare into his eyes, as you have. Besides, I doubt we would be looking for the same thing, don't you know."

"What are you saving it for," asked Green, "when there are some real men around here?"

Hall was furious, but before he or Katherine could answer, a voice came from the back of the room—a voice cold as arctic ice.

"You abuse the hospitality of this house. Away from this place you may do as you please, but never here."

Six pairs of stunned eyes focused on John Ryder. No one had known he was there. They looked first at him, then across the room to the library door. It had been closed all evening. It was still closed. For the first time anyone could remember, Ryder wasn't smiling.

Ever since men first sat around the fire sucking the juice out of thighbones, women have been the brighter of the species. Katherine had never met a holder of The Gift before, she didn't need to. After hearing Ryder's voice, and looking at him, she knew. The signs were unmistakable. She was awed and relieved and a little afraid.

Ryder crossed the room to stand in front of Katherine's chair. She wouldn't look at him. "Come, Katherine." With a gentle knuckle under her chin, he slowly lifted her head.

"John, I...we've been so worried. Are you all right?"

"You might be surprised. I'll tell you about it when I can." For a long moment, they looked at each other, all else forgotten.

"Isn't that just ducky," said Colonel Cameron. "How did he get in here? Eavesdropping, I suppose. Really, Andrew, in your own home, of all things."

Cameron started across the room. "Are you going to permit this? First, he takes over the house and now he's got his grubby hands all over your daughter. Look at him, he's filthy. I'll take care of this."

Hall had been staring at Ryder. True, the man was a mess. His clothes were dirty and torn. He was also wet, dripping all over the priceless Oriental carpet, but Hall wasn't the least bit disturbed.

"That's enough, Brooks," he said. "Do shut up." Cameron froze in his tracks.

Ryder came over to Hall's desk and stood looking down at the seated man.

Yes, thought Hall. There it is again. It had been more than thirty years since he had last seen that expression in someone's eyes. He had despaired that he ever would again.

Despite the dirty, wet clothing, there was an aura about Ryder, a presence. He didn't do anything, he just stood there. The hardened planes of Ryder's face, and the haunted gray-blue eyes, looked back at Hall with an "I've spit in the eye of the devil and here I am" expression.

"Yes?" asked Hall.

"Yes," replied Ryder. "Whatever you left me in that cup seems to have done the trick."

Hall became deathly quiet, staring at Ryder as if he had never seen him before. "What cup?"

It was John's turn to stare. "I didn't imagine it."

Andrew slowly shook his head.

"Something make you wet your pants again, boy?" asked Green.

"I tried," said Ryder, still talking to Hall, "to jump the pond."

"Where?"

"In the middle."

"There are limitations. What did you expect?"

"I expected," said John, with the faintest of smiles, "to get wet."

"I see you haven't lost your questionable sense of humor."

"I'm not so sure."

It was a different John Ryder who now turned to face the trainers. Mahmut Asim and Harry Tanaka were watching with alert expressions. Colonel Cameron was still standing in the center of the room. His hunter's antennae were out—something had changed.

"It seems," said Cameron slowly, "that our little trainee has cut his baby teeth."

Still looking at the four trainers, Ryder smiled. It was a smile of recognition and understanding. There was something predatory about it. "Now, for the challenge."

"No, John," said Hall, "If you mean what I think you do, I will not permit it. It is too soon."

Ryder raised his hand. "No!"

No one talked to Andrew Hall like that. Except for the fire crackling in the fireplace, the room was still. Ryder opened his mind to Hall. After a moment, Hall nodded and began to smile.

Ryder walked over to the game table and picked up the heavy oak cribbage board. "Gentlemen," he said, addressing the trainers, "over the past months, as you have studied me, I have studied you. I know how you work, how you think, your philosophies of life."

Ryder looked at Harry Tanaka. "And, of death. It was your job to train me, but you did more than that. Now it is your turn." Ryder looked around the room until his gaze met Green's.

"I'll start with you."

"Pretty cocky talk for a guy who's soaking wet."

"Nathaniel Hawthorne Green, survivalist," continued Ryder, "the man who's constantly looking for an edge. An educated man with a short fuse."

Green sprang to his feet. "I'm in your face, boy. I don't need an edge for the likes of you."

Backed by two hundred and forty pounds of anger and frustration, Green unleashed a straight overhand right to Ryder's head.

It never arrived. With a crack, Nathaniel's fist stopped in midair against Ryder's hand. The hand didn't move. Green might as well have hit one of the oaks out in the meadow.

"You led with your right," said Ryder, watching Green.

Everyone else was watching, too. Green was bent over in pain, clutching his right hand. Ryder put the cribbage board back on the table—the heavy, solid oak cribbage board that Green had just punched out.

Picking up the deck of cards, Ryder said, "In the old days, when knights wore armor, it was hard to tell the players without a scorecard. So the good, honest fellows developed a system. They wore their coats of arms on their tunics and on their shields. It was a statement. In battle, you knew exactly who your opponent was. If you had a grudge against one particular man, you went looking for his coat of arms. You called him out."

Ryder began shuffling the cards. "Silly and old-fashioned maybe, but it was all up front. It was a code by which men lived and died. In those days, a man stood for something and he wasn't afraid to say so."

Ryder looked at the four trainers. "Why am I telling you all this? Simple—you don't have shields or tunics, so here's what we're going to do." He shuffled and cut the cards. "There are four aces in this deck, one for each of you. We'll call them your coats of arms."

Ryder riffled the cards twice and cut again. In his hand was the Ace of Clubs. Asim and Tanaka were staring at Ryder's hands.

"The Club or Cudgel," continued Ryder. "It has always amazed me, Nathaniel, how quickly you resort to physical force. If something doesn't fit or conform, you smash it until it does. Since you have taken such a fancy to the pond outside, then the pond it shall be."

Green was watching Ryder with hooded eyes, still waiting for the feeling to return to his hand.

Asim and Tanaka were waiting, too. There! Ryder shuffled the cards again. They both were staring at Ryder's hands like a pair of hungry wolves. Ryder riffled the cards several times, then cut the Ace of Hearts.

"The Heart—a symbol of the cup that Christ used at the Last Supper. How many Crusades were there to free the Holy Land from the Infidel? Mahmut, this one's yours."

The second ace was too much for Harry Tanaka. He reached over and took the cards from Ryder's hands. He fanned the cards and felt their edges. He held several up to the light, then riffled the pack, watching the backs of the cards.

He handed the cards to Ryder. "Do it again," he commanded.

"Of course, Harry. You're next anyway." Again the shuffle, the riffle, and the cut. In the palm of Ryder's hand was the Ace of Diamonds.

Tanaka snatched at the card. "Nobody can do that—it's a trick. You cheat."

"No trick, Harry. If I told you how I did it, you wouldn't believe me anyway, so why bother. The Diamond—cold, hard, unyielding. No matter, every diamond has its fracture line, and so do you."

124

Green stood glowering in the background while Asim and Tanaka re-examined the cards. Cameron had returned to his seat at the game table and was studying Ryder.

"It won't be necessary to bother the others with this," he said. "We can settle this between ourselves."

"Oh, no, you don't," interrupted Green. "He belongs to me. " Green was rubbing his knuckles. "You can have what's left over."

"Absolutely not," said Colonel Cameron. "I have first go and that's all there is to it."

"Gentlemen—gentlemen," said Ryder. "It's not going to be that easy."

"You can't imagine the pleasure this is going to give me," said Cameron.

"You really think so?" said Ryder reaching for the cards that Tanaka had put back on the table.

"Satisfied, Harry?"

Tanaka only grunted.

For the last time, Ryder shuffled the cards—two crisp riffles and the cut. Ryder tossed the pack down on the table. He still held one card, face down, between his thumb and first two fingers.

Cameron watched with a bored expression. "That's not going to help. Tricks won't save you."

"Sorry to hear you disapprove. And I so thought you'd appreciate my act. That's why I saved you for last. Colonel Brooks Cameron, the British edition of the Desert Fox, a little gray around the muzzle, but cunning and deadly all the same—this is for you, Old Chap—the boss card."

With a snap, Ryder turned the card over and flicked it through the air. It landed, face up, on the table in front of Cameron. "The Sword, the Ace of Spades—you know what they say about those who take up the sword, don't you, Brooks?"

Ryder stood looking at the four men. "Strange how things work out sometimes, but there you have it." He paused before continuing, "Gentlemen, in case there is any doubt, I'm calling you out—now—tonight. I will not wait another day."

He went back to Hall's desk. "In one hour, send them all out!"

Hall was incredulous. "At the same time?"

"Exactly."

"They're here just to train you. John, you must reconsider. The wraps will be off; they'll try to kill you."

Ryder's face was hard. "It's what they've wanted all along. They have to know the power of The Gift. They'll never leave it alone until they do. Andrew—one hour—see to it!"

Katherine was standing with her back against the closed library door, barring the way. "Don't worry," Ryder said softly.

"John, listen to my father—please don't do this. If you have any regard for me, you will stop right now. They aren't worth it."

He touched her lips with his finger. "I'm sorry."

"It's just not fair."

"Fair has nothing to do with it."

"So—you think you got it," said Green. "Now you're the main man. Shee-it! You're going down."

Ryder gently moved Katherine to one side, opened the door, and turned back.

"You know you're going to die out there," said Cameron in a flat voice. "You might get away from one of us, but not all four. You're already a dead man."

"No, Brooks, you have it wrong. I'm not trying to get away from any of you." There was a gleam from Ryder's eyes. "I'll be waiting."

Chapter XIX

Midnight. Andrew Hall sat at his desk. He could hear the trainers talking in the great hall. It was going to be a long night.

Katherine was pacing the floor. She went to the library door and closed it. She gestured to the book on the seat of her chair. "If I had read this, I wouldn't believe it for a minute. The whole thing is criminal. John hasn't got a chance and you know it. Those men out there are killers. And don't tell me about tradition or the Code or anything—none of it is worth a man's life."

"My dear, you have become personally involved—"

"What if I have?" Katherine was struggling for control. "I know there's no future in it, but one doesn't plan these things." Her eyes flashed. "We serve only The Gift and can never think of ourselves. The Gift has given him to me and The Gift will take him away." She paused, and when she continued, her voice was lower. "I shall never again see him alive."

Hall sighed. He was toying with the deck of cards from the game table. "Perhaps you've already had more than you've any right to expect."

"Meaning?"

"You know the answer to that, as well as I do."

Katherine pointed to the cards that Hall held. "Sleight of hand is one thing, being hunted by professional killers is quite another. The trainers have had years to polish their skills. By comparison, John is a rank amateur."

"You must have faith. John doesn't have to learn what he already knows—it's all there. He didn't realize it before, now he does. Tonight, we have to risk a little to gain a lot. Consider it a gambit."

"Gambit! I thought we were talking about a man's life?"

"It's a chess term."

"Thank you, Father," said Katherine sarcastically. "I am familiar with the expression."

"Sorry, my dear, of course you are. What I mean to say was that, for the new holder of The Gift, tonight is analogous to an opening gambit in chess. In other words, he must sacrifice material at the beginning in order to create an advantage later in the game. When done correctly, the result is inevitable."

"How can you sit there so smugly and refer to a man's life as a game? I don't understand, maybe I never will. This obsession with The Gift, to the exclusion of everything else. Don't you see what you are doing? Those animals out there in the hall—they enjoy this. Brooks, Nathaniel and the others—they want to destroy him. Oh, why bother—" Katherine turned and headed for the door. "If you won't put a stop to this, I will!"

"It's too late—they've already gone."

Katherine stood in the doorway. The great hall was empty. After a moment, she looked squarely at her father. "If he dies," she said softly, "if he dies, then it all dies with him. It will be the end of everything. Even if another should appear in my lifetime, I will have absolutely nothing to do with him. Nothing!"

"You are upset—"

"I mean it."

Hall sat looking at the cards. In her own way, Katherine was as much of an absolute as John Ryder.

"I'm sorry," he said.

Katherine took one last look at her father. "I'll be in my room," she said.

Hall knew there would be no sleep for her tonight. His heart was heavy—she had so much to learn. He rose and went to the woodbox to put more wood on the fire. Then he poured a brandy and turned the lights out, one by one, until only the desk lamp remained. He went back to his desk and settled himself once more. He opened the humidor and selected a cigar. After a sip of brandy and a puff on the cigar, he was ready. He rubbed his hands together and picked up the cards.

In the light of the desk lamp, Hall's strong fingers shuffled and riffled the cards. Then, one after the other, he cut the four aces from the deck. Yes, he thought, it was easier for him than for his daughter. He knew something that Katherine didn't. He knew what was out there in the night.

A quarter moon hung low in the frosty night sky. A faint breeze stirred the trees. Down by the pond, the ducks were restless. An owl returning from hunting in the meadow flared off from his nesting place. There was nothing to be seen, there was nothing to be heard, but something was there in the darkness...

Chapter XX

It was a night of dark shadows. One of the shadows moved. Harry Tanaka, dressed in black, was advancing noiselessly down the gravel drive toward the meadow. To do so, he had to pass one of the first large oak trees that gave the meadow its park-like appearance. In the tree, standing along one of the thick lower branches, well out from the trunk, Ryder was waiting.

As Tanaka passed beneath him, Ryder dropped silent as the great owl, but instead of grasping talons, Ryder landed softly in the grass behind Tanaka.

"Here——" he said.

Tanaka was true to his training. Without pause, he whirled, drew his long sword and thrust, in the samurai version of a quick draw. The *ihai-jutsu* move had won many a contest, but not this one.

Ryder's bladed hand flashed as he struck the side of Tanaka's sword, breaking it in two. Tanaka dropped the useless weapon and drew its companion. That sword, too, was shattered.

Immediately, he took a step and leaped in an airborne side-blade kick. Ryder seized Tanaka by the ankle, spun around once, and threw him up into the nearest tree. Then, to Tanaka's horror, Ryder was up in the tree with him.

Raising the twisting body of Harry Tanaka above his head, Ryder threw him out of the tree.

When Harry hit the ground, Ryder was already back around on the other side of the duck pond, concealed in the tall grass that grew by the water's edge. He knew Green would pass this way.

Sure enough, here he came—Nathaniel Hawthorne Green, survivalist. Ryder hadn't disturbed the nesting ducks and geese, and neither did Mr. Green. Green, who could track a puff of smoke across a pool table, never suspected. The cackling of geese might have saved Rome, but they didn't do a thing for him.

The first hint that Ryder was anywhere near was Green's inability to move his legs. He had time for only a glimpse of disembodied hands around his ankles before he was yanked off his feet.

Hall had once described Green as the kind of man who went walking alone, at night, in New York's Central Park, just for the hell of it. He had an inner rage and the ability to make those who crossed him regret it.

When Ryder stood up, so did Green. He unleashed a short snapping right to Ryder's head that would fell an ox.

Ryder moved his head to the side, just far enough so that Green's fist didn't make contact, but close enough so that Green's knuckles brushed his cheek. By the time Green's arm reached full extension, Ryder's right hand was socketed deep in Green's exposed armpit, and the fingers of his left hand found their grip above Green's left hip.

Ryder raised Green above his head, stepped to the side of the pond and drove Green's rigid body waist-deep into the mud at the bottom of the pond.

The sound of Green hitting the water scared the hell out of the ducks. In the ensuing uproar, a flock of fat hens and drakes who hadn't been airborne in months went tearing off across the pond with panic in their wings.

"Stay put, Nathaniel," said Ryder quietly. "I don't want to see you again tonight."

Ryder returned to the pavilion for the bow he had used earlier that night. It had a pull of well over two hundred pounds.

Ryder selected four arrows. Unlike the usual broad-headed hunting arrows, these had movable barbs that lay close to the shaft while in flight. The entrance wound they made was comparatively small, but any attempt to dislodge or withdraw them made the barbs swing out at right angles to the shaft. The resulting wound was formidable.

Ryder waited near the center of the meadow. An hour had passed. Except for an occasional protesting quack from the direction of the pond, the night was still.

After he'd finished with Green, he'd taken his time. Ryder knew that Asim and Cameron had heard the noise. He'd meant them to. He also knew that neither would come charging in. As hunters of men, the two relied only on themselves.

Ryder's attention returned to one particular tree. Isolated in the center of the meadow, it was a huge old oak with an enormous trunk and branches that reached high into the air.

Asim was standing close to the trunk, hiding in the tree's shadow. Ryder had watched him come all the way across the meadow, darting soundlessly from tree to tree.

Asim remained close to the tree for some time, eyes searching the darkness. He knew Ryder was near, he could feel him. He'd hunted big game all over the world, using his compound bow. He'd hunted the Cape buffalo and had faced the charge of the tiger and the Kodiak bear. And he'd hunted men. But it had never felt like this.

Asim had heard the splash in the pond and assumed that Green had thrown Ryder in again—this time, for good. He had waited for a signal, but it never came. His eyes flicked around the meadow.

When it happened, Asim couldn't believe it. The last sound he'd expected to hear was the double cluck children make with their tongues when urging an imaginary horse to gallop. Asim saw what he'd seen before, but failed to recognize.

Ryder was standing alone in the park, well away from any cover, and in plain sight. It was a hunting trick Asim had used himself, when the wind was right. The game might be suspicious but, if you remained absolutely still, they didn't identify you—recognition depended on movement. Asim had never thought to try it on a man.

The second shock followed on the heels of the first. Ryder was looking at him down the shaft of an arrow held firm in a fully drawn bow.

Asim knew which bow it was. If he had a suspicion before, he was certain now. Only one man could use that bow and stand easy with the arrow pulled full back.

Asim threw up a hand in a vain effort to protect himself. He heard that lethal hiss and was slammed back against the trunk of the tree with an arrow through the palm of his hand. The pain was excruciating.

Using his free hand, he struggled to get loose, then to stop what he knew was coming next. Again, he was thrown back against the oak, the other hand pinned like the first. He braced his feet in a desperate effort to wrench free. Two more shafts came in rapid succession, one through each foot. Asim was spread-eagled against the side of the great oak.

Although he was writhing in pain, Asim didn't make a sound. He closed his eyes, waiting for the final shaft to free him from his agony, but it never came. When he opened his eyes again, he was alone with his pain. The place where Ryder had stood was empty.

Back at the pavilion, as he put the bow back in its place, Ryder was already thinking about Cameron. He knew the Colonel would find the others. He wanted Cameron to know exactly what he was up against. Colonel Brooks Cameron, the last and worst of the four—the man most determined to see Ryder dead.

As soon as he came out of the pavilion, he spotted Cameron. Around the house, down the drive, and across the meadow they went. When Cameron moved, Ryder moved with him. When Cameron stopped, so did Ryder. If Cameron was a tree, Ryder was a stone wall. If Cameron moved with the silence of the Ninja master, Ryder was thought itself.

He heard the almost inaudible snick of the .45 Colt Commander being cocked when Cameron found Harry Tanaka's unconscious body. Ryder was on the other side of the pond when Cameron discovered Green, and close enough to see the expression of disbelief cross his face when Cameron got his first look at Mahmut Asim.

Across the meadow they drifted. Sometimes Ryder trailed behind, sometimes he was on one side of Cameron or the other, always paralleling the hunter's path. Finally, at the end of the meadow, on a steep wooded slope carpeted in leaves, he was ahead.

He watched Cameron easing his way up the slope, heel to toe, in the ancient way. Not a leaf rustled. Every living thing gives off an aura, a life force. The antelope cannot see the lion, but he knows it is there, all the same. The quick and the strong, those whose aura burns the brightest, survive until they meet a need stronger than their own.

On a hillside, waited the greatest life force of all, but there was no aura, no glow to warn Cameron. The professional killer, the consummate hunter of men, walked right up to Ryder and never saw him.

Ryder's left hand found the back of the hunter's neck with a paralyzing grip. With his other hand, Ryder set about removing the weapons that Cameron was carrying. First, he plucked the Colt Commander from numb fingers.

"I'll take this, if you don't mind. Now let's see what else you've brought along."

132

Cameron made a move toward his armpit and Ryder increased the pressure on his captive's neck. Cameron went limp and Ryder removed the Smith & Wesson.

"Be still and stop wiggling. I know you don't like to be touched, but that's your problem."

Cameron wore a commando knife at the back of his neck, with the scabbard concealed between his shoulder blades. Ryder tossed the knife on the growing pile of weapons. He ran his free hand over Brook's body.

"I know you've got the damn thing—"

Still holding Cameron by the neck, Ryder lifted him to feel his legs.

"That's more like it," he said as he removed the Granger knife from a sheath strapped to the Colonel's right leg.

Ryder set Cameron back on his feet and examined the blade. He'd seen the weapon before, but Cameron would allow no one to touch it, not even Andrew Hall.

Cameron had carried the knife since he'd been assigned as an advisor to a special training unit in the United States and had visited T.R. Granger, Jr. at his shop in Macon, Georgia. Cameron had finally met someone with his own exacting standards of quality.

The result was a custom-ground piece of steel with a flattened handle. Cameron was of the opinion that the knife was the finest possible and, like the .38, he was never without it.

Ryder dropped the Granger on the pile of weapons. Cameron winced and made a convulsive attempt to break free.

Between his prisoner's legs, Ryder found a hardness that Cameron could never have possessed, even on his best day. Ryder unzipped the Colonel's pants and reached inside. Under his boxer shorts, Cameron was wearing a dance belt, the artistic version of an athletic supporter. Ryder's fingers found and removed a .22 caliber Derringer from the elastic support cup.

"Last line of defense, Colonel?"

Cameron closed his eyes. It was the final indignity.

Ryder gave Cameron a good shake. "I owe you for that crack on the head."

Cameron looked into Ryder's eyes and shuddered.

Ryder took a slow breath and let it out. "Brooks, you can thank your stars for Andrew Hall."

Ryder let go and Cameron fell to the ground to stare at a hole under the roots of a nearby tree.

"Probably fox or badger," said Ryder, as he reached behind the tree and brought out two Persian sabers that he'd concealed there earlier.

"Stick your head in the hole, Brooks."

Cameron didn't move, his face a mask of horror.

"No, I'm not going to kill you. Your only worry is if anything still lives in there. Move it!"

Cameron crawled slowly and painfully to the hole and did as he was ordered. One after the other, Ryder placed the swords against the back of Cameron's neck, driving them deep into the ground until their points found the roots of the tree. The sabers held fast, crisscrossed over the Colonel's neck.

Ryder sat back on his heels to admire his handiwork.

"There, that does it. The swords are sharp. Be still and you won't get hurt. Move and you have only yourself to blame."

Ryder stood up.

"Brooks, don't ever come looking for me again!"

The challenge was over.

Be not pleased, for you are still an infant and an infant you shall remain. What use the skills of men when I am here.

Chapter XXI

The fireplace was cold. The last red ember flickered and winked out as the sound of hurrying footsteps came down the stairs of the great hall. Hall looked up to see the first pale gray light at the window. The long night was over.

"Father, you must come," said Katherine. "There is something moving out there and I think it is a man."

The grandfather clock in the hall was striking the hour. Katherine and Hall almost collided with the ever-present Bentwood. He helped them on with their coats and Hall motioned for him to follow as they rushed from the house.

Their feet were noisy on the white gravel drive as they hurried to the figure at the foot of the garden. It was Harry Tanaka. Harry, using his left elbow, was crawling toward the house. His useless right hand was tucked under his belt.

Hall knelt and tried to help him sit up. Harry looked at Hall with accusing eyes and teeth locked in pain. "I have been master for many years," he whispered, "but no more. My shoulder is broken and something else... inside." There was blood on Harry's lips.

"What about the others?" asked Hall. "Have you seen anyone else?"

Harry didn't answer.

"Let's get you up to the house," said Hall. "Can you walk?"

Harry shook his head. "He broke my swords"—Harry looked at Andrew—"with his hands. He threw me up into a tree. He threw me out of a tree." Harry tugged at Hall's sleeve. "It is finished—please." With that, Harry let go of Hall's coat and toppled over into the bushes, out cold.

A nervous sound escaped from Katherine, something between a sob and a giggle.

Hall felt Harry's pulse. It was strong and regular.

"Bentwood, please get James and the others. Also contact Doctor MacDonald at the clinic—he's standing by."

There would be no questions asked and no reports filed. There wouldn't even be a raised eyebrow, as Doctor MacDonald went about his work. The Doctor's research had long been underwritten by Andrew Hall. Doctor MacDonald's clinic was small, but lacked for nothing. The Doctor had also done a turn in the army. He'd seen wounds before.

Hall eyed his daughter with concern. "Why don't you go back to the house and wait until this is over."

There was a rebellious glint in Katherine's eyes. "Oh, no, you don't. I'm not leaving until I know."

Hall was pleased. She, too, had changed. Hall could see the difference in the tilt of her head and the set of her jaw.

The ducks were gathered at the far end of the pond, paddling back and forth, nervously twitching their tails, protesting something. The something was Nathaniel. The only part of him that showed was his head and shoulders.

"Good morning, Katherine—Hall. Looks like it's going to be a fine day." Nathaniel had a strange expression on his face.

"Isn't it too cold to be swimming at this time of year?" asked Hall.

"I didn't have much say in the matter."

"Mr. Green," said Katherine, "why are you sitting in the water? You must be chilled to the bone."

"Correction. I am not sitting, but standing." Nathaniel raised his arms. "See—no hands."

"But it's only two or three feet deep there," said Katherine.

"I'm aware of that. I'm stuck in the mud. I've been trying to get out, but it's complicated. Both my ankles are in bad shape and I'm not sure about my hip." Nathaniel grimaced. "No leverage."

Hall noticed that Nathaniel's face had a grayish cast, and what he had supposed were drops of water on Nathaniel's forehead were actually beads of perspiration. Nathaniel seemed to be in great pain.

Katherine had to ask. "But how did you get in there?"

"Early this morning, I was incarcerated in this prison of mud by your Mr. Ryder. It has been a sobering experience."

Katherine spoke from behind her hand, trying to hide her smile. "Mr. Green, you sound like a professor."

"I was, at one point in my career, and may be again. I think I would enjoy a life of tranquility and reflection—ivied halls and all. Assuming that I ever get out of here."

Hall motioned to Bentwood, who was standing by. "We'll see to it directly, Nathaniel. By the way, you didn't run into Mahmut or Brooks, did you?"

"I only saw Harry."

Katherine had walked out into the meadow and couldn't hear the two men. "I can't keep this up much longer," said Green through clenched teeth. He was shivering now.

Hall spoke softly. "Tell me, Nathaniel, would you say that John is operating at a level necessary to compete against professionals?"

"Any number of adjectives come to mind. I'm in here and he's out there. A thesis on the subject should not be necessary."

Hall permitted himself just the hint of a frosty smile. "My daughter is right—you do sound like a professor. Be patient, we'll have you out of there directly. Bentwood will see to your needs."

Hall hurried to catch up with his daughter.

"That giant of a man...stuck in the mud," said Katherine. "I thought it would be John."

They were well out in the meadow when Katherine suddenly clutched Hall's arm. "My God, look over there!"

Alone in the center of the park, spread-eagled against the side of an oak tree, was Mahmut Asim. Asim was alive and conscious, but there was no way he could have gotten free by himself. He had struggled to get free and had torn his flesh badly. He hung on the side of the tree, pinned like some enormous butterfly, the prize of the collection—species Homo sapiens.

Doctor MacDonald had arrived with the ambulance. A sedated Nathaniel Green was already inside. It had taken four men to dredge him from the mud.

"How is Harry Tanaka?" asked Hall.

"You mean the Oriental chap? Well, he has internal injuries. I can't be certain until I have him at the clinic, but he should recover. Broken shoulder, of course. Fortunately, the man is as hard as a rock."

Hall was impatient. "You haven't seen Brooks, by any chance?" he asked Asim.

"I saw nothing. Don't expect me to train my son for this." Asim turned his face away.

They found Brooks, stomach down, among a thicket of trees, on the side of a hill at the far end of the meadow. Slipping and sliding on the carpet of leaves, Katherine and Hall pulled themselves up the steep slope, holding onto half-grown saplings.

It was gruesome. The body didn't have a head and bloodied claw-like hands clutched metal where the head should have been.

Katherine was looking nervously around in the leaves for something she didn't wish to find, when the body moved.

Hall knelt beside Brooks and brushed the leaves away. "If you can hear me, squeeze my hand." The hand squeezed.

"Listen," continued Hall, "I'm going to get you out, but we have to be careful. The swords are stuck fast and I'll have to break the blades. Just don't move!"

Hall exerted slow, even pressure, up and away from the back of Cameron's neck. He broke the blades, first one, then the other, and pulled Cameron from the hole. Hall turned him over on his back.

Cameron was blue from the cold and his face was scratched. He had lost some hair, but as far as Hall could tell, there were no serious wounds.

Breathing deeply and squinting against the light, Cameron passed his tongue over dry, parched lips. "Bit stiff to the pin, don't you know. You wouldn't, by any chance, have a drop on you?"

"It so happens, my old friend, that I do." Hall pulled a silver flask from his inside coat pocket and helped Cameron to sit, leaning back against a tree. He held the flask for Cameron to drink. "Easy now, not too quickly—there's plenty. Ease off for a second, will you."

Katherine looked at the two men and saw that the situation was normal, or what passed for normal these days.

Cameron was coming along, thanks to liberal doses of brandy. Color was returning to his cheeks. He looked at Katherine. "I'm surprised to see you here. After last night, I thought you were off me for good."

"For Father's sake, I'm glad to see you alive. I suppose I should feel sorry for you, but I don't. You got what you deserved. It could have been worse."

Cameron eased himself to a more comfortable position. "See, Andrew? Men are the romantics. Women are merciless, they get right to the blood and guts of things."

Hall wasn't interested in small talk. He would not be put off any longer. "Tell me!"

Cameron rubbed his hands together and blew on them. He looked out over the park as if he could find the words out there. "You wouldn't believe it." He paused to look at Hall. "Or maybe you would. The man is not human. His strength is incredible." Cameron massaged the back of his neck. "I saw the others, after he got them. Are they alive?"

"So far."

"He saved me for last. Bloody hell, Andrew. He was toying with me." Cameron paused for another drink. "I knew he was there." Cameron looked around at the brown leaves drying on the ground, and then at Hall, seeking reassurance. "No man, not even Nathaniel, could surprise me here, in all these leaves. I never saw him and I never heard him."

"How did you hurt your hands?"

Cameron examined his bloody fingers and broken nails. "I tried to scratch away the dirt so I could get out from under those swords. The soil was too hard."

"But where is he?" asked Katherine. "He wasn't at the house when we left and we haven't seen him since. Is he injured, lying out there somewhere?"

"No," said Hall thoughtfully, "I know where he is. There's only one place he could be. Katherine, stay with Brooks until I can get someone." Hall looked at his daughter. "Please—"

"Yes, Father," she said meekly. Hall didn't believe her for one second. It was going to be hell around here.

"I can walk," protested Cameron as he made an attempt to stand.

"I'm sure you can." Hall placed a restraining hand on Cameron's shoulder.

"We just want to make sure. Be a good fellow and stay put for a bit."

"If you insist—" Cameron lay back against the slope. "Rather have the company of a beautiful lady any day."

"I have nothing to say to you and, if I must stay here, at least make yourself presentable."

Cameron looked confused.

"Zip up your fly!"

With a smothered oath, Cameron made a grab for the front of his pants.

At the bottom of the slope, Hall stopped and looked back. Katherine, stood, her arms folded, while Cameron was staring straight ahead. His face was red. Shaking his head, Hall hurried back to the house.

Bentwood was waiting in the great hall. "M'lord, have you found Colonel Cameron?"

Hall explained where Cameron and his daughter were, then headed for the back of the house. He entered the sitting room and closed the door with care. He went to the fireplace, paused for a moment, then squared his shoulders and placed his hands on the mantle. The wall swung slowly open. Hall hurried down the sloping corridor.

The cavern was empty, but the spotlighted sword no longer hung over the Round Table. Instead, it had fallen and was embedded, point first, in the thick wood. A length of twisted cable was attached to the handle. Hall reached out to touch the frayed metal strands. They were still warm.

Chapter XXII

The morning flight from London to Frankfurt landed on schedule. Ryder had only a carry-on and cleared customs quickly. Once through the double doors of the customs shed, he was confronted by a crowd of impatient people behind a waist-high metal barrier. Although it was early, the transatlantic night flights were due and friends, relatives, and international business associates were waiting.

Ryder turned right and walked to the end of the barrier, scanning the sea of faces for some sign of recognition. Hall had said it was arranged.

He noticed a short, sturdy man with rimless eyeglasses, standing away from the crowd, watching him. The man hesitated, then approached.

"Herr Ryder?"

"Yes, I'm John Ryder."

"My name is Hasselbach...Klaus Hasselbach. If you will follow me— your auto is outside."

In the center of the street was a cement island for temporary parking and unloading. Herr Hasselbach stopped beside a red Porsche that Ryder had been eyeing as they crossed the road. It was hard to miss. It looked like no other Porsche John had ever seen.

"May I ask if you have driven a Porsche before?"

Oh-oh, thought Ryder, here it comes—that German propensity, that overwhelming need, to explain things. "Yes, I have—the older 356C and several of the 911 models."

"This is a 930."

"I know."

"But this is entirely diff—"

Ryder stopped him by holding out his hand. "I'll manage, thank you."

Without hesitation, Herr Hasselbach dropped the keys into Ryder's open palm.

"The registration is in the glove compartment. The auto has been prepared to Herr Hall's specifications."

It was clear that Herr Hasselbach disapproved of anyone daring to advise the Porsche factory in Zuffenhausen on such matters. He sighed as he touched the car with the tips of his fingers.

"Not too fast until the oil pressure is up—the machine is very quick."

Ryder walked once around the car. He might have known. When he had informed Andrew that he was returning to Heidelberg, Andrew wasn't pleased.

"You can't leave."

"I'm too close to all of this. I must think and I need time away from here."

"There is no time."

"You keep saying that, but we've gone on for months and nothing has happened."

"Not yet, but it will."

"And because of this danger you won't tell me about, I can't go to my son?"

"That is correct."

"Andrew, you'd better be right. You're still playing your own private game and I trust you about halfway." John studied Andrew's face for a moment. "I'll go to Heidelberg."

When Hall realized that Ryder was adamant, he offered to put a car at Ryder's disposal.

"Make it a 930 Porsche."

Hall didn't miss a beat. "What color?"

"I was kidding. They only make these things to order. Besides, it would cost well over a quarter of a million dollars—"

"I'm aware of that—what color?"

"How about red."

"Done."

"Won't I be just a little conspicuous?"

"Not at all," Hall replied dryly. "No one remembers the driver, only the auto."

Ryder opened the car door. "Herr Hasselbach, may I drop you somewhere?"

"*Nein, danke.* I will take the underground back to Frankfurt. *Gute Reise!*" With a last look at the Porsche, Herr Hasselbach took reluctant leave.

Ryder couldn't help but wonder how easily the German had just turned a very expensive piece of equipment over to a total stranger. He shrugged. Then again, knowing Andrew, why not.

Ryder opened the door and slipped into the driver's seat. He adjusted the seat for legroom, scanned the rearview mirrors, fastened the seat belt, and checked the diagram on the gear shift knob to see what changes had been made since the last Porsche he'd driven. There were five speeds forward.

The engine fired immediately. Holding steady at three thousand rpms, Ryder drove under the overpass that connected the Sheraton Hotel with the terminal. The car's exhaust sounded like dried peas in a can with a heavy turbo undertone.

Porsche was one of the world's two most distinctive-sounding automobiles. The other was Ferrari. Even without seeing them, they could never be mistaken for anything else. He reveled in the stiff suspension. The Porsche felt glued to the road; it was like driving a board with wheels.

At the traffic circle, Ryder took the exit marked Karlsruhe and headed south in the direction of Heidelberg. As usual, long stretches of the autobahn were under construction. In ten more years the whole country was going to be wall-to-wall cement.

He had to stay in the lower gears to keep the revs up. When he'd driven his first sports car, he had been disappointed. He'd tried to drive it like a normal car, not realizing that you had to run at high rpms. It was unnerving at first, but the performance machines only came alive at the top end of the tachometer.

He was on the old Frankfurt-Mannheim Autobahn, built in the glory days of Adolf Hitler's Third Reich to facilitate rapid troop deployment.

Construction ended short of the Heidelberg cutoff and traffic was light as he started up the long, sweeping curve to the left that connected with the new autobahn. He checked the rear and side mirrors, and took a quick look over his shoulder as he slid into traffic.

At these speeds you didn't get a second chance. He was in the left lane, tacho climbing steadily and falling off slightly as he went up through the gears. The throws were short and quick.

It was ridiculous. He worked it out in his head, converting kilometers to miles. He was doing the equivalent of one hundred forty miles an hour and the car wasn't even trying. It was cruising and the faster it went the more stable it became.

Germany was the only country in the civilized world without a speed limit. Ryder pressed a notch harder on the gas. In a car like this, it would be easy to run out of guts before you ran out of pedal. He thought of the sports cars in America, so heavily detuned they were a joke. He pressed harder.

It was over much too soon. The blue-and-white sign said Heidelberg-Schwetzingen. He swung over into the right lane and started gearing down, using the motor to reduce speed. It wasn't necessary with four-wheel disk brakes that worked so efficiently, he just liked the sound. The on-board computer system went to work, shifting power to the front wheels and cutting in the anti-skid function.

At the top of the exit ramp he turned right toward Heidelberg, crossing back over the autobahn. At the next light he turned right again toward Kirchheim.

It was the back way to Martin von Friedenthal's house, avoiding the traffic of the inner city. He crossed the old railroad bridge that separated Kirchheim from Heidelberg, drove past a police station, and entered Hasenleiser.

Hasenleiser was a section of Heidelberg that had grown up around a former German Army base that was now home to the U.S. Army 130th Station Hospital. The modern apartment complexes and shopping center broke with the usual white stucco walls and red-tiled roofs.

The school that Ryder was passing was all glass and polished green stone. It housed two indoor swimming pools, used as much by the adults of the community as by the school children. He'd had gone there with the von Friedenthals.

Martin von Friedenthal had built a long, low, flat-roofed house at the edge of the development. He had been delighted to sell the family monstrosity, as he called it, on the Philosophenweg.

Ryder had liked the lovely old house with its big, high-ceilinged rooms that looked across the Neckar River at the traditional view of Heidelberg— the Old Bridge, the Holy Ghost Church, and the castle ruins on the far hill.

Years ago, von Friedenthal's father had put up a sign on the front gate warning, in four languages, of a savage dog loose somewhere on the property.

It was the only way he could keep the camera-crazy tourists out of his garden. The dog was imaginary.

Von Friedenthal had sold the house for a ridiculously high price to a young couple more concerned with atmosphere and status than inconvenient flights of stairs and horrendous heating bills.

Ryder pulled up in front of Martin's house and gunned the motor before turning the key. What a sound. Beethoven lived. Liesel von Friedenthal was standing in the doorway with a shopping basket over one arm. She set the basket down, then took Ryder's hands in hers, kissed his cheek, and held him at arm's length. "How nice! Martin said you'd be here this morning."

"I hope I'm not imposing—"

"Of course not, you are always welcome. Now that you're here, I hope that you will spend the holidays with us." Liesel smiled at Ryder, then noticed the Porsche for the first time.

"What a lovely red automobile! Wait until Martin sees this." Liesel gave Ryder's hands a squeeze. "But why are you standing out here?"

"I'm talking to a lovely lady."

"Don't be silly. He's downstairs as usual. Go on—you know the way. The girls will be home from school soon and I have shopping to do."

"I'll drive you."

"Men! You and Martin—you never go anywhere without your toys."

No matter how often Ryder visited, he was never prepared for the sight of Martin in his railroad room.

It began years ago, as Martin told it, at a chess tournament in the United States. After the tournament was over, a friend had taken him to see a model railroad club layout. He hadn't known that such a thing existed. To his astonishment, the friend had asked if von Friedenthal would like to take the throttle of a high-stepping passenger train in full dress. Like Toad of Toad Hall, he was hooked.

Ryder suspected, despite Martin's denials, that the real reason for building this new home was to provide expansion room for his trains.

A number of architects had thrown in the towel trying to maintain the structural integrity of the building and still meet von Friedenthal's specifications.

He'd done battle with every bureaucrat in Heidelberg who refused to give permission for building such a house. Minor government officials are infamous the world over and, in Germany, they have refined bureaucratic red tape to a fine art. But, to von Friedenthal, the term impossible didn't exist.

He was at them like a terrier with a rat. In the end, they practically begged him to take his signed, approved plans with all the pretty stamps and get the hell out. He could build any damn house any damn way or where he pleased—if he would only leave them in peace. They would even come over on weekends and help—if he would only go away.

The problem was the railroad room—a room forty by sixty feet. Von Friedenthal absolutely refused to have any support columns as required by law for a living space of that size. They would spoil the view and detract from the realism of the background scenes painted on the walls. The lights had rheostats and when turned down, the moon and stars came out and tiny lights winked on in all the miniature houses. Von Friedenthal gave the same meticulous attention to his layout as he would to an opponent's undeveloped center pawn.

America had introduced him to this way of life, so an American layout it must be. In that miniature world, the time would always be 1927. There were towns, tunnels, harbors, forests, mountains, and mines, where trains ran over, under, and through.

In the midst of his creation, wearing bib overalls, engineer's cap, red bandana, and puffing on a pipe that made more smoke than a helper engine on a steep grade, sat God.

"I thought I heard a terrible noise outside," spoke God. "And I said to myself, that must be John Ryder, who's stolen a tank from the army motor pool."

"It's one hell of a tank."

Martin glanced at the clock. "Just in time—the Bridgeport freight is due in five minutes, so take your seat." Martin slapped his thigh. "Now that General Hartley isn't around, we can have a good operating session—just the two of us."

Chapter XXIII

"Can I help you, sir?" asked the MP, standing up from behind his desk. Ryder didn't look like the usual visitor to the command building. He wore a sports coat and turtleneck instead of a business suit and tie, and he carried a nylon gym bag instead of a briefcase.

Ryder glanced over his shoulder to the guardroom off the foyer. He didn't know what signal had been given, but two large young men appeared in the doorway. They were dressed like the one behind the desk, all starched and pressed, with creaking leather, thick double-soled patent leather boots, and .45s heavy at the hip.

"Sir!" insisted the MP again, fingertips balanced carefully on the desk top. "Please state the nature of your business." The two other MPs had shifted so that Ryder was now the center of a triangle.

"I'm here to see Major General Hartley."

"Identification please, sir, and is the General expecting you, sir?" asked the MP in the same neutral tone.

"Yes, he is." Ryder reached for his wallet. The MPs were alert as he took the wallet from the inside breast pocket of his jacket.

The MP behind the desk relaxed slightly when he saw Ryder's American passport. The other two went back to the guardroom. No apologies were offered.

"Sir, how come you didn't use the information center at the main gate?" asked the MP, reaching for the telephone. He remained standing.

"Following instructions, soldier."

The MP spoke quietly into the telephone. The answer he got seemed to satisfy him and, as he hung up the telephone, he took his seat again. Consulting Ryder's passport, he began filling out a slip of paper.

"Sir, this is your installation pass. We will retain your passport while you are on the Kaserne. Please sign your name on the back where I've put the X. I'll examine your bag, if you don't mind."

Ryder knew it wouldn't make any difference if he did.

"Please have the General's office countersign the pass when you are ready to leave. Your passport will be returned to you when you surrender the pass to the person at this desk. Your escort, sir."

Ryder turned to the MP waiting behind him. He'd known he was there—anyone would. Those metal cleats on the polished stone floor sounded like the Queen's horse guard.

"Follow me, sir—right this way."

On the second floor, the MP stopped at a doorway. "General Hartley's office, sir."

An attractive, well-groomed, middle-aged lady sat at a large desk. "Mr. Ryder, how nice to meet you. My name is Gladys Moran. Please have a seat. The General will be right with you. May I offer you a cup of coffee?"

"No, thank you, not before a squash match."

"Of course, how silly of me."

The General had made it very plain when she was first interviewed for the job. His noon squash match took precedence over everything else, unless the missiles had been launched.

She was expected to have the court reserved for the General, Monday through Friday, whether he used it or not, and to have a suitable opponent standing by. Weekend games involved anyone she could coerce or blackmail.

Fortunately, there were always those who liked to drop the words into the happy hour conversation "as I said to the General on the court today..." Mrs. Moran had been in government service long enough to know the drill— she'd never let the General down.

Mrs. Moran patted her hair. John Ryder wasn't what she'd expected. Yesterday, when the General hung up the phone, he'd instructed her to get hold of someone in Public Affairs or the Stars and Stripes—whatever.

He wanted information on a John Ryder—who played chess or something. The General had a nose for such things and knew there had to be something on record about the man. It was no surprise when the answer came back.

A retired Lieutenant Colonel, now a double-dipping GS type, who had brought the after-lunch office nap up to state of the art, had the clippings. It turned out that John Ryder was a chess grand master, with what was popularly referred to as a brilliant future.

Mrs. Moran smiled shyly at the man seated on the other side of her desk. Oh, my goodness, she thought, he has the nicest smile. She patted her hair again, but before she could say anything, General Bob appeared in the doorway to an inner room.

"Good! Right on time. Come on in, I'll only be a minute." The General turned on his heel and spoke over his shoulder. "I was surprised to get your call. I thought you'd run out on me. Martin said you'd had to go back to England."

"Unfinished business, General. I just got in yesterday."

Ryder followed the General into a large, well-lighted room. Expensive wall-to-wall carpeting, bought with end-of-year funds, complemented an informal seating area of couch, easy chairs, and cocktail table. There was also an imposing desk.

The desk had a table pushed up endwise against the front of it, with three chairs on either side. The General was fond of calling it his mini conference room. A stand with several flags stood in one corner.

"This is Lieutenant Colonel Thomas Dash," said the General, indicating a trim officer who was just standing up from one of the chairs. "Colonel, this is John Ryder. He plays chess." The General spoke as if he had a mouth full of sour owls.

"Mr. Ryder," said the Colonel, "it's a pleasure to meet you. I've heard of you, of course."

General Bob looked sharply at Lieutenant Colonel Dash. "You play chess, too?"

"Not like Mr. Ryder."

As Ryder took the Colonel's hand, he found himself smiling.

"The Colonel here," said the General, "is one of the men in this man's army who make the whole thing work."

The General was right. Lieutenant Colonel Dash was not trade school, would probably not make general, or even full colonel. He was one of that ten percent, officers and enlisted alike, who still considered God and Country a working premise. He was a professional in the best sense of the word and would have been surprised if anyone made a fuss about it.

"If you'll excuse me, General, I'll get to work on that report. Mr. Ryder—a pleasure," said the Colonel and left.

"He doesn't have much to say, does he."

"No, and that's a welcome change around here, let me tell you," said the General, taking his hat from a coat rack, "We'll walk over and give you a look around. I usually wouldn't waste the time, but I can get away early today."

They went back downstairs, this time to the basement. With a "we'll use the side entrance," the General led the way past the barber shop, a small mess hall and the message center. Once outside, they cut between Buildings Three and Twelve, heading toward the red clay parade field in the center of the Kaserne.

"There've been some great ceremonies on that field," said General Bob, marching right along. "The British Army of the Rhine used to send over a band and Scottish pipers to celebrate the Queen's birthday. They'd put their swords on the ground and dance. Looked silly—grown men in skirts—but the music can get to you. Almost makes you want to pick up a sword and have at it."

Ryder smiled to himself.

"Now that building over there," said the General, pointing, "the one that connects the other two, is our command center where we would go if things ever got hot." He made a motion with his hand, dismissing another point of view before it was expressed.

"I know that everyone thinks that Russia is an economic and political mess. The trouble is now the whole damn world thinks they can play puss-in-the-corner, while we reduce troop strength. There're still missiles out there and no one knows where they're pointed."

They were heading for the rear of the Kaserne, when the General spoke again. "That's the German canteen on the left. If it wouldn't make such a stink with the local nationals who work on the base, I'd close the place down. They have a table in there, they call it a *Stammtisch*, with the names of a lot of my sergeants painted on it." The General was indignant.

"Hell of a way for a military man to spend his time—sitting around drinking beer for lunch!" The General's face cleared. "That brick building by the back gate is where we're going."

As they approached the one-story structure, the General took a key from his pocket and unlocked the door. They entered a narrow room with lockers along two walls and a gray painted wooden bench down the center. All the lockers had locks on them.

"Kind of bare, but better than nothing." The General dialed the combination lock and opened the door. A rack attached to the inside of the locker door held a number of squash racquets.

"Pick out one you like. Toilet is up front, showers in the back. Use any of the clothes hooks on the wall. You don't have to worry about your wallet—only officers use the court."

General Bob was dressed and on the court before Ryder.

"Get a move on, fella. Only got an hour, so move it."

In the warm-up before play, Ryder returned the ball easily, right down the middle of the court, waist-high, first to the General's forehand and then, when they switched sides, to his backhand. The General did the same. No one was giving anything away.

"You ready?" asked the General in a honey-sweet voice, trying to conceal his impatience.

"Sure—go ahead and serve."

General Bob wasn't one to waste time on amenities. Besides, he liked to serve, using a big three-quarter arm overhead smashing serve, aiming the ball right at Ryder. Moving smoothly to one side, Ryder took the ball off the back wall and returned it down the left side, close to the wall.

The General moved well for a big man and had been known since his West Point days as one who really blooded the ball—low, smashing alley shots that barely cleared the tin on the front wall, shots that sounded like the crack of doom.

As a member of the Academy team and later, as a junior officer, he had been nationally ranked. There were several aspects of the General's game that kept him in that rarified company longer than most.

Along with his innate ability to hit the ball hard, he was also extremely accurate, both forehand and backhand. While most players become erratic when they push past their natural limits, the harder the General hit the ball, the better he was. This ability to hit the ball hard and accurately was coupled with an iron will to win.

He never entered the court for mere enjoyment or exercise. As far as the General was concerned, that was a copout. Whenever one man went up against another, it was War. It was even worse now that he had only one hour. What with changing, showering, and dressing, he had to squeeze in every point he could.

The most unique feature of the General's game had come about quite by accident. As the son of a General, and with a long family history of military service, young Robert had attended one of the country's top military prep schools. It was brought to his attention that squash was the only quality game for a serious, career-minded future officer, and he took to the game with a vengeance.

So much so, that he had never forgotten the flicker of fear he saw in his opponent's eyes after one of his first wild, uncontrolled swipes at the ball. The racquet had barely missed the boy's head. The future general filed that bit of information away, and thought about it from time to time.

As his ability to play the game progressed, so did his particular style. While most squash players use wrist action and a tight, controlled swing, young Robert used complete arm extension and a full follow-through, much like a tennis player.

The eighteen-by-thirty foot court suddenly became a very small place indeed, when you played the Hartley boy. The sound of the air though the racquet head was enough to make you weak in the knees.

He was warned about his play, but he never hit anyone, at least not hard, and no school commandant was going to sideline one of the country's best players. For his opponents, the thought of that racquet head was as good as a loaded gun.

Young Robert controlled the ebb and flow from the T in the center of the court. After a trip to New York to watch an exhibition by two touring Pakistani professionals, he came to the conclusion that the player who could stay on the T the longest, won.

The opponent who tried to hit the ball and still stay outside the radius of the Hartley racquet felt like he was playing with a man-eating plant growing in the center of the court.

It was an impossible task, except for the very foolish or the very brave. Now that he had those two stars on his shoulder, it was even easier. A solid belt on the behind was a good reminder to stay the hell out of his way.

General Bob went to work on his man, but it didn't turn out as he expected. Before he knew what had happened, the score was seven to two in favor of Ryder, and the General had broken a heavy sweat.

He couldn't get a handle on the man—it was like having a pillow fight in the dark. He was off balance and couldn't seem to get set enough to take the offensive.

When he tried to bull Ryder out of position, the man wasn't there. Neither was the ball. That was another thing. It wasn't how hard Ryder hit the ball, but where.

The ball didn't seem to be traveling that fast, but the General was off the T at full stretch, trying to get his racquet on the thing. There was none of that getting set, picking the ball off the back wall, and creaming it down the line.

The General could only get to the ball on the dead run, and he had the sneaking suspicion that his two points were due more to luck than to anything he'd done.

If he were deep and to the right, the ball was short and to the left. He would recover a drop shot, only to have the next ball return to exactly the same place. Back on his heels, trying to get to center court, he could only watch helplessly as the ball rolled dead at his feet. Ryder won the first game fifteen to five.

The General left the court for a quick toweling off. He was sweating like a racehorse. His legs were good and he was able to get his breathing under control, but it was time to get serious before things got completely out of hand.

Playing Ryder was like playing smoke. He hadn't been able to hit the man even once with the ball—just to let him know ol' General Bob was there.

Officers who played the General wore their squash bruises like decorations. These particular decorations, which were not admired by the officers' wives, looked like sunrises, or better yet, sunsets.

Where the ball struck, the flesh was traumatized and remained a perfect white, but radiating out in all directions from this white circle were all the colors of the rainbow. The mark left by a well-hit, hard rubber ball traveling at over a hundred miles an hour, lasted for weeks. They were terrible-looking things and pleased the General no end.

As the General dried the handle of his racquet, he revised his game plan. A good crack on the calf of the leg with his racquet head ought to cool Ryder down.

It had worked before with some young, smart-assed officer who thought he was going to run the Old Man off the court. Instead of hitting the ball along the side wall, he would accidentally hit the ball into the center of the court, and when Ryder came in after it, the General would be waiting.

The General reentered the court, closed the small inset door and prepared to receive Ryder's serve. He noticed that Ryder didn't seem to be sweating. Never mind, he would be. What turned General Bob's resolve to steel was that bemused smile. Now you're going to get it, you peckerhead, thought the General.

It all went wrong. True, the first part went just fine. He hit the ball into the center of the court where he was waiting, primed and cocked.

Ryder came drifting in after the ball, but before the General could fire, Ryder hit the ball down the right-hand wall, the General in hot pursuit. He tried it again. Ryder picked the ball off with a half-volley, this time sending it down the left side.

The Two Star soon came to the conclusion that he was never going to be able to hit Ryder with the racquet, much less pick the spot.

Whenever Ryder had to come near the General, he came all the way in, inside the radius of the General's swing, so close General Bob could have kissed him, if he were that sort of guy, and if he didn't have something else on his mind at the moment, like that goddamned black rubber ball.

The game became a kind of out-of-sync ballet, with the General moving faster and faster, and Ryder hardly moving at all. Any good racquet player must anticipate. Off would go the General to where he knew the ball would be, only to meet the damn thing on a parallel course two feet away and going in the opposite direction.

He didn't have a chance in hell of getting his racquet on the ball. Worse yet, he would arrive at the point to take the ball, only to look up and see the thing rolling dead on the other side of the court.

Somewhere along the line, the General began to question the validity of the information supplied by Public Affairs. There was no way this guy could be a chess player. More likely he was the reincarnation of Hashim Khan.

Just wait until he got his hands on the clown who supplied that crap about John Ryder. General Bob was going to tear a strip off him six inches wide. The second game ended with a score of fifteen to two. The General didn't win.

Toweling off, the General was furious at himself, at Ryder, and at the world as a whole. The last game was going to be all-out war. He had never, in all his years, at any level of competition, been shut out.

Winners tell jokes and losers say "deal the cards." General Bob growled through clenched teeth. "Serve the ball, for Christ's sake."

The third game was a disaster. The General received a lesson in basics—volleys, half-volleys, drop shots, crosscourt shots, and angle shots. There were shots he had never seen before.

The General became confused. If he moved to cover the front, a lob hit with surgical precision would drop in a back corner. He began looking for shots that existed only in his mind.

It got so bad that the General became rooted to the spot, while seventeen parts of him tried to go seventeen ways at once. Everything canceled out, leaving him to watch a knee-high ball go right down the middle of the court untouched.

Or worse, he would hit an outright winner, really crushing the ball with all his pent-up anger and frustration, knowing there was no way it could be returned, and back it would come, just out of reach. General Bob never got to serve.

He watched as Ryder prepared to serve the ball for what he knew would be the last point. It was a nightmare. The game and the score were bad enough, but what really shook the General was the way the man moved.

It was all done in absolute silence. Sure, the ball and the racquet made noise, but Ryder didn't. There were no grunts or sharp exhalations of breath, and no sneaker slap or squeak when Ryder changed direction or stopped. He moved in an eerie stillness, doing things with a squash ball that were impossible.

General Bob never saw the last point. There was a blur and a terrible double crack—first when the racquet hit the ball and then, when the ball hit the back wall of the court.

Panting like some large, wet, shaggy dog, the General could only stare at the pieces of squash ball at his feet. The thing had exploded.

The General had seen broken balls before. He liked doing it himself, but those were in halves, down the seam, not in pieces. Stupid, but all he could think was that it had been a new ball, too.

Now that the game was over, General Bob didn't know if he could make it out of the court. He didn't want to think about his pulse rate, and he regretted to the bottom of his soul all the cigars and whiskey sours he'd ever had. There was a terrible taste in his mouth. The sum total of the world's paté and glazed duck was sitting on his wishbone.

Then Ryder had him by the shoulders, helping the General from the court. "Sorry, General, I had no way of knowing. I can no longer play these games."

General Bob didn't have the slightest idea what the man was talking about, but the arm around his shoulder gave him strength.

It had always been his wish to die in battle or, barring that, on the squash court—short and sweet with none of that lying around in some hospital bed all wired up to a machine going *beep, beep, beep, be....*

Slumping on the gray wooden bench, the General began to feel better. Guess it wasn't his day for a heart attack, after all. He was half right. It was Major General Robert E. Hartley's day to die, but it wouldn't be from a coronary.

Chapter XXIV

In the Officers' Club, on the second floor of the Casino at Campbell Barracks, Heidelberg, Germany, it was Happy Hour.

"TGIF, Dave."

"Hey, babe, you know it. Waddya drinkin'?"

"No way, Dave—you're late, gotta get you caught up. Besides, I'm buying. Fritz? Beers for my friend."

The German bartender, whose name wasn't Fritz, and his wife, who waited table, had heard it all before. The voices and the laughter were always louder on Friday nights, but the tips would be good, especially tonight. The eagle had crapped—payday. For the men and women at Campbell, the week was over. Monday would never come and the room was packed, the older officers without their wives, the younger ones with. About a third of the crowd was civilians. The men were either GS types or representatives of companies under government contract. The women were mostly unmarried secretaries, or school teachers full of the romance of a year in Europe. They had the watchful eyes of the hunter, and the air was sharp with brittle laughter.

On the bar, and at each table, were bowls of popcorn. It had been an unseasonably mild day, so the balcony doors were open. People were outside, seated at the white wrought-iron tables that overlooked the parking lot at the front of the Casino.

Except for the Duty Officer, the Message Center, the MPs at the main gate, and some shift workers at one of the computer divisions, the Kaserne was deserted. Later, there would be a movie at the theater downstairs, but for the moment all was quiet. The war was over until next week.

Second Lieutenant Daniel Carlson and his wife Debbie were seated at the front of the balcony. They couldn't help noticing the military sedan passing by the Post Office, the Chase Manhattan Bank, and the Accounting Division. When the sedan turned, they saw the red standard with two silver stars. The sedan stopped in front of the Casino, just below them. It was unusual for a general officer to be at the Casino after hours. He might come to see a movie, but then he would be in civilian clothes and driving his own car.

"Who is that, honey?" asked Debbie.

"Looks like General Hartley. I don't recognize the civilian with him." The Lieutenant thought for a moment. "I wonder what the hell the General's doing here."

"Dan, please don't swear. It sounds terrible, honey." Debbie Carlson secretly enjoyed her husband's swearing. In between meetings of the Officers' Wives and German-American clubs, she indulged a passion for romance novels.

She would never admit it, but her husband was not the man she'd first imagined, when all she could see was the uniform. She would have preferred a more—how was it that Rhea, the heroine of Dark of the Moon, had put it?—yes, that was it, a more "ruthless and relentless" lover. Oh, my—yes.

Debbie just adored happy hour and being around so many men in uniform. Too bad they could only afford to go out once a month, but that would change as soon as Dan got his promotion. Maybe it was just as well for now. A room full of men seemed to make her nervous, for some reason. Silly of her, but she had to go to the bathroom all the time.

Debbie turned in her chair to look through the open double doors to where General Hartley was now standing with the man. She caught her breath. He was smiling and looking right at her. She knew at once, in her heart of hearts, that his smile was for her alone.

His eyes were magnetic; she couldn't look away. Oh, God...Rhea. He wasn't even in uniform, but he was so handsome, she could swoon. She would have, too, if she knew how, and if she didn't have to go tinkle again.

"What's it going to be, John?" asked General Bob.

"Beer will be fine."

General Bob was pointedly ignoring the chorus of "Take my seat, General" and "This place is empty, sir." He remained standing, bellied up to the bar that wasn't crowded anymore, at least not where he was. "If a man's going to drink at a bar, then he ought to do it standing up. Two beers, bartender," said the General, holding up two fingers to make sure. "That's one thing they know how to do in this country—make beer. I'll give 'em that."

Ryder nodded. He was watching a slender, frizzy-haired blonde out on the balcony, obviously the wife of the studious-looking lieutenant. She acted nervous, clutching her purse with both hands and sitting on the front edge of her chair. Ryder watched as she took off at a lope.

"Well, the wines aren't bad," conceded the General, who thought privately that only French wines had any real value. He'd studied French in school and could read the labels. "And some of the cars are all right."

"I'm glad to hear that you think Germany is more than cuckoo clocks and beer steins. It must be comforting to the local nationals."

General Bob looked closely at Ryder's face. He still wasn't sure about the man. It had taken all afternoon, but little by little he had worked the noon hour squash match around in his own mind. By the time he had Mrs. Moran call and invite Ryder to join him for a drink, he'd justified his defeat. Not really a loss, mind you, more like showing a man of Ryder's obvious caliber a good time. It was hard, though, to play down one's game, to lose gracefully.

The milk of human kindness was giving the General a warm feeling in his gut. He sighed. It was too bad that beer gave him gas. What he did for the service! No sacrifice was too great. Besides, it was good for public relations. It wasn't so great or so good that the General hadn't picked tonight's territory with care.

His third encounter with Ryder was going to be different from the first two; there was more than one way to win the war. He was too old a campaigner to use neutral ground, like a local Gasthaus, and asking Ryder to come home with him was out of the question.

These days, with the children gone, he never knew how the wife was going to react. No, the Officer's Club was perfect. The General rarely went there, but for tonight it was ideal—his kind and all that. The stage had been set.

"I've asked Colonel Dash and Colonel McPherson to join us. McPherson is a member of my staff, too. I knew you wouldn't mind." The General didn't wait for Ryder to offer an opinion.

"Should spend more time with the men—give myself a chance to get away from the pressures of the office. Be good for you, too, John. Colonel Dash plays chess and all that stuff. You two have something in common." The General looked over John's shoulder.

"Ah, here they come now,"—he glanced at his watch—"right on time."

When the General had offhandedly suggested that it would be nice if Colonel Dash and Colonel McPherson could join Ryder and himself for a drink, they didn't have a hell of a choice. Of course, he'd understand if they had other plans; after all, it was short notice. If they couldn't make it, they shouldn't give it another thought. Like hell—it was a command appearance.

"Good to see you, men," said the General. "Name your poison."

The military game is played exactly like the corporate one. In the time it took the two colonels to walk from the head of the stairs to the bar, the drink of the evening had been established.

"Beer, please, sir."

"Beer's fine, General."

"Relax, men. We're off duty."

Sure, babe, just like pigs fly.

"Yes, sir."

General Bob was pleased. "John let me introduce Colonel McPherson. Mac—this is John Ryder. My people tell me he is quite a chess player."

Colonel McPherson was a large, ruddy-faced, lean-forward-in-the-fox-hole type.

"Yes, sir; I know, sir."

General Bob rocked from the balls of his feet to his heels and back again. One hand was behind his back at parade rest, the other held his glass beer stein. He found it hard not to be doing something—movement was action.

The area of the bar around the General was filling up again. The direction and strength of the social wind had been tested and found reassuringly warm and mild. The General was in a good, if not to say expansive, mood and seemed to invite company. Soon he was at the center of a group of officers.

"Honey, you'll never guess who I had a drink with at the club tonight. There's big things down the road, just you wait."

Wait she did—from Guam, to Georgia, to Germany. "I married you for better or for worse, but dear God, Kansas?" Pack and unpack. A dozen apartments, either on the economy or in one of the ghetto military housing developments. *Fuck you, Krauts* in black spray paint on the side of the dumpster out back was the local goodwill message. A hundred snack bars, hair in curlers, and a thousand solitary meals. "Sorry, honey, but I'm going to be late again tonight."

If she was worth her salt or if some well-meaning senior officer's wife took her aside, she came to realize her importance to her husband's career.

160

Long before big business started interviewing the wives of hopeful executives, the military wife had been hard at it.

"Dear, why don't you get that nice young Lieutenant Hartley in your division? He's a bright young man and has such a charming wife. You know, she raised six hundred dollars at the bazaar last week."

Her duty was clear. First off, she joined the Officers' Wives Club, where the inexorable march of the years and her husband's rise in rank coincided with her seated progress, row by row, from the back to the front of the room.

If she was very smart or very lucky, she picked the right one from the Academy, the exception, the one who got his star. Finally, it was the front row. The reward for a job well done.

Her husband was an officer and a gentleman, by act of Congress, and she was his lady. Never, never Major and Mrs. Hartley, but Major Hartley and his Lady. Power corrupts, and it was hard not to abuse her husband's authority, especially since he got those lovely stars. She'd pinned them on, herself.

It was hard to remember when she was a second lieutenant's wife and on a strict budget—besides, who wanted to? What the hell, she'd earned a few perks, even if the care she took in applying her lipstick was inversely related to her gin intake. They also serve who stand and wait. Well, no one ever said you had to wait alone. Mr. Gilbey was fine, dependable company. He never told.

"John, how about we get you a refill," said General Bob. "You boys still okay? Mac, did you hear what this fella did to me on the squash court today?" asked the General, in his best hail-fellow-well-met voice.

Colonel McPherson knew all right. The General's secretary, Mrs. Moran, had confided that the General had been in a filthy mood all afternoon, snapping at people and slamming things around.

Why, he'd even had that nice George Sweeny from Public Affairs behind closed doors for over half an hour, yelling something fierce, and that new Captain Lewis had practically been in tears.

Colonel McPherson glanced at Colonel Dash. Nobody's fool, Colonel Dash was busy studying the design on his beer stein. McPherson was nobody's fool, either.

"No, General," he lied, "I haven't. As you know, I was over in Building Fourteen all day, going over the plans for this year's maneuvers. Didn't hear a thing—why?"

"I know you won't believe it, but this son of a gun beat me."

"General, I find that hard to believe." Mac looked at Colonel Dash for confirmation. "Tom?"

"So I understand," said Colonel Dash carefully. "Would you care to tell us about it, General?"

The General smiled benignly. Colonel Dash and Colonel McPherson relaxed a fraction; the ball was safely back in the other court.

"Just met the man a few days ago," said the General to a rapt audience. The officers crowded around, not too close, but there was a bit of jockeying. Each wanted to get as close to the flame as possible.

"Met him at the home of a friend of mine, Doctor Professor Martin von Friedenthal. I'm sure you've heard of him—one of the greatest chess players, World Champion and all that. He tells me that John here plays a pretty fair game himself."

Colonel Dash almost laughed out loud. John Ryder's brand of chess had little to do with the kind played around Campbell, when the plastic seventy-nine-cent PX special was dragged out for a lunchtime game.

"John," continued the General, "is what they call a grand master and he's the up-and-coming future champion. Going to show those Ruskies a thing or two, aren't you, boy?"

"They might take exception to the idea, General."

"Imagine me, losing to a chess player." General Bob's voice was filled with wonder. He still couldn't and neither could anyone else. The General's squash record was well known. Rocking back on his heels, the General went on.

"We had us quite a tussle, could have gone either way. In fact, for a while there, I thought I had you."

John watched the General pause to take a drink of beer.

"You have to admit that you had a lot of lucky shots. Talk about missed hits, boys! I never saw so many dinks in my life, but it happens that way, sometimes. There's no holding a fella when it starts going right for him." The General rocked again. "We'll have to play a rematch real soon."

He meant it when he said it, but it would be a frosty day in hell before he let himself get caught again on the court with John Ryder. He didn't care what that jerk in Public Affairs said, and he didn't care about his precious newspaper clippings, either.

The General looked around, daring anyone to dispute his word. "Of course, I get a little rusty with the level of competition around here; it's hard to stay sharp. Well, no excuses—win some, lose some. A toast, boys. To John Ryder. Today, he was the better man."

Ryder could almost hear what the officers were thinking. That General Bob was sure some kind of guy. Must have had an off day. The General was human after all. Never realized he was such a great sport. The General's warm camaraderie was infectious. An officer at the edge of the group had to ask.

"What were the scores, General?"

General Hartley looked first at the nametag and then at the man. The look was enough.

"Zimmermann," said the General softly. "That's a German name, isn't it?"

As soon as he could, the officer excused himself, saying he was late for dinner. All the way home he would wonder why the hell he had to open his big fat mouth.

Ryder knew what the General was doing and, in a way, had to admire him. General Bob was trying to get his balls back. Next, he would be lifting a figurative leg. No trespassing—this is my turf, here is my mark. I'm the bullmastiff around here, so watch it. Let him, thought Ryder. I owe him that.

"So there you have it, men. I wanted to buy John a drink and congratulate him. He's had a helluva day, haven't you, boy?" General Bob clapped Ryder on the back—the ultimate sign of approval, the laying on of hands.

Ryder nodded, but he was looking at Colonel Dash. "Like the man says, Thomas. Win some, lose some."

"It's like that, sometimes," answered Colonel Dash.

"Sorry." Ryder and Colonel Dash weren't talking about a squash match, but the General.

"It's all right, we'll weather the storm," replied Colonel Dash, "we always do."

"If you gentlemen are through with your private little conversation," snapped the General, "we'll drink up and be on our way. Got to get John to the von Friedenthals by seven. Frau von Friedenthal gave me the word. To-night, in John's honor, she's making her special sauerbraten."

"Mac—Thomas—" said the General, "you boys take your time and fin-ish your drinks. Remember, we've got that briefing first thing in the morn-ing."

Colonel McPherson offered his hand. "A pleasure to meet you, John."

"Thank you," said Ryder taking the Colonel's hand, "and you, too, Thomas. Keep the faith."

"We do our best."

The General retrieved his hat from a table at the head of the stairs.

"Well, you fellows seemed to hit it off pretty well."

"A fine couple of men, General."

"Obviously. They wouldn't be on my staff, otherwise," said the General, leading the way back down the stairs.

Crossing the lobby, Ryder could see the General's driver standing by the open rear door of the staff car.

The General waved off his driver.

"Forget the door, Sergeant—we're running late. Got to get this boy home, it's almost seven. Jump now!"

Thinking about nothing in particular, Ryder was ducking his head to enter the sedan when he suddenly stopped. Straightening up, he was trans-formed in a split second. Eyes wide to gather the light, nostrils flared to catch the scent. He glanced quickly up at the balcony and around the parking lot. He could feel it. Danger!

A computer specialist with an armful of printouts, taking a shortcut across the parking lot, stopped dead in his tracks, frozen against the back of a pickup truck. Jesus H. Christ, he thought. That cat by the General's sedan looked like he was going to come right across the roof of the car and tear his throat out.

That's exactly what the man looked like—a great big cat. Man, those eyes. The specialist was pinned against the metal grillwork of the dog cages bolted to the bed of the truck. Afraid to move, he opened his mouth to say that—whatever it was—he hadn't done it, when the man did something strange.

Ryder again glanced up at the balcony. Colonel McPherson and Colonel Dash had come out to see the General off. Colonel Dash saluted Ryder with his glass, but Ryder didn't answer. Twisting away from the sedan, he took one running step and launched himself in a headlong dive back toward the Casino entrance.

For reasons he would never be able to explain, Colonel Dash also turned and dove for the rear of the balcony, stretching out for all he was worth and leaving his beer stein momentarily suspended in midair.

Watching Ryder, his mouth hanging open in disbelief, General Bob stood with one hand still holding the open door of his sedan. The last thing his brain had time to register was the sound of breaking glass. When the bomb went off, he never heard it.

Chapter XXV

The trunk of Major General Hartley's sedan had been packed with high explosives. The car disintegrated. Afterward, there was a moment of silence, an eerie stillness, broken by the sound of metal rain as pieces of Staff Car 312 started returning to earth. Then the screaming began.

The brick support columns of the balcony could not resist the force of the explosion which was directed up and away from the staff car. The columns buckled and the balcony collapsed, turning into a giant slide, to dump the dead, the dying, and the wounded onto the street below.

Colonel Thomas Dash, face down, slid feet first to the ground. Regaining his balance, he stared at the remains of the General's sedan. In the midst of the smoking debris, where the largest single pieces were the motor block and the frame, stood the Sergeant from Tennessee.

Caught, at the instant of explosion, bending over the right front bumper to remove the cover from the General's standard, the Sergeant was still alive. Although he was in obvious shock and covered with grime, there there wasn't a mark on him. His jaws were slowly working on a nonexistent chew.

"Are you all right?" asked Colonel Dash.

"I think so, sir. Jus' let me see to the General."

"Never mind that, Sergeant. I'll attend to him. Get to the phone in the lobby and see if it's still working. Call the Duty Officer and explain what's happened."

Colonel Dash took the Sergeant by the shoulders and looked into a vacant pair of eyes. "He's to notify General Briggs at home. Recommend we go on full alert. If you can't get in through that mess at the door, use a window. They all seem to be broken anyway. Move out, soldier!"

Muttering under his breath, Colonel Dash said, "Yeah, I'll see to the General." Glancing around at what was left of the sedan, he added, "that is, if I can find him."

Lieutenant Colonel Dash took charge. The first jeepload of MPs that screeched to a halt were sent for first-aid kits and fire extinguishers. Able-bodied survivors who found their way outside the building were put to work. Colonel Dash quickly identified those with CPR and first-aid experience.

In a matter of minutes, a semblance of order was restored. No one stood around. For the moment rank was forgotten. Senior officers who had never been in combat followed Colonel Dash's lead.

"Sir, help Captain Fowler over there if you will...another turn on the belt should do it...Colonel, hold this pad on that pressure point...careful Major, she's got a compound fracture—just pull her dress down so she's decent and don't let her move."

The Colonel was no paper soldier. With a steady calm, he gave people a sense of purpose, a direction. As he moved among the wounded, he had a word for everyone.

"Hang on, soldier—only a few more minutes...I know it hurts, but try to stay calm, ma'am—help is on the way." No longer alone, the wounded were relatively quiet. Finally, there was nothing more to do; now it was hurry up and wait.

Colonel Dash looked around at the still forms, faces covered with uniform jackets and handkerchiefs. The dead would wait. There was time for them now, all the time in the world. No more staff reports, no more parties. "Come on for Christ's sake, Melba, we're going to be late." It was the beginning of eternity.

"TGIF, my ass!" he said softly to himself.

What a mess. It was like war, only worse, because it had been so unexpected. The sight was bad enough, but just as bad was the smell. The smell of blood. In large quantities, it rolled over you, wrapping you in a cloying, clinging odor that didn't wash off. In the fading daylight, he watched the dry, parched concrete, a gray vampire, suck up the last of life.

There was a disturbance, a minor upheaval in the Casino entrance. Out of the rubble of brick, plaster, and splintered lumber rose the figure of John Ryder, like some terrible golem freed again to the night. In the gathering darkness, his eyes blazed, lit by an inner fire.

Colonel Dash scrambled over the debris toward the dirty, bloodied figure. How in God's name could he have forgotten? "John, are you all right? Here—let me help you."

168

As Colonel Dash came within reach, Ryder's hand shot out to grip the Colonel's upper arm. He yanked Colonel Dash to him, almost tearing his arm from his shoulder.

"No, John, wait. It's me, Thomas Dash." In spite of the light in Ryder's eyes, Colonel Dash could see the man was out on his feet.

"John, you know me—we had a drink together and talked about chess. There's been an explosion and you've been hurt."

Ryder stared at the Colonel, scrutinizing every feature. Then the light faded from his eyes and he collapsed. Colonel Dash was barely able to catch him as he fell. The Colonel could only use one arm, the other had been broken.

The waiting was over. The parking lot in front of the Casino was alive with sound, light, and movement. Army ambulances went screaming off down Roemerstrasse toward the 130th Station Hospital. Helicopters woofed in and departed with the wounded that the 130th couldn't handle. Landstuhl and Stuttgart had been alerted and were standing by for the first casualties.

The MPs were assisting a cleanup crew with the body bags. Charles Goodwin, fresh from police school and on his first overseas tour, found Colonel McPherson. One look at the headless body, still holding the handle of a shattered beer stein, sent the MP, bent over at the waist, to the nearest bushes on the double. Mother of God!

The worst thing that had ever happened to him was a dislocated shoulder playing football. Hell, coach got him over on the sidelines and had popped that sucker right back in and sent him out to play linebacker again. Nobody'd told him about anything like this.

"Come on, son," said Colonel Dash, who'd been watching, "there's a job to do. We can't be of help if we lose control of ourselves."

"Sorry, sir."

There would be eighteen closed-coffin services. A number of wives would have nightmares, wondering if it really was their husband in the box. Debbie Carlson would. They put the Lieutenant back together as best they could. The only unbroken part of Dan were his glasses, which they found alongside the road that ran behind the Kaserne.

Debbie had been in the lady's room again when the bomb went off. She would move back home to her parents and later marry Joe Ingalls, the local independent insurance agent. For the rest of her life, whenever she saw a military uniform, she would feel ill.

They found the remains of the computer specialist in the back of the pickup truck. He'd been neatly diced and strained through the undamaged steel grillwork of the dog cages bolted to the bed of the truck.

The Sergeant from Tennessee paid his dues. First, he visited each of the eighteen graves. Then he retired and methodically drank himself to death. That staff car and its passenger had been his responsibility. He never did get rid of the ringing in his ears.

The big problem was the body of Major General Robert E. Hartley. A so-called buddy of Charles Goodwin had been searching on the far side of the parking lot, back of Building Twenty-two.

"Shit, Chuck," he called, trying to send the young MP back to the bushes, "there's another chunk way over here."

"Screw you, Herb," said Charles Goodwin, a lot older than he had been an hour ago.

Around the Stammtisch in the German canteen, officers were not always treated with kindness. The story grew that, if you listened real carefully, shortly after twelve noon each day, when the wind was right, you could hear the sound of a hard rubber ball on the squash court across the way.

Sometimes, especially after a few rounds, one of the regulars would lean over and say, "You know, they never found all of him."

Maybe not, but it was true that, for months afterward, until the current crop of squash players had rotated to their new assignments, the squash court remained unused between the hours of twelve and one.

At last the parking lot was empty—the wounded gone and the dead gathered up. One by one the lights went out. The Kaserne was on full alert. Heavily armed men patrolled the fences and kept watch from rooftops. There would be no movie tonight.

Chapter XXVI

Someone was calling. He didn't want to listen, but the little-girl voice kept right on. He drifted reluctantly up from the warmth.

"Dan! Dan!"

"Sorry, miss, but you'll have to leave."

"No, I won't," said the little-girl voice. "You can't make me. That's my husband. Dan, wake up and tell them."

"He can't hear you and he's not your husband. Your name is Carlson. You're the wife of Second Lieutenant Daniel Carlson. The man in the bed is John Ryder."

"No! I don't want to hear any of this. That's my husband. Just ask Rhea—she knows."

He opened his eyes. A blonde woman was standing at the side of his bed. Bed? What was he doing in bed? He wanted to ask, but it wasn't worth it. Should he know her? There was something, but it didn't matter. He closed his eyes and the numbing mists took him.

"Dan...Dan!"

It would be light soon. They had been riding all night through the rain. He was more uncomfortable than tired. The leathers itched and the furs smelled. Shifting the lance to his left hand, he flexed cramped fingers and looked at the man riding beside him. His hard-eyed companion acknowledged the glance with a nod; they were almost there.

Turning in his saddle, he looked back at his army, heads lowered and shoulders hunched against the rain, some asleep in their saddles. A miserable band, but they would have to do. Not as many as he would have liked, but when he got past this next battle, he would have more men than he would ever need again.

As they approached the plain, the trees started to thin. At the edge of the forest, he reined in and the horses behind followed suit. It was time to wake the troops. Pursing his lips, he gave a piercing whistle. Heads came up and men stirred, easing stiff muscles and cursing. It was a good sign. His army, wet and sore, was in a temper. They would fight well, taking their dis-comfort out on the enemy. There would be no morning meal—hunger gave the men an edge.

He listened to the subdued voices of his troops when they saw the campfires out on the plain. Greatly outnumbered, they were apprehensive, but they'd learned not to question. If he led, no matter where, they would fol-low. He looked again at the man riding at his side—the man who was father, brother, friend, and teacher, the man who had given him The Gift.

Not for the first time, he wondered what lay behind those hard eyes, what they saw when they looked back at him. Did they see a boy who was not yet a full-grown man, a boy who was sometimes afraid and unsure of himself?

Leaning over in the saddle, he and the hard-eyed man clasped fore-arms. There was nothing to be said. They kicked up their animals and rode out onto the plain at the head of a growing wedge of horses and men—first at a walk, then at a trot and, when they heard the warning cries from the camp, at a gallop.

The wedge broke as each man tried to be the first to close with the enemy. No matter how often he had explained the strategic advantage of holding formation, and no matter how often his men had acknowledged the wisdom of the plan, the minute the charge began, all was forgotten.

They streamed across the plain toward the enemy camp at full gallop. He held his place out front, riding easily with his lance couched and ready. But something was bothering him. For some reason he wanted to call the hard-eyed man Merlin, but that wasn't his name, no more than he was... Arthur?

His lance broke in the charge and he drew his sword. It was his favorite weapon, given to him by his teacher. When he swung the sword above his head, it had a life and voice of its own. A bond had been formed between them and he was never easy when the sword was out of sight. Wherever he put his head down for the night, the sword Excalibur was always close at hand.

His horse collapsed from under him in a hail of arrows. He was un-touched. Already, in drafty halls and around campfires, they spoke of the great sword and of its owner. How none could stand against them, how no blade could pierce his flesh and no arrow could find its mark. Leaning closer, so the night couldn't hear, they whispered of the hard-eyed wizard and of... *magic.*

With strong, slashing strokes, he destroyed all that stood before him. Wood, leather, and iron were no match for this devastating force. He drew the enemy, each wanting to be the one to defeat him, but neither soldier, chieftain, nor prince, wise in the ways of battle, could stand against him. There was no skill, no technique, that could turn aside the power of his blade.

They came at him in great numbers, trying to overwhelm him, to bury him with the sheer weight of bodies. He laughed and cut them down. Those who lived would do their part in spreading the legend of what had happened on that gray, rainy morning.

The voice of the hard-eyed man was in his mind. Behind you! Whirling, sword high, ready to strike, he was blinded by the light.

Light was everywhere. The sun blazed huge in a vast, cloudless sky. The world was alive with raw color. His sword, along with thousands of others, reflected the sun as it was held up, silhouetted against the endless blue. He shouted "Death to the Infidel," then staggered slightly.

Lowering his blade, he regarded it with narrowed eyes. It was the same as always, but for a moment there, he had the strangest feeling—a vision of a battle on a gray, rainy morning. Curious—it hadn't rained since they'd left home and the battle was still to come. The image faded.

It must be the heat, it was like an oven inside his armor. He wouldn't be the first to start seeing things, and it wouldn't do to become careless, now that the goal was in sight.

Stretching out before them, safe behind great walls, lay the city. They could see the domes and the flat-roofed houses, and the sprawl of the bazaar. Rising tall and slender were the minarets used to call the faithful to worship. *Shahada*—there is no God but Allah, and Muhammad is his messenger.

The eyes of the men glistened. For the first time, they saw the church of the Holy Sepulcher and, hazy in the background, the Mount of Olives, where Jesus had gone to pray. It was June 7, 1099 and the city was Jerusalem.

The 13,000 men who stood upon the Hill of Joy were as splendid as the city itself. Armor shone, sparkling in the sunlight. Banners and pennons fluttered bravely in the breeze, and on the brilliant white tunic of each and every man blazed the scarlet sign of the cross.

He looked at the city shimmering in the distance. At last! Final preparations would begin tomorrow, but tonight he needed a bath, something to eat and time to ready himself for the coming battle.

It would be a relief to shed his armor in the safety of his tent. Even then, he had to be careful. The closer they came to their goal, the more time they spent quarreling amongst themselves.

He hoped they could give the Infidel as good a measure. Ah, well, it was a small price to pay. With nothing more on his mind than looking forward to the pleasing coolness of evening, he started to sheath his sword and was fighting for his life.

There were five of them in the light of his servant's torch. Blades drawn, they stepped from the shadows of a darkened shop front, directly into the path of his manservant, barring the way.

The attackers had seen the light as he and his man started across London Bridge. The wooden shops that lined the sides of the bridge were closed at this hour. Not that it would have mattered. Danger awaited the unwary London traveler in 1665.

The torchbearer stepped to one side. His only task was to hold the light and stay out of the way.

The five men, all dressed in black, formed a half circle around their victims, who had their backs against a store. On signal, they all lunged to skewer this innocent, who was only now drawing his weapon. It was disappointing that neither of the two had tried to flee—it added a bit of sport.

Anyone who ventured out at night, much less attempted to cross London Bridge, got what he deserved. From the looks of the well-dressed gentleman, this spot of work was going to pay handsomely. They'd soon be in a nearby tavern, tankards in hand. Pity, though, the two didn't cry out or beg for mercy.

For the briefest of moments, the finest swordsman in all of Europe stared at his blade as if he had never seen it before. He parried easily, avoiding the first thrusts, his blade flickering and dancing in the light and shadows cast by the torch.

Cut to the hard and thrust to the soft. His blade whispered its approval. It didn't have the voice that another sword did. Strange—he'd been thinking about Excalibur as they'd started across the bridge.

It was over quickly—five passes and the sigh of his blade as each time he struck home. Cleaning his weapon, he paused to study it again and he was holding a Very pistol.

The trench was a quagmire. He wondered how much longer the wooden bulkheads were going to hold. The shelling didn't help matters any. The Major looked at his watch. The daily bombardment was due to start any time now. The faint smell of mustard gas hung in the air and there was the occasional moan of a bagpipe.

The Black Watch couldn't wait. They scared the hell out of the Boche. Even when the Germans couldn't see them, they could hear them and knew that, once started, they would keep coming to the last man.

Earlier in the war, the Major had seen for himself. The charge had faltered, broken, and turned back, except for a single piper marching across the smoking, pockmarked fields, straight toward the German lines, blowing his pipes for all he was worth. Not even the Major could save him.

The firing became sporadic, then stopped, as those on both sides of the line listened in disbelief to that caterwauling, discordant, hair-raising, magnificent noise—the same call that brought the clans down from the highlands to the side of the Bonnie Prince.

The piper marked time in front of the barbed wire that protected the German trenches. Finally, a fifteen-year-old from Wiesbaden, with boots and helmet too large for his malnourished body, could take it no longer. He fired one double-bar, song-ending shot. The piper fell. The air escaping from his bagpipes moaned and died like the dreams of Prince Charles Edward that day on Culloden Moor.

After a moment of shocked silence, the Allied lines went crazy. Bayonets fixed, they came boiling out of their trenches toward the German lines at a dead run. For some, that was exactly what it turned out to be. The rest smashed and stabbed their mindless way for two hundred yards before sanity returned. A week later, they were right back where they had started, staring vacantly at the same wooden bulkheads and trying to stay alive, the piper forgotten.

The Major would never forget and neither would the man in the hospital bed. Asleep? Dreaming? Remembering how, as a child, he had awakened himself when he had a bad dream, he tried to reach up and pull his eyelids open. He couldn't move. He had become an unwilling witness to history.

One after the other, the pictures flashed through his mind—images of other places and, sometimes, in other tongues. Later, he would remember and understand, but for now there was nothing he could do but watch. Gradually, the scenes slowed, then stopped.

He was a boy again. He was on a bridge, looking down the rails, watching the freight train straining its way up the long grade out of the town where he lived. He felt easy. He was twelve years old and had been planning this all spring. It was the first week of summer vacation and the best feeling in the whole world.

As soon as the engine had passed, he unhurriedly swung over the railing to stand on the outside of the bridge. He watched the freight cars passing beneath him, getting his timing right. Launching himself, skinny arms flailing to keep his balance, he plumped down, square in the middle of an open canvas-covered grain car, nice as you please. It was just as he had imagined. He threw back his head, looked at the sky, and laughed.

At the top of the grade, where the train went the slowest, was a trestle. Before it reached the trestle, the track curved through a cut in a hillside. Hanging from the grab irons on the side of the grain car, he wondered if getting off would be as easy as getting on. It was. He stepped smoothly to the cinder roadbed and moved away from the train. When the caboose went by, he was just some kid waving from the bank alongside the track.

Now for the rest of it. The trestle stretched out for several hundred feet, spanning Fletcher's Gorge. Along one side of the trestle was a walkway with a pipe metal hand-rail. The railing needed painting and he could rub the rust off with the ball of his thumb. No matter, it had to be done.

He was able to step from the bank to the top of the railing. Standing with one foot on the bank and the other on the railing, he looked out along the rusty, uneven fence. His toes curled in his sneakers. He took a deep breath, arms stretched wide for balance, and stepped out onto the railing.

He started slowly. He'd practiced on the fence that ran around the church, but it wasn't like this, at all. As he moved farther out along the railing, he realized that a strong, gusty wind was blowing down the gorge. He

176

almost stopped, but that would spoil everything. He had come too far and was too stubborn to give up now.

A third of the way across, he made himself look down to the bottom of the gorge. After a moment of wild arm-waving, he got himself back under a measure of control. Out in the center of the trestle, the wind was really kicking up. In spots, he had to lean out into the wind, away from the trestle, to keep his balance. If the wind suddenly stopped blowing... He made himself think about it.

After that, it was easy. He was across to the other side before he was really ready. He didn't want to let the moment go; it was important.

Jumping down from the railing, he turned and started back across the trestle, back toward town, disappointed that it was over. No one had seen him, no one knew. That was the way it should be. What he had done was for himself alone. He would never doubt again. Sure, he would be afraid, but the running from himself and from others was over.

Skipping from tie to tie, he wondered what else he could do this summer to test himself. Next fall, the guys who waited for him in the schoolyard every day were in for a surprise. He thought about the train and the trestle and hopped four ties.

The little-girl voice was calling again. "Dan! Oh, Dan, wake up! It's me—Debbie. Open your eyes and talk to me. I don't know what to do. There's been a terrible accident and you're in the hospital. I thought you were dead. Please, Dan, say something."

"Mrs. Carlson! You have to stop sneaking in here like this. Mr. Ryder is a very sick man and this sort of thing isn't helping matters any. If you continue, I shall have you forcibly removed and held for psychiatric evaluation. Now—out you go!"

"Oh, God...Dan!"

"Mate in five, young man. No? Here, let me show you. *Nein!* That way is even worse, mate in four. So...like this. There, now you see? You show promise," said the chess player who, except for a word here and there, sounded more British than German.

"There's much to learn if you intend to play seriously. You could, you know," said the chess player, looking at the position of the chess pieces on the board. "I've never seen a defense quite like that before—most interesting. I wonder what you'd do with the white pieces. Maybe I'll find out…yes, definite promise." The chess player leaned across the board so that he couldn't be overheard. "Tell you what—I won't be much longer. Wait for me and we'll have a cup of coffee together and talk. Yes?"

At last the room was empty except for the two men seated facing one another on metal folding chairs. "I hope you like your coffee with cream and sugar," said the chess player, pouring coffee from an oversized thermos into two plastic cups.

"Careful, it's still hot." After setting his cup down, the chess player extended his hand. "Now's the time for introductions. I am Martin von Friedenthal, and you are…let me see…" The chess player consulted a slip of paper. "Here it is—the sixteenth board. You are John Ryder. Correct?"

Ryder nodded in agreement, took a drink of coffee, and looked at the three long tables, placed so they formed a U. On each table were eight chessboards, twenty-four in all. Martin von Friedenthal had given an exhibition in simultaneous play.

Chess pieces, like discarded toy soldiers, told of battles over for now, but not forgotten. Games would be replayed and moves reconsidered.

"If only I had played queen to bishop four…" "I don't care if he was world champion, no one that age has the right to play like that—must be older than God, damn old buzzard anyway…" "Now, on move fourteen, if…"

The damn old buzzard took another sip of coffee and indicated the tables. "I always enjoy these events. I meet so many nice people and sometimes, every once in a great while, someone like you." Von Friedenthal leaned over.

"Yes, I know you lost today, but who wants to win all the time. The fun would be gone, *nicht?* Your play made an impression on me. I was hard-pressed to break through your defense. No, I mean what I say. No matter what else we may do, on the chess board there is only truth—you must learn that. I think you have possibilities and should do something with such a talent." Von Friedenthal beamed. "I make it a rule never to offer advice, but since it's my own rule, I can break it, can't I? Go home—think about what I have said."

Von Friedenthal handed Ryder his card. "If you should decide to become serious about the game, write to me at my home in Heidelberg and I'll tell you what to do." Von Friedenthal paused, looking at the scattered pieces with unseeing eyes, then leaned closer to look directly at Ryder.

"You are someone I thought I'd never meet. No, don't say anything, just go home. When one is young, it's easy to say something in the flush of enthusiasm that you may later regret." Von Friedenthal smiled to take the sting from his words. *"Auf Weidersehen*, John Ryder—until we meet again."

He was John Ryder, grand master, playing chess with Martin von Friedenthal in England. Held in a place between sleep and consciousness, he realized that what he saw had already happened but, for some reason, he had to live it again.

Images, like flickering pieces of film, flashed through his mind, finally ending on a frosty night in the Cotswolds. The man in the hospital bed turned and twisted, attempting to escape The Gift. At first he tried to cry out, then he smiled, reveling in his newfound strength. Among the shadows, battles had been fought and won.

Now that Ryder had seen through the eyes of Arthur, past fused into present, body and mind became one. The healing was over.

Ryder stood in the meadow, looking up at the stars, but all he could see were Katherine's eyes. The man in the hospital bed saw them too, growing larger and larger until they filled the sky.

Ryder woke. He opened his eyes and she was there.

Chapter XXVII

It took him a moment to realize that this was no dream. She was very real. Seated in a chair by the side of his bed, Katherine was reading. He saw her profile framed by her hair. Maybe he'd stay this way for a century or two and just look at her.

There was another person, standing over by the window, watching him. It was Andrew Hall. When Ryder had first met him, he'd been impressed with how still Hall could be. He had none of the mannerisms that other people acquire along the way. Hall smiled slightly and nodded.

Ryder regarded the part of the room he could see without moving his head. It wasn't necessary. There was no mistaking those institutional green walls and the smell. He was in a hospital. He turned his gaze back to Katherine. He wasn't the first, nor would he be the last, to lose his head over Katherine Hall.

While she was still in her teens, photographers, model agencies, and talent scouts had gone wild over Katherine's beauty. It got so bad that Hall had hired a gentleman whose sole duty was to look after her. Dressed in suits from Huntsman and shirts from Hildreth & Key, he was the titled son of a noble family that had, as the saying goes, fallen on hard times.

He always remained conveniently in the background. Earlier, he'd studied with a martial arts expert in Japan and had the unheard of privilege of living in the master's home.

The titled young nobleman was most proficient at breaking boards, bricks, and bones. He had a smile that could charm the knickers off the ladies and the grip of an anaconda.

There had been more than one social occasion while still chatting about the ballet or the races at Ascot in his fruity public-school voice, he'd escorted a randy guest to the front door with one languid arm draped around the man's shoulder and two steely fingers of the other hand buried in the pressure point just above the man's elbow.

It tended to make the guest walk on tiptoe and feel weak in the knees at the same time. The young man was very good at his job and very well paid.

Unfortunately, he, too, fell under the spell of Katherine's eyes and was dismissed at the moment of attempted indiscretion, when Hall threw him through a window. He was thankful that he wasn't cut by broken glass. He was also thankful to be alive.

The window through which he had exited Hall's London townhouse was located second floor front and he'd landed on the roof of his own Jaguar parked at the curb.

After his release from the hospital, the titled young man took up with a Roumanian countess who was a professional houseguest. Their needs were simple—the best food, wine, and clothing that six continents could provide. They lived very well.

The turning point for Katherine had been a skiing holiday at an exclusive resort in the Swiss Alps. An Italian movie mogul, a giant in the industry, famous for his avant-garde films, had been seated with his party at an outdoor table, taking the sun. When Katherine crossed the terrace on the way to the lobby to check in, the movie mogul took one look and began acting as if he were having a seizure.

His companion of many years, a well-known, somewhat long-in-the-tooth actress, almost had one herself. She still hadn't gotten that bastard to the altar. She had overlooked his little diversions, as he liked to call them, but now she wondered if she'd waited too long. She also wondered about Italian courts and their views on cohabitation as grounds for inheritance. The thoughts were short-lived.

Showing a surprising turn of speed, the rotund mogul went sprinting off to the desk to learn who the new guest was. Katherine's holiday became a nightmare. She was still too inexperienced in the ways of the world and it was more than she could handle.

Her companion, a school chum, was enchanted with movie people. She was easily distracted, per the mogul's instructions, by one of the young men in his party, thereby clearing the decks. The great man gave Katherine the full treatment.

Doubly motivated, the mogul was indefatigable in his attentions to the girl. Katherine's beauty, combined with her fresh innocence, kept him in a constant state of rut. A half step behind was the knowledge of the kind of movie he could make.

The idea had haunted him for years. The more he saw of Katherine, the more certain he was that he had at last found the one woman who could star in what would be the pinnacle of his life's work—his celluloid monument. He became quite emotional when he thought about it and tears would come to his eyes.

At first, Katherine was flattered by the idea of being a star. "No, *cara mia*, superstar," he corrected. She considered it for a fleeting moment, and that hesitation gave the mogul a chance to move in—flowers, candy, lavish gifts, hourly phone calls, the works. He tried to ply her with liquor, but discovered the young lady had a cast-iron stomach, while he gulped antacid pills.

Only on the slopes or in her own room was she ever out of his sight. He kept after Katherine, assuming that her growing silence was the beginning of submission. The thought drove him wild. A man possessed, he redoubled his efforts.

The worst for Katherine was the night she spent alone, locked in her room. Her school chum was sleeping elsewhere. Armed with her ski poles which, should it prove necessary, she fully intended to use, Katherine spent the night dressed and sitting cross-legged in the middle of her bed.

The movie mogul had tried to bribe the concierge for a key to Katherine's room, but was firmly informed that the hotel wasn't that sort of place.

Until morning's light, Katherine had listened to the mogul scratching at the door and whispering to his *cara mia* about all the wonderful things they could do to and for each other, if she would only open the door. He was most explicit. Why not? It had worked before when all else failed—besides, didn't she want to be famous?

She didn't want to be famous and she wasn't about to open the door, but the night did harden her resolve never to allow herself to be placed in such a situation again. She decided it was time she stopped having to pay for how she looked.

The worst for the movie mogul came later that same morning. He was seated outside on the terrace at his usual table, having breakfast with the beautiful people, including the actress and Katherine's school chum.

He'd gotten himself into such a state that he couldn't sleep anyway. There was the promise of a crystal day. He began to appreciate it, especially now when he saw Katherine approaching his table.

She was dressed for the slopes, but he knew she was there to ask his forgiveness. The night hadn't been wasted after all. His mouth was dry with the thought of what was to come. He knew he would be the first. He imagined the slivers of sunlight sneaking around the blinds of her darkened room, the last wisp of silken clothing dropping to the floor, honey-colored skin...

Aroused to instant lust, the mogul started to stand up while he still could. Katherine stopped him with a light touch to his shoulder. It was the first time she had allowed any physical contact between the two of them. The mogul felt his heart pound. Startled, he sank down again to look at her with hot, reproachful eyes.

She smiled. It was a smile that rivaled the sun-kissed mountain peaks. Speaking slowly and distinctly, in a street Italian that no proper young English lady had any right to know, Katherine told the movie mogul exactly what she thought of him.

Smiling all the while, she analyzed, in graphic detail, his deviant sexual preferences, his gross physical and mental infirmities, his advanced age. If the fates so decreed, she concluded, she would sooner mate with the village goat. Each word dropped like a stone in the clear mountain air.

Katherine announced to her stunned audience that if she ever were to disrobe in public, it wouldn't be to make a movie and most assuredly not for the likes of him.

Now, she intended to finish her holiday, what was left of it, in peace and if she caught him so much as looking in her direction, she would geld him on the spot, making certain to use the dullest blade she could find. If he didn't understand her, she was prepared to repeat what she had just said in French, German, or English.

With blanched cheeks and bloodless lips, the movie mogul watched Katherine's departure amidst a round of applause from the Italian-speaking guests, who quickly translated what Katherine had said for the others on the terrace. French and German tourists, and a couple of Americans, added their approval. The movie mogul had endeared himself to no one.

The applause drowned out a howl of anguish from an Italian waiter who had been trying to walk, watch, and listen, all at the same time. He was so engrossed in the spectacle of the great man getting his, that he ran full tilt into the butt end of a low railing that edged the terrace.

If anyone had thought to look, they would have seen the waiter, six feet below the terrace, hunching along in the snow like a giant inchworm, trying to sooth the fever in his groin.

Through centuries of war, pestilence, and famine his family bloodlines had remained strong. Tears ran down his cheeks. To have it end like this, here in the snows of Switzerland, the last of his line—*tutto finito*! If truth were told, his concern had less to do with history than with the fear that his delivery system, necessary for carrying on the family bloodlines, had been damaged beyond repair.

The movie mogul checked out the same morning and Katherine had a marvelous time for the rest of her holiday. Her school chum never forgave her and neither did the Italian waiter, at least not until later that evening.

After a hot bath, and using a copy of a girly magazine that some guest had left behind, the waiter ran an equipment check on his delivery system. To his intense relief, he discovered that it was fully functional. He was so happy. With forgiveness and love in his heart, he ran a second equipment check, just to make sure.

The movie mogul married the actress and started making spaghetti westerns. Among the paparazzi, who know about such things, it was said that theirs was a marriage of the spirit.

"Hi!"

Katherine didn't look up. She needed a moment. Of all the men in all the world, why, oh, why did it have to be someone who said "Hi?" She raised her head to look calmly at the man in the hospital bed.

"Must you? You've been lying there like a limp noodle, scaring me— us—half to death and that's all you have to say?"

"How long?"

"Ten days. I liked you better without the beard."

Ryder sat up with a start. He fingered the stubble on his chin and looked to Hall for confirmation. Hall nodded.

"Shouldn't you be lying down?" asked Katherine.

"No," said Ryder. He looked at Hall again. "I seem to remember a building falling on me."

"That is quite correct."

"Anyone else hurt?"

"Eighteen dead—scores injured."

"Jesus, what happened?" Before Hall could answer, Ryder held up his hand. "Don't tell me." He could see the pictures in his mind—it was all there. "The General?"

"Dead."

"Anyone else I know?"

"I believe you met Colonel McPherson."

"What about Thomas Dash?"

"He made it with nothing more than a broken arm. He comes by every day to see how you're doing."

"Who else?"

"Well, the General's driver was fortunate."

"The Sergeant is alive?"

"That's what I said. Quite amazing when you think about it. Pieces of automobile scattered over half of Campbell Barracks, the Sergeant standing right next to the point of explosion, and he doesn't have a scratch on him. Brooks tells me it happens that way sometimes."

"What about the other people at the Casino?"

"John," said Katherine, "must you? This can't be good for you."

"I have to know...Andrew?"

"The explosion killed just about everyone at the front of the balcony. There were also several people in the parking lot who didn't survive. All in all, a bloody mess. One would think you would stop being caught out like this."

"Stuff it, Andrew, will you."

"I can excuse the incident in my dining room," continued Hall, "since you had yet to receive The Gift. This time, however, is a bit much. Haven't you learned anything?"

"Your concern is overwhelming. Just let's say I wasn't expecting it and leave it at that."

"You must always expect it. No place is safe for you now. Safety is a state of mind—do try not to forget that."

"I've got the lumps, not you."

"You shouldn't have them in the first place. I told you it was too soon to leave, but you insisted. I didn't find you after all these years to lose you to something as ridiculous as an explosion. If you had stayed at Hall House and had taken the time to learn about the abilities you've been given," he added, "then this wouldn't have happened."

"You're going to keep right on, aren't you?"

"Can you read my mind?"

"No."

"Or Katherine's?"

"Stop it, you two," said Katherine. That would be the last thing she wished.

"Father, put a lid on it, will you. As for you, John Ryder—lie down and be quiet. You haven't been conscious for five minutes and you've got everything up in the air. We thought you were either dead or dying. You shouldn't even be sitting up. Lie down and stop making such a fuss."

"You sound like me Mum."

"It's utterly ghastly when an American tries to sound British."

Ryder winked at Katherine. "I'm not going to lie down. If I weren't wearing this hospital gown, I'd get out of bed right now."

"You wouldn't dare—"

"Is that modesty or simply an expression of your concern?"

"*Humph!*"

"I thought so," said Ryder looking into Katherine's eyes. God, she was lovely. Damn and double damn Merlin and his code. For two cents. . .

"So, where am I?" he said instead.

"The U.S. Army 130th Station Hospital," answered Hall. "You've passed the place any number of times."

Ryder nodded. "I need a shower, a razor, and my clothes. By the way, where are my clothes?"

"Probably burned by now," said Hall. "You were a mess."

"There you go again." Then Ryder remembered. "Jesus—Liesel's sauerbraten. She's got to be mad as hell."

"Don't worry about Frau von Friedenthal." Hall paused. "She has other things on her mind at the moment."

Before Ryder could ask what Hall was talking about, an army nurse with maple leaves on her collar, bustled in. "Here now, finally awake, are we?

We shouldn't be sitting up in bed, now should we. We're going to lie down, like a good boy, and have our temperature and blood pressure taken."

Firm, strong hands that had subdued more than one difficult patient gripped Ryder by the shoulders to press him back. He didn't move. The hands pressed harder. Ryder still didn't budge. The nurse looked at Katherine, trying to create a bond—we against them, sisters under the skin. She didn't receive any encouragement.

"You people will have to leave," said the nurse.

Katherine looked at her father.

"As you wish," he said.

"Cowards," said Ryder, "deserting a sinking ship." He had time for one last parting shot at their retreating backs.

"Don't forget my clothes," he yelled.

"Clothes?" said the nurse, closing the door to his room. "You're not going anywhere until we say you are."

Ryder swung his feet over the side of the bed. "Want to bet, Major?"

The Major came to stand at the side of Ryder's bed, close enough so he could read her nametag. Woodhouse. She placed sturdy hands on sturdy hips. With fifteen starched and scrubbed years in service, she was a formidable sight. The only imperfection, if one could call it that, was a strand of hair that had escaped from the tightly pulled-back bun.

"Look, buster, I'm in charge here. I know you're a VIP, but you're a patient, in bed, and you're going to do what you're told. Now, lie down!"

Ryder wasn't five years old anymore and he had long ago lost his reverence for the medical profession. "Your bed?"

"You know what I mean."

"Yes, Major, I'm afraid I do. Everyone keeps telling me to lie down. I was brought here when I couldn't do anything about it. Save your ministrations for someone who needs them."

"Lie down, you're a sick man," fretted Major Woodhouse.

"No!"

She brightened. "Of course, that's it. You're still out of your head. You've been carrying on, laughing and babbling, for days. It's been driving the doctors crazy."

"What did I say?"

"A lot of nonsense—stuff no one could understand. They had a shrink sitting by your bed taking notes, until Mr. Hall arrived. You also spoke in tongues."

"I what?"

"You know, talking strange. Sometimes it sounded like German or something; the next time it would be some language no one had ever heard. I'm not sure if you need a doctor or a priest."

"Woodhouse, I'm not dying."

"It's not dying I'm talking about."

Ryder looked at her. "You think I'm possessed?"

"Anyone with your vital signs is not normal. Your pulse rate and blood pressure have the doctors looking in books they haven't read since medical school. There've been more people standing around your bed, scratching their heads, than you can imagine. For that matter, I'm not at all sure you're human."

Ryder started to stand up. "I've overstayed my welcome."

Major Woodhouse reached for Ryder's shoulders again, but he caught her hands in his. She tried unsuccessfully to free herself.

"Enough, Major."

"If you don't lie down, you will be restrained."

"Major," said Ryder in a level voice, still holding her hands, "I'm not going to be restrained; the time for that has passed. There are not enough men, women, or large dogs in this hospital to do that."

"But the explosion—you've been unconscious for days."

"I promise it won't happen again—I'm all right." Ryder smiled at her and reached up to tuck that stray wisp of hair back in place. "Besides, I'm a civilian; I don't belong to the club."

Maybe the smile did it, or maybe she recognized a resolve in his eyes just as strong as her own. "Well..."

Ryder smiled again. "Please," he added softly.

"All right, for now," said Major Woodhouse, "but forget that foolishness about your clothes."

"Whatever you say, nurse. And kindly leave the door open."

Still she hesitated.

"*Shoo—*"

For the first time she saw him as a man. Major Woodhouse left the room trying to tuck that wayward wisp of hair back and doing something she hadn't done in a long time—she was smiling.

"John?"

"Come in, Thomas."

"Well, it's about time you were able to sit up and take nourishment. How are you?"

"I'm fine, thanks. How's the arm?"

Colonel Dash fingered the cast. "It itches sometimes, but at least they fixed it so that I can use my fingers. It's a simple fracture."

"I did that, didn't I?"

"Yes."

"I appreciate the honesty. I wouldn't hurt you; I didn't know what I was doing. My reaction was meant for someone else."

"I hope to God. I never want to see a pair of eyes like that again."

"What can I say?"

"Nothing—I probably wouldn't believe you anyway. You're something other than a chess player, but I don't want to know. Right?"

"Right."

"We could talk about your physical condition."

"Do you know something I don't?"

"Not really, but your case had been giving the doctors fits, until Andrew Hall showed up. If it wasn't for him, I can't imagine what might have happened. He's not an American, is he?"

"No, British. Why?"

"I'd have sworn he was a senior member of Congress or some other heavy hitter. You should have seen everyone tiptoeing around, especially after the call from Washington."

"That's him."

"The doctors were ordered to extend every courtesy. You were his responsibility and they were to follow his instructions without question. Very mysterious. He told the doctors to leave you alone—no medication, no x-rays, no intravenous feedings, nothing. If they couldn't defer to his wishes, you would be moved. Since his arrival. he's watched over you day and night. The man doesn't sleep."

"Now I know why I'm ready to eat a moose. Anything else?"

"That's about it. Hall got some static at first, but in his own quiet way, things went exactly as he wished. The telephone call from the White House didn't hurt."

"It wouldn't have made any difference, believe me."

"If you say so," said Colonel Dash, holding up a hand. "I know—I shouldn't ask about Andrew Hall."

"Right."

"His daughter's a real beauty, isn't she."

Out of the corner of his eye, Ryder saw Katherine's head in the doorway of his room. She must have heard.

"If you like the type—"

Katherine made a face at him and disappeared.

"If you can say that," said Colonel Dash, who had his back to the door, "I know you're still a sick man. Better lie down."

"Not you, too."—Ryder glanced at the now empty doorway—"Sorry, that wasn't for your benefit,"—he raised his voice—"just for the eavesdroppers." There was a satisfactory gasp from the hall.

"Okay, Thomas, what else is on your mind? You've been uneasy since you got here. Is it the arm?"

Colonel Dash shook his head.

"Me?"

"No, it's not that."

"Security? I suppose there's all kinds of people waiting to get at me?"

"You'll have to make a statement and go through debriefing, but your relationship with the General and the reason for your visit to Campbell have been established. It's a shame that you had to be involved."

"Well, then, what's the problem?"

"The problem is Doctor von Friedenthal."

"What—Martin? You've got to be kidding."

"I'm afraid not."

"Come on, Thomas. Martin's the finest man I've ever known. He's not mixed up in any of this. I'll stake my life on it."

"You'd lose. Martin von Friedenthal is right in the middle of this, but not in the way you think."

"Don't diddle, Thomas, you're not the type."

"All right, I'll give it to you straight. We've received a letter from a group claiming responsibility for the bombing. And there has been another incident."

"Not another bombing?"

"No, not that. The same group that sent us the letter, sent one to the von Friedenthals. Two days ago, they kidnapped his daughters."

I built a funeral pyre to light the night sky, but still you live.

Chapter XXVIII

The door opened before Ryder could ring the bell. "Ach, Herr Ryder, *Guten Tag.* I thought it was more reporters, until I heard the auto. Not many drive such an expensive automobile."

"Fräulein Grimm."

"I was just cleaning the steps, but come in, please. Be careful, the marble is wet. Frau von Friedenthal is in the"—Fräulein Grimm paused, searching for the word—"*ach, ja,* in the kitchen and the Professor is downstairs."

Ilse Grimm, part-time cleaning lady and full-time student at the University, was showing off her English. She had come to von Friedenthal's attention in one of his political science classes.

Von Friedenthal had discovered she was very bright. Raised on a small farm, she had none of the social graces, but she was a willing worker, so he had taken her on to help around the house.

The regular cleaning woman, who von Friedenthal had inherited from his father, still insisted on working. She was stiff of knee and didn't see into the corners anymore, but the von Friedenthals, father and son, were her life.

Years ago, Martin had tried to pension her off, saying it was his turn to look after her, but she wouldn't hear of it.

It was an arrangement, thanks to von Friedenthal, by which everyone benefited. The old lady came on Mondays, Wednesdays, and Fridays. Although she never said so, her attitude was, "See, the house looks better than ever—and with only three days a week. What would you ever do without me?"

The von Friedenthals had a spotless home and Fräulein Grimm, who worked on Tuesdays, Thursdays, and Saturdays, and to whom von Friedenthal paid a generous wage, had the feeling of earning her own way. The only problem was keeping the days straight. Sometimes it got a little dicey when the old lady became confused and showed up while Fräulein Grimm was in the house.

Ryder stepped carefully across the marble foyer and jumped the three steps leading to the upstairs part of Martin's house. He found Liesel in the kitchen, hands covered with flour. She was kneading dough.

"I saw you through the window," she said. "You lost weight in the hospital."

"I know."

"I'm preparing dinner; you'll join us."

"I couldn't impose, Liesel. I should have phoned before I came, but I just heard about the girls."

"They are such good children. They will be home from school soon, so I'd better hurry and get this in the oven."

"Liesel—"

"You run along now—Martin is downstairs. I'll call you when everything is ready and the girls are home. You must eat."

Liesel kept working at the counter, her back toward Ryder. She had her shoulders hunched as if expecting a blow. Liesel refused to look at him. If she kept busy, kept to the safety of doing the routine things, everything would be all right. Nothing had changed. "Go now—please."

Ryder found von Friedenthal downstairs in the railroad room, seated at his workbench. The only light was the fluorescent lamp above the work area. The model railroad was still. The houses and factories were dark, the engines as lifeless as the look in von Friedenthal's eyes.

"I thought you were still in the hospital."

"I just got out," said Ryder, recalling the three-ring circus it caused when he'd announced he was leaving. "I came as soon as I heard."

Ryder was shocked. Martin had suddenly become an old man with bowed back, sagging jowls, and prominent liver spots on the backs of his hands. His clothes seemed too large. The bright, inquisitive mind had let the mainspring of the soul run down.

"Here, take a seat. You've lost weight."

Ryder sat on a stool at the side of von Friedenthal's workbench. "Listen, Martin, I just got that upstairs. My weight is not important; I'm alive and I'm here. Liesel won't talk about what's happened. I hope I'm not going to get the same routine from you."

Von Friedenthal looked at Ryder with pain-filled eyes. "How can you?"

"I seem to remember, not so long ago, a visit to this fair city and a talk with a friend of mine—a tough old bird who survived imprisonment during the Second World War—a man who's taken everything life has thrown at him and returned the favor in spades. Where is this fellow who told me the mind was the only thing that mattered?"

"You've changed. There is a hardness, a cruelty, about you that you didn't have before. If you were my friend, you couldn't say these things." Von Friedenthal stared down at his hands.

"I always loved children, but I thought it would never happen for me, until I met Liesel. You're young. You cannot imagine what a blessing it is, at my age, to be a father. Those girls are my life and now they are gone, and I can't do anything to help them."

"What about the police?"

"They do nothing."

Ryder sat toying with a paperweight from von Friedenthal's workbench. It was a multi-colored glass egg, flattened at one end to keep it from rolling. "Tell me."

"What is there to tell? Karen and Silka didn't come home for their noon meal. Liesel called the school and several of their friends' homes. No one knew where they were. Karen and Silka are good girls and never late.

"Liesel and I went to the school. We didn't find them, but just as we were leaving, we met one of Karen's classmates. She said she saw the girls earlier, getting into a gray Mercedes. I'm sorry to say we didn't believe her because that is something the girls would never do. When we returned home we found the letter."

"Go on."

Von Friedenthal sat hunched over, elbows on knees, looking down at the floor. He shook his head slowly. "We know these things exist—bombings, killings, murder really. It's like cancer—until it happens to you, there's no way to understand. You read about it, you see it on the television, but it is not the same."

"What did the letter say?"

Still with his elbows on his knees, von Friedenthal put his hands up to shield his face. As he spoke, his shoulders shook. The old man was crying. "The police have the letter," he said finally, in a dead voice.

Ryder waited.

"But I remember," said von Friedenthal. "How can I ever forget?" He still held his head in his hands, staring at the floor.

"'Children,'" quoted von Friedenthal, "'are the tomorrows. They will lead the way out of the capitalistic darkness of oppression to a new world. Children, with their fresh new minds, will know the truth. What better proof is there than two children of an elitist pig joining us to become the symbols of a new front. Now, pig, they belong to the people. You will not see your children again until we unfurl our banners of freedom.'"

"Martin, that says exactly nothing."

"There was more, but it's all repetitious. The letter was signed 'Tomorrow's Children.'"

"Was the letter written in German or English?"

"English."

"I wonder why?" said Ryder thoughtfully, then added, "That's all? No death threats, no demands for money?"

Von Friedenthal wouldn't look at Ryder. "You say that's all. Don't you understand? My daughters are gone. Just like you, the police ask questions and do nothing. I'm very tired; I think you'd better leave."

Ryder stood up. He looked first at the paperweight in his hand, then at the top of Martin's bowed head.

"I'll leave all right, but understand this," he said in a voice that von Friedenthal had never heard before, "someone has gone too far."

Ryder held the glass egg in a closed fist for a long moment, then put it carefully on the workbench. If von Friedenthal had raised his head, he would have seen Ryder's eyes—the same eyes General Hartley had seen in this very room, the same eyes Colonel Dash had seen in the Casino rubble.

"You'll have your daughters back, my old friend,"—Ryder placed his hand on Martin's head—"I promise you."

Von Friedenthal watched with tear-filled eyes as Ryder left the room. For the first time since he had received that damnable letter, he felt like having a pipe. As he took the jar down from a shelf, he noticed something on his workbench. He poked at it with his finger. It appeared to be a mound of finely granulated, colored sugar.

He reached into his pocket for a handkerchief. He wiped his eyes, gave his nose a good blow, and looked at his workbench again. It was still there.

Von Friedenthal packed his meerschaum, pressing the tobacco down hard with his thumb, staring all the while at the multi-colored mound of glass.

Humming softly under his breath, von Friedenthal lit his pipe. He deliberated laying a little more track on that new narrow gauge branch line. He had a lot to think about.

In the hallway outside the railroad layout, Ryder found Fräulein Grimm closing the door to another room.

"Herr Ryder, I was just changing my clothes. I have a class in one hour and I must hurry."

"Here, let me help you with your coat."

"Why, thank you, Herr Ryder, you are most kind."

"May I offer you a ride? I'll be going right by the University."

"I thank you again. I didn't ride my bicycle today; it has a flat tire. Now I'll have time to eat. Lunch is a luxury I seldom have time for when I come to the von Friedenthals."

Ryder followed her up the stairs and outside to where his car was parked.

"Such a lovely auto," she said, as Ryder held the door of the Porsche. "You must be very proud."

"I never thought of it like that." He checked to see that she was safely settled inside the low-slung car.

He went around to the driver's side and eased himself into the formfitting seat. The engine fired with a satisfactory snarl. Ryder waited until the oil pressure gauge began to rise, then swung the Porsche around in the cul-de-sac and started off down the street.

"Well, Fräulein Grimm, what do you think of all this?"

"Think of what? *Ach, so!* You mean the von Friedenthals. Terrible! He must have done something very bad."

"Who?"

"Why—Professor von Friedenthal, of course."

"That old man never hurt anyone in his life."

"I don't know. Around the University, there are some who say…you know…about the war."

"And what does that have to do with Karen and Silka? During the war Martin was a prisoner of his own country, for Pete's sake."

"I do not understand—for Pete's sake?"

"I used to talk like that. It doesn't mean anything."

"You Americans seem to do many things that do not mean anything." They were on Kolbenzeil, driving past the back gate of the 130th Station Hospital. Pointing to a soldier on duty, she continued. "Like that soldier."

Ryder looked at the soldier, who was wearing combat gear and had a rifle slung over his shoulder. "What about him?"

"Normally, there's no one at this gate or the one in front. After a few weeks, when things calm down again, the soldiers will be gone. All that's needed is patience."

"You seem to know quite a lot about it."

"I use my eyes, Herr Ryder. I ride my bicycle from the University. I have passed this gate many times. I see no more than anyone else."

"You can't expect them to remain on alert all the time—"

She didn't answer, but asked instead, "Is that the hospital you were in?"

"Yes."

"Did you like it?"

"Not very much."

Waiting for the light to turn green so he could turn onto Karlsruhes-trasse, Ryder glanced at Fräulein Grimm. Still warm from her household chores, she had a noticeable body odor. Large, work-reddened hands lay quietly in her lap.

Ryder had never seen her wear anything but dark shapeless sweaters and nondescript skirts. She had a tall, angular body and strong facial features that fell just short of being masculine. She didn't shave her legs, wore no makeup, and had brown shoulder-length hair. Except for a pair of quick, bright eyes, she was a study in muted colors.

What the hell, he thought, she's in the University, she ought to be smart. There had to be something going on upstairs, though some parents might dispute that.

For years, until public pressure forced a change in rules, the German universities had been jammed with professional students, sons and daughters who found school an acceptable way of life, just as long as the monthly checks kept coming.

There were fathers who considered the check a small price to pay if it kept Junior and his weird friends the hell out of the house. Other parents suffered in silence, while little Willi attended the occasional lecture to keep up appearances and recuperated from the rigors of academe with days spent sunbathing along the banks of the Neckar and nights trying his very best to drink his favorite *Bierstube* dry.

Ryder drove off down the street, the Porsche's tires slipping in and out of the recessed rails of the streetcar tracks.

"Now what was that bit about Martin, again?" he asked.

"It sounds strange when you call him that."

"That's his name."

"Not to me—"

"No, I suppose it wouldn't be for me, either, if I were his student. Now, how about it."

"You mean about the war?"

"Yes, Fräulein Grimm. about the war."

"No need to get upset; I really don't know anything. Some students say their fathers told them Professor von Friedenthal was put in prison because of things he said about the Third Reich and because he helped some Jews escape."

"What does that have to do with Karen and Silka? And don't give me all that business about the sins of the father."

Ilse looked puzzled.

"Forget that," said Ryder. "What I meant was, how can a bombing at army headquarters and the kidnapping of two children be put down to Martin and the Second World War? Back then, he was just a boy."

"I know nothing about the bombing, but Professor von Friedenthal is a very well known man. He was the world chess champion. Also, he is a famous scholar and has written many books. Everyone would know."

"You're telling me that two little girls were kidnapped so that everyone would know?"

"That's what they say."

"The magical *they*. Who are they, this time?"

"People—students—at the University."

"Do you think Martin is a good teacher?"

"I don't always agree with what he teaches."

"I don't think Martin, excuse me, Professor von Friedenthal, cares whether you agree with him or not, just that you think for yourself."

"Oh, Herr Ryder, I do—I always have."

James L Diffin

Ryder turned left, drove through what used to be the old train tunnel, turned left again, passed the American Express office and, working his way across town using the one-way streets, headed for Theaterstrasse. "Who are these students? Do they have names?"

"I don't know—who remembers such things? Besides, the University is very large and I don't know everyone. I don't attach much importance to what people say. If you're so interested, you should talk to them yourself. I don't have the time."

"I might just do that," said Ryder, stopping the car. "Here we are. It's a shame that little girls have to be involved in someone's stupidity."

For a moment, Ilsa looked as if she had something to say. Instead, she got out of the Porsche and came around to Ryder's side. "Karen and Silka are such good girls," she said. "I don't think anything bad will happen to them."

"You'd better be right."

"It's not a very nice world you leave us, Herr Ryder."

Ryder had to smile. "Maybe I'm not done with it yet, myself. However, I'll take your advice about talking to some students. Any suggestions where I should start?"

"Why you, Herr Ryder? Shouldn't you leave that sort of thing to the police?"

"I'm involved whether I want to be or not. For one thing, I have a distinct aversion to being blown up and, for another, anything that involves Martin, involves me."

Ilse stood looking down at him as if debating what to tell him. "There are several places in town where students like to go. Maybe they will talk to you, maybe not. If you're serious, you can at least try. Two of the best places are the *Gasthaus zum Löwe* and Charly's Pub. In the pub, they even play chess. You might find it interesting."

"Charly's Pub? You're joking."

"Herr Ryder, you will find that I don't joke."

"Well, thanks for the advice. Take care of yourself."

"I suggest you do the same, Herr Ryder. It's a dangerous time we live in. You never know when the next bomb might go off."

The Porsche motor ticked over quietly as Ryder watched her walk away across the cobblestone street with long, no-nonsense strides. She didn't look back.

200

Chapter XXIX

It was a crisp, windy evening, so Ryder decided to walk. He did some of his best thinking on his feet. Besides, it had rained and the air smelled clean. Von Friedenthal had introduced him to walking, and there was something pleasantly hypnotic about it, once you got into a rhythm and really started moving out.

He was wearing his Harris tweed jacket, but no topcoat. Although it was December, he'd spent enough time in Europe to know the climate was temperate and far different from the violent seasonal changes of the northeastern United States where he'd grown up.

From the hotel steps, he looked across to where the Porsche waited, red satin skin gleaming in the lights of the hotel. The Porsche was in the first parking slot directly across from the hotel entrance for two reasons. One, the doorman could keep an eye on it and two, the car was a testimony to the type of guest who frequented the hotel.

Passing the Dresdner Bank, he looked at the Mengler building across the street. It was the tallest structure in Heidelberg and passed as the town's one and only skyscraper. He could see the lights from the Chinese restaurant on the second floor.

That damn Martin. Ryder nodded to himself. The man never forgot anything. He knew that Ryder was a Scotch whiskey drinker. Martin drank Scotch himself, but he also knew that, on special occasions, Ryder enjoyed a martini.

On one of John's early visits to Heidelberg, Martin suggested that there was an excellent Chinese restaurant in town and had let nature take its course. Ryder thought it a fine idea and had asked the von Friedenthals to be his guests that evening for a Chinese dinner.

It was with a certain air of anticipation that Martin watched the waiter place the cocktail in front of Ryder. He could barely sit still as Ryder raised the glass, said "Cheers!" and took his first swallow.

The "what the hell?" was quickly followed by an apology to Liesel. Ryder could tell by her smile that Martin had told her to expect something unusual if John should happen to order a martini.

"You knew, didn't you?" said Ryder with a grimace. "You rotten old man."

"There was a possibility," admitted Martin.

Much to the delight of both von Friedenthals, Ryder took a second taste. His expression and the ensuing "Whaa!" brought tears to Martin's eyes and giggles from Liesel. It also brought disapproving glances from several of the more staid diners. The waiter appeared.

"Is everything all right?"

"You're kidding."

"No, sir."

"You call this a martini?"

"Yes, sir. A martini cocktail—just like you ordered."

"No, it's not."

"I have been serving these drinks for years. No one has ever complained before."

"They were probably too stunned."

"One minute, sir. I will call the manager."

The manager came and so did a charming Oriental lady, who was either the owner or his wife—Ryder never did get it straight. His German was adequate, theirs was not.

They tried their very best, they really did. After all, Professor Doctor von Friedenthal was a famous man and a valued guest. The management wasn't too sure about Ryder.

He seemed to have some strange ideas about making martinis. However, after much smiling and nodding, and close attention to his instructions, the waiter again placed a martini cocktail in front of Ryder.

"Compliments of the house, sir."

"Thank you."

The eternal optimist raised his glass to the von Friedenthals, said "Cheers!" and took a long sip.

"Ah-ha!"

The waiter was pleased. "Are you ready to order now?"

While they waited to be served, Ryder looked out of the window. It had been raining and several umbrellas were waiting at the corner for the next streetcar. He could see Martin's smiling reflection in the glass.

Ryder mentally paraphrased Rafael Sabatini. What was more fitting in a mad world, than to be seated in a Chinese restaurant in Germany, served by an Italian waiter while listening to Elvis background music, and drinking a martini made with sweet vermouth? The second cocktail was exactly like the first.

Every time Ryder was in Heidelberg, he always found an excuse to go to the Chinese restaurant. They knew him now and a martini would be placed in front of him as a matter of course. Smiling and nodding in agreement, they still made their martinis with sweet vermouth.

Ryder knew that if right now, tonight, he crossed the street and climbed the stairs, it would happen again. There are some things that never change.

He turned right at Bismarckplatz and started down the Hauptstrasse, the main street of Heidelberg. Except for delivery trucks and vans, the street had been closed to traffic. The trolley tracks has been pulled up and the road resurfaced, pedestrians only.

He felt uneasy. The bright, festive Christmas decorations along the street and in the store windows contrasted sharply with the sense of evil that was always with him now. Sometimes it was so bad he thought he could almost hear voices—one voice in particular. Ryder fervently hoped it was only his newly heightened awareness and not something else.

There were couples out strolling and window shopping. Farther down the Hauptstrasse, the people were younger. Heidelberg is a university town and the streets were full of students. No one paid much attention to him, except for a speculative glance or two from some of the girls. It was obvious that he wasn't one of the enemy—he wasn't a parent or the police.

He crossed the street and cut through the parking lot between the Holy Ghost Church and the Town Hall. Once a week there was a farmer's market in the lot, but tonight it was full of cars.

Heidelberg, like so many other old European cities, had lost the battle to the automobile. Even at night, parking spaces were at a premium. The lot was full and the nearby streets had cars, bumper to bumper, parked half on the sidewalk so those who were still looking could squeeze by.

James L Diffin

Behind the Rathaus, on one of the narrow side streets that led down to the Neckar River and the Old Bridge, was the place Ryder was looking for—Charly's Pub. It was a Gasthaus that had made an attempt to look English and failed.

As Ryder entered, faces turned to look at him. He was judged safe and the antennae were put away for the moment. It was still early and the place was less than half full.

To the right of the door, was the bar. The rest of the room was filled with tables, each with a light hanging over it. There were English hunting prints on the walls and mirrors with *Dewars* and *White Horse* printed on them.

At the bar, Ryder asked for a beer and when it came he took a table by the window. Damn, the stuff was good and bore little resemblance to the liquid brewed in the States.

He looked around the room. There were some students and some who made their living from students. The students, in their jeans and army surplus jackets, looked like GI's and a couple of GI's, who had taken the trouble to learn a little German, looked like students. There were two men in civilian clothes at the end of the bar who had to be the police. The question was— whose?

At a table in the middle of the room, two American soldiers were putting the make on a couple of German girls. The guys were giving it the hard sell, but their German wasn't that good and, if what Ryder overheard was an indication, they weren't going to score. The girls giggled. They would stay only as long as the beer kept coming.

At the table next to his, a chess game was in progress. The player on Ryder's side of the table was getting his clock cleaned. The two played quickly, slamming the pieces down or using them to knock the captured chess figures from the board.

They played chess like Germans play *skat,* the national card game. That game involved slamming the table as hard as possible with your fist when playing a card and arguing at the top of your voice after every game.

"*Scheisse!*" With a violent gesture, the losing player scattered chess pieces across the table. Several fell on the floor. He wouldn't surrender, but played on to the bitter end, still hoping for a miracle. It didn't help matters any that his opponent was methodically capturing one piece after another, instead of going for the checkmate.

204

Turning sideways in his chair so he could get his hand into skintight jeans, the loser pulled a crumpled twenty mark bill from his pocket and threw it on the table. He saw Ryder's smile.

"What are you laughing at?" he demanded. "Think you can do better?"

"Perhaps."

"What?"

Ryder wanted to talk with some students, but this wasn't what he had in mind. He continued to look across the room toward the bar, ignoring the boy.

"Listen, shithead, I'm talking to you."

Ryder raised an eyebrow, but said nothing.

"*Verdammt*! That does it!" The boy shoved the table back and jumped to his feet. "Don't you ignore me!"

"All right, then. Go away."

The boy couldn't believe what he was hearing.

"Nobody speaks to me like that, not even my own father. Besides, you talk funny. You an American?"

Ryder didn't answer.

The boy got louder. "I might have known it, a stinking *Ami*!"

The other patrons were watching and the bartender-owner was getting nervous. He sighed as he raised a hinged section at the end of the bar. Trouble, he thought, and it wasn't even Saturday. That damn Stefan.

"What's the problem here?" he asked, leaning heavy hands on the table.

"The only problem I have," said Ryder, "is that my glass is empty. I can't speak for Junior, here."

The boy made a move, but was stopped by a brawny arm. "Not in here, Stefan," said the bartender.

"Come outside, *Scheisskerl!*," yelled the boy.

"I'm not going anywhere with you."

The bartender addressed the other student at the table. "What started all this?"

The student grinned and pointed to Ryder. "He won't talk to Stefan."

"That's it?" asked the bartender, relieved. "There's not going to be any trouble?"

Ryder raised his glass. "Only if I don't get some more of this fine beer."

Ryder couldn't have appeared more relaxed. The bartender was reassured. "At once," he said, flicking a cloth over the table with a practiced motion.

Stefan stood, his hands clenching and unclenching. He still wanted to fight, but there was something disturbing about the American. He was too calm. Stefan slumped back down in his seat. The last time he had gotten into trouble, he hadn't been allowed in Charly's until the fall term. It was the best bar in town. All the guys came here.

"You're still a shithead."

"How about a game?" the other student asked Ryder. "You do play chess, don't you?"

"I play."

"Well, how about it?"

The bartender was back with Ryder's beer. "If you make any trouble, Stefan, it will be the last time you come into my place. You understand? The last time."

Stefan slouched in his chair.

Ryder figured that since he had come this far, he might as well keep on with it. By now everyone must be wondering what a lone American was doing in a student hangout. He wasn't a tourist, he wasn't military, and he wasn't local.

"It wouldn't be fair."

"Why?" asked the student. "Don't you know the moves?"

"I make my living playing chess," said Ryder, remembering how the student had tortured Stefan. "You wouldn't enjoy it."

"That's nice," said the student, who didn't believe a word. "Why don't you try me?" He began setting up the pieces. "You can even play white."

The student had a sideline at school—playing chess for money. Stefan's twenty marks had already disappeared from the table. The student normally spotted the first move. He seldom lost and that, almost always, was deliberate. It kept the suckers coming back for more. Besides, he was thinking of trading his Alfa Romeo in on a new BMW. "By the way, how much are we playing for?"

"You play for money?" Ryder acted shocked.

"Just a few marks. Puts spice into the game. Anyway, you said you made your living playing chess."

Smiling to himself, Ryder shook his head. Hustlers, regardless of nationality or race, were the same the world over. There probably wasn't a game going where someone wasn't making a buck, peso, or kopek out of it.

When Ryder had first moved to New York City, fresh from his hitch in the Navy, and eager to try college, he'd found a Checkers and Chess Club on the second floor of a seedy building on 42nd Street. It wasn't really a club, but that's what they called it. You paid a dollar to get in.

In one large, dingy room, that might once have been painted yellow, with strips of gray paint hanging from the ceiling, were three long rows of tables. Ancient wooden checker and chess pieces were set up on oilskin fields. It was a horrible, smelly place, with dirty, nicotine-stained ashtrays, but Ryder was intrigued—New York, the big time.

According to the rules of the club, you rented the board and the pieces on time, and the loser of the game paid. Ryder played several men who were hanging around. He won easily.

Then he went gunning for the owner of the place, a toothpick-in-the-corner-of-the-mouth, gray little man with disillusioned eyes and bad breath. Ryder didn't know it, but he'd just met his first professional hustler.

The gray little man inquired in a dusty voice if this was Ryder's first trip to New York. Reluctantly, he allowed Ryder to talk him into playing a game. When Ryder left that day, he hadn't won, but he had the feeling he should have. He paid for the time and that was it.

He was back the next day and he paid again. The third day, with the hook well set, the question of playing for money came up. Ryder was never quite sure how it happened, but it was a great idea. Imagine, playing chess for money! Why not? He was just getting hot. Didn't he win a game yesterday and again today?

The hook had such a gentle barb that Ryder never felt it until he couldn't pay his rent at the end of the month. Where the hell had his money gone? But he didn't care, he was obsessed. He had to beat that gray little man who drove him to distraction with those rubbery lips working that toothpick from one side to the other.

Every day, when the gray little man came to unlock the club, Ryder was waiting. Finally, he learned. He got thrown out of his room and he half starved to death, but he learned.

James L Diffin

Now he remembered the gray little man with fondness. After he'd started playing serious chess, he went looking for revenge. The club was padlocked. Downstairs, where they sold adult videos, someone said they thought the guy who rented the room upstairs had died.

"Well, how about it?" the student asked again. He had sized Ryder up. No rings or jewelry that he could see, but the man had a deep tan and wore clothes of good quality.

"A hundred marks too steep for you?"

"You want to play me for a hundred marks when I told you I make my living from this game?"

"Sure, man." The student was amused. His chess prowess was well known around the University. When he had said "A hundred marks," those at nearby tables, who had been watching, smiled. That ought to take care of the "I've warned you twice."

"Two hundred," said the student in a loud voice, attracting attention from nearby tables.

"Can you afford it?"

"Don't worry about me,"—the student grinned—"just take care of yourself."

Ryder moved over to the table and turned the board around so that the student had the white pieces. It wouldn't be quite the same without the toothpick.

Stefan couldn't contain himself. "Now you're going to get it, shithead. Give it to him, Ulli!"

Chapter XXX

Ulli slammed the pawn down on queen four, only it wasn't queen four at all, but the palm of Ryder's hand. Ulli watched in disbelief, as Ryder's hand closed over the pawn and Ulli's fingers. He tried to pull his hand back, but nothing happened. He gave a good yank. The hand on queen four didn't budge, neither did Ulli's fingers. He looked at Ryder. No one in the room, including Stefan, who had pulled up a chair to watch, had seen Ryder move.

"No, Ulli," said Ryder, "not with me. Don't do that again. When you play this game, treat the pieces with respect."

Ryder released Ulli's fingers and signaled the bartender for another beer. Charly's Pub was starting to fill up and there were whispered conversations about Ulli's two hundred mark game.

Ryder noticed that the two German girls who had been drinking with the GI's were gone and the soldiers were quietly getting sloshed, though that's not the story they would tell.

"You guys wouldn't believe the two chicks me and ol' Ralph picked up last night. Some of that real hot German stuff, let me tell you. No, I ain't pimpin' for you guys, so don't ask me where it was. Go find your own. Now, like I was saying, they had this great pad, see. Mattresses and pillows all over the floor. You know, things like that. When we turned out the lights, why man, she damn near bucked me clean off. Four of us crawlin' around in the dark, all naked. Almost nailed my buddy one time. I tell you, it was almost more'n me and ol' Ralph could handle. Now ain't that right, Ralph?"

Ulli put the pawn down carefully on queen four. He was beginning to suspect that he was playing a weight lifter and not someone who said he played chess.

Ryder also played pawn to queen four.

In short order, Ulli was in trouble. The average chess player, who sets up the board to play the moves out of the Sunday newspaper, solves the mate-in-three problems, and keeps a couple of chess books gathering dust on the shelf, nurtures the delusion that, given the chance, he could stay with the big boys. Simple. One way was to trade off. Force the exchange. He might go, but not until well into the end game. And who knows? He might get lucky.

It doesn't work like that, not even for the hustlers. The cute little coffeehouse opening swindles and traps are seldom successful in catching real bears.

By the tenth move Ulli was already teetering and two moves later he lost the first move tempo. He'd started playing with one arm thrown carelessly over the back of his chair. Now, the game had his full attention. It was impossible that he could be in trouble after so few moves, but he was. He sat, head in hands, and watched as Ryder kept right on with his development, ignoring Ulli's offers to exchange pieces.

The beginning of the end came with a simple pawn move, challenging Ulli's control of the center. After that, things came unstuck in a hurry. He discovered that if he took the pawn, he was in trouble and, if he didn't, he was in worse trouble.

There was also long-range pressure on his king's side, so he castled long. It didn't help. Two hundred marks, he thought. At ten or twenty marks a game, that was a couple of good nights' work. Charly's Pub had suddenly gotten warm and Ulli was sweating. His chair felt hard as hell. Ulli looked across the table. With both elbows on the table and his hands around his beer glass, Ryder didn't seem to be paying that much attention to the game. He must have been, however, because the moment Ulli let go of a piece, Ryder made his own move. Ulli was in a temper, but didn't dare show it. Instead, he stared holes in the board, frantically searching for possibilities, while that stupid guy just smiled, looked around the room, and drank beer.

Every time Ulli captured a piece, there was another one to take its place. It was called a four knights game, but as far as Ulli was concerned, all four knights had belonged to the other fellow.

Ryder moved his one remaining knight. "Checkmate."

Ulli looked at the board, then at Ryder. "Another game."

"I think not."

"Another game—this time for five hundred marks."

The crowd that had gathered around began to drift away. There were better things to do. Ulli had come a cropper, was all. Couldn't happen to a nicer guy.

"I haven't seen the two hundred marks yet."

Ulli threw his wallet down on the table and dug into its contents. "Here—two hundred marks," he said tossing the money on the chessboard. "We play another game."

Ryder picked up the crumpled bills. He counted the money, stacked it and placed it in front of Stefan, who was still staring at the board.

"Take it, it's yours. Maybe it will make up for some of the money you've lost. In the future, try not to bet on games you know little about."

"How come you're so smart?"

"I'm not. It cost me a lot more than this to learn my lesson and it took a lot longer."

Stefan hesitated, then picked up the money. "I suppose I should say thank you."

Ryder almost smiled. "Don't say something you'll be sorry for."

Without another word, Stefan pocketed the money and left.

"Five hundred marks."

Ryder looked at Ulli. "You still here?"

"Five hundred marks." Ulli was setting up the pieces again. "I'm ready for you now."

Ryder caught the eye of the bartender, raised his glass and looked around the room for Fräulein Grimm. He thought he'd caught a glimpse of her at the bar during the chess game. Now, she didn't seem to be there.

While he was scanning the room, a man had taken Stefan's place. He had a reddish-brown beard and a white scarf tied around his neck.

"Go ahead and play him," said the beard.

"And who might you be?"

"Play," repeated the beard.

"Why?"

"Because I said so, that's why."

"Not good enough."

"Listen," said the beard, reaching for Ryder, "you do wha—" The words stopped with a click.

Ryder's hand was beneath the reaching grasp to close around the woolen scarf. The click was the sound of the beard's teeth closing when his chin hit the top of the table. His whiskers did little to cushion the blow.

The beard first tried to sit up and then, when that didn't work, to stand. His chin remained firmly anchored to the table. His fingers fumbled under the table to where Ryder held the scarf. It didn't help. He sat, bent over, with his face about three inches from the chessboard.

The bartender set Ryder's beer down on the table. "What's the matter with him?"

"Don't ask me," said Ulli, his eyes wide. "Ask him."

The bartender shook his head and walked away.

Still holding the scarf, Ryder took a long drink of beer. He'd wanted to attract someone's attention and he had. Earlier, he'd seen the beard talking with Fräulein Grimm at the bar. Evidently, someone wanted Ryder to stay. He put down his beer.

"If I let you go, do you think you could mind your own business?"

Breathing noisily, the man looked at Ryder with moisture-filled eyes. He blinked and two fat tears slid down his cheeks to join the others that glistened on his beard.

"I take it that means yes."

The man blinked again.

"Good." Ryder released the scarf and wiped his hand on his pants leg. "You really ought to wash that thing."

The man left the Gasthaus rubbing the back of his neck.

Ryder turned back to Ulli. "Now, what about you?"

Ulli was pale but persistent, "You must play me for five hundred marks."

"Don't be silly, I don't have to play you at all, much less for five hundred marks." Ryder glanced around the room.

"Tell you what. I seem to have some time, so we'll play again. To make it interesting, I'll give you a spot."

"I don't want a spot."

"First of all, you'll play white again."

"Five hundred marks," chanted Ulli.

"Do all you students have one-track minds?"

Remembering the bearded man with the scarf, Ulli didn't push it. "How'd you know I was a student?"

"As I was saying, you'll play white. I imagine you're the kind of guy who likes to make it look good by spotting a rook, so we'll do that, too." John took the queen's rook and set it to one side.

Ulli couldn't help himself. "A thousand marks."

"Where does a student get off having that kind of money?"

Ulli looked toward the Gasthaus door where the bearded student had disappeared and didn't answer.

"Now—we'll take off the queen, as well."

"Not even Professor von Friedenthal would do that," sputtered Ulli.

"You're right. Martin would probably throw in the other rook, too."

"You know Professor von Friedenthal?" It was like knowing God.

"Yes, and if he ever heard of what I was up to, he'd never forgive me. Tell you what—win or lose, you keep your money. If I lose, I'll pay you fifty thousand marks."

"You insult me."

"Don't be silly, Ulli. A hustler can't afford it."

Ulli looked at the smiling turn in the corner of Ryder's mouth. When Ulli won this game, his reputation would be made. In the telling, of course, there would be no need to mention the queen and rook advantage. He might drop around to the BMW showroom tomorrow and pick up a color chart. He favored silver.

Ulli turned to call a couple of the guys. A little moral support couldn't hurt. He knew he wasn't popular, but the guys would take his side any day.

"No,"—Ryder stopped him—"this is between you and me." Ryder had seen that Fräulein Grimm was back. A crowd around the table would make it impossible to keep track of her.

Ulli almost made the mistake of slamming the pawn down again, when he noticed Ryder's cocked eyebrow. "What's your name, anyhow?"

"John Ryder."

"The American grand master?"

"Yes."

"But why didn't you say so?"

"Don't be dense. I told you I played chess for a living and you chose not to believe me. You were too delighted with the idea that you had a live one on the hook to care what my name was."

"But I just read in the newspaper that you were in the hospital in critical condition. You were in that bombing at Campbell Barracks. What are you doing here?"

"Drinking beer. Are you going to play that pawn or not?"

"What?" Ulli looked blankly at the pawn in his hand.

"They said you were dying."

"Play the pawn."

With the advantage of a queen, rook, and first move, Ulli put the pawn down gently on queen four. He could afford to be kind. What did he have to fear? The greatest chess player in the world couldn't give those odds and expect to win.

Ulli decided to take his time and enjoy himself. This was going to be fun. With his crushing superiority, he'd bring out his pieces, sticking to the tried and true. This was no time to get cute. He wouldn't rush things.

Ulli didn't care if John Ryder *was* a grand master—he was going to take control of the center and squeeze that bastard until the blood ran.

His development went off without a hitch. He had pawns at both king and queen four, knights and bishops well posted, he'd castled, and his rooks were strong at king and queen one. He was ready.

On the other side of the board, Ryder had chosen a passive development. He was weak in the center with both king and queen pawns on the third rank. He had fianchettoed both bishops and castled. His king's knight was at king two, the queen's knight was not developed. The queen and queen's rook were missing. White's position was overwhelming.

Now that he thought about it, Ulli decided to go ahead and order that silver beauty tomorrow. With the extra money, he would get the red leather interior. It would look fantastic with silver. While he was at it, he might as well get those special aluminum rims and Dunlops—really dress it up.

Ulli was astounded by Ryder's apparent lack of concern. The American played almost without looking at the board, as if he had done this a thousand times. He seemed more interested in the room, crowded now with people coming and going, constantly milling around. The loud voices contrasted with the whispered proposals, for and of the flesh.

"Forty marks an ounce? You're crazy. Only last week I paid—" "So I told my old man, if he wanted me to take the exams, he had to get off my back—" "Then she tells me she's pregnant...tries to hang me with that—" "Listen, you put straight pipes on that bike and the cops are going to—"

Ulli savored the moment. He was ready for the big push—an all-out attack on the queen side, where the black pieces without the queen and rook were helpless. Fifty thousand marks! Ulli could feel the padded leather steering wheel.

Hold it, he thought. He'd made that mistake before. First a probe with a knight, just to make sure. It looked too easy.

The knight beat a hasty retreat. All right, then—he would double his rooks behind a pawn push and smash through. Ulli was going to run the king right off the board. Now for the big squeeze.

It was like squeezing water. Ulli pushed his pawns, only to have them interlocked with Ryder's so he couldn't move forward or capture. Ryder had countered the attempted exchange that would free the board. Ulli found his doubled rooks, the most powerful combination on the board, useless behind a wall of his own pawns on the queen side—a wall that couldn't move.

A minor delay. Recalling the Maginot Line from the Second World War, Ulli would take a leaf from history and flank Ryder's defenses. Instead of overrunning Belgium, he would smash through the lines at the center of the board.

This time, Ulli broke through, but those two undeveloped enemy knights, that he hadn't thought much about, were now loose behind his own lines. First, the knights sneaked in and then, the bishops. Ulli got Ryder's one remaining rook, but it cost him a bishop, a knight, and two pawns.

Sharp exchanges followed quickly. Ulli pushed hard, but the exchanges were made only when Ryder was ready. Ulli was one move away from the game-breaking play, when he fell into a three-way fork. Not only was he in check by Ryder's knight, but he also had a rook and his queen on the hook. Ulli braced himself.

He couldn't believe it. After moving his king out of check, Ryder ignored the queen and rook, and made an entirely different move. After a moment of hysterical relief, Ulli saw why.

Not only were his queen and rook still in danger, but Ryder's last move again threatened Ulli's king. How the hell had he gotten into this? He'd put out one fire, only to have it break out someplace else. He didn't understand how Ryder did it. The man didn't have that much material left, but what he did have was lethal.

End game. It was down to a knight and a bishop against Ulli's bishop and his precious queen. At least he'd saved that. It was more than enough. The board was wide open and Ulli set off to chase the black king. The more Ulli pursued the king, the better he liked it. Just like old times.

Check after check brought Ryder's king across the board to where the white king waited. Every so often, the queen check would be blocked by the intervention of a bishop or pawn but, in the end, the black king was there, on bishop eight. It had traveled completely across the board.

At last, thought Ulli. Now that he had Ryder cornered, he could bring his bishop into action for the final mate.

"Check," said Ulli.

Ryder countered the move by promoting one of his last two pawns to the eighth rank, interposing it between the white queen and his king.

"Queen, please," said Ryder.

The move not only blocked the check, but pinned Ulli's queen against his own king, forcing a trade-off.

"It's all over, Ulli—the rest is academic. You can't free your bishop soon enough to stop my other pawn from queening."

Ulli sat staring at the board. There had to be a way, there just had to. Finally, he looked up at Ryder with questioning eyes.

Ryder pushed his chair back. "I must go."

"You can't," pleaded Ulli. "We play for anything you want, but don't go."

Ryder had seen Fraülein Grimm leave and watched her, through the window, walking toward the corner.

Ryder tossed a five mark coin on the table. "Sorry, old man, there's a lady I must speak to."

As Ryder stood up, Ulli grabbed his arm. "I won't let you go."

Ryder's hand slapped down on Ulli's wrist and squeezed. Ulli gasped with pain.

"You've made two mistakes tonight," said Ryder, "don't make a third. If you would take the time, you have the makings of a first-rate player. Try it. You might surprise yourself."

Fräulein Grimm had already turned the corner when Ryder spoke. "I'll see you home."

Taken by surprise, she stopped in her tracks with a gasp of fright.

"Guilty conscience?" asked Ryder.

"No, you startled me, that's all," she said. "I'm not used to people sneaking up behind me in the dark." She started walking again.

"I saw you leaving Charly's Pub and thought I should see you home."

"That's very gallant of you, Herr Ryder, but I have been walking these streets—alone—for quite some time. It's perfectly safe—this isn't America."

"You're so right," said Ryder. "In America, we haven't fully acquired your taste for car bombings."

"My taste? What do you mean?"

"Whatever you want."

Chin down, hands in her pockets, Fräulein Grimm continued up the street toward the Hauptstrasse. She glanced at Ryder.

"No coat, Herr Ryder? It's chilly tonight. You'll catch your death." Her voice was expressionless. "I thought you were still playing chess. I find it difficult to believe that a man of your reputation would stoop to playing chess with a student. Such a waste of time."

"I found the evening most revealing, Fräulein Grimm. You never know what you're going to find in a place like Charly's and I enjoy playing the game with almost anyone. That's one of the attractions of chess."

"Why are you here tonight? The questions you want answered have nothing to do with chess, Herr Ryder, but with a far more dangerous game. It could prove fatal."

"Is that a warning?"

"Oh, no, Herr Ryder, you misunderstand. I'm a student. How should I know about such things? It's only that you almost died once. I would think you'd be more careful and not go looking for more trouble. Like tonight—you, a well-known man, hanging around a student bar. It makes people wonder."

"No one knew or cared who I was. Well, almost no one, but thank you for your concern."

They walked a few more steps in silence before she spoke again. "Did you get your answers?"

"Perhaps—although the people in Charly's Pub weren't exactly communicative."

"Maybe it's the way you act, Herr Ryder, always so sure of yourself. As you Americans would say—it rubs people the wrong way."

"I seemed to have rubbed one of your friends the wrong way."

"I have many friends."

"I bet you do—like the guy with a full beard and an urgent need for a bath. I saw you talking to him at the bar."

"It's entirely possible, Herr Ryder. I talk to many people, but your description doesn't bring anyone in particular to mind. As I said, I've many friends."

"Anyone with a knowledge of explosives?"

"If I did, I wouldn't talk about it."

"Would you talk about kidnapping?"

She stopped and turned to face him. "That's enough, Herr Ryder. I've worked for the von Friedenthals for over two years and Karen and Silka are like little sisters to me. They'll come to no harm."

"I hope you know what you're talking about."

"The letter was signed 'Tomorrow's Children,' was it not? Does that sound like someone who hurts children?"

"It doesn't mean a thing. Besides, kidnapping hurts, Fräulein Grimm. It's something those little girls will never forget. And how do you know who signed the letter?"

"Professor von Friedenthal told me." She started to cross the Hauptstrasse and spoke over her shoulder. "Goodnight, Herr Ryder. I cannot stand around talking on street corners all night. I must get up early tomorrow morning."

"Along with Tomorrow's Children?" asked Ryder, crossing the street after her. "Don't give it a thought. I've come this far, I'll see you the rest of the way home."

She stopped in the middle of the deserted street. "You must stop following me." She had grown increasingly agitated. "You must leave me alone."

From one of the side streets, down by the river, a motorcycle started up, revving motor loud in the night. The presence of evil stirred in Ryder's mind. At the sound of the motor, Fräulein Grimm turned the other way and went loping off down a wide cobblestone street, almost at a run.

"You leave me alone now," she said to Ryder, who was moving easily at her side.

"Nothing like a brisk stroll before bedtime." The sense of evil was overwhelming and Ryder's eyes searched the darkened windows and doorways.

218

Fräulein Grimm stopped to confront him, but before she could say anything, a motorcycle shot out of a side street, crossed the Hauptstrasse and headed directly toward them. Fräulein Grimm started to run.

There was no time for her now. The way the bike was coming at Ryder left no doubt in his mind. There were two of them, the driver and the person sitting behind him. They wore space-age helmets with dark visors, but what interested him the most was the object in the passenger's hands—it looked like an automatic weapon.

Ten yards away, the driver turned the bike. Ryder saw he had been right. The short, ugly machine pistol glistened with dark intent in the light from the street lamps. It was one of those Polish jobs that fired an incredible number of rounds a minute from an oversized clip as large as the weapon itself.

As soon as the bike changed direction, Ryder moved. There were several trees that had survived modernization, growing out of the cobblestones. When the biker made his pass and the bullets started to fly, a tree was between Ryder and the gunman. There was a shower of bark as the rounds buried themselves in the wood.

When the biker wheeled for another pass, Ryder was behind the next tree, working his way back down the street. The bike roared by, the bullets flew and Ryder was off and running again.

Close to the corner of the Hauptstrasse was a statue. An iron fence surrounded it, protecting it from cars and tour buses. Ryder dashed across the last open space, hurdled the fence, and took cover behind the monument. The bike headed toward him.

Ryder peered around the stone. If the bike stopped to discharge its passenger, he had to be ready. It was immediately apparent that the biker had no intention of closing with Ryder.

Instead, he circled the monument, just outside the metal fence, like a band of rampaging Indians around a wagon train. As fast as the bike went, Ryder kept pace, always keeping the monument between them.

It was a classic stalemate. They couldn't get to Ryder and, at the moment, he couldn't get to them.

Skidding wildly on the cobblestones, the biker had his hands full, while his passenger fired relentlessly at the monument. Slugs sparked the granite, then went whining off into the night.

James L Diffin

The biker made one last pass, the passenger emptied the clip, and the two went tearing off along the Hauptstrasse.

As Ryder stepped down from the monument and vaulted the fence, he saw the bike turn left at the Holy Ghost Church. He could hear the biker going up through gears as he reached the road down by the Neckar. From the sound, they were headed upriver, toward Neckargemünd.

Ryder looked for Fräulein Grimm, but she was gone. The street was empty. No lights had come on in the surrounding buildings. Nothing moved. The evil presence that lived in his mind had retreated. Then, in the distance, he heard the faint ta-tooing of a police car.

Chapter XXXI

Andrew Hall's room, like Ryder's, was a spacious, high-ceilinged square, with an adjoining bathroom nearly as large. Although no one spoke of it, the hotel was proud of the fact that Hitler used to stay there whenever he was in town. For some, the old days weren't far from the surface.

"I know it's late," said Ryder, "but we have to talk."

"Come in—I've been expecting you." Hall was wearing a silk dressing gown over his shirt and trousers. "What can I do for you?"

"I want you and Katherine to leave."

Hall didn't seem overly concerned, as he closed the door. He indicated a chair and returned to his own. The adjacent end table held an ashtray with a lighted cigar. Hall put a marker in his book and placed it on the table.

"Do I have time to pack or is the hotel on fire?"

"They made a try for me tonight. It wasn't an accident; they set me up and came looking for me."

"And?"

"As you can see, they didn't get me."

"I should certainly hope not."

"It got a little tight. No one ever shot at me with a machine pistol before."

"Did you hurt anyone?"

"No, they got away. Fräulein Grimm was with me—part of the time."

"The student who works for the von Friedenthals?"

"She was in the Gasthaus tonight. I was playing chess and only got to talk with her afterward, outside, on the street. She was with me when the shooting started."

"Think she may have something to do with this?"

"I'm not sure, but at the moment she's the only lead I have. We're wasting time."

"Do I have time to pack?"

"Let the hotel take care of it."

Hall flicked the ash from his cigar. "You're serious. Need I remind you that I have been looking after things for quite some number of years now."

"That may be true, but I can't afford to take a chance. As long as you and Katherine are here, I'm vulnerable. They know who I am now and, if Fräulein Grimm is mixed up in this, what I'm after."

"Are you referring to Martin von Friedenthal's children or are you planning an act of vengeance?"

"Not vengeance—justice, but only after Karen and Silka are safe."

Hall studied Ryder for a long moment, then put down his cigar and picked up the telephone. He spoke quietly, then hung up.

"My plane will be ready to leave as soon as we get there. I think you are overreacting but, since you are new at this, I'll humor you."

"Thanks." Ryder smiled wryly. "We've been seen together, and both of you have been to Martin's house. People talk. If they know me, they know about you." Ryder stood up.

"Go back to England, Andrew, and take your daughter with you. Tomorrow may be too late. I'll go now and tell her."

Hall took one look at Ryder's face and nodded.

Katherine opened the door on the second knock. She was wearing a long white nightgown with matching robe. "If you're going to stand there and stare, I'm closing the door."

"I've just come from your father's room."

"Making the rounds, are we? Oh, all right, come in. This had better be important."

"You're leaving."

Katherine folded her robe around her, sat on the side of the bed, and crossed her legs. "Oh?"

"Start dressing; I'll get the car. Don't bother to pack."

"Quite the efficient little busybody, aren't we. Are we eloping or is this just a sudden brainstorm?"

"There's not much time. Andrew will be ready in fifteen minutes. You are both going back to England."

Katherine sat watching the slipper on one lazily swinging foot.

"I suppose I'm doing this badly?" said Ryder.

"I would say that you were," she agreed.

"Sorry—they tried to kill me tonight. I can deal with that, but not if I have to worry about you."

"I am my father's daughter."

"Yes, I know, but there's no magic that I know of, even for a Druid priestess, that can stop a bullet."

Katherine had spoken before she'd really heard Ryder's words.

"Who tried to kill you? Oh, John..." She looked at him, then smiled. "I'm sorry, but all this sounds so melodramatic. You know, women and children to the lifeboats—"

"This isn't a game. These people, whoever they are, mean business. They proved it tonight." Briefly, he told her what had happened. "I can't watch over you and find Martin's children."

She rose and came to stand in front of him. "Do I mean that much to you?"

Ryder put his hands on her waist. Their eyes met. Then he drew her close and kissed her. She was a sleep-warm, silky softness.

With her arms around his neck, Katherine returned his kiss. Her mouth opened to him and Ryder felt the almost imperceptible thrust of her hips—the ageless flaring of loins, the readying.

He didn't know who broke the embrace.

"You're not well," she said, touching his brow. "There is moisture on your forehead." She rested her head against his chest. Katherine seemed to be generating a lot of body heat. "I'm sorry." She stepped back and looked up at him. "How can I undo a thousand years?"

"I don't know, but I'm ready to kick Arthur and Merlin right in the slats."

"If only you didn't have The Gift."

"To hell with the damned Gift! You know...I..."

"Yes, we both know. It may be difficult for you to believe, but this is just as hard for me." She smiled suddenly and touched him with a soft caress. "The only difference is mine doesn't show."

"Sorry—"

"Don't be. And don't give me the bit about liberated womanhood or I'll start screaming. How's that for a Druid priestess? Tradition, my foot." Katherine made a face and spoke in a hollow voice. "The code—is—inviolable!"

Ryder had to smile. "Jesus—you sound just like Andrew."

"That's better." She kissed his hands, first one, then the other, looking into his eyes all the while. Truth? Beauty? Love? Old-fashioned words for old-fashioned values. Silly, inconvenient concepts in a computerized, throwaway world.

"You know, if you don't marry, it will be the end of Merlin's line—the end of everything."

Katherine's voice was firm. "So be it."

"You'll change your mind—you must."

Katherine searched Ryder's face, trying to memorize every feature. "Never!"

"What about Andrew?"

"When the time's right, I'll tell him. If I must live with his code, a code not of my choosing, then he'll have to accept mine."

"You mean that?"

"I never meant anything more in my life. Now, get out of my bedroom and let me get dressed." Katherine held one of John's hands to her cheek. She was smiling, but her eyes were moist.

"Go," she whispered. "Just how much more of this do you think I can stand? Get the hell out of here before I change my mind."

Ryder rose noiselessly and slipped on his shirt and pants. It was after one in the morning and someone was standing in the hall outside his room. German hotels, especially the older ones, have double doors, one inside the other, to provide a degree of soundproofing.

But, even in sleep, he'd heard people passing in the corridor. This was different. Although it wasn't the malevolence he'd felt earlier this evening, he stood carefully to one side as he opened the doors.

"Do you sleep in your clothes?" asked Katherine.

"I thought you'd gone."

"Obviously not."

"Where's Andrew?"

"By now—in England."

With her hands deep in the pockets of her coat, Katherine was staring at Ryder as if she'd never seen him before.

With a glance down the hall in either direction, he took her arm. "I don't know what the devil you're doing, but don't just stand there. Come inside where it's safe until I can get you out of here."

She pulled her arm away. "I've already been through this with father. No one is going to tell me what to do."

"But—"

"Don't waste time!" She looked down at his bare feet. "Finish dressing—I'll wait for you downstairs."

Katherine walked to the elevator, pushed the button, and stood looking back at Ryder until the elevator doors slowly closed, hiding her from view.

Ryder threw up his hands in exasperation, dressed in record time, and was racing for the stairwell almost before the elevator reached the ground floor. There was no one in the lobby, but the front door was just swinging shut. He tossed his key on the reception desk, startling the night man who'd been quietly dozing.

Ryder stood at the top of the hotel steps, looking for Katherine. He saw her at once. She was standing next to the Porsche.

"Do you realize the chance you're taking?"

"The door—please."

He held the car door for Katherine and then came around to the driver's side. As he slid behind the wheel, he began to ask a question.

"Please don't talk—drive!"

"Any place in particular?"

"Yes—"

Following Katherine's curt instructions, Ryder drove through the deserted streets of Heidelberg, crossed the Neckar by way of the Friedrichsbruecke, and headed up one of the steep roads of the Heiligenberg, the Holy Mountain.

Ryder kept the Porsche in second gear. Almost at the top, just past the lookout tower, was a car park.

"Stop here."

"Do you care to tell me what this is all about?"

"No." Katherine opened her door and started walking toward the amphitheater. Ryder had no choice but to follow. She continued past the amphitheater and finally stopped at the ruins of the Monastery of St. Michael. The monastery was at the very top of the mountain.

Katherine looked at Ryder with an unreadable expression before walking away across the worn stones and encroaching grass to an iron gate set in a wall.

"Open it, please."

"You've been here before?"

She didn't answer.

Ryder swung open the protesting gate. "After you."

They were in what had once been a garden, but even in the darkness Ryder could tell that the grasses and growing things were far different from those on the other side of the wall.

"You must shut the gate."

When he turned back to Katherine, she was standing in the center of the garden, facing him. The sky had turned sullen and the clouds were lighted from within by an occasional luminous flash. There was no sound of thunder, only the silence of dark lightning.

Ryder did not know the woman who spoke.

"This garden is sacred. It existed long before those who built the walls, long before the ancient Romans or the still more ancient Celts. It is a place of rites and rituals—ceremonies of death…and of life." She was staring at Ryder, fixing him with those great eyes now turned night-black.

Still watching him, she began to remove her clothes. She didn't tease, she did nothing provocative, she simply undressed. At last, she was naked, her clothing scattered at her feet.

"Now it's your turn."

"It's December—"

"There is no winter here."

Ryder hesitated and, for the first time, Katherine smiled the smile of love. It was a smile without subterfuge, reflecting the pure joy of being, without reservation. He took off his clothes.

She pointed to a large block of stone. "Be seated. There is a throne upon which I would rest."

Only after Ryder took his place, did she move. She stopped before him, close to but not touching him, and Ryder feasted his eyes. She was everything he had imagined and more. There was a scent of spring and of sunshine, but still he made no move to touch her.

"Are you afraid?"

"Everyone I love, dies."

"Your strength?"

"That, too."

"It is of no matter. If I must die, I would die of you," she said, settling her weight feather-light on Ryder's thighs. She took his head between her hands, kissed his lips, and then held him to her.

Ryder kissed first one breast, then the other, and finally lifted his face to Katherine's waiting mouth.

In the beginning, their joining was slight as he stroked her back and hips, marveling at the silken touch of her. He held himself under tight control and Katherine sensed his reluctance. With a savage thrust of her hips, she came down on him full weight.

She winced and gave a soft, high-pitched cry. She remained still, her hands clutching his shoulders. Her brow cleared and the look of pain disappeared. There was pleasure in her voice.

"I have need of you and if the stallion will not take the fence, he must be spurred." With that she raked his back with her fingernails.

Ryder stood up and carried Katherine to where the grass grew thick. There they lay together. He took her in anger and fear—and love.

The night became a place of discovery and rediscovery and of lengths and textures and of smoothly sliding muscles under velvet skin, while overhead the dark lightning flashed.

Katherine was surprisingly strong and when, at long last, Ryder fell back, she stretched full length upon him. There was no place from lip to toe where they did not touch. Katherine's hair had come undone and covered Ryder's face like raven's wings.

"This is our moment, my beloved man," she said, kissing him softly. "No one can ever take this away, no one."

Before Ryder could speak, Katherine put her fingers over his mouth. "Hush, John Ryder. I shall always love you with all that is in me. Be still now and know that it is enough." She passed her hand lightly over his face and gently closed his eyes.

"Sleep, my prince, for we are in the Garden of Paradise, and all things are possible. Sleep in my arms and I shall watch over you."

Ryder fell asleep.

And while he slept, Katherine wept silent tears. One fell on Ryder's chest and she kissed it away.

"Sleep deep, my love. For the first time, my powers fail me. I see nothing ahead. There is only darkness, and I fear you shall never know peace again."

Katherine placed her hand over Ryder's heart and felt it slow as he fell into a still deeper sleep, safe in her arms, while she smiled down on him.

You have taken what was not yours to take. The night may hide you and the power of the garden shield you, but return to the land of men you must. There shall be no redemption.

Chapter XXXII

Clementine wanted to run, so he let her. Ryder had to smile. Giving names to automobiles was like talking baby talk to a pet parakeet. When he'd first seen her, with her flared wheel wells and wide tires, the name had popped into his mind—Clementine—and he remembered the words of the old song, *herring boxes without topses*. The name clearly had nothing to do with the car's sleek potential, it was just that she had those lovely big feet. Jesus, he thought, if anyone knew, they'd put him away.

Just before the Walldorf-Wiesloch Kreuz, Ryder decided to take the Stuttgart autobahn that went past Heilbronn. He laughed out loud as the Porsche leaned into the curve. Since his sixteenth birthday and his first Plymouth, there had been a number of ladies in his life—a Volkswagen named Elsa, a Volvo called Alice and several sports cars with more exotic names.

The cockpit of this beauty was all leather and rich pile. Clementine had more than her share of switches, lights, and dials. She was a four-wheel-drive computer mounted on rubber.

Ryder's eyes flicked restlessly over the gauges—oil pressure normal, rpm steady, no problem up ahead, and nothing in the rearview mirror. The auto was made to be driven at speeds and the steering wheel fit the hand without blocking his view of the instrument panel. The seat was an example of engineering excellence.

It was midmorning on a Tuesday and traffic was light. Ryder glanced in the rearview mirror, remembering another time, when he'd almost jumped out of his skin after such a glance. Suddenly, without warning, a Lamborghini Countach was sitting two meters from his rear bumper. The driver didn't flash his lights or blow the horn, but sat there, rock steady, behind Ryder, who had been doing 125 miles an hour in a 911T Porsche.

When Ryder eased the Porsche over to the right lane, the Countach had flashed by and disappeared up the road with awe-inspiring speed. Ryder wasn't the only fast lumber on the road. After that, he kept an eye on what was going on behind him.

He checked the gauges again. The blue-and-white signs flashed by—Sinsheim, Steinfurt, Bad Rappenau, Kirchhausen. Now he was on the long sweeping curve connecting the autobahn to Würzburg. The road widened into three lanes and the Porsche had more room to do her work. Clementine seemed to be saying "Hurry! Hurry!"

Using all the powers at his command, Ryder refused to think about last night. Instead, he chose to concentrate on his driving. Why torture himself, remembering something he wasn't even sure had happened.

This morning, as usual, he woke at six. His internal clock still thought it was time for his daily training session with Harry Tanaka. Today had been no exception. He'd opened his eyes and sat up in bed with a start.

He was alone in his hotel room with absolutely no memory of how he had gotten there. He dressed and went looking for Katherine. The Porsche was parked in its usual spot. The desk clerk informed him that Miss Hall and her father had checked out the previous evening.

He thought he'd lost it until he'd gone back to his room to shower and change. He flinched when the water hit him. He checked his back in the mirror—there were scratches.

Later, as he was soaping himself, he discovered a purple mark on his chest where no mark had been before. It looked suspiciously like the silhouette of an acorn and, no matter how hard he scrubbed, it wouldn't come off. He knew that Katherine had marked him. He remembered tears.

The Porsche swerved slightly. He'd have to be more careful. He decided to think about something else and settled on Kommissar Brunner.

Ryder's earlier debriefing by the American military authorities was, after all, only a formality. However, this morning, his session with the German Kriminalpolizei had been quite another matter.

While he was in the hotel dining room having breakfast, a uniformed policeman arrived, much to the displeasure of the hotel management. The policeman invited Ryder to stop in at police headquarters just across the plaza, if it would be convenient, to answer a few questions.

He had been ushered into a bare room on the second floor. A large heavyset man rose as Ryder entered the room.

"So glad you could make it. This won't take long. A routine matter, I assure you. I'm Kommissar Brunner. I'm sort of the dogsbody around here.

Please, this seat here. Coffee? No? Don't mind him—he's taking notes. Don't let it concern you. This is just an informal get-together. Smoke? No? I envy you. Now, to the business at hand."

Kommissar Brunner took a seat behind a bare wooden desk. There were no telephones and no papers. "Shocking, isn't it? I mean the bombing and now the von Friedenthal children. I must say you are looking surprisingly fit after what you've been through, the hospital and all. Ah, I almost forgot—would you like an interpreter? It'll only take a moment. No? Good. Your German is excellent. I'm sure we will have no problem."

Kommissar Brunner rattled on. It would be easy, with all the chatter and all the fuss about getting Ryder settled, to underestimate him; that is, if you didn't notice his alert black-button eyes.

"Let me see if I understand you correctly. The reason for your original appearance at the Kaserne was for a squash match. Of course, how stupid of me. Fascinating sport, I'm told. Never had time to play the game, more's the pity."

Slowly and methodically, by the numbers, Kommissar Brunner covered a broad range of subjects—Ryder's relationship with Martin von Friedenthal, how Ryder had first met General Hartley, and how he happened to be at Campbell Barracks when the bomb went off. Nodding his head in agreement, the Kommissar went on.

"You played squash again that evening? Oh—the officer's club. How nice of the General to invite you for a drink. Now, about the unfortunate incident that followed. Any ideas? Did you see or hear anything unusual?"

"Not really."

On it went. The Kommissar was most patient and low key. If it weren't for the eyes that never left Ryder's face, he might have been deceived. They went over the story again. Then the Kommissar branched off into the kidnapping and the letter.

"And how regrettable that you are connected with both affairs. What a dreadful coincidence! Now, just so I understand, please tell me again how you met General Hartley."

Ryder repeated the story word for word.

"Herr Ryder, if I didn't know better, I would say you had rehearsed all this. No? But no one says the same thing exactly the same way every time. Of course, how could I forget? See, I told you I was stupid. A chess grand master never forgets, correct?"

"That's hardly true."

"So, I think that is about all. We will have your statement typed and you can sign it and leave. Sorry about any inconvenience this may have caused, but you understand. Sure you won't have some coffee while you wait?"

"No, thank you."

"Oh, before I forget—just one small matter, Herr Ryder. You know, something to talk about while we wait. It has been reported that you were playing chess in a Gasthaus yesterday evening. Naturally, Herr Ryder, you have every right to do so. But, after you left, there was an unpleasant incident in the vicinity—a shooting—and I thought you might have seen something. No, again? Too bad."

They went over it again and again. Ryder decided that the person who was supposed to be typing his statement had to be the world's slowest typist. Finally, there was a knock at the door. A uniformed man entered and whispered in the Kommissar's ear.

"Please excuse me for one minute, Herr Ryder. I'll be right back."

When Kommissar Brunner returned, he took his seat behind the desk and sat contemplating Ryder. Gone was the air of easy informality.

"That was a call from Bonn. It seems you have friends in high places, Herr Ryder. That's all, for now. Please wait outside until your statement is ready. Sign it and go. Do not try to leave Germany without permission; we would be forced to detain you."

Ryder almost missed the Bietigheim exit. He reduced speed and swung over into the right lane, dropping from fifth gear to fourth, then third, while Clementine snarled her reluctance.

In Bietigheim, he asked for directions from an old man with a cane and an impenetrable dialect. Ryder didn't understand him, so he stopped at the next gas station and got directions to the Grimm family farm.

He knew it was a slim lead, but it was the only one he had. As soon as he'd left police headquarters, he'd called Martin von Friedenthal to ask for Fräulein Grimm's address.

By the time he got to her room in the student quarter, she'd already cleared out, still owing a month's rent. The irate landlady was more than happy to supply Fräulein Grimm's home address, especially after Ryder had corrected the financial oversight.

He turned off the paved road into a farmyard. The faded stucco house sagged comfortably with the weight of years. He shut off the motor and climbed out of the Porsche.

In the silence that followed, Ryder looked around. The barn was really a series of sheds, leaning together for support. Parked beside one of the sheds, he could see a tractor still hitched to a wagon piled high with sugar beets.

Scattered around the yard, between the house and the barn, were galvanized tubs, rusted pieces of farm machinery, dozens of empty flowerpots, and two wooden chairs with the seats missing. Chickens, clucking their disapproval, scratched in the dirt. From somewhere out back came the squeal of pigs.

Behind the barn were the fields. The earth had recently been plowed in preparation for an early spring planting and the freshly turned furrows were speckled with crows. From a line of trees at the far end of the field came the taunting cries of the guard birds.

It was a sad, tired place dressed in faded greens and browns. There were no songbirds and no flowers. Like the couple standing in the doorway, the time for that had passed.

"Herr Grimm, Frau Grimm," said Ryder, approaching the couple, "I'm here to see your daughter."

"We have no daughters. Who are you and what do you want?"

Grimm spoke with a heavy dialect. Both Grimms watched Ryder with closed faces and suspicious eyes.

It was easy to see where Ilse Grimm had gotten her height. Frau Grimm was a heavier version of her daughter, towering over her husband. She was a muscular woman, with large breasts squeezed into a faded blue dress. She wore an unbuttoned tan cardigan and below the hem of her dress Ryder could see work trousers tucked into rubber boots.

Herr Grimm, a short, stocky man with no neck, was one step away from obesity. He was dressed for the fields in a heavy shirt, work pants and boots, and he wore a hat with a narrow brim. An unlighted cigar hung loosely from his lips. He was staring at the Porsche.

"Go away!" said Grimm. "Leave! We don't talk to strangers."

James L Diffin

Von Friedenthal had taught Ryder the trick of dealing with his countrymen. For the most part, Germans are an orderly folk, with an overwhelming need to conform. They respect authority and live by the rules. To not be part of the system is unthinkable. It didn't matter where you were in the system, but only that you were part of it.

It was obvious to Ryder that he wasn't going to be treated kindly, much less asked in, so he sat down on a front fender of the Porsche and put one foot on the bumper. Herr Grimm looked stricken. "We have nothing to say. Go away or we will call the police."

Ryder admired his shoeshine. "Call the police, by all means. I'm rather surprised they aren't here already."

The Grimms looked uncomfortable, the threat to call the police forgotten. This kind of authority made them nervous. The man with the Porsche was too sure of himself not to be somebody important.

"Police? Here? We've done nothing."

"Perhaps not," said Ryder, "but you're wasting my time. I've asked about your daughter Ilse. Is she here?" His tone left no room for argument.

"No."

"You're sure?"

"Yes," said Frau Grimm. "Our daughters don't come home anymore. Ilse did, at first, when she went away to university, but not now. She brought some others from school and they sat around and talked bad things. Papa told them to stop and they went away. Ilse has never come back."

"What do you mean, bad things?"

She looked to her husband for support, but he only stared at the Porsche and Ryder's foot on the bumper.

"We don't understand about such things," said Frau Grimm. "They talked about how there should be no government and no laws." She looked shocked at the idea. "They said people are the government."

"I find it strange that you haven't once asked if something is wrong. Ilse might be sick or in trouble—she might even be dead."

"She might as well be," said Grimm with a hard face. "The last time we telephoned her, she told us she never wanted to see us again. She said she was ashamed of us. She was going to move and we shouldn't try to find her."

"You mentioned daughters. Ilse has sisters?"

"Yes, one."

234

Ryder flicked imaginary lint from his slacks and, in a voice where patience was running dry, asked, "Well, then?"

"Her name is Gertrude. She lives in Garmisch-Partenkirchen and owns a ski shop." Frau Grimm looked at her husband again. "She doesn't come home, either."

"Is she close to Ilse?"

"They were—once."

"Does Gertrude share Ilse's political views?"

She looked puzzled and picked at a fingernail. "I don't know, she never said."

"Is she married?"

"I don't know." Her eyes glistened. This wasn't the way it was supposed to be.

"Do you have your daughter's address in Garmisch?"

"Yes."

"May I have it, please?"

"Are Ilse and Gertrude in trouble?"

"Not that I know of," said Ryder. "I have some questions that must be answered, that's all."

She hesitated. Ryder sat on the fender, watching the chickens. It was obvious he wasn't going away.

"All right," she said, "I'll get it." She disappeared into the house.

"Sorry to bother you like this," said Ryder to Herr Grimm.

Herr Grimm didn't answer. He was still looking at that foot. Ryder knew the problem.

In a country where the make of automobile is the measure of a man, where the Audi passed the Volkswagen, the Mercedes passed the Audi, and the Porsche passed everything, where touching another automobile's bumper while parking is a fighting offense, that foot was as out of place as a nun at a nudist camp. He left his foot where it was.

Frau Grimm was back, still holding the stub of a thick pencil. She offered Ryder a yellow piece of lined paper. He glanced at the address, folded the paper, and put it in his pocket.

"Herr Grimm, Frau Grimm—I thank you for your trouble."

The two stood motionless as Ryder turned the car, headed back to the highway, turned left, and was soon lost to sight.

Chapter XXXIII

It was a shame. The German government couldn't or wouldn't pass a speed limit for the autobahns, but every time Ryder drove the roads these days, more of the 130 Kilometer signs had appeared. One day they weren't there and the next day they were. Those red-and-white signs spelled the death of the sports car.

They had widened the autobahn around Stuttgart, but it was still a mess and traffic crept at a snail's pace. Ryder left 81 and got on 8 at the Stuttgarter Dreieck, heading toward Munich. Holding steady on the long climb, where the north and southbound lanes split around the mountain, he thought about it.

The halcyon days of the Ferrari, the Maserati, and the Lotus were almost over. Soon the roads in Germany would be just as tame as those in every other industrialized country. With their teeth pulled by detuning, the exotics would become a parody of themselves.

Climbing the steep, winding road, Clementine buckled to and Ryder decided to enjoy it while he could. Maybe the next time he came to Germany it would all be over.

At the tunnel entrance on top of the mountain was a sign—*Licht*. Ryder switched on the headlights and flashed through the tunnel. He dropped into fifth gear again and began to move. The bright red Porsche fled across the flats around Ulm like a ship before the wind. Clementine was doing what she had been built for and there was nothing that could catch her now.

Inside the cockpit, his eyes were constantly moving. At these speeds, it didn't pay to nod off; you only got to do it once. Check and check again—the road ahead, the road behind, and the instruments. The sign for Augsburg blurred by and then Dachau. Right out there on the highway was a sign for the place that some still claimed had never existed.

Ryder had visited Dachau once. It was a national shrine, a memorial to man's inhumanity to man. He'd seen the silent ovens and those infamous showers.

"Don't be afraid, child. If they were going to hurt us, they wouldn't bathe us first, now would they? Come, hold my hand, you silly girl. Yes, I know you're cold, pet, but you'll soon be warm, I promise. No, Mommy's not crying. My love."

Just before Munich, Ryder pulled into a gas station. The attendant asked the question.

"Full?"

"Please."

"Don't see many of these," said the attendant, cleaning the windshield. The second question wasn't far behind.

"How fast?"

"Fast enough."

"I've done a little Formula V racing, but nothing like this. Does she handle like the other Porsches?"

"Better."

"I thought so. Great color," said the attendant. He sighed. "Maybe I'll win the Lotto someday. Here's your ticket. Pay inside."

Skirting the edge of Munich, Ryder got on the Garmisch autobahn and let Clementine have her head again. It wouldn't be long now.

There they were. Whenever Ryder saw the Alps, it was like the first time all over again. The Himalayas were higher, so were the Rockies, but there was something special about the spine of Europe. The name alone brought pictures to mind—Hannibal and his elephants, the Roman legions, invading barbarians, even Adolf Hitler, were all part of the history of those great gray rocks.

Garmisch-Partenkirchen comprised two ancient towns that had incorporated in the mid-thirties. Although it was now an international tourist resort, Garmisch managed to retain much of its old-world charm.

There was something for everyone. The town had never gotten over the fact that it had been the site of the 1936 Winter Olympics. You could skate in the Olympic ice stadium, ski downhill or cross-country, or attend a mountain climbing school. Even more popular was just plain walking.

Of course, the conventional walking costume could hardly be called plain, consisting of leather knickers, long woolen socks, heavy hiking boots, jacket, velour hat with brush and don't—for heaven's sake!—forget the walking stick.

There was trout fishing in frigid streams, the railway ride to the top of the Zugspitze—Germany's highest peak, swimming in the Wellenbad with its artificial waves and, if you had anything left over for the evening, a number of fine restaurants and a flourishing casino.

Towering above the narrow streets and onion domes of the churches were the mountains—the Alpspitze, the Dreitorspitze and, tucked around the corner, the Zugspitze. Garmisch was a place to recharge the batteries, to draw strength from the deep quiet of the forests and the brooding peaks above.

The shops were doing a brisk business and, as Ryder turned the Porsche onto the main street, the sidewalks were crowded. He passed the Post Hotel, the casino, and something he thought he'd never see, at least not in this town. On the left side of the plaza, behind the taxi stand, was one of America's secret weapons.

Ryder had to wonder how they'd gotten it by the village fathers. Maybe, as in the States, it had something to do with broadening the tax base. Plump in the middle of all that old-world charm were the golden arches of McDonald's.

Just past the plaza, on the right-hand side of the street, Ryder spotted the address he was looking for. There were no parking spaces nearby, so he turned down a side lane and found a spot alongside a stream where a covered wooden footbridge spanned the water.

The afternoon air was frosty and the gray sky held the promise of snow. Ryder walked briskly back to the shop.

"May I help you?" asked the salesgirl. She was dressed in ski pants, sweater, and some kind of furry aprés-ski boots—a walking advertisement for the store. Her accent said she was local.

"Don't you get warm, dressed like that?" asked Ryder.

The salesgirl looked down at her clothes. "Oh, my, no," she said. "It's just that we have such lovely things here, I can't resist." She leaned toward Ryder. "Employees get a special discount."

"With that tan, you must ski a lot."

She laughed. "Everyone in Garmisch skis. If business keeps on growing like this, the owner is going to make me assistant manager. Then maybe I'll have more—" She stopped.

"Sorry, sir," she said. "How may I help you? We've just unpacked a brand-new shipment of ski clothes. May I show you? No? Some pants, perhaps?" She indicated her sweater. "How about one of these Norwegian sweaters? You wouldn't believe how soft they are."

"Very nice," said Ryder. "I wish I had the time, but I'm here to speak with Fräulein Grimm."

"You're not selling something, are you? We're terribly busy." She couldn't help herself and leaned forward with a conspiratorial whisper. "Fräulein Grimm is with an important customer right now—von Braun. You've heard of the family?" The salesgirl looked at the man with the blue-gray eyes. "Sure I can't help you?"

"Some other time, perhaps."

"If you are selling something," said the salesgirl, "you should know that Fräulein Grimm sees salespeople by appointment only. We are much too busy; you must call first."

"I'm not selling and I'm not buying," said Ryder, "but I'm certain that Fräulein Grimm will want to see me. Please tell her it concerns her sister. I'll wait."

"Her sister? I didn't know she had a sister." Looking doubtfully over her shoulder, the salesgirl left.

The shop was a series of small rooms packed with merchandise. As the business had grown, so had the demand for space. The store next door had been rented and a doorway knocked out to join the two. The process had been repeated until the whole building had been taken over. Every bit of space was packed with things you couldn't live without.

There were skis, poles, bindings, boots—boots for skiing, for climbing, for walking, or looking like you did. The aisles were narrowed by extra showcases, tables, and racks. There were walking sticks by the dozen, socks, long and short leather pants, jackets, dirndls, capes in loden green or gray, and imported Scandinavian sweaters. There was a room with nothing but hats, and you had to be an expert to tell which were for men and which were for women. Under one of the glass countertops were silver and pewter holders for the decorative brushes worn on the velour hats.

On it went, room after room. The inventory was staggering—mountain climbing gear, ropes, pitons, ice hammers, tents, and even windsurfing boards and kayaks. There was a case full of compasses. Through the maze of aisles, customers wandered with glazed eyes.

Ryder had gone back to the front of the store and was studying a case of binoculars, when a short, stout woman marched up to him and demanded, in a no-nonsense voice, "What's this about my sister?"

It was easy to see which parent Fräulein Gertrude Grimm favored. She wasn't as heavy as her father, but she had the same chunky, neckless body. Except for her long hair, her eyeglasses, and the way her sweater fit, she was her father all over again.

"Is it always like this in here?" asked Ryder.

"Business is very good, thank you. Now—don't waste my time. Who are you and what do you want?"

"My name is John Ryder. I've just come from Heidelberg. I'm a friend of the von Friedenthals. Your sister Ilse works for them. I'm looking for her."

"I read the papers, Herr Ryder. I know all about the trouble with the von Friedenthal children. I must say, it is touching that you have come all this way, just for a cleaning lady."

"I'm not being altruistic, Fräulein Grimm. Two little girls have been kidnapped. My concern is for them."

"You'll excuse me. This has nothing to do with me."

"No, I will not excuse you."

"I could call the police."

"It must run in the family."

"What's that supposed to mean?"

"That's what your parents first said when I talked to them this morning."

"You've been to the farm?"

"That's how I got your address."

Gertrude Grimm regarded Ryder from close-set eyes, safely hidden behind oversized pink-tinted lenses. He had the feeling that he was being priced and the profit margin calculated to the second decimal place. She reached a decision.

"Follow me."

Without waiting for a response, she headed for the back of the store. The stretch pants she wore were being put to the test. Ryder wondered how long the material could hold out against the relentless onslaught, as her buttocks clenched and unclenched with each stride.

She opened a door. "Now we can talk."

They were in a small courtyard behind the store. There was a table and chairs and on sunny days the girls had lunch out here. Fräulein Grimm didn't offer Ryder a seat. Instead, she crossed heavy arms over her chest. Her stubby fingers made her hands look like paws. The barricades were up.

"You're an American, aren't you?"

"Yes."

"Say what you have to say, Herr Ryder, so I can get back to work."

"There must be more to life."

"We do what we have to. I will probably die someday in one of my shops, helping foolish people spend their money on foolish things."

"How about getting away, or spending time with your friends—or your family?"

"You did that very well," she said. "Just the right amount of interest and concern. If I answered your question, you would have what you came for—am I not right? No, you don't have to say anything." Gertrude shrugged.

"I live to work. I keep no husband or pets, but I do read. I read about an American chess player who almost got himself killed. Everyone knows Doctor von Friedenthal and now we know about his children. My sister works for him. I don't have to read between the lines and I don't believe in coincidence. You are that same John Ryder."

Ryder nodded.

"You think my sister had something to do with the kidnapping?"

"There's that possibility."

"Have you spoken with her?"

"I tried to, but she seems to have disappeared."

"Perhaps she's in danger herself. Maybe she has also been kidnapped. Have you thought of that?" Her voice was rising.

It was clear that Gertrude Grimm had a lot of emotion bottled up. "I can understand your feelings," he said.

"Do you? What could you possibly know about it? I've been working for as long as I can remember. At first, I didn't mind; it was fun. You saw the farm. It wasn't always the way it is now."

She relaxed for the first time since he'd met her. Her face was softer. "On a farm there is always something to do, but we all worked together. You never saw so many flowers." She paused for a minute.

"It sounds nice." Ryder smiled in encouragement. He had to keep her talking.

Gertrude went on as if she hadn't heard. "I was the oldest, so I took care of Ilse. My sister was always full of questions. You know the kind of questions a child can ask. No one can answer them, much less another child. Ilse would go to our parents and say she had asked me such and such and I couldn't tell her. It made little difference that my parents didn't know the answers either, but somewhere along the way, I became the dumb one and Ilse the smart one."

The air was cold and Gertrude shivered, vigorously rubbing her upper arms. "It was decided that when I finished school at fifteen, I would learn a trade. Living on a farm can be a good life, but there's no real money to be made from a small place, so I would help send Ilse to university by working. I wasn't consulted. It was decided around the kitchen table one night after I was in bed."

Gertrude pulled out a chair and motioned for Ryder to join her. "The day after I left school, I was apprenticed to a large department store in Stuttgart. The teen years? Dates, parties, and friends were not for me. I worked all day in the store and came home at night to my chores on the farm. I even helped Ilse with her schoolwork."

Gertrude's voice was firm with resolve. "I spent twelve years at the department store, but I, too, was learning. I went from clerk to supervisor to department manager. I had no formal schooling for those positions, Herr Ryder, just the ability to work hard. I never refused to stay after hours or work on weekends. I made myself indispensable."

The expression on Gertrude's face began to harden. "I was the dutiful daughter—work and more work, all to give everything to my sister. No new clothes, unless absolutely necessary, no auto, not even a moped. All those bus and trolley rides and the hours spent waiting for them. That's when I started to read. You could say I was educated courtesy of the public transportation system."

Still hugging herself, Gertrude remembered. "And while I was working and learning, Ilse became an activist. Ban the bomb, save the whales, equality for students, anything. A protest of any sort and she was in the front row, banner high, though it was more often a cardboard placard and a grease pencil. At first, it seemed harmless and we all enjoyed the stories she told. Ilse can be quite engaging when she wants to be."

With a faint smile, Gertrude continued. "After she entered the university, she became—how did she put it?—oh, yes, she became politically active. She used words and slogans without knowing what they meant. Then she stopped coming home so often and whenever she did, there was trouble."

Gertrude began picking at a fingernail. "We never had much to say to each other, but she was my sister and I tried to understand. Our parents were confused, but they still gave her every penny they could spare—of their money and of mine. It had to end."

Her voice was bitter. "One day, it exploded. Ilse told us she was ashamed, that she couldn't bring any of her friends home, that our parents were no better than the beasts that worked the fields and a mutt like me should have been smothered in my cradle. She left my mother in tears, begging her not to go. My parents would do anything, if she would only stay."

Gertrude looked up at the mountains. "It was just too much. I left home that same day. I lived in a small pension in Stuttgart until I could train someone to take my place at the store, then I came here. That was three years ago. I mortgaged my soul and went into business for myself."

Gertrude looked directly at Ryder for the first time. "I had a partner and we slept in the back of the store. We worked fifteen hours a day, but she couldn't take it, so I bought her out and worked twenty hours a day. Now, I own the building and have two other stores besides this one."

"Fräulein Grimm," said Ryder, "I'm impressed."

"I didn't tell you because of that."

"I know."

Fräulein Gertrude Grimm nodded her head in acknowledgment. "You're a very good listener, Herr Ryder. You didn't say a word. I shall lie in my bed tonight and wonder why I've told you all this."

"Do you ever go home?"

"Only once."

"Have you kept in touch with your sister?"

"Yes and no. She calls and asks for money."

"And do you give it to her?"

Gertrude looked uncomfortable. "Yes."

"After all that?"

"She's still my sister."

"Do you have any idea where I can find her?"

Gertrude looked up at the great gray peaks silhouetted against the gunmetal sky. The answer wasn't there, but in her heart.

"Not really," she said after a time. "Ilse is involved in so many things and she has many...I suppose you could call them friends."

"When you say involved, do you mean organizations and things like that?"

"Yes."

"What, for instance?"

"The only one I remember—" She stopped. "This is absurd. The only one I can remember right now is really silly. Ilse is absolutely fascinated with the history of the American West."

"You mean cowboys and Indians?"

"Exactly. She belongs to a Wild West Club."

"No."

"There are quite a number of Western Clubs here in Germany."

Ryder could only stare at her.

"I mean it," said Gertrude with the first hint of a smile. "There are Europeans who still think that America from New York to the Mississippi is the Mafia and from the Mississippi to San Francisco all cowboys and Indians. It comes from American films and from television. Some wonder why John Wayne was never elected President. It's the romance of the American West; we Europeans eat it up."

"Where men are men and women are women?"

"Ilse couldn't get enough of it. She even has a gingham dress, button shoes, everything."

"How long ago was this love affair?"

"It's still going on, as far as I know. It's the place I'd try, if I wanted to find her. They have a ranch outside of Heidelberg, down along the Neckar toward Mannheim and they meet"—she stopped speaking and looked at the date on her watch—"the second Tuesday of each month and that's today."

"A ranch?"

"Don't sound so skeptical. That's what they call it."

"In Germany?"

"Why not? Every year the clubs get together for an annual roundup. They come from all over Germany, even from France. It's very authentic. The French Indians are especially good, I'm told."

Ryder had the fleeting thought of "Home on the Range" sung in German.

"I'm sorry I can't be of more help, Herr Ryder, but I really must get back to work."

"I appreciate your time."

As they went back into the store, Ryder asked if he could use her telephone to make a long distance call. Collect, of course.

Chapter XXXIV

"The turnoff is just up ahead, Herr Ryder."

"By the split rail fence?"

"That's the place. Be careful, some of the ruts are deep. They keep it that way on purpose—more authentic."

"Why do you say *they?*" asked John. "I thought you were a member."

"I am, but I don't come around much anymore. It's not the same as it used to be."

"How's that?"

"Oh, I don't know—it's a different crowd now. There are some new members and they keep pretty much to themselves. Many of the old-timers have left and there's been talk about starting a new club. It's too bad; I'll miss the place. We have it fixed up real nice. You'll see."

Ryder glanced at the man seated beside him. He supposed that somewhere in the western United States—it didn't even have to be the western part—there was someone riding in a Porsche, dressed in a cowboy outfit. But they never, thought John, looked like his passenger.

Before Ryder had left Garmisch, he'd telephoned Martin von Friedenthal from Gertrude Grimm's office. He'd explained to Martin about the Wild West Club and the meeting that evening. No matter how, Martin had to get Ryder an invitation.

Just outside Garmisch, Ryder had topped off the Porsche's gas tank and checked tire pressures. Once he got started, there would be no stopping.

The trip back was different. On the way down, Ryder had been motoring quickly, enjoying the thrill of driving a fine machine at speeds. Now it was all business and he was going flat out. You can't redline a Porsche in top gear, but Ryder got close.

Keeping a sharp lookout in the reduced speed zones, Ryder exceeded the 130-kilometer limit by a significant margin and, in the unmarked stretches, his foot was on the floorboard.

He still found it difficult to pass the green-and-white police cars on the autobahn without coming unstuck. He had to remind himself that they couldn't care less how fast you were going, only that you kept things moving.

Traffic was relatively light and, except for a truck that pulled into the passing lane when he was about a hundred yards away, there were no problems. It occurred to Ryder that if one of the Dunlops decided to let go, they would be picking up the pieces for a week.

At the Stuttgarter Dreieck, John elected to use the autobahn that went past Karlsruhe, instead of the way he'd come this morning. It would enable him to avoid the heavy traffic around the northwest side of Stuttgart.

When he got to Heidelberg, Ryder parked in front of his hotel, telling the doorman not to touch the car, he'd be leaving again in a few minutes. At the desk, he learned that von Friedenthal had called. As soon as he got to his room, Ryder called Martin back.

"Four-thirty," said von Friedenthal, "you pick up Herr Kramer in Sandhausen. You know where that is, don't you?"

"All I need is the street address."

"Forgive me, but I have to ask. Do you think you are on to something?"

"I really don't know—"

"Seems like an odd place to be going."

"You're telling me!"

"John?"

"I know, Martin. It's going to be all right."

"Be careful, I wouldn't want anything to happen to you, too."

"It's after four already and I'm curious to see what Old Shatterhand will look like."

"Karl May will never forgive you."

Old Shatterhand and Winnetou were two fictional creations of Karl May, an author of Western novels who'd never left Germany, a fact that hadn't affected the popularity of his books one bit.

As Ryder started up the walk to the house on Waldstrasse, the front door opened and out stepped Old Shatterhand.

Old Shatterhand was wearing a cream-colored Stetson with a braided chin strap. He had on a plaid shirt and a black leather vest. A bandana was tied around his neck and his cord pants were tucked into hand-tooled, high-heeled boots. On the heel of each boot was a heavy roweled spur. Around

248

his middle was a wide black gun belt, holding a single action Colt .45. The holster was tied down with a leather thong just above his knee.

"Holy Hannah!"

"Pardon?" asked Shatterhand. "I'm sorry, but I speak only a little English. You must be Herr Ryder."

"I hope I'm not putting you to any inconvenience," replied Ryder in German.

"Not at all, Herr Ryder. I was delighted when Professor von Friedenthal called. He is a very famous man, but he talked to me himself. I'm almost ready," said Herr Kramer. "Please come in; it will only take a minute."

After meeting Frau Kramer, who kept nervously wiping her hands on her apron, and downing a shot of homemade pear schnapps strong enough to grow hair on an egg, they left.

Following Herr Kramer down the walk to his car, Ryder wondered if the steam had stopped coming out of his nostrils. Any American who thought he could drink a German under the table could forget it—they were weaned on the stuff.

Outside, children were playing in the street, riding bicycles and roller-skating, but no one took the slightest interest in Old Shatterhand.

It was quite a sight for a peaceful little German town, but what really ripped it was the way Old Shatterhand walked. Maybe it was the boots, or maybe he'd seen one too many westerns, but whatever it was, he looked like he was going to fall on his face any second.

Easing over the ruts in the lane, between rows of bare-branched apple trees, Ryder still had to wonder where all this was leading. Ryder had a dry taste in his mouth. Did he know what in the hell he was doing?

There was a gate at the end of the lane, with a sign over it that said RANCH.

"It's not very original, Herr Ryder, but we couldn't agree on a name, so that's what it's always been."

The sign looked as if it had been branded and the wood was stained and weather-beaten. On the other side of the gate was a field of parked cars. There were the usual Volkswagens, several campers, and a fair share of Mercedes sedans, squatting foursquare, like their owners. Ryder eased Clementine in beside a yellow 911 Porsche and a pair of motorcycles.

Under Ryder's watchful eye, Kramer exited the Porsche without tearing anything with his spurs and the two started toward the ranch house.

Time had missed a beat. Strolling around the grounds of the ranch were cowboys of every imaginable variety and some that passed imagination. Ryder had the urge to pinch himself. It seemed as if each cowboy had dressed to suit his own fancy and his own pocketbook.

Evidently, each man had his own dream of the American West, but it was a West that had never existed. The only thing they had in common was that they all wore guns. Some even had two, riding low in tied-down holsters.

It was hard to overlook the women. There was a scattering of gingham dresses, as well as the more authentic black skirts and high-necked, long-sleeved blouses. Several cowgirls wore leather skirts and, like the men, wore guns.

Ryder was curious. "I don't see any children?"

"The club is only for adults. Maybe later, if we start over."

"What about all these weapons?" Ryder asked. "I thought it was next to impossible to own a handgun in Germany, unless you were a member of a gun club."

Kramer laughed and patted his holster. "These aren't real, Herr Ryder; no license is required. They may look authentic, but they are only replicas. They could not fire live ammunition."

"Yeah, right."

"I'm serious. For instance, my weapon was custom-made for me by a member of the club. He is a machinist. See the brass trigger guard? The gun is an 1851 Navy Colt. Not the real thing, of course, but it has the weight and action of the original. Here, let me show you—I'm very good at this."

Kramer took a step back and went into his gunfighter's crouch. "Hands up!"

With a practiced flick, he drew and attempted to cock the single-action Colt. He couldn't. Looking down at the weapon, he discovered why.

Ryder's hand was around the cylinder, preventing it from turning, and holding the barrel down at a forty-five degree angle. This accomplished two things—the weapon couldn't be cocked and it wasn't pointed at Ryder.

Kramer was so surprised, he let go of the gun. "I was only trying to show you my quick draw. It's perfectly harmless. I told you the gun isn't loaded with real bullets and it can't shoot."

"Maybe so, Pardner," said Ryder, "but I've been taught to never allow anyone to point a gun at me if I could help it."

He reached out and dropped the Colt back into Kramer's holster. "Here—if you wish, point it at a tree or the house or your wife, but not at me. I'd appreciate it if you left that thing in the holster while I'm around. Except for my tailor, I dislike anyone telling me to put my hands up."

To the casual observer, nothing had happened. Herr Kramer had been showing his gun to a guest, but he looked so crestfallen that Ryder relented.

"Don't take it so hard, Old Shatterhand," said Ryder. "You did your trick, I did mine. If it's any consolation, and if you want to do it the right way, the first rule is don't stand within arm's reach when you draw. If you're going to do that, use a club."

"I thought you were a chess player like Professor von Friedenthal?"

"I used to be. Now—how about showing me this ranch of yours."

Ryder's smile and easy manner soothed Kramer's ruffled feathers. "Follow me, then. Over here is the barbecue pit and, behind that, the chuck wagon."

Kramer spoke to a couple of men in white aprons, tending a bed of burning coals. He smiled at John. "I hope you brought your appetite?"

"Sounds good. I seemed to have misplaced lunch today."

"Around back is the bunkhouse," Kramer continued. He opened the door of a small building and stepped inside. There were bunks—beds, really—around the sides of the room. The walls were unfinished. The only decorations were some centerfolds which would have given a long-ago cowboy sleepless nights. Kramer pointed to one of the two doors across the room.

"We have lockers, a shower, and a toilet. Many of us come directly from the office and change here. I work in Mannheim and coming right from work saves time. Sometimes I even stay overnight." Kramer couldn't contain himself. "It's really something, isn't it?"

Without waiting for an answer, he led Ryder through the second door. "This is our tack room."

Inside, wooden pegs along the wall held lariats, bridles, even a horse collar. In the center of the room, resting on a hitching rail, was a row of Western saddles.

"We don't keep horses here, but for special occasions we bring some in from a local stable." Kramer gave a hitch to his gun belt. "How about a drink? All this talking has made me thirsty."

As they circled the main building, Ryder noticed a wall of heavy planks buried upright in the ground with the painted outline of a man.

"I give up," said Ryder.

"That's where we practice knife throwing. Would you like to try?" Kramer asked.

"No, thanks. Knives make me nervous."

The main building, or ranch house, as Kramer called it, was a good-sized structure, complete with front porch and rocking chairs. As they mounted the steps, Kramer greeted a number of people. He seemed well liked and Ryder attracted little attention. Someone was always bringing a friend or relative. As long as the food and drinks were paid for, guests were welcome.

"Wait until you see this," Kramer said, opening the door. Ryder took one step inside and stopped. The room was noisy and full of people.

It wasn't a ranch house at all, but an Old West saloon. A bar, complete with brass rail and cuspidors, ran along the back of the room. There were tables with low-backed wooden chairs and a faro table with black-frocked dealer. In an alcove, behind a beaded curtain, was a pool table.

A potbellied stove in the center of the room glowed red in the smoke-filled light from heavy chandeliers. Steer horns hung on the walls. Someone had even made a chair out of them. Ryder noticed that no one was sitting in it.

On the wall to Ryder's right was a large painting of a reclining nude. She looked across the room to the opposite wall, to where a buffalo head stared back in glassy-eyed disbelief.

There were women dressed as dance-hall girls and the tinny sound of a piano cut through the din. Ryder finally located it in a far corner. No one was seated at it, but the keys were clicking merrily along, all by themselves. Ryder felt glassy-eyed himself.

"I knew you'd like it. Come on, let's get that drink."

There was room at one end of the bar. John got his first look at the bartender—waxed mustache, slicked-down hair, and a collarless shirt with sleeve garters.

The bartender finished drawing beers for one of the dance-hall girls and made his way to where Old Shatterhand and Ryder waited. Drying his hands on a towel, the bartender leaned one elbow on the bar. *"Wie geht's?"*

Ryder almost burst out laughing. He had to remind himself that he wasn't here to pass judgment on European views of the romantic Old West; he was here to find two little girls.

"Anything wrong?" Kramer asked,

Ryder shook his head and ordered two beers.

After the bartender brought the beer, and had drawn one for himself, Kramer introduced Ryder.

"It's not often that we get Americans in here," the bartender said. "What do you think of the place?"

"I've never seen anything like it," said Ryder looking around the room. When he got to the buffalo head, he almost lost it again. "Where did you manage to get all these...these things?"

Kramer answered before the bartender could. "We order from magazines and many of us have relatives in America. We did a great deal of research, too. This is probably the finest saloon of its kind in all of Europe."

"I'll bet it is," said Ryder, pleasing Kramer and the bartender no end.

The bartender spoke to Kramer.

"We haven't seen you around lately—"

Kramer glanced at Ryder before answering. "It's just not the same anymore. Sometimes we can't even come to the ranch when we want to." He scanned the bar. "There are people here in the middle of the night. I know, I've seen them."

He lowered his voice. "I had to work late and decided to stay at the bunkhouse, instead of driving all the way home. When I got here, there were men loading a van. The way they did it made me afraid. There were no lights and they kept their voices down." He shook his head. "I never told anyone. I went home and tried to forget about it."

"It's probably a good thing you did," said Ryder.

The bartender looked pensive. "And I thought it was just me." He wiped the top of the bar with his cloth. "I haven't wanted to admit it, but it's true. I have so much invested, I'd hate to give it up. It's the only hobby I've got."

He shrugged. "Maybe things will get better."

"Some of us have been talking about starting over in a new location," said Kramer. "Would you be interested?"

The bartender took another swipe at an invisible spot. "Maybe—listen, I've got to get busy, we'll talk later."

The bartender left and Kramer turned to Ryder. "He's one of the old gang and has put a lot of time and money into the ranch. He has the food and drink concession. Everything above cost goes right back into the ranch."

Indicating the room, Kramer said, "Maybe it's not much to you, having the real thing in the States, but it means a lot to us."

"Herr Kramer," said Ryder, "what you have here is one of a kind." Ryder nudged one of the spittoons with his foot. It made a brassy *thunk*.

As if in response, there was a loud clanging from outside. People drifted toward the front door until the room was almost empty. Even the bartender disappeared. Only two other men remained at the bar.

One of them wore fringed leather gauntlets, but otherwise they weren't dressed as elaborately as the rest of the cowboys. They seemed interested in their reflections in the mirror behind the bar.

"That was the dinner bell," Kramer said. "It's not cold tonight, so we're going to eat outside, sitting around the fire. Let's go."

"Fine," said Ryder, "I'm starving. How about you boys?"

The two cowboys didn't answer, but continued to stare into the mirror until the room was empty. Then they turned to face Ryder for the first time.

Kramer tugged at Ryder's sleeve. "Let's go," he repeated.

"You talk too much," said the cowboy with the gauntlets. "Don't bring strangers around and then start complaining. Get out, if you don't like it."

Kramer was indignant. "See! See what I mean," he said to Ryder. "That's exactly why so many are leaving. Who voted you into the club, anyway?"

"Just get out," said the cowboy with the gauntlets.

"Sure is a sweet-talking son of a gun, isn't he?" commented Ryder to no one in particular.

"Mind your own business, if you know what's good for you."

Ryder glanced around the room. The place was deserted. "Don't you think you're letting all this atmosphere go to your head? You've misplaced a hundred years somewhere along the line. You look silly."

Leather gauntlets had backed away from the bar so that he and the other cowboy were side by side, facing Ryder.

"How dare you insult my guest!" said Kramer. He tried to push past Ryder, but stopped with a hand against his chest.

"Let me handle this," said Ryder quietly, never taking his eyes from the two men. "It's not you they want."

"But—" The pressure of Ryder's hand eased as Kramer stepped back.

Ryder straightened up and came to the end of the bar, confronting the two cowboys, who weren't cowboys. He looked at their faces. Neither were they bankers, accountants, or salesmen. Ryder had known ever since he'd stepped up to the bar. Andrew Hall had pounded it into his head—know your enemy! The weapons in their holsters were just that—weapons. They weren't Starr, Remington, or Colt replicas, but the real, double-action thing.

For anyone with half an eye, the way the men held themselves was a dead giveaway. It showed as plainly as if they wore signs. A loaded gun gives a man an added dimension, an awareness that he's not like other men.

The second cowboy spoke. "Come on, Gunther, let's get it over with before someone comes back."

"You're right, Kurt. You take care of the bigmouth and, as for you"—he faced Ryder—"this time I won't miss."

He took a step backward. Kurt stepped back, too. Ryder stepped forward.

They went for their guns. Hands flashed to their hips, but the holsters were empty.

Ryder was standing in front of them, clutching the two weapons. He looked confused.

It was obvious that Ryder didn't even know how to hold a gun, since he held the weapons backward, muzzles pointed at the ground in the same position in which they'd been removed from their holsters. Ryder acted like he had a live rattlesnake in each hand.

"Get him," said Gunther. The two men jumped to wrestle Ryder to the floor. Kramer started to help, but changed his mind when he got a backhand across the mouth.

Ryder somehow managed to get a table between himself and the two cowboys. Kurt came charging around one side, Gunther the other, only to find another table in the way. Seemingly bewildered, Ryder was still holding the guns upside down.

Gunther swore. "You stupid shit!"

They came after Ryder, throwing tables and chairs to the side. Ryder seemed to be moving awkwardly, but there was always one more table between them. Finally, he was in the center of the room with only one table left.

"Now you're going to get it, asshole," hissed Kurt. He stopped.

Ryder was standing next to the potbellied stove. Using the butt of one of the guns, he flipped the stove door open, tossed the two weapons on the fire and slammed the door shut again.

"Do you know what you just did, you dumb bastard?" yelled Gunther, leaning both hands on the table in front of him. "Do you?"

"Sure—I just threw your guns in the fire."

"Those guns were loaded with live ammunition." Gunther was shouting.

"Goodness, I didn't know that." Ryder looked as if he might faint. "It's a good thing I got rid of them."

Kurt was getting nervous feet. "How long before that ammunition starts going off?"

"How the hell should I know?" answered Gunther.

In the stove, an expanding coal chose that moment to give a healthy snap. Gunther and Kurt froze.

"Live ammunition...is that dangerous?" asked Ryder.

Another coal snapped. That did it. Gunther and Kurt went charging out the back door of the saloon. Ryder stood by the glowing stove and watched them go.

"Get out of there!" Kramer's voice came from behind the bar. "You're going to get killed!"

"Am I?" said Ryder, strolling back to the bar. "You can stand up now. It's over."

"But you heard,"—Kramer's Stetson, suspended three inches above the bar, didn't move—"there are real bullets in those guns."

Ryder began standing brass cartridges in a line along the bar. Wide eyes focused on each in turn, until all twelve were accounted for. Ryder flicked a finger and down went the brass casings, like dominoes.

Kramer stared at Ryder. "But I didn't see you do anything."

"You weren't supposed to."

"They got away—"

"For the moment."

"I'm calling the police."

"Here we go again—the answer is no."

"Those men are dangerous, they were going to kill us."

"They only thought they were—there's a difference. I've met those two before, but they weren't dressed for horseback riding." A pair of motorcycles started up outside.

"I thought so." Ryder nodded.

"Okay, stand up now and pay attention. I let them get away. Straighten the place up and, no matter how difficult it is, say nothing to anyone. It's important. None of this happened."

Ryder smiled. "If you can keep quiet, you'll have your club back the way it used to be." He passed his hand over the bar and the cartridges were gone. Kramer gasped.

Ryder smiled again and moved to the same door that Gunther and Kurt had used.

"Maybe next time I can stay for dinner. I'd like that."

Chapter XXXV

As Ryder was turning onto the main road, he immediately spotted Gunther and Kurt. They'd stopped alongside the pavement to change clothes. Each had his own bike. Gun belts and Stetsons were hastily removed, stuffed into saddlebags, and replaced by fatigue jackets and helmets.

There was a lot of gesturing. It was obvious that there was a difference of opinion. They looked back in the direction of the ranch, but Ryder didn't think they spotted the Porsche. It was still light enough for him to run without headlights.

Transformation complete, the two set off again. They looked no different from any other biker. At Heidelberg, instead of continuing into the main part of town, they turned left over the first bridge, then right, to follow the road along the Neckar. Across the river, the floodlit red sandstone castle stood watch from the hill above the city.

At Ziegelhausen, the bikers turned left, heading up into the hills, past the white stucco houses with their red-tiled roofs.

The road climbed steadily into the Odenwald. It was night now and the only lights came from the two motorcycles; there were none from the pursuing shadow. In the cutbacks, Ryder used the gears to slow down and, in one place, the hand brake. "Sorry, old girl," he muttered under his breath.

They crested the ridge and started down the other side. It was harder going downhill, but Ryder did his best to keep a safe distance behind the cyclists and to keep his foot off the pedal so the brake light wouldn't go on.

They were deep in the Odenwald now. There was only an occasional house and, once, a startled driver on his way home from having a few beers with the boys. He saw a Porsche running without lights; at least, he thought he saw a Porsche.

The sound of the horn hadn't been lost on Gunther and Kurt and they slowed. Ryder had to use the hand brake again. After a bit, the bikers accelerated and Ryder kept them on a longer leash. It was a good thing he did.

On a curve in a heavily wooded area, the brake lights of the two bikes came on and stayed on. Ryder used the hand brake again, but this time it wasn't going to work. As he debated giving the brakes a quick stab, the taillights went out and he saw the headlights of the bikes turn off into the woods.

As Ryder rolled by, he could see the lights flickering and bouncing down a dirt road through the trees. Farther around the curve, he found a place where he could pull Clementine off the road and under some trees, so she couldn't be seen by a passing motorist. Ryder knew you didn't leave a Porsche like Clementine parked along the road and not expect some questions.

Before opening the door, he took the precaution of switching off the overhead light. He stepped out, removed his jacket and left it on the seat. The door closed with a faint click. He stood beside the car for a time, absorbing the pungent smell of the pine forest and listening. Clementine gave a couple of cooling pings and the silence moved in.

Ryder moved away from the Porsche and became one with the forest. He felt a faint flutter of anticipation as he set off through the trees, keeping parallel to the main road.

Just before he reached the spot where the two cyclists had turned off, Ryder headed into the woods. Over the years, the pines had laid down a thick carpet of needles. In these well-groomed German forests, the woodsmen had been busy and there was no underbrush. Not that it would have made any difference. Neither stag, nor rabbit, nor any creature of the forest night could have been more silent.

Still in the shadows, Ryder paused at the edge of the tree line. The field in front of him dropped sharply to the valley below. Moonlight was reflected in the stream that wound along the valley floor. The road that he'd been following led down to a grove of trees where a spiral of smoke rose from an unseen chimney.

Ryder spotted two shooting stands along the tree line on the opposite side of the valley. It was something he'd seen before, but somehow, this time, it didn't look right.

Keeping to the shadows, he checked his own side of the valley. Same thing. There were two more shooting stands along the edge of the trees.

They reminded Ryder of the watchtowers that guarded the border between East and West Germany and that was the problem. The stands were too regularly spaced. He'd better find out if things were as innocent as they looked.

Ryder smelled the man before he saw him...tobacco. Someone was up in the shooting stand. Ryder stood at the base of the tower and looked up.

The tower, built on poles cut from trees, was designed to blend with its surroundings. This stand was about nine feet from the ground. It had a roof of rough-hewn wooden shingles and waist-high sides to conceal the hunter. Across the supporting stilts, short pieces of wood had been nailed to form a ladder. Ryder knew there would be a seat of some kind up in the stand, to make the long hours of waiting easier.

He rubbed his thumb over one of the logs. The scent of tree sap was strong. The stand was new. New or not, there was no reason for it to be occupied.

It was too dark for hunting and the morning was still many hours away. He moved carefully away from the stand. He could see the vague outline of a head and shoulders, and smoke continued to drift out from under the wooden roof.

The second stand was like the first—it was new and there was someone in it. Any doubts he might have had were gone. While it was possible for one screwball to be up a tree at this time of night, two was stretching it.

Ryder leaned his weight against one of the support poles. The tower was well built and there was very little give. He had his foot on the first rung of the ladder when there was a sudden loud crackling from the stand above his head. He was back under the stand, out of sight, before he realized what it was.

The radio transmission was brief—everything was quiet, and damned boring, at post number four. What interested Ryder was the sign-off—Tomorrow's Child. He wondered how often the men in the towers checked in. Every fifteen minutes? On the half hour? The hour? He knew it was ten o'clock and all was well.

Willi, who was sitting with a scoped rifle across his knees, had started to turn when Ryder broke his neck. He'd heard nothing and died with a look of mild curiosity on his face.

Ryder caught the body and eased it to the floor, along with the rifle. The tower was empty, except for a thermos and a two-way radio on the wooden seat. After a quick look around, Ryder was sliding through the woods again, back to the first shooting stand.

The second man died without ever knowing what happened. He also had a scoped rifle and a radio and he, too, died of a broken neck. Without pause, Ryder was up into the tower, then away, gone as quickly as he had come, this time toward the head of the valley.

There was no way he could get across the open fields to the other side of the valley without being seen. If there were guards on this side, it was certain that the other two stands were occupied as well.

Ryder skirted the edge of the field. Running without a sound on a carpet of pine needles, he burst into the next shooting stand without stopping. The third man died as quietly as the others.

The man in the last stand had just come to the top of the ladder, intending to relieve a full bladder, when Ryder appeared before his startled eyes. He died with his hand on his zipper.

Ryder left the cover of the woods for the first time and raced down the open field to the trees by the brook. He had to chance it.

As soon as the first man died, there was no turning back. Nothing happened. Ryder slid into the trees alongside the water and stopped. Tobacco again. From the shadows, sparks arced, then vanished, as a butt hissed out in the water.

Ryder eased through the grove of trees, searching the grounds around the house. He was alone with the smoker. The stucco farmhouse needed a coat of whitewash. In the garage behind the house were a Mercedes, an old blue Ford Taunus and two motorcycles. The bikes were still warm.

The guard didn't suspect a thing. Compared to Colonel Cameron or Nathaniel Green, he was a rank amateur. Besides, he was bored. It was cold tonight. It was a waste of time; nothing ever happened.

Duty in one of the towers was bad enough, but at least you could sit down. It was ridiculous having to stand around like this. No one could get across the fields without being seen by someone in one of the shooting stands. He stamped and he fretted—and he died.

The windows were shuttered and the house was dark, except for a dim light visible through the opaque glass panel in the front door. The door was locked and there was a faint protest of tortured metal as Ryder forced the latch. Then he was standing in the hall, listening.

The house was quiet. He couldn't hear anyone, but he knew they were there. The light came from behind another glass-paned door at the end of the hall.

That door wasn't locked and the handle turned easily. No one was in the room. There were two overstuffed chairs, a floor lamp with red tassels hanging from the shade and, across the room, an old-fashioned radio console with a portable television set on top of it.

In the center of the room, beneath a bare ceiling light, was a dining table covered with a white cloth. The table held a sprawl of magazines, a two-way radio, and a chess set. It was one of those pseudo-Florentine sets with large red and white plastic pieces that were supposed to look like ivory.

On the opposite wall, open double doors led into the next room. Someone spoke from the darkened doorway.

"Good evening, Herr Ryder. I've been expecting you. I don't know how you managed to get by the guards outside, but it doesn't matter now. The important thing is that you're here."

Ryder started across the room.

"That's far enough, Herr Ryder. Please be seated at the table, and keep your hands in sight."

In the light from the overhead bulb, Ryder saw what he'd come for. He sat down and placed both hands on the table.

"Very good." Ilse Grimm was sitting on the side of a double bed. On top of the bedcovers, fast asleep, were Karen and Silka. Ryder felt the tension leave his body.

"Fräulein Grimm—how nice to find you home. Perhaps I should have called first?"

"I don't suppose you brought anyone with you?"

"No, I'm alone. Are the girls all right?"

"You can see for yourself—they're sleeping. A little something in the food. They eat and then sleep. When they wake up, they eat again. It works perfectly."

"So much for Tomorrow's Children."

Ilse glanced down at the girls. "We all must do our part, Herr Ryder, each in his own way."

"Doped to the gills?"

She chose to ignore his remark. Instead she looked at him with a small, crooked smile on her lips. Her eyes were unnaturally bright. "This is nice— so cozy, don't you think? You could be the father, seated at the table. And I'm the mother, putting our children to bed."

Ryder felt the ghost of a shiver between his shoulder blades. "If you're my wife, then I should call you Ilse."

"Very good...John." She tasted his name for the first time. "Now where was I? Oh, yes, I was putting the girls to sleep, while my husband, the famous chess player, is working on a new opening. Go on, John—begin."

"Whatever you say, dear." He moved a pawn.

"I cannot see from here," said Ilse, "but you did play your king's pawn, didn't you?"

"How do you know that?"

"It's a wife's duty to take an interest in her husband's work. You always open with that move."

A clock ticked somewhere in the house.

"Creature of habit?"

"Oh, no, not you, my husband."

"I'm pleased that you care. And I thought you didn't even play. Come— show me."

She smiled. "But I haven't finished putting the children to bed. You go on with what you are doing, dear. Go on, now."

Ryder moved a red pawn from the opposite side of the board.

"So nice—" She spoke in a singsong voice. "As soon as the girls are asleep, I'll join you. You'll play chess and I'll sew or read. Later, I'll make some tea."

"How about now?"

"Really, you men are so impatient. You know I can't leave the children until they are asleep."

Ryder moved another chess piece, his hand remarkably steady.

"We'll watch some television before we go to bed," Ilse continued, "and later we will make love. You'll fall asleep afterward. You snore, you know."

"I do?"

"It only makes me love you more."

The scene was domestic as all hell—the snug little house deep in the woods—the room, the woman, and the children sleeping in the darkened bedroom.

It wasn't so dark, though, that Ryder couldn't see the 9mm Walther P1 that Ilse was holding to Karen's head. It didn't take Colonel Cameron's weapons recognition course to know which model it was. Ryder had identified it as soon as he had stepped into the living room. He'd had a cap gun just like it when he was a boy.

It was domestic, all right. A great little gadget to put the kids to bed with—worked every time. It also worked well enough to keep him powerless, anchored to the table. Ryder shook his head and moved a knight.

Ilse spoke. "You don't like my game?"

"That's all it is—a game and you can't win."

Her voice became firm.

"Of course, I'm going to win. We've only just gotten started and look what's already happened."

"My compliments, Ilse. Eighteen innocent people dead and now you've kidnapped two children."

"I still don't know how you got in here." She looked down at the Walther in her hand. "Gunther and Kurt should have killed you in town. If I had been doing the shooting, I wouldn't have missed. The fools almost got me instead." She raised her voice.

"Gunther! Kurt! Get in here!"

Ryder had known they were there. He'd heard them trying to be quiet in the hall behind him. He shifted around to see Gunther and Kurt in the doorway. Each of them was holding an automatic weapon.

"Don't you two ever run out of guns?" said Ryder, moving bishop to bishop four.

Gunther stepped into the room and struck Ryder with the barrel of his gun, raking it across Ryder's cheek. The sight ripped a furrow which rapidly filled with blood.

"You want to play," said Gunther, "we'll play." He drew back to hit Ryder again, then stopped.

Ryder was looking at him with eyes Gunther had never seen before. For the moment, he was mesmerized, seared by the intensity of that look.

"That's enough!" said Ilse. "There'll be time for that later. Kurt, keep an eye on our guest. Gunther, search Herr Ryder and then contact the guards and find out how he got in here. If those idiots are drunk or sleeping—"

Careful not to get in the way of Kurt's gun, Gunther searched Ryder as roughly as possible. He was disappointed when he didn't find a weapon. Next, he picked up the radio and tried to raise the towers. There was no answer.

"Forget that," said Ilse. "I never did trust those things. You're going to have to go out and see what's happening. And while you're there, check back to the main road,"—Ilse looked at Ryder—"just to make certain our guest is telling us the truth."

"What about him?" asked Gunther, indicating Ryder. "The others won't be here until morning. Let's kill him now."

"No, not yet. First find out what's going on outside and then we can have the pleasure of dealing with Herr Ryder."

"I'll get my bike and be right back."

"For God's sake, Gunther, think! If there's anyone out there, do you want him to hear you? You'll have to walk. And check on Wolfgang, too."

Gunther looked at Ryder. "When I get back—" He raised his machine pistol.

"Gunther!"

"Okay, I'm going—"

"Before you leave, wake Rolf and Helmut. Tell them to make a pot of coffee and something to eat. This may take some time."

After Gunther left, Ilse spoke to Ryder. "First Charly's Pub, then the ranch, and now here. You enjoy taking chances—"

"Not really," said Ryder, making another move with a chess piece. "It's all so predictable and all so boring."

"Boring?" snapped Ilse. "You call Tomorrow's Children boring, after what we've done?"

"That's what I said." Ryder was at his condescending best. "You people remind me of kids, trying so hard to be different. Too bad you all wind up looking and sounding exactly alike. Someone should assign numbers for identification purposes."

It almost worked. The gun pointed at Karen's head wavered. "You're trying to make me mad," said Ilse, with a nervous laugh.

266

"You're already quite mad." Ryder moved another chess piece.

The gun wavered again.

"While we're waiting," said Ryder, "I'll tell you a story—the story of Tomorrow's Children."

"You talk too much," said Kurt, from the doorway.

"Let him," said Ilse. "I want to hear this."

Ryder moved another piece. By now, Ilse and Kurt hardly noticed. "Tomorrow's Children..." he began. "I wonder how you came up with that name."

"Never mind," said Ilse.

"You're right, it doesn't matter. It's only a name, and not a very good one, at that. There's no zing to it."

"You bastard!"

"Listen, Ilse! Fascist! Capitalist! Socialist! Tomorrow's Children! Do you hear? Maybe you could call yourselves Tomorrow's Childrenists. How's that for a name?"

"I'm going to kill you myself."

Ryder's hand paused in midair. Then he set the chess piece down. "I'm glad you said that, Ilse. It's just become a no-limit game."

"Another one of your Americanisms," said Ilse. "I don't know what you mean."

"You never will."

The gun in Ilse's hand was shaking. "Come on, Gunther," she said under her breath. "Hurry up!"

"If he had any brains," said Ryder, "he'd keep right on going, but he's stupid enough to come back."

She ran her tongue over her lips. "And when he does—"

"I know, Ilse, but it's still boring."

She looked as if she might snap. "How I hate your kind," she whispered, looking at the gun inches from Karen's head. "You and the von Friedenthals and all the rest."

"Don't let him bother you," said Kurt. "He'll get his, soon enough."

For the moment, it was as far as Ryder dared push her.

"Tomorrow's Children," he said. "Two lovely words."

"What?"

"That's right," said Ryder. "Tomorrow is a word full of promise—a golden tomorrow, when all things will be perfect. And aren't children our hope for the future?"

"Yes, for a perfect Germany."

"No, Ilse, you're a fraud. You use people. It worked with your parents and with your sister and now it works with characters like Gunther and Kurt."

Ilse scowled, but didn't speak.

"Of course it works. Remember? As soon as you discovered that you were a little smarter than the rest, that made you different."

"I'm smart enough to know," said Ilse, "that I'm not just another sheep to be led."

Ryder raised a clenched fist. "Right on!"

"Are you making fun of me?"

"Oh, no, Ilse, never that. You aren't the least bit funny. You're something special and I take you very seriously."

"I am special."

"Of course you are. Look at your folks. They worked and did without, just to send you to school. After all, a mind like yours had to be given every opportunity. Even your sister helped. How is she, by the way?"

"How should I know?"

"She called you today. Maybe she didn't speak with you, but she let you know that I was asking questions, and that I'd be at the ranch tonight."

"She's nothing but a fat cow."

"But she's still your sister and, for some mysterious reason, she still cares for you."

"She doesn't know any better. Don't waste your breath on a bourgeois little shopkeeper."

Ryder shook his head. "And you'll go right on using her, won't you?"

"You're as bad as she is," said Ilse. "Save the bleeding-heart philosophy for someone else."

Ryder continued. "I deliberately telephoned Martin von Friedenthal from Gertrude's shop. Anyone that organized would know how to contact you. I hated to do it to her after what she's already gone through with you."

Ryder looked up from the chessboard to stare directly at Ilse. "In the end, Karen and Silka are all that's important."

Ilse smiled and looked down at the gun in her hand. "I counted on it."

"That makes us even, because I counted on you, too. When Gunther and Kurt showed up at the ranch, I knew it wasn't coincidence. But I'm getting ahead of myself."

Ryder moved a knight, posting it strongly at queen five, and spoke to Ilse. "So off you go to university and meet other students who don't like anything, either. You learn all the buzzwords—the slogans of the moment. Freedom now! Throw the foreigners out! Germany for Germans! But what you're selling has nothing to do with freedom. I could go on, but it's so incredibly boring."

Ilse glared.

"The really neat thing," said Ryder, "is that you can keep going from one 'ism' to the other until they're all mixed up together. Just great! You can be against everything, because in the end it doesn't mean a thing."

"You know nothing about it."

"Don't be too sure."

She didn't answer.

Ryder went on. "You decide to organize and, like little kiddies, it has to be a secret society."

Ilse sat up straight. "We're not children."

Ryder ignored her interruption. "Now you have an organization, but unfortunately it's no good, because no one knows about it. How can you be against all these things, if no one knows? What to do? I can see the bunch of you, all sitting around scratching your heads."

"It wasn't like that at all."

Ryder studied the board. The red pieces were putting up a strong defense. Almost as an afterthought, he added, "Then someone has the bright idea—no small accomplishment, I assure you—of setting off a bomb. It makes a lot of noise, it kills people and, best of all, it gets a lot of attention. True, it's not very original, but what a great way to burst onto the scene. You'll be able to take your place right alongside Baader-Meinhoff and the Red Brigade."

"We stand alone. We—"

"Spare me," interrupted Ryder. "You are about to hit me with another of your platitudes. Let me finish. It's not going to take much longer."

269

Kurt, brandishing his gun, was about to speak, but Ilse silenced him with a look.

"And on the subject of bombs," said Ryder, "who are your demolition experts?"

"Gunther and Kurt, of course."

"And where do students learn about explosives and firearms?"

"We've been well taught."

"I should've guessed," said Ryder with a shrug. "Now, about this bomb. Where to put it? What's always controversial, represents authority, and makes an easy target in the bargain? The military, of course. You probably thought of it one day while riding your bicycle past army headquarters."

She looked startled.

"I'm not doing so badly, after all," said Ryder.

"A lucky guess."

Ryder moved pawn to bishop seven.

"Somehow, you managed to get that bomb into General Hartley's sedan—"

Ilse broke in. "It was simple. The General was at the house."

"The von Friedenthals?"

Ilse was delighted. "That's exactly what I mean. See, you don't know so much, after all. I kept the driver busy, while Gunther and Kurt worked on the auto. We had planned it differently, until the General started coming around so often to play trains."

"Martin would love that."

"Fortunately, the von Friedenthal house is the only one at the end of the street," said Ilse. "No one saw us, and that stupid driver thought I was offering him more than a cup of coffee."

"Where was Frau von Friedenthal when all this was going on?"

"She was sitting out on the back balcony, sewing. Once she gets started, she doesn't notice anything."

"Tell me—how'd you get hold of Karen and Silka?'

"I met them after school and asked if they would like to go for a ride. I told them their parents had given permission. I gave them some candy we had prepared. They still had some in their mouths when they fell asleep."

"You'd make one hell of a mother."

Switching the pistol, Ilse flexed the fingers of her right hand. "Kurt owns the auto and this house. If it hadn't been for all your nosy questions and your meddling—insisting on walking me home—I wouldn't have had to disappear so soon, but it's working out for the best. If you'd told anyone, you wouldn't be here alone."

"Don't be too sure of that."

The pistol was again in Ilse's right hand. "All we had to worry about was you and here you are. When Gunther returns, we'll take care of that problem. We'll find that Porsche of yours and dispose of it, too. If you want to finish your story, you'd better hurry up."

Ryder moved a rook. "Gunther is taking longer than I expected—he must be out of shape."

"He'll be here soon enough," said Kurt.

"The last part of my story has to do with a revelation. After the bomb went off, people went nuts. The U.S. and German military went on alert and the police started carrying automatic weapons. You couldn't turn around without running into the lens of a television camera, and the world press gave the incident front-page coverage. Your government in Bonn sat in special session. No car could exit the autobahn without being stopped and searched. Everyone was talking about it. In fact, that's all they talked about."

Ilse blinked like a satisfied owl.

"You learned, after you got over your own initial misgivings and the coffeehouse bull, and actually did the job, what all the other terrorist gangs have learned. You discovered the power of fear. Not the little qualms you'd experienced, but blind, bleating panic. What a trip! All that fuss about a few pounds of explosives."

"It was more than a few pounds," said Kurt.

"The idea scares people spitless, because explosives are so unselective. Folks who have no reason to be afraid are paralyzed. No one is after them, but the thought is never out of mind when they are in public. They can't walk through a parking lot without wondering if that innocent looking old VW Beetle over there is going to blow up in their faces."

Ilse looked like she had been given an award.

"You used the term yourself," said Ryder. "Helpless, harmless sheep—"

"—who have grown fat at the expense of the people," she finished. "You and your autos! It's time you were made to pay."

"You're breaking my heart, little girl," said Ryder. "Trouble is, you're not little girls and boys anymore. Kurt over there is pushing thirty, and so is Gunther, and you're no teenager yourself. You should have learned something useful by now, you've been in school long enough."

"Wait'll I wire your ass up with a couple of sticks of dynamite," said Kurt, "and you'll find out what I've learned. We'll see how brave you are when you watch the fuse burn down."

"That's what it's all about, isn't it?" said Ryder. "Terror is power. You clowns don't really want a new world. You wouldn't have the foggiest notion of what to do with one if you had it. You blow up a bunch of innocent people and hide behind the words Tomorrow's Children."

"They were part of the military complex," said Ilse. "They deserved to die."

"What about Karen and Silka?"

"Have you ever attended one of Professor von Friedenthal's lectures?"

"As a matter of fact," said Ryder, "I have."

"The man should have been put in a gas chamber along with the Jews."

"Sounds familiar."

Ilse nodded at the children. "This way is better. I've seen how he looks at them. Now, he will never know—"

"You plan to kill them, too?"

"After we make some video cassettes. Children will say anything you tell them to. When we have no further use for them..." She shrugged.

"And you'll go right on your merry way," said Ryder, "spreading joy wherever you go. You'll join your oppressed brothers and sisters, making people's lives as miserable as possible. The sheep, as you call them, will be milling around, afraid to act because they don't want to get hurt."

"You learn quickly," said Ilse. "We've already been contacted."

"I'll bet you have," said Ryder, "by every ding-a-ling outfit from Ireland to Iraq to Japan, with a couple of stops in between. They'll supply the arms and the money and you'll all be one big, happy family. You'll be patient. After a time, when nothing happens, everyone will relax. When things are back to normal, the wolf will raid the flock again."

"Exactly," said Ilse. "It's so easy. For practice, we waited for a rainy day, stole a car with military plates, flashed a card and drove right onto the Kaserne. Those stupid crash barriers are a joke."

Ilse let out a derisive laugh. "No MP is going to get wet if he doesn't have to. They stayed in their little huts and waved us right through. Afterward, we took the auto back to Patrick Henry Village. No one knew it was gone. When the General started visiting the von Friedenthals, it was even better."

Ryder moved another piece.

"Do you think I joined a Wild West Club because I'm so in love with America? That's ridiculous! I used them. It's the easiest thing in the world to cross international borders with all that junk."

"Guns and all."

The words came tumbling out in a torrent of hate. "No customs inspector is going to paw through the clothes, the saddles, and the fake guns as long as you have the proper documentation. They think the whole thing is silly. You'd be surprised at what can be hidden in the trunk of an auto if it's packed full enough. With a van, they throw up their hands and walk away."

"And the sheep will be off and running again."

"With our plans, Herr Ryder, the next time will be even better."

"There's not going to be a next time." Ryder smiled. He was the least dangerous person in the room. "You see—I'm not a sheep and I'm not a wolf; I'm something you've never met before."

"You're a fool like everyone else."

Ryder could hear running outside. "I've given you every chance, but it's no use. If you were caught and put in prison, there'd always be the possibility of your getting out."

"I'll never go to prison."

"I know." Ryder picked up a red chess piece. "The Queen—the single most powerful figure on the board," he said pensively, holding the gaudy plastic, feeling its solid lead-weighted heft. "Sometimes, in a whole game, she only moves once."

"You're in no position to make threats, Herr Ryder," said Ilse, moving the gun closer to the sleeping head. "There's nothing you can do."

Someone was in the front yard. Ryder was surprised that no one else in the house seemed to notice. "Until tonight," he said, still examining the chess figure, "I'd never killed a man,"—Ryder looked at the sleeping children and at Ilse and the gun—"or a woman. What you've done, and what you plan to do, is unforgivable."

"We were following instructions. The von Friedenthals and their kind are bad enough but, Mr. Genius Grand Master, Karen and Silka are here because of you."

Ilse's laughter bordered on hysteria. "You should see the look on your face."

The front door banged open and Gunther came running down the hall.

"They're dead!" he yelled. "Up in the towers, they're all dead!"

Gasping for breath, Gunther leaned against the wall by the door, holding his gun in one hand and pieces of a black plastic radio in the other.

"That bastard killed them all."

Ilse straightened with a jerk.

"Wolfgang?"

"Dead, too." Gunther dropped the pieces of plastic and turned his gun toward John.

"You know what he did? He put Wolfgang on my motorcycle. He's sitting out in the garage right now, riding my bike—and he's dead." Gunther crouched, leveling his weapon. "You son-of-a-bitch!"

"No!" screamed Ilse, swinging the Walther toward John. "He's mine!"

She was bringing the weapon up with the shooter's two-handed grip, when there was a flash of color from Ryder's hand and he was up and away from the table.

Gunther died from a smashing blow to the breastbone. He was still standing, firing his weapon into the floor, when he died.

Kurt never got that far. In one smooth, liquid motion, Ryder slid around Gunther and seized Kurt by the face, slamming his head against the doorjamb. Before Kurt began his slide toward oblivion, Ryder was down the hall toward the kitchen, looking for Rolf and Helmut. He found them.

Ryder entered the bedroom. There was a quiet. Death was here. Lying on her back across the foot of the bed, her right arm hanging over the edge, Ilse was still holding the Walther. A grotesque green eye in the center of her forehead stared blankly at the ceiling.

"Check and mate," said Ryder. "To hell with Tomorrow's Children."

He took Ilse by the left wrist, rolling her over to dump her body unceremoniously on the floor, and sat down on the edge of the bed.

"You were wrong about the rest, Ilse, but you did do one thing right."

Karen and Silka were still sleeping. Shots had been fired, people had died, and the children slept on. It was just as well.

Ryder leaned over to smooth a lock of Silka's hair, but he was thinking about his son Matthew. Seeing the girls like this made him realize there was no real shelter, no safety, from evil.

Who had brought him to this farmhouse and the two sleeping children? He was a pawn who'd yet to see the face of his opponent.

"Come on you two," he said gently. "Time for us to go home." He hoped it wasn't too late.

With a child cradled against each shoulder, Ryder left the house, walked up the road through the fields, and disappeared into the trees at the top of the hill.

Chapter XXXVI

In a restaurant at the Frankfurt airport, John Ryder was waiting for his flight to New York. As he turned to the last page of the International Herald Tribune, someone took a chair from his table and sat down.

"Good morning, Kommissar Brunner," said Ryder from behind the newspaper. "Won't you sit down?"

The sarcasm wasn't lost on the Kommissar. "I thought I told you not to leave Germany without permission," he said.

Ryder folded the newspaper and tossed it on the table. "By the numbers—always by the numbers—" He shook his head. "What may I offer you?"

"You're drinking tea."

"You must be a detective."

"Make it tea."

Ryder signaled a waitress who had been hovering nearby. "I've been expecting you."

"I can't think why," said Kommissar Brunner heavily. "What happened to your face?"

"It's just a scratch. I heal quickly; it will be gone in a couple of days."

"How did you get it?"

"Oh, horsing around. You know how it is."

"You're telling me that we can play this game all day."

"If you wish—"

"*Verdammt!*" Kommissar Brunner banged his fist on the table. "Listen—" The Kommissar ground to a halt when he encountered the look in Ryder's eyes.

"That's better," said Ryder. "Why don't we start over. Let's sit here and converse like civilized people until my plane leaves."

"You're not going anywhere," said the Kommissar. "And you can hardly refer to yourself as civilized."

Ryder was the voice of reason. "You're attracting attention and, more importantly, a man of your years should give some thought to his blood pressure."

Kommissar Brunner leaned back in his chair and took several deep breaths. "You're doing this on purpose."

"All I'm trying to do is finish my breakfast. Here's your tea."

The two men watched as the waitress set a second pot of tea down on the table. She turned over a cup that had been resting upside down on the saucer and poured. She placed the cream pitcher and the sugar bowl next to the Kommissar. She kept fussing until he growled at her and she went away.

"Why aren't you using one of Mr. Hall's private airplanes? It is my understanding he places great value on you."

"I come and go as I please."

The Kommissar poured a liberal portion of cream into his tea and stirred. "There are some very serious questions you must answer."

"The only thing I must do," said Ryder, "is, one day, I must die. Nothing else."

"Speaking of dying, can you explain the ten bodies—the victims of violent crime—that I have on my hands?"

"No more than I can explain the eighteen that the American military authorities have on theirs."

"Like that, is it?"

"Just like that."

"You expect me to believe you know nothing about these deaths?"

"Why should I? I'm a chess player. The only violence I'm familiar with takes place on the chessboard. No one's ever died, that I know of. Some of us may feel like killing ourselves after a stupid move, but that's about it."

"As you know, the details haven't yet been released to the press, "—Kommissar Brunner paused and took a sip of his tea—"but it seems there's a homicidal maniac on the loose."

"By whose definition?"

"Ten people," said the Kommissar reflectively, "all of whom died horrible deaths."

"In this day and age and here, in this land of law and order."

Kommissar Brunner looked up from his tea. "What kind of man are you, John Ryder? We have ten mutilated bodies and you're being flippant."

"You're wrong—I see no humor in mutilation."

"There's no other word for it. You see, they weren't shot or stabbed. Someone apparently used his bare hands."

"Perhaps it was a personal matter—"

"Five died of broken necks," continued the Kommissar relentlessly. "If it wasn't for a smashed two-way radio, we might have missed four of them entirely. There was another who died of massive internal injuries, one with the back of his skull crushed, one without a mark on him, and another who had a refrigerator door slammed on his head."

There was the hint of a smile on Ryder's face as he refilled his teacup.

"It's not funny." A throbbing vein on the Kommissar's forehead looked as if it might burst.

"You're damn right it isn't funny. It wasn't funny when those people died at Campbell Barracks. I know, I was there. It wasn't funny when Martin von Friedenthal's children were kidnapped. Involving children isn't humorous at all, Herr Kommissar. You might ask Martin how amusing he thought it was."

"That's another thing."

"What now?"

"No one will talk to me. I know you were at the Grimm's farm and I know you were in Garmisch. But no one has anything to say. While I'm at it, Herr Ryder, if I couldn't arrest you for anything else, I could charge you with driving 250 kilometers an hour in a 130-kilometer zone."

"I'd wondered about that."

"We're not fools here."

"I never thought you were."

Kommissar Brunner leaned his forearms on the table. "And then there is a certain Herr Kramer. You know him, of course?"

"We've met."

"What did you do to him?"

"Not a thing that I know of. Why?"

"I went to his home in Sandhausen. He said he was the fastest draw in Germany—until you came along. Now what's that supposed to mean?"

"Think nothing of it, Herr Kommissar. I showed him a trick, that's all."

Kommissar Brunner was tracing lines on the tablecloth with his spoon. "There was a police report of a red Porsche driving without lights in the Odenwald on the night in question. Normally, I wouldn't see a report like that, but all stations were told to call in any unusual occurrences. Driving a 930 Porsche without lights is not considered usual."

The Kommissar looked up from his artwork. "Of course, you wouldn't know anything about that. And while I'm at it, that's a very expensive auto for a chess player to drive."

"Let's say I have independent means, Herr Kommissar."

"What about the Odenwald?"

Ryder leaned back in his chair, crossed one leg over the other and seemed interested in getting the crease in his pants just right. "If you're referring to Clementine, Herr Kommissar, I imagine there is more than one red Porsche in all of Germany."

"Clementine?"

"That's her name—the Porsche, I mean."

The Kommissar looked off across the restaurant. "We have examined the undercarriage of Clemen—" The Kommissar stared at Ryder for a long moment. "We found a type of grass caught in the undercarriage of the Porsche," he said finally, "that only grows in the Odenwald."

Ryder shook his head. "Herr Kommissar, you can do better than that."

"And then there's the matter of Doctor von Friedenthal," said the Kommissar, marching doggedly forward. He was going to touch all the bases or know the reason why.

"Yes?"

"All of a sudden, just like that, his two daughters are back."

"I know, I saw them."

"In the Odenwald?"

"Even though the newspapers and television are full of little else, I saw Karen and Silka at their home."

"The children are back, but I'm not able to speak with them. The von Friedenthal family physician will not permit it. He claims they were drugged. And Doctor von Friedenthal says only that he heard a noise at the front door and, when he opened it, there they were."

"Perhaps," said Ryder, reaching for the sugar, "that's just the way it was."

The overhead light came on, the front door opened, and the old man stood blinking in the harsh glare.

"Well, Martin, aren't you going to invite us in? I haven't had a thing to eat since yesterday morning and I'm starving. Oh, by the way, I found these two out in a pumpkin patch. Recognize them?"

Give von Friedenthal credit. His back straightened, his voice firmed, but he did seem to be having trouble with his vision. Perhaps the light over the door was too bright. "Why, John," he said, "what happened to your face?"

"Never mind my face. Do you think it's a good idea to be standing out here, chatting like this?"

"I'm sorry, please come in. I'll tell Liesel you're here."

Von Friedenthal held the door open so Ryder could enter.

"Strange you should mention it, but pumpkins have been on my mind for quite some time now." Von Friedenthal closed the door carefully behind John. "The…ah…pumpkins haven't been damaged in any way, have they? They're very fragile when they're small."

"No," said Ryder, carrying the children up the stairs to the main part of the house, "I don't believe so. A little wilted perhaps, but I think you'll find these two will be as good as new once they're back in their own patch for a day or two."

"Martin," called Liesel from another part of the house, "who is it?"

"It's all right, darling," said von Friedenthal, "just a man with some pumpkins."

"Did you say pumpkins? At this hour?"

"Yes, my love," answered von Friedenthal, his voice suddenly husky. "I think you'd better come and see."

Ryder finally got Liesel and von Friedenthal together on the couch in the living room at the same time. Liesel had a tendency to keep running down the hall to check on the girls. They had begun to come to during the ride home, but they were still groggy.

After the girls were settled, Liesel fixed a sandwich and a glass of milk for John. She insisted on cleaning the wound on his face, making a big production out of sterile cloths and antiseptic, but he wouldn't let her put a bandage on.

He sat on a chair facing them. "Listen—there's not much time, so let me say this and then be on my way. Karen and Silka are safe in their own beds, but as soon as I leave, call your doctor and have him take a look at them just to be sure."

He smiled. "I know I don't have to tell either of you what to do, but you must be prepared for the storm of public attention that will descend on you as soon as this gets out."

Von Friedenthal put a reassuring arm around his wife's shoulders. The years had dropped away and he was very much himself again. "I foresee no problem that we cannot handle," he said. The tone of his voice was all the answer Ryder needed.

Martin von Friedenthal had faced adversity before and would again, if necessary. As a young man, during the Nazi regime, he'd watched friends being loaded into box cars at the railroad station and had been beaten when he tried to interfere.

They came for him that same night and von Friedenthal disappeared. Repeated attempts by his father to find him led to a warning that if the old man didn't stop making trouble the same would happen to him.

One day, three months after the war in Europe was over, there was a knock at the front door of the von Friedenthal home, overlooking the Neckar. Martin's mother opened the door to a ragged, malnourished, red-eyed stranger who smelled bad. Normally a kind person, she started to close the door, because the man frightened her. It frightened her even more when he asked, "Mother—don't you know me?"

He'd spent the last three months making his way across Europe, hiding from the Russians by day and walking by night. During the war, he'd been a prisoner in one of the more infamous camps in Czechoslovakia. It was only by a fluke that he'd been freed.

The Russian commander who "liberated" the camp was a chess enthusiast. War and nationality were irrelevant when he met the young, world-class chess player. However, when it became clear that von Friedenthal had no intention of playing chess for Mother Russia, the commander had released him.

He deleted von Friedenthal's name from the camp records and provided him with food, a map and, best of all, his freedom. There were only two conditions.

If von Friedenthal were captured, he was to swear he'd never met the commander and, if the fates allowed, some day the commander would play a game of chess with von Friedenthal in Heidelberg.

In the rebuilding years after the war, von Friedenthal had often thought of the commander, but he never saw him again.

Ryder leaned over and lowered his voice. "There's one thing you can do."

"You have only to ask."

"You're going to have to lie for me and make it stick, no matter what."

"Is that all?"

"It won't be easy. You may as well know the worst of it—people died tonight. I'm not going to give you a speech, but I killed them."

"Because of Karen and Silka?"

"Because someone used them to get at me and because of the 1938 Crystal Night philosophy."

Von Friedenthal's eyes were clear and untroubled as his arm tightened around Liesel's shoulder. "When I lost Karen and Silka, I gave up. I never shall again. You gave me back my life. There is nothing to concern yourself with."

"Don't speak too quickly, old friend," said Ryder. "I want you to be ready when a certain Kommissar Brunner comes calling and, rest assured, he will."

"Leave the Kristallnacht advocates and the Kommissar to me," said Professor Doctor Martin von Friedenthal.

Ryder's eyes sparkled as he raised his teacup. "Kommissar, I imagine you had an interesting meeting with Doctor von Friedenthal."

Kommissar Brunner looked shocked. "You're not going to drink it black, are you?"

"Just like my heart, Herr Kommissar."

"I never saw such a mess in my life," grumped the Kommissar. "Von Friedenthal was bad enough by himself. Then I started getting calls from Bonn—all very specific. I was not to harass a national treasure...as if anyone could harass that man."

Kommissar Brunner drew a final line on the tablecloth, then placed the spoon carefully on the saucer alongside his empty cup. "I don't know who is worse, Doctor von Friedenthal or you," he said gloomily.

Then he brightened. "Of course, there is the matter of the fingerprints."

"Come off it, Herr Kommissar. That's almost as bad as your 'Odenwald grass.'"

"I could keep you in prison and forget about you, that is, until you talked."

"I thought that sort of thing went out of style back in the 1930's."

Kommissar Brunner lost his temper again. "Don't talk to me about the thirties!" he yelled. "Talk about today. I have ten bodies on my hands that must be explained."

Ryder leaned forward. "Better dead than in prison, where some fine night after another terrorist attack, they'll haul your official ass out of bed because more blameless people are going to die if you don't release the prisoners. Herr Kommissar, I'm through talking. Arrest me or button it. And, when you leave, take your two assistants, waiting over there by the door, with you."

Surprisingly, Kommissar Brunner wasn't upset.

"So, you noticed. I wondered if you would. They still have a great deal to learn."

Kommissar Brunner put his hands on the table as if to stand up. "Unofficially, and off the record, and speaking hypothetically, of course, does it have to be this way?"

"Kommissar Brunner, you never did anything unofficial or off the record in your life. But, hypothetically speaking, the answer is yes."

"For how long?"

"For as long as it takes."

Kommissar Brunner sighed, rose heavily from his chair, and stood looking down at Ryder. "You have a high regard for Doctor von Friedenthal?"

"Not a high regard, Kommissar. I love that old man."

"Strange, he says the same about you." Kommissar Brunner shook his head. "Ten bodies and we are discussing love."

Slowly, he offered his hand. "I don't agree, I never will. There must be another way."

Ryder rose to take the Kommissar's hand. "Then find it."

Kommissar Brunner looked into Ryder's eyes, then turned and started out of the restaurant. He stopped after a few steps and came back.

"Forget something?"

"No, I didn't and neither did you. I've been told, by people who know, that you never forget anything."

"Is that a crime, Kommissar?"

"I was at the house in the Odenwald. In all my years of dealing with death, I've never seen anything like it. I told you about nine of them and you know there were ten. A chess grand master, who routinely thinks seven or eight moves ahead on the chessboard, is unable to count to ten?"

"You did seem stuck on the number, Kommissar, but otherwise I didn't think about it."

"Because you knew all along."

"Your story."

"Broken necks, heads in refrigerators, and one who was so terrified, he died of fright."

Ryder waited.

"When I first saw Fräulein Grimm, she was lying on the bedroom floor—dead." Kommissar Brunner rolled his head around on his shoulders, trying to loosen tightened neck muscles. "It still bothers me to think about it. She was watching me with a huge green eye in her forehead...horrible-looking thing."

He suppressed a shudder. "No one knew what it was until the autopsy. The pathologist says what he found is physically impossible. That green eye was the felt base of a chess piece that had been driven into Ilse Grimm's brain."

Kommissar Brunner took a long slow breath. There! He had finally gotten the last of it off his chest. "What do you have to say to that, Mister Grand Master who can't count up to ten?"

Without another word, Kommissar Brunner turned and left the restaurant. In the back seat of the police sedan, on the return trip to Heidelberg, Kommissar Brunner folded his hands comfortably over his stomach, closed his eyes, and prepared to do some heavy thinking.

Although he would have denied it with his dying breath, for the first time in years, Kommissar Brunner was a man totally at peace with himself.

Once again, John Ryder, you have escaped. You grow too strong. You destroy my temple and seek to hide. A far place will not ease the weight on your mind. It is time to discharge your debt, so I now lay claim to what is mine. I will wait no longer.

Chapter XXXVII

He was being watched. Ryder was awake, but didn't move. It was the first time since his training had begun that he'd slept past six o'clock. Close to his ear was the ticking of a clock, while from somewhere back in the house came the comforting chuff of a washing machine. Outside the sliding glass doors of his room, blue jays were yelling about something. Ryder could smell the sulphur water from the lawn sprinklers and remembered—Florida.

He turned his head to look toward the doorway of his bedroom. Lying on the floor in the hallway was a massive black dog with his head on his paws. As soon as Ryder made eye contact, Lord Byron, the family Newfoundland, began to move his feathered oar sweep of a tail from side to side on the rug.

Sitting on the side of his bed, Ryder nodded. Immediately, By, as he was called, rose and came to sit in front of Ryder. Ryder scratched the dog's chest and By looked everywhere in the room but at Ryder, who gave the Newf a playful shove. Lord Byron went belly up, throat exposed in one-hundred-forty pounds of abject surrender. Ever since Ryder's arrival last night, there was a new leader of the pack.

Ryder slipped on a pair of jeans, pushed back the sliding glass door, and stepped outside. Before he could close the door again, Lord Byron wriggled through with surprising agility for a dog of his size. He threw himself down and sighed, as if the effort had been too much.

"Easy for you to say," said Ryder. By looked away.

The two were on a wooden deck that ran the length of the house. The house itself clung to the side of a bluff overlooking a creek and wetlands. On the level below was another deck with a glass-enclosed swimming pool.

There were no other houses in sight, but Ryder could see several rooftops through the trees. On the far bank of the creek, like a priest blessing his flock, a cormorant stood and spread his wings to dry in the rays of the early morning sun.

After a shower and shave, Ryder went looking for someone, but the house was four levels of emptiness. In the kitchen, he found a note from Wanda stuck to the front of the refrigerator with a pink magnetic bunny.

She had a planning committee meeting this morning and in the afternoon she was scheduled for volunteer work at one of the local hospitals. After a morning of preschool, the children would be at the hospital day-care center with her. The keys to the extra car were on the table by the front door. She'd see him tonight.

Ryder searched the cabinets and finally decided on toast and shredded wheat. He created a mess. He made a derisive noise and By, who had followed him into the kitchen, looked troubled. Newfs apparently worried about everything.

Leaning against the kitchen counter, Ryder ate his breakfast and thought about his sister-in-law.

Even though it was well into the evening, Wanda had insisted on meeting Ryder's flight in Jacksonville. She greeted him with a sisterly peck on the cheek and several nervous little pats on the back.

"It's nice to see you again," said Ryder, "but you really shouldn't have gone to the trouble. I could've rented a car and checked into a motel."

"Oh, we wouldn't think of it. We've moved into a new house and there's plenty of room." Wanda tucked her arm under Ryder's and steered him toward the stairs leading down to the baggage claim area.

Ryder held up his carry-on. "This is it."

She looked pleased. "I guess you aren't planning to stay very long."

"Not really."

"But you'll stay for Christmas? It will make Matthew so happy."

Ryder wasn't sure what she meant, but now was not the time. "Perhaps—"

"Of course, you will. We insist. Heaven only knows the next time you'll come to visit."

With a proprietary air, Wanda guided Ryder to the parking lot and to a dark blue Cadillac. It suited her. She spent a good deal of time in the pool and on her exercise bike, but she was no longer girlishly slim and had the first hint of a double chin. She was still a striking-looking woman and knew exactly what she wanted. She made sure her husband Slade got it for her—her car, her house, her boat.

She could barely conceal her pride when she told people that her boat was the longest one in the marina. They always stayed in sight of land, but

288

she loved the parties at the Yacht Club, where the toilets had those cute little signs, INBOARD and OUTBOARD, over the doors, and where you could get all dressed up and be admired.

Ryder thought of Stacey and wondered how two sisters could have been so close and yet so different.

"It's late," he said. "If you're tired, I'd be glad to drive."

She looked shocked. "Oh, no—no one drives my car but me."

All the way back to St. Augustine, she chatted brightly. But whenever Ryder asked about Matthew, she said as little as possible and changed the subject.

"Sooner or later we're going to have to talk about my son. Is something wrong?"

"Of course not, silly. He's grown so much, you'll hardly recognize him. It's been almost a year now and Matthew is part of the family."

"Did you tell him that I was coming?"

Wanda was saved from answering when they turned off U.S.1 into an impressive subdivision. Ryder could see the lights of substantial homes among the trees and shrubbery.

"Slade built most of these houses and ours, too," said Wanda, as she pulled up in front of a three-car garage. The house itself was floodlit. There were colored lights in the trees. On the lawn, Santa and his reindeer blinked on and off.

"Lovely, isn't it?" said Wanda. "Folks drive by all the time just to admire. You can't really see the house from here. There are four levels right down the side of the hill to the creek." Wanda giggled. "The kitchen is higher than the living room and there's a heated swimming pool. According to Slade, it was a devil of a job to build on the side of a hill, but wait until you see. It's so pretty and all the furniture came from New York."

Ryder rinsed his breakfast dishes, put them in the dishwasher, and went down to the next level. There was a black woman in a white uniform plumping cushions and humming to herself.

"Good morning."

The woman whirled around, eyes wide. She was clutching her chest.

"I didn't mean to startle you. I'm John Ryder, Wanda's brother-in-law."

The woman let out her breath in a rush. "Mister, you oughtn't go snea-kin' up on folks like that."

"Maybe I should wear a bell—"

"You and the cat." She pointed. "That's him—Dracula."

At one end of the sofa, a fat orange-colored cat was sitting on his paws, sound asleep. He was wearing a collar with a small silver bell.

"He stays out all night and sleeps all day. That's why I gave him that name. I put a bell on his worthless hide, 'cause he used to sneak up on me and scare me half to death. I think he liked to hear me holler, but I fixed him good and he don't bring me dead birds no more."

She looked around the room. "I'm through in here, so I'll go finish the laundry." With that, the woman in white started up the stairs, muttering to herself about scarin' folks.

The room was starkly modern. There was a great deal of chrome and glass. There were no books. Standing beside the stone fireplace, almost touch-ing the ceiling, was an artificial Christmas tree. At the base of the tree were piles of colorfully wrapped packages.

Ryder was restless. He didn't feel like taking a swim, and the thought of waiting around all day held little appeal, so he took the car keys and, to the Newf's delight, whistled up Lord Byron.

Things had changed since he and Stacey last visited. New shopping centers and strip malls overshadowed the faded signs for lube jobs and well-drilling services. Legions of stoplights has grown like toadstools after a spring rain. Ryder picked up lunch at a drive-through. By was pleased with his hamburger.

There was still the long afternoon and Ryder headed out toward the St. Johns river, past tin-roofed shacks bowed under the weight of more kids, tears, and drunken beatings than a house could stand. Ryder slid the station wagon into a curve before he remembered what he was driving. There was a thump from the back as By lost his footing.

"Sorry, By. I was thinking of something else." There was the oar sweep of a forgiving tail, but By didn't stand up again.

The afternoon passed slowly. Ryder found a small park beside the river and let By loose for a sniffing orgy. Afterward, they followed the William Bartram Trail along the river and finally headed back on State Road 16. At the turn, the body of a bandit-faced raccoon lay by the side the road, small black feet folded together like a naughty child turned innocent in sleep. Overhead, hawks and buzzards rode the thermals over America's cement game trails.

At the hospital parking lot, Ryder cracked the windows of the station wagon so Lord Byron could have some air, then went to sit on a bench by the entrance. It wasn't long before he heard Wanda's voice.

"There's your father, Matthew."

He looked up to see Wanda and the children coming toward him. The twins, Slade Wallace III and Vanessa, were Matthew's age, while Janine was a year younger. They all looked at Ryder with curiosity. Matthew was a quiet, dark-haired child with large eyes and a grave expression.

Without thinking, Ryder grasped his son under the arms and tossed him high in the air. It was a game they used to play, much to Matthew's joy. This time it was different. Matthew let out a scream of fright and went running to Wanda. He wrapped his arms around her leg.

"John!" exclaimed Wanda. "Be careful! You're terrifying him."

"Why? It's a game Matt and I used to play by the hour. He loves it."

"Obviously not. And his name is Matthew."

"I know, I gave it to him."

With ice in his heart, Ryder crouched down to talk to his son. "Hey, old man, don't you remember me?"

Matthew wouldn't look at Ryder and hid his face against Wanda's skirt.

"What do you expect?" said Wanda. She didn't sound displeased. "He doesn't see you for nearly a year and then you frighten him almost to death. Don't cry, Matthew, it's just your father."

Matthew was watching Ryder with one round eye.

"Do you want to ride home with me?" asked Ryder.

The eye disappeared.

"I've brought Lord Byron."

Matthew pressed his face tighter against Wanda.

"Sorry, old man. I won't frighten you again."

"Well," said Wands brightly, "let's all go home and take a swim, shall we?"

The children went racing to Wanda's car.

"You be careful, hear!" called Wanda. She looked pleased. "We'll meet you back at the house, John. I'm so going to enjoy your visit."

Ryder was sitting in a chair watching his son, who was carefully keeping the heated swimming pool between them, when a large raw-boned man with sun-streaked blond hair appeared. Slade Wallace Peavey II was not one of Ryder's favorite people, but he stood up just the same.

"Well, boy," said Peavey, offering his hand, palm down, as if bestowing knighthood, "it's been awhile."

Peavey, who squeezed rubber balls to improve his grip, seized Ryder's hand and put on the pressure. There was no reaction. Ryder knew all he cared to know about his brother-in-law.

Slade Wallace Peavey II was a financial success. He'd taken his father's piddly-assed, one-man contracting business and his father's reputation, built on over forty years of quality work at a fair price, and had struck out on his own with a burning desire to get to the top of the pile.

It wasn't that he cut corners, exactly, but why give the customers a lot of stuff they'd never see? Peavey sailed as close to the wind as the law almost allowed. He was big on visual gimmicks, especially in the kitchen and bath. He sold a lot of houses.

Peavey believed in diversification and, in addition to his contracting business, he was also into lumber and land management. He and the boys had fine-tuned the art of contract bidding. He was also into a couple of things that didn't appear on the company books.

Peavey belonged to the requisite number of local civic organizations and had held office in most of them. He'd reached that station in life where he could pontificate the obvious with great authority and people listened.

Ol' S.W. was thinking about public office and the boys in Tallahassee were interested. It was time to get back to the Southern brand of Democratic politics like it used to be—before things had gone totally to Republican hell.

Peavey took his hand back. "Sun's over the yardarm. How about a drink? And for Christ's sake, don't say tea."

"Scotch will be fine."

"Damn it, boy, that's almost as bad." Peavey raised his voice. "Hey, babe!"

Wanda was at the shallow end of the pool with the children. "Yes, hon?"

"Bring us menfolk a couple of drinks while the brothers-in-law find out where it's at."

"Sure, hon." Well, why not? After all, he'd only belted her twice in all the time they'd been married, and he was sorry afterward. The first time had cost him the boat and the second time, the house.

Peavey was watching his wife walk away. She was wearing a bikini. "Fine-looking woman, ain't she, boy?"

"Slade—"

"Yeah, boy?"

"Two things—"

"What's that?"

"Stop calling me *boy*—and knock off the corn-pone routine."

Peavey grinned. "You'd be surprised the business us country folk can do when we put our minds to it."

"Give it a break."

Peavey was feeling ugly. Wanda, breasts swaying with her Miss America walk, looked just as good coming toward him and it hadn't rained in weeks.

Slade Wallace Peavey II had had little sexual experience in high school. It wasn't that he'd planned or wanted it that way, but things never seemed to work out.

He thought he had it made the night of his senior prom. He finally got Mavis Hayes in the back seat of his dad's Chrysler. He'd rounded third and was streaking for home when Deputy Sheriff Bubba Dawkins banged his nightstick on the car hood and pinned the lovers with his flashlight.

Peavey never knew how he got over the front seat and behind the wheel with his pants down. He'd sped away to hooting sounds of laughter and had single-mindedly gone looking for another place to park.

It was useless. Mavis was hysterical and kicked up such a fuss, he'd had to take her home.

It was a small town. He'd known Wanda in high school, but she'd cut him dead. Peavey went away to college and lost his virginity, while Wanda attended a local school.

When Peavey returned, he went into business with his father. About that time, Wanda's younger sister Stacey got married, and Peavey started building houses. Suddenly, there was Wanda.

They dated. Peavey made his move—nothing. On a good night, he might get to fondle her breasts through her clothing, but it stopped right there. He couldn't stand it and asked her to marry him. To his surprise, she said yes and they honeymooned in Disney World

It rained all the time and they stayed in their room. He never imagined it could be like this. Now that the ring was on her finger, Wanda was insatiable. As the rain beat down, she was a mewling, moist furnace of mouth and thigh. Business was going to go to hell when they got home.

It was a typical glorious Florida day, without a cloud in the sky, when they returned. The honeymoon was over. It wasn't that she refused him, she seldom did. But it was just not the same.

Peavey was really starting to move now, building several houses at the same time. The only delay was the day it rained and he had to send the crews home. He was moping around on the sofa trying to figure how to catch up, when Wanda landed in his lap. It was Disneyworld all over again and they never left the couch.

He'd met the delivery date, brought in the houses on time, and had started six more. It was a gamble. He had all his plates in the air at the same time, but if he could pull it off, he'd have rounded the corner. The stress had given his dad a fatal heart attack and Peavey was on his own.

Before he could get the roofs on, it started to rain, and rain heavily. He had waited as long as he could before he sent the boys home. Wanda jumped him in the garage, scaring the hell out of him. They wound up rolling around on the cement floor, while the rain thundered down.

It rained for four days. Afterward, Peavey had to work from dawn to late at night. He drove the men, seven days a week, with threats and pleading, but he met his deadlines.

While Peavey hammered and sawed and measured and fitted, he thought about Wanda. He was beginning to get the idea.

The next time it rained, he was ready and, sure enough, Wanda was after him. It seemed that rain drove her crazy. At first, Peavey was ecstatic. If water did it for her, Peavey was game for anything.

He damned near drowned her in the tub and the next time out he kept her in the shower so long she looked like a prune. He even rigged up a lawn sprinkler aimed at their bedroom windows and timed to go off when the two of them were in bed. Nothing, absolutely nothing. No matter how inventive he was, Peavey couldn't push Wanda's button.

Then it rained, Wanda went crazy, and Peavey came to know the terrible truth. It had to be the real, falling-down-out-of-the-sky, God-given stuff. There were bonus points for thunder and lightning.

So it was with mixed emotions as a builder and a lover that Peavey listened to the weather forecast on the eleven o'clock news every night. He supposed he was the only man in the state of Florida who prayed for a hurricane.

"You boys have got ten minutes," called Wanda from two decks up, "to get yourselves changed and to the dinner table."

Ryder couldn't believe it. Seated in the formal dining room, amidst Wanda's best crystal, china, and silver, Peavey was wearing a karate gi. He saw Ryder's look.

"Know what this is, boy?"

"I thought we talked about that."

"Okay, okay...but pretty snazzy, huh?"

"I've seen one before."

"Right after dinner, I'm driving to my karate club in Jacksonville. I work out two, maybe three times a week. See this here. I've got a black belt. You should come along and get some exercise. We don't get any chess players."

"Not this time, thanks."

Peavey looked satisfied and turned his attention to his food. He ate with the same single-mindedness as he built houses. First he attacked the meat, then the potatoes and, finally, the vegetables. He didn't talk.

"I wish you'd slow down, Slade," chided Wanda. She wanted to impress Ryder. She was wearing a hostess gown and inquired in her best lady-of-the-manor voice if he would like some more wine.

"I'm fine, thanks."

"Please help yourself to seconds. I've made a fuss just for you."

"Where are the children?"

"Oh, they don't eat with us. Sarah is serving them in the breakfast room and she'll get them ready for bed. It's been a long day."

"I'd like to see Matthew before he goes to bed."

"You just leave everything to Wanda," said Peavey with his mouth full. "She's a great fixer-upper."

"I believe you." Ryder looked at Wanda. "I wanted to wait until I could speak to you both together. I can't thank you enough for looking after my son these past months, but you might as well know this now. I'm taking Matt back to England with me."

Wanda dropped her fork with a crash, her best china forgotten. "What? What was that you said?"

"I'm taking my son to England."

"Why?"

"To live, of course."

"You can't do that!"

"I've arranged for his passport. All we need is a photo."

Wanda's eyes blazed. "No!"

"What do you mean—no?"

"I've never forgiven you," hissed Wanda, "for having Stacey cremated."

"It's what she wanted." Stacey and John had talked about it when the reality of the act had seemed a lifetime away.

"You didn't even have the human decency to have her buried properly, so I could visit her grave."

"You didn't know Stacey very well, did you?"

"She was my only sister and you took her away and destroyed her. Matthew is the one part of her I have left, and now you want to take him, too. I won't let you."

Wanda shook her head in disbelief. "You disappear for almost a year. No one knows where you've been or what you've been doing, and then you have the nerve to show up here and tell me what you're going to do."

"I can understand how you feel, but you have no choice."

"We'll see about that. Slade, do something," said Wanda. She stood up and ran from the room.

Peavey took another drink of wine. "Don't like the stuff. Tastes like horse piss. Look, sport, we've talked about it. Wanda wants to keep the boy.

We'll do right by you and adopt him all legal-like. I'll even treat you fair and throw in a little something extra just for you."

"You mean money?"

"Why not? You chess players don't make any real money and a fella can always use a couple of extra bucks."

Slade dropped his voice for some man-to-man talk. "Maybe this will get her off my ass. She's been at me for months now and I've come close to popping her one, but I can't afford it. Lord knows what it would cost me the next time around."

"How much?"

Peavey had figured it right. "I bet a hundred thousand sounds pretty good to you right along about now."

"Not as good as Matt riding a pony and chasing some fat ducks I know."

"I'll get him a pony, if he wants one," called Wanda from the floor below. "And Lord Byron loves him."

Peavey sighed. "All right, sport—two hundred thousand."

Ryder tossed his napkin on the table. "I think this discussion is over."

"Two hundred thousand it is. Good man."

Ryder couldn't afford to lose his temper. He stood up and leaned on the table. "Slade," he said quietly, "I'm going to say this just once—Matt is coming with me."

A telephone began to ring, as Peavey glared at Ryder. Peavey was used to telling people what to do. He stood up. "The boy stays."

"I think not."

Peavey came around to Ryder's side of the table and assumed a Praying Mantis stance. "I'm warning you. You can have it either way, but you're leaving without the kid. We know all about that bombing business in Germany. You're not fit to be his father."

Peavey was closing the distance when Ryder held up his hand. "Slade! Don't do it! If you come at me woofing and hopping around, I'm going to slap you right out of those fancy pajamas."

Peavey laughed and was settling deeper into his stance when Wanda burst into the room.

"There's a terrible man on the phone," she said looking at Ryder. "And he wants to talk to you. He says the call is from England."

"Where's the telephone?"

"In the living room, on the desk."

As Ryder went downstairs he could feel the presence. He thought he'd left it in Europe, but he could feel evil emanating from the telephone. When he picked up the receiver, the presence was stronger.

"Hello?"

"It is time we met," said a voice, in an accent unlike any Ryder had ever heard. It was the voice of evil that lived in his mind.

John paused. "You know where to find me."

The presence flared like a sunspot, but the voice remained soft and unhurried. "You will come to me."

"Listen—"

"No—you listen."

"John,"—Katherine's voice was urgent—"don't come, he has the—"

"Hello? Katherine?"

"She is here and well—for the moment. Andrew's plane is standing by at the airport."

"I'm not going anywhere."

"Of course, you are. If I come to you, it will mean the Halls are already dead."

The telephone clicked. Ryder stood staring blankly out of the window.

"Who was that?" asked Wanda. "And just who, if I may ask, is Katherine?"

"I have to go. There's a plane waiting for me. I'll leave your car at the airport."

Wanda was triumphant. "You won't be here to see Matthew open his Christmas presents."

Ryder turned away in pain.

"Don't you come back, boy," said Peavey. "I'll have a court order waiting."

Ryder's eyes focused on Peavey. Until the day he died, Peavey would never be closer to death than he was at this moment.

As Ryder drove north to the airport, he felt sick to his stomach. A full moon was rising out of the sea, pale and mysterious, and as remote and unattainable as Katherine herself. In the west, the sun had set and the horizon was blood red.

Chapter XXXVIII

Bentwood was dead. He lay sprawled on the squares of black-and-white marble in the great hall, a fallen paladin, his head twisted at a grotesque angle. Ryder straightened Bentwood's legs, folded his arms over his chest, and closed the staring eyes.

The steel door to the sitting room had been ripped from its hinges and flung against a wall. Across the room, the open door to the cavern hung crookedly.

As Ryder started down the sloping tunnel, the sense of evil grew stronger. All the lights in the cavern were on, including the spotlight over the Round Table. Seated at the table were Katherine and Andrew Hall, Colonel Brooks Cameron and, in Arthur's place on the far side of the table, another man.

Ryder paused in the entrance, his eyes searching the dark places.

"Come in. You have nothing to fear," said the man at the far side of the table. The words were spoken softly, almost whispered.

Ryder did not move.

"You may approach. We have been waiting for you."

Katherine opened her mouth to speak, but stopped when the man raised his hand. "It is not necessary—he knows."

Still looking at Katherine, Ryder walked to the table. "Are you all right?"

She was pale, but her voice was steady. "Yes," she said quietly.

"Then why are you here?"

"You should be talking to me," said the man. The presence grew in Ryder's mind, but still he ignored the man in Arthur's chair.

"Katherine?"

"You shouldn't have come."

"We both know the answer to that. Please leave us."

There was a flash of evil and Katherine flinched. "I...I can't."

"We'll see." Ryder looked next at Hall.

"All this time I thought it was you."

"I know."

"Why didn't you tell me?"

"Would you have believed me if I had?"

"Where did he come from?"

"An aberration from the past."

Ryder continued to stare at Hall. He could feel a warning tentacle of thought touch his mind. "And Brooks?"

"Don't talk around me," snapped Cameron. "I can speak for myself."

"Well?" asked Ryder, his attention still on Hall.

Colonel Cameron slammed the palm of his hand down on the table. In the cavern silence, it sounded like a pistol shot. "It's because of me that we are here. I knew I would beat you in the end." His tone was righteous.

Ryder looked at Cameron. "I warned you."

"You touched me."

"Bentwood is dead because I took a weapon out of your jockstrap?"

"It was humiliating. No one touches me."

"Who else is dead?"

For the first time, Cameron looked doubtful. "I don't know."

Ryder turned finally to face the man across the table. The walnut-sized knot of evil that lived in his mind grew heavier.

"Perhaps I should ask this one."

The man sitting in Arthur's chair was unforgettable. He was brown and his skin was dry and cracked. He had no hair on his head and no eyebrows. Even the backs of his hands resting on the table were hairless. He wore a long-sleeved shirt buttoned at the throat.

"You are?"

"Elo will do." Elo's thin lips didn't seem to move and Ryder wasn't sure if he'd actually heard the words or if they were only in his mind.

"What sort of name is that?"

"It is the only one you could understand."

"A name to go with the man?"

"You see me as I am. Others do not."

"Are you responsible for the destruction out there?"

Elo nodded.

"And Bentwood?"

Elo's glance flickered toward Hall. "Yes."

"Why?"

"I left him for you to find."

Ryder studied Elo, looking deep into his eyes. Harry Tanaka had taught him to know his enemy, to penetrate the depths, to the core of the man. Ryder found only emptiness. Staring into Elo's unblinking eyes, Ryder noticed for the first time that he had no eyelashes. A childhood memory, long forgotten, stirred.

Ryder had been in the reptile house of the city zoo, face close to a glass case. One of the great constrictors was awake. Ryder was mesmerized by the snake's eyes. There was no hate or anger or passion. There was only an unswerving, soulless purpose. It was his first look through the gates of hell.

Ryder tore his gaze from Elo and looked around the cavern. Why not? It had started here and here it would end.

Hall read Ryder's thoughts. "Careful, he also has The Gift."

"Gift?" asked Elo. "If that's what you call it, then I *am* The Gift."

He stood up and Ryder tensed. "No, not yet," said Elo.

He turned his back to Ryder and glided up the steps to the stone altar where Excalibur rested. He moved like no man Ryder had ever seen. Elo picked up the sword and came back to the Round Table.

"I have known about you for a long time," he said to Hall, "but I did not realize you had managed to save all these things. If I had, I would have come sooner."

"You wouldn't be here now," answered Hall, "if you hadn't had help."

"Ah, yes, the good Colonel." Elo walked around the table, past Hall and Katherine, to stand behind Colonel Cameron. "He had no choice. I willed him to come to me. He is mine now. I possess him."

"That Sunday, when you thought I'd gone shooting, I finally met the real holder of The Gift." Cameron spoke to Hall. "I did it for you."

Hall shook his head. "Will you ever know what you have done?"

"I already do, and so will you once we get rid of John Ryder."

"But you are of no further use to me," said Elo, raising Excalibur high over his head. There was a whirr and a flash of steel as Elo split Colonel Cameron open from crown to breastbone, instantly transforming the smiling man into a monstrosity that spouted a fountain of blood. Colonel Brooks Cameron fell forward against the table, twisted, and crumpled onto the cavern floor.

James L Diffin

It was so sudden, so brutal, so cold-blooded, that no one was able to move. Elo was walking back up the altar steps as if nothing had happened.

Ryder looked only at Katherine. She was staring at him, transfixing him with her eyes as if he was the one remaining truth in a world suddenly gone mad.

"You have shamed the sword," said Hall. "It is the first time in fifteen hundred years that it has been used with dishonor. You'll pay with your life."

"Now that I've seen this place, I rather like it," said Elo, ignoring Hall.

"Too bad you won't be able to stay," said Ryder.

Elo placed the bloody sword on the altar and came back to sit down. The feeling of evil was growing. "Who is going to stop me?"

"I am."

"Ah—" Elo rested his elbows on the table and stared at Katherine and Hall over steepled fingers. "You two are the spawn of Merlin?"

"As you well know," said Hall.

Elo looked first at Ryder and then at Katherine. "She's safe for some time to come. I, too, must have a successor."

"Never in this life," said Katherine.

"Leave them alone," said Ryder.

Elo turned his unblinking eyes toward Ryder. "You couldn't protect your own wife; how do you expect to save these two?"

"What has my wife got to do with this? She died in an automobile accident." There was a note of doubt in his voice.

"Did she?" Elo could have been discussing the weather. "We have known about you people for years. However, things change, and that is why I'm here."

"What about Stacey?"

"According to our calculations, your son would be the next to have the power."

"Matthew?"

"No, not him, the other one."

"Jesus! What other one?"

"The one she had in her belly."

Ryder was stunned. "I didn't know."

"I did."

"There was an autopsy—"

302

"And?"

"Nothing was said about a pregnancy."

"The report read what I wished it to read."

"You killed her?"

"An opportunity presented itself and I used it."

Ryder was beyond anger. He had gone to a place in his mind where he'd never been. "Why have you been following me these past months?"

"Our calculations were incorrect. It wasn't one of your sons who would have the power, but you. I was curious to see what you would do with it."

"And Tomorrow's Children?"

"One of many interests. They had their chance and were unable to settle the matter of John Ryder. That's why you're here."

"So it all comes down to this?"

"You pose more of a threat than the others did."

"You've killed a holder of The Gift?" asked Hall.

"Yes, two of them—Major Collins and Brian Harwell."

"Major Collins died during the First World War."

"I know."

Ryder remembered his dream and the muddy trenches. He took a deep breath and slowly let it out. The presence was steadily growing in his head like a tumor.

In the blink of an eye, Ryder was across the top of the table, but Elo was lizard-quick. He fled to a rack of weapons with Ryder a step behind.

They fought—steel upon steel. The sparks flew as battle-axe crashed against sword. The noise was deafening. Ryder was a tireless force. Long minutes, then hours passed, and still they fought, raging back and forth across the cavern, their shadows huge against the cavern walls.

No matter how quickly or strongly he struck, Ryder was fighting a reflection of himself. And all the time, Elo's expressionless eyes stared at him from behind mirrors of flashing steel. Handles broke and steel shattered under the relentless blows. Immediately, another weapon was seized in its place, until all the racks were empty.

Then, they fought with their hands. Ryder used everything he'd ever learned, but Elo countered. Karate, boxing, even his wrestling skills were useless. At one point, Elo had his shirt torn off. Except for the dry cracks in his skin, Elo's chest was featureless. He had no nipples.

Slowly, Ryder was forced back, the evil presence in his mind weighing him down. Elo was merciless coiled steel. Ryder retreated, stumbling up the stone steps, and was pressed back against the altar with Elo's hands at his throat.

"I had no intention of killing you quickly," said Elo. "That would have been too easy. You must fear death before you die."

Ryder's hands were on Elo's wrists, trying to pull the choking fingers away. The pressure only increased. "You lose, I'm not afraid."

Ryder's vision was turning dark. His tongue was numb and the ringing in his ears was like a thousand discordant wind chimes. His stomach knotted. Elo was breathing heavily and his breath smelled like an open tomb.

From a great distance, Ryder heard Hall's voice. "Open your mind!"

"No!" Ryder struggled to speak. "I must keep him out—"

The pressure on his throat strengthened. It wouldn't be long now. Hall's voice came from somewhere in Ryder's head.

"By the power of Arthur—!"

Ryder was bent back over the altar, his shoulders touching Excalibur.

"Now it is time," said Elo.

The black came rushing in and with it came something else. In Ryder's mind, a pinpoint of light flickered. Slowly, it grew, fighting the darkness. It was brighter now and with the light came the voices of the holders of The Gift, and with them—their strength.

Ryder opened his eyes. Elo's face was inches from his own, eyes fixed with an intensity that would consume him.

Inch by inch, Ryder's back began to straighten until he stood erect. He ripped Elo's hands from his throat, spun him back against the altar, seized Excalibur, and thrust the blade home.

Elo stood impossibly straight, rigid as death. Slowly, he turned sideways and fell back, sliding down to sit with one shoulder against the altar. Elo looked down at the hilt of the sword with disbelieving eyes. He stroked the handle with the gentle touch of a lover and whispered.

"At last you're mine."

Elo's voice was so faint that Ryder could barely hear him, but the presence of evil was so strong in his mind that he took an involuntary step backward.

Elo looked up. "You finished me."

"Yes, I did."

"Then," whispered Elo, "we die together." With an impossible strength, Elo ripped Excalibur from his body and hurled the weapon straight toward Ryder's heart. If it hadn't been for the awareness of evil in his mind, it might have worked. Ryder caught the blade in midair.

"Give it back," said Elo, coughing. His lips were stained red.

"It was never yours."

"You think this ends it, don't you." Elo smiled, then coughed up a torrent of blood. He threw his head back and let out a great cry. The sound reverberated and crashed around the cavern.

At last, it was silent. Ryder squatted on his heels to study Elo. Elo's eyes still held the same expression, but the weight of evil in Ryder's mind was gone.

He rose and carefully replaced Excalibur on the altar, first wiping the blade clean on one of the banners that had been torn from the wall. Ryder staggered back to the Round Table and dropped into a chair.

"Andrew, what the hell happened?"

"You were never alone, you just needed to be reminded."

"That's not what I asked. Are there any more like him?"

"No."

Ryder gazed at Katherine before speaking. "This is the end of it?"

Hall was confident. "It's finished."

"You knew about him, didn't you?"

"Yes."

"No more surprises?"

"None."

"Andrew, you're a lying sack. You owe me one hell of an explanation."

"And you have lain with a Druid priestess."

Ryder stood up. "Mind your own business."

Hall also stood up. "This is my business, as a father and as a custodian of The Gift."

"Stop it right now!" said Katherine, as Ryder started around the table. "Hasn't there been enough violence? Father, I make my own decisions."

"Do you wish to unleash that upon the world again?" Hall gestured toward the altar and the body of Elo. "After all the years of training, how irresponsible can you be?"

Katherine's chin came up as she faced her father. "There had to be something for me even if it was only for a few hours. Don't worry, I have no intention of conceiving." Katherine touched Ryder with her eyes. "Although nothing in this world would give me greater pleasure."

Ryder was reeling with weariness. "I had better get some answers from both of you or I'm going to bring down the temple—no more half-truths and no more things left unsaid."

Ryder sat in Arthur's chair and looked up at the altar. "You can begin by telling me about Elo."

Hall looked around the wrecked cavern and at the dead. "Do you think this is the place for Katherine?"

Before Ryder could answer, Katherine said, "But Father, this is my heritage. My place is here, especially now."

Hall sat down next to Katherine and the two, father and daughter, stared at Ryder across the Round Table.

"I love you, Katherine." Ryder spoke quietly. "I can walk away from this, if you'll go with me."

"She can't, any more than you can," answered Hall.

"Then you'd better tell me why."

"Everything I have told you about The Gift is essentially true." Hall shifted uncomfortably. "However, The Gift doesn't reappear at random, as I may have led you to believe. Only when there is great danger does The Gift return. A sort of check and balance. We don't lose, but neither do we win. We survive, grow and, hopefully, learn."

"And Elo?"

"Very near the beginning, there was a Druid priestess who slept with a holder of The Gift. They thought their joining would be the start of something new, something wonderful. Instead, it unleashed a darkness upon the world. For every true holder of The Gift, there has been a shadow image, an Elo."

"Why did he wait so long?"

"Arrogance, perhaps. I shall burn the body in the proper manner and return him to where he belongs."

"Hell?"

"Heaven and Hell are religious concepts. I'm speaking of good and evil. It is the core, the very essence of mankind. It is what the Round Table was all about."

Ryder looked at Hall for a long minute. "So, you don't have all the answers after all." He gave a heartfelt sigh. "I suppose the rest of my life will consist of trying to pry the truth out of you."

Ryder put his head down on the table. "I don't want to even think about it. But, no matter what, as soon as I've rested for a moment, I'm leaving to get my son."

Amid the ruin and death in the cavern behind Hall House, he closed his eyes and slept.

Epilogue

For John Ryder, the twenty-ninth holder of The Gift, it was the beginning. On the other side of the world, it was an ending.

Somewhere below Easter Island, in the warm waters of the South Pacific Current, he slept. Always on the surface now, soothed by the slow, eternal roll of the sea, he dozed, basking in the sun. But even in sleep, he was alert. The ocean was alive with sound. From time to time, he raised his head. He saw the spouts of a family of whales heading south toward the Antarctic. Over on the horizon, rays of sunlight were shining through a rainsquall. Cloud shadows, like great ships, sailed across endless seas. He had not eaten for many weeks. No longer hungry, he was waiting.

Then it came. He heard, at last, the silent call. Without question, he began the final dive. That, too, was his way. Down through the sparkling top waters he swam, toward the twilight of the mid-depths where old combatants, the giant squid and the sperm whale, were to be found. At this depth, the light faded quickly and was soon gone. As he thrust down into the black, he saw flashes of light that told of the presence of monsters, some small and some not small at all. Deeper still.

Then there was nothing, no light, no sound, no living thing. For the first time, he entered the total void of the deep. His movements slowed, then stopped. His great body drifted gently toward the ocean bed. His last thought was of his birthplace, of the boat, and of the two men, especially the one....

THE END